The Wild Trumpet Call

Bedside Books
An imprint of American Book Publishing
P.O. Box 65624 Salt Lake City, UT 84165
www.american-book.com
Printed in the United States of America on acid-free paper.

The Wild Trumpet Call

Designed by Melissa Montoya, design@american-book.com

Publisher's Note: This is a work of fiction. Names, characters, places, and incidents either are the product of the author's imagination, or are used fictitiously, and any resemblance to actual persons, living or dead, events, or locales is entirely coincidental.

ISBN 1-58982-238-2

Tragarz, Jules H., The Wild Trumpet Call

Special Sales

These books are available at special discounts for bulk purchases. Special editions, including personalized covers, excerpts of existing books, and corporate imprints, can be created in large quantities for special needs. For more information
e-mail info@american-book.com.

The Wild Trumpet Call

By

Jules Tragarz

To Jim Hadjin, whose inspiration and literary insights fueled the animating spirit of this book.

"When one is young, one must see things, gather experience, ideas, enlarge the mind."

—Joseph Conrad, *Heart of Darkness*

"Every man strives instinctively for a citadel and a privacy where he is free from the crowd, the many, the majority."

—Friedrich Nietzsche, *Beyond Good and Evil*

Chapter 1

Jim Stahr emerged from the Waverly Place Building in the late afternoon and stood staring across the street at the wide expanse of Washington Square Park, which traditionally served as a campus for most live-at-home students at New York University. Impulse, not reason, made him shake off indecision, look sideways to check for oncoming traffic, and sprint across the street, his textbooks pinioned to him by the pressure of his right hand. But he decided not to enter. Throngs of students milled around him, some leisurely strolling, others moving with quick purpose. Yet he was in no hurry.

He stood fixed in place, baffled as to what to do next with his time. It was Friday, and he wanted nothing more than to be free of all academic concerns. Breathing in the late September air only intensified what had arisen earlier that day as a cogent need for movement and change. Again, caprice took hold, making him twist free of the teeming students and scurry back to the other side of the street. This time, though, there were no signs of hesitation as he hastily made his way toward Broadway. Just as he reached the busy street, a bus skidded to a halt, blocking his way. He plunged behind it and dodged his way between horn-tooting vehicles. As he reached the opposite side, he began jogging in the direction of Tenth Street. His disquiet began to diminish as he neared Stephan's Tavern. Something in the fall air, he told himself, was inciting this craving to escape the ordinary and routine. Maybe, just maybe, being in the company of strangers would rid him of this yearning for new horizons. This had proved to be a panacea in the past.

The loud thumping of a polka blasting out of a jukebox greeted his entry into the saloon. As soon as he laid his books on top of the long wooden bar, Stephan, the tavern owner, placed an empty glass under one of the taps and began filling it with beer. Seating himself on one of the swivel-top stools, Jim waited, hoping the beer would help rid him of his churning restlessness. After taking several deep gulps from the glass, he let out an audible sigh and pivoted around to survey his surroundings.

His interest quickly focused on a group of Polish laborers who stood in a tight circle nearby. Though he could not understand what they were saying, their antics and guffaws accompanied by the slapping of open palms on the badly scarred, unpolished counter drew his full attention. His troubling absorption with himself was supplanted by an all-consuming preoccupation with their good-humored exchanges. The vivaciousness of these men sprang forth with a robust contagion, and he found himself grinning openly as he continued watching them.

After a while, three of them shouted their good-byes and quickly slipped outdoors. The few who remained regrouped into a tighter circle, their gaiety suddenly exhausted, their faces no longer frolicsome but sedate. As their voices lowered and grew more serious, his mind returned to the concerns he had pushed aside. After emptying his glass, he withdrew some coins from his leather jacket and deposited them atop the bar. He wiped his lips with the back of his hand, took hold of his books, and sauntered out. The bartender acknowledged his leaving with a nod of his head.

Daylight was now in full retreat, leaving behind a penetrating chill. He strode eastward on Tenth Street. As he neared Second Avenue, St. Marks-in-the-Bowery came into view, its short steeple awash with light stemming from a nearby streetlamp. As he had done many times in the past, Jim stopped, leaned against the church's protective iron railing and stared up at the new apartment building across the way, its three stories towering imposingly over the squat structures situated nearby. On every past occasion, he had found convincing reasons not to enter and had turned away with a shrug of his shoulders. This time, however, the desperate need to search for something that could animate his mind and senses made him cast aside all former pretexts for not setting foot inside. Clasping his books tightly to his chest, he walked briskly across the street.

Clearly displayed on one side of the entrance was an orderly listing of the building's tenants. He quickly found Peggy Troy's name and her apartment number. After pressing the button next to it, he waited, unsure whether this is what he wanted to be doing. Receiving no response, he reacted with feelings of dismay and relief. Just as he turned to leave, words crackled out of the intercom.

"Who's there?" The question had a peremptory quality that left him no choice but to reply.

"It's Jim Stahr." There was an obvious lack of virility in the sound of his voice.

A chuckle preceded the reply, "Friday's miracle."

Jim heard a half-suppressed laugh as the buzzer sounded. He pushed the heavy door open, walked into the entrance hall and climbed the stairs to the second floor. Peggy stood waiting for him in the open doorway.

"You've made so many promises to stop by my apartment these past years—what made you suddenly decide to pop in unannounced?" she greeted him.

"Formality was never my strong point," he shot back without bothering to respond to her query.

"That's for sure." Her words left a trail of lyrical delight.

Peggy motioned him to enter and led the way through a corridor that ran tunnel-like from the front door to the living quarters in the rear. The first thing that caught Jim's eye was the simplicity of the furnishings, their specific locations seemingly an attempt to fill empty space rather than to achieve any balance in decor. The room manifested a sense of impermanency.

"Would you like some coffee?" Peggy asked with a smile.

"Beer would be preferable. That's if you have any."

She nodded affirmatively and started for the kitchen, informing him at the same time that her roommate was studying in one of the adjoining rooms.

Jim followed behind her. "What's she like?" His query lacked real interest.

"Who?"

"Your roommate."

Peggy remarked jovially. "She's somewhat shy but intelligent. You'll find her interesting." There was no trace of jealousy in her words.

Peggy removed a bottle of beer from the refrigerator, removed the cap with an opener that lay atop the kitchen table, and handed it to him. He took a hurried swig from it before continuing his disinterested questioning.

"Is she also graduating in February?"

"Yes," she mumbled as she filled a cup of black coffee from a pot that stood boiling atop the stove.

"By the way, Jim, have you got any ideas about how to stay out of the rut after we graduate?" Self-disgust was more apparent in her question than any expectation of helpful counsel. She started back toward the living room, taking care not to spill the coffee from her brimming cup.

"Never ask a loser how to win," he said, his negativism manifest, yet stripped clean of any self-pity. Jim felt at ease in the kitchen and would have preferred to remain there, but he unenthusiastically followed her into the adjoining living room.

"We've had years of discussions about the world's ills, but never a word about ourselves—as individuals, that is. Do you realize that?" she declared aggressively.

Jim did not comment. Instead, he seated himself on the floor using the base of one of the couches as a back support. He sat observing Peggy as she lit a cigarette and searched for an ashtray. They had known each other since they had enrolled as freshmen more than three years ago. It now dawned on him that his knowledge of her was vague. Their acquaintanceship had been limited exclusively to gatherings in the school cafeteria, and always in the company of a number of other intellectually inclined students, none of whom partook in any of the organized activities of the university.

Apparent to him though, were traits that indicated her family was financially well off. She visited them regularly in a town north of the city known for its large houses that overlooked the Hudson River. To the practiced eye, the clothes she wore always fit with an enviable perfection, and their quality was obviously superior to those worn by all the others in their group of friends. In addition, what obviously set her apart from the rest of them was her private school way of speaking, which to the untrained ear could easily be mistaken for a waning British accent. The subject of money never entered into any of her conversations, nor did she ever sport her affluence in any offensive manner. Her dealings with all those who participated in their daily gatherings in the school's cafeteria were always straightforward and without any show of aloofness. On the contrary, she was always trying to please, and willing to help, if asked. Yet, she kept a tight silence on the subject of her family, perhaps to downplay her pride, or shame, of them. No one could be sure. As to how she had spent the war years, all he knew was what someone in the group had told him—that she had been awarded the Bronze Star Medal for bravery while serving as an army nurse in France. Although rumor had it that she had participated in the rescue of some wounded infantry men while under enemy fire, Jim deliberately kept his curiosity in check as to what she had done to merit this military honor. Any probing on his part to uncover such information could have opened up the possibility of having to provide details about his own combat experience as a teenage foot soldier. This was the one subject he would never discuss with anyone. The actions he had taken one day in Belgium had left him with feelings of shame, which to this day were quick to surface whenever anyone touched on the subject of personal courage. And whenever they did, he adroitly found an excuse to leave. Much to his satisfaction, their unorthodox alliance of friends had early on reached a tacit agreement not to talk about their wartime experiences, except in jest.

Jim watched as she placed her cup and an ashtray atop a nondescript table before she plopped into a chair next to it. Peggy returned his searching look before saying accusingly: "Come to think of it, I've never heard you talk about the future."

"I've never had to before," he answered, unperturbed.

"Why's that?"

"Well, ever since I got out of the army, all that I was concerned about was my studies. Nothing else mattered."

"I guess that was as good a way as any of avoiding the future."

"Maybe you're right," he said. "But the university was the best that has ever happened to me. And, I have to admit, I'm going to hate leaving it."

"So will the rest of us," she said, defeat having overpowered her former assertiveness.

"What a generation! A childhood nurtured by poverty, thanks to the Great Depression," he mused aloud.

"And becoming adults—the hard way. Thanks to the big war," Peggy interjected.

"And who said that the discipline of study was a soft touch?" Jim asked rhetorically. "Well, who wouldn't want to be free to choose after all that?" he added before taking a swallow from the beer bottle gripped in his hand. She smiled at him in a way that signaled her agreement with what he had just said. "No doubt, there'll be plenty of constraint in the workplace to tie us down. Free to think...free to act...ha! In this world, no one is actually free." His words were imbued with a defiance that surprised Peggy, her look of concurrence having encouraged him to continue discoursing on the same subject with less self-restraint in articulating his opinions.

There was a moment of hesitancy before Peggy started to voice her own gloomy reflections. "I guess that's one way of putting it. Maybe we'll all become just a bunch of simple subway straphangers." Drawing deeply from her cigarette, she arched her neck backward and sent a stream of smoke into the air. Her eyes remained fixed upward, looking intently at the thinning, irregular formations. "Oh, if only I could be one of those who could escape the trap!"

In answer to her entreaty, he remarked acidly, "Peggy, you're asking for the moon."

Her head snapped down, a muffled anger having replaced her musings.

Jim knew it was spiteful to continue along this pessimistic path. Nevertheless, to his way of thinking, there seemed no other way to indirectly reveal that his claims of being a self-directed individual were nothing more than pretense. He could not deny to himself that he lacked the courage to strike out alone in a society in which togetherness was the binding ingredient. "There's some herd instinct in each of us," he went on, "that makes us stampede into conformity's corral in order to have our spirits branded with the collective motto—'We Follow!' Can't you see that?" The tone of his question was argumentative but quickly turned to disgust when he added, "In the end, you have to admit that even the most defiant of society's individualists get tamed by responsibility."

"Must you always look at everything analytically?" she shot back at him, unable to contain her growing ire. "Where are your hopes, your imagination?"

"Where they belong!" The reply resounded sharply. "I can't afford to be a dreamer." Swinging the bottle up to his mouth, he gulped from it, and then placed it on the floor next to him. Without making any effort to mask the scorn imbedded in his words, he continued, "Do you know what kills off more creativity than anything else? It's that all-consuming drive to be somebody. That's what! If you're going to succeed in life, play the game—and by the rules, mind you. And all along the way, it's hammered home that you've got only one choice—to win." He ended on a cynical note. "In the end, there's no room for losers."

"We can't all be somebodies," Peggy retorted. "Some of us have to be nobodies. Anyway," she went on, a hint of humor beginning to color her speech, "the somebodies would be nobodies if we nobodies did not take the trouble to make them somebodies."

Both of them burst out laughing.

"Look, Peggy," he began in a soothing apology, "all I'm trying to say is that it takes neurotic gall to be a true runaway from the crowd, and most of us don't have it."

She drew on her cigarette before calmly concluding, "If you're correct then it makes all of the rest of us nothing more than ordinary and conventional…just a bunch of other nonentities. You don't leave the common folk much of a choice, do you?" She took one last puff on her cigarette before twisting the lit end into a nearby ashtray.

"Not all of them," he stated emphatically. "There're still the odd ones. They've dropped out of the race to achieve what we term success, and they make up the incompatible minority in our cultural barrel." His voice trailed off pensively.

A girl stepped silently into the room, stopped, and threw a hasty glance at Peggy Troy. Unwilling to disrupt the conversation, Peggy nodded a greeting to her without extending an invitation to have her join them. She, in turn, acknowledged her roommate's unspoken wish by positioning herself in the doorway of her room, intent on remaining as inconspicuous as possible.

"Who are those 'odd ones'?" Peggy asked. She bent forward, her curiosity having been aroused by what he had said.

"Oh, I never gave a thought as to what they could be called." He seemed at a loss for words and began to scratch his face. "They're the rare breeds that have been around since people have walked on two legs."

A period of silence followed. When he did begin speaking again, Jim's words took on a more positive bent. "They have no name...only a mission. Perhaps it would be best to refer to them as life's perennial wayfarers. They take any road that leads away from boredom and toward discovery, even about themselves."

"Did you say away from boredom?" Peggy questioned with a newborn enthusiasm.

He disregarded her inquiry and kept on speaking. "They're the ones in search of a domain where life is an animating experience."

"Now, that's more like it, Jim. I'm willing to trade that place for the Fountain of Youth."

"Like buccaneers," he went on, "they want to ransack life. Scrutinize its vitals. Gorge out with their senses and reason the very marrow and substance of living."

"Who are these people?" Peggy leaned forward to ask with a quizzical look.

"I guess you can categorize them as the monomaniacs of life. For them living is just a constant pursuit of the uncommon, the innovative," Jim explained.

"What's wrong with that kind of madness?" Peggy demanded with a show of eagerness.

Jim was pleased that he had managed to dispel her anger and rekindle her curiosity. Now, he reasoned, would be the appropriate time to allow reality to enter and play its role in the discussion. "Well, like all single-mindedness, there's always a flaw in the structure. All you have to do is look for it."

"How?"

"It's not a matter of how, but why," he started to explain "because these explorers are consistently in search of the new. Unfortunately, for some of them, this affliction with living life to the fullest doesn't allow time for any altruistic respites...like sharing the knowledge they've acquired."

Peggy laughed. "It sounds like they're on a learning spree that has no ending."

"I guess in a way they're like addicts all right, only their drug is human experience. When they can't satisfy their real need for newness, they become wasted spirits, barren and insipid."

"I wouldn't mind being hooked like that. Would you?"

A startled expression flared up, his eyes taking on the appearance of someone caught in the process of committing some unforgivable wrong. "Maybe, just maybe...I am," he implied quietly. Only there was no way of concealing his realization that he, too, was just one of the conventional many.

His earlier compulsion to seek the new and offbeat had fizzled away. In its place, weariness crept in, giving rise to an urge to leave. When he stood up, he caught sight of Peggy's roommate standing in the doorway behind him with her arms crossed, staring back at him with a look of despair. His former expression of self-satisfaction changed to that of surprise, then to embarrassment, as if the revelation of his most innermost thoughts had been overheard by some unwelcome eavesdropper. Peggy, noting his loss of composure, quickly got out of her chair and strode over to him and, without her customary grace, hastily introduced her roommate, Gennie Connors The look of despondency in the girl's eyes made him put off shaking her hand. He nodded his recognition of her instead. Turning back to Peggy, he thanked her for allowing him to visit and shuffled into the long corridor that led out of the apartment.

After carefully closing the door behind him, Jim plodded down the stairs, refusing once again to make use of the elevator. He started back to his parent's apartment in Brooklyn. His former craving for novel distraction had vanished, his own words having reduced this imperative demand for novelty to the solidity of windblown ashes.

Chapter 2

A bell signaled the end of class. Jim Stahr gathered up his books and strolled out of the room. A short distance down the hall, another student approached and stopped in front of him. The man who blocked his way was obviously a number of years older than Jim, tall and powerfully built, with wide shoulders and muscular arms. Yet there was a languor in his greeting, which was more reflective of having dealt with chronic pain from a physical injury rather than from any overexertion in some physical endeavor.

Nearly three years ago when the tall man had learned that Jim had also been caught up in the horrific Battle of the Bulge, a kinship had formed between them—a secret sharing of a wartime event in which defeat seemed more a reality than any chance of victory. Jim was the only one to whom he had revealed the source of his persistent headaches, the cause being the result of a head wound sustained during that terrible winter conflict. Left unspoken between them, however, was the emotional damage done to Jim Stahr at that same time and place. He, too, had been a casualty. His was a hurt, however, that left no visible scars or any other outward sign of injury. But hidden underneath the boldness of his habitual verbal assertions concerning how best to set right the world's shortcomings, was the recognition that his spoken words safeguarded a lack of self-confidence about his fortitude to carry out these same measures. He could not dismiss the fear that resolution would fail him, as it had done once before, in that wartime battle in the heavily wooded Ardennes forest. That incident had cast off the last threads of his youthful innocence and had left him drained of hope and purpose. He came home from the war weighted down with the need to find a moral sense—a direction—that would give meaning to his life. The knowledge he hoped to glean from his studies at the university was the avenue he had chosen to help light the way through the dark corridors of self-doubt in search of himself.

"Wait a minute, Jim. I want to say good-bye."

Jim looked up at Lacy Hutchins with a crooked grin before snapping back cockily, "Who're you kidding?"

Lacy didn't return the smile.

Jim was quick to note that his friend's appearance was unusually sedate and expressionless. As they walked together, a crowd of students barged their way between them, forcing Jim to fall back. Trailing behind Lacy, his attention focused on the gray stripes that ran indiscriminately through the short strands of hair that looped and curled like matted shrubbery around his head. Whenever his friend passed directly under any of the overhead lights, the dull texture of his dark skin assumed a polished glow. Putting aside his meaningless observations, he sped forward and once again began walking alongside his college chum.

"When are you coming back?" Jim's question had the assurance of one merely seeking confirmation.

"To be honest with you, I don't know if I can say, even if I wanted to."

Jim stopped walking and spun around to face his companion. "What in the hell do you mean by that?" His query reflected shock more than surprise.

Lacy shook his head and said nothing.

They started down a stairway with quick bouncing steps. At the bottom, Jim started toward the cafeteria, which had been their habitual free-time destination during their years at the university. Lacy grabbed his arm. "No, Jim, not today. I'm not in any mood for bull sessions or for any more good-byes." The words flowed out listlessly, the last of them barely perceptible mumbles.

"I don't feel like talking much either," Jim lied. "I'll walk you to the station."

They followed the crowd of students out the door, both maintaining their silence as they sauntered along University Place. When they crossed Eighth Street, Jim tried to elicit a reason for his friend's decision to terminate his studies just months short of graduation.

"Don't you want to get into law school? Leaving now doesn't make much sense."

"I wouldn't be leaving right now if it weren't for these pains in my head. I can't seem to study anymore." Lacy put two fingers above the bridge of his nose and rubbed the area softly.

Jim watched him for a while, but decided not to pursue the subject further. His thoughts wandered back to the day when Lacy had humorously boasted that while other army sergeants may have had a brassy manner, gold in their teeth, and lead in their ass, he had the added distinction of having silver in his head. Now these same words seemed to lack even a shred of jocularity.

They passed Tenth Street without speaking. Frustrated by the failure of his efforts to uncover the true cause for Lacy's abrupt departure, Jim attempted to probe once more.

"The least you can do, old buddy, is to tell me where you're headed. Don't pull that silent John Wayne squint-eyed bit on me." He had resorted to a verbal expedient bred in the inner city's ghettos by conveying concern through the wisecracking manner of the urban poor. It had served as an effective means in the past to show interest in the welfare of those who harbored that special pride of self-reliance that poverty breeds.

"I'm going south—just south." The reply was free of the jadedness that had filled Lacy's speech since they first met in school's hallway

"South!" Jim exploded. "Of all the directions to go, you choose south. You're a mystery, a real mystery."

Using the palm of his free hand, Lacy began to massage his forehead. "Damn headaches...damn headaches," he moaned.

"Well, if someone asks where you've gone, what do you want me to tell them?"

"Tell them nothing. I'm coming back...just wait and see," Lacy said with conviction.

They strolled slowly up the street, the pencil-gray clouds blocking out whatever optimism the sun's light could have contributed to easing their gloomy exchanges.

When they reached the White Rose Saloon on Twelfth Street, Jim stopped and went over to peer through the tavern's plate-glass window. The only person he recognized was the bartender, who was going about his tasks with a look of complacency. Jim turned to face Lacy and asked, "How about a drink?"

Lacy shook his head.

"It's on me. What do you say?"

"No, Jim, no thanks. When I come back, I'll take you up on it. There're people waiting for me right now."

Jim Stahr looked inside the tavern again and quickly concluded that the dreary interior was no place to bolster sagging spirits. He turned and hurried back to where Lacy stood waiting for him.

Again, silence prevailed until they reached Fourteenth Street. They stopped and watched the flood of people passing in a steady stream before them.

"Do you want to wait until the rush hour is over?" Jim asked.

"No, I have lots to do before I leave."

"Well, I'm going to wait," Jim stated emphatically. He stared glumly at the throng of humanity jostling toward the subway entrance in front of the May Company.

"Look, I've got to go," Lacy said without looking at him, his face pointed toward the crowd.

"Well, if you've got to…then that's the way it has to be. You can bet that I'll still be here when you come back."

Lacy turned to face Jim, extended his hand, and said quietly, "Sorry, Jim, but I'm not in the mood to say much. I'm feeling low. So low, in fact, that I have to reach up to touch bottom. I'm not sure what they'll do to me at Walter Reed. That's the hospital that put the metal plate in my head in the first place." He reached up and passed his hand over the lengthy scar that showed through his closely cropped hair. "I have to be in D.C. tomorrow. I hope they know how to get rid of these pains in my head. Anyway, you needn't worry. I'll be back…wait and see." With a wave of his hand, he shouldered his way into the mass of pedestrians just as they bunched and slowed, preparing to descend into the subway station.

Just as his friend disappeared from view, intuition gave rise to a fearful premonition, one Jim could not quell. When he began walking away, it was without any thought as to the direction he was taking.

Chapter 3

The cafeteria was strangely subdued, and the unusual absence of contending voices lent an air of disquiet to these familiar surroundings. Jim Stahr checked the nearby tables and the line at the food counter but did not see anyone from his group that habitually gathered here. Maybe they had all decided to go to the Automat on Broadway. He quickly dismissed this notion. Over the years, in the breaks between classes, they had always congregated in this section of the school's dining hall. The disparate group had agreed long ago that it was this place, within the school walls, that afforded them the freedom to express their ideas and feelings openly. Here they were isolated from nonacademic observers and could enjoy the privilege of education—free discussion—without fear of judgment or ridicule from others.

Sitting by himself, he felt like an exile from all things that he considered customary, desirable and good. As he sat debating whether to stay or leave, he spotted Nick Grigoris coming toward him, his legs moving with their usual heaviness. Nick neatly deposited his books on the table and, without a word of greeting, sat down. Withdrawing the cigarette that dangled from the corner of his lips, he turned his head to scan the nearby tables. The manner in which his gaze swept around the room had the practiced air of a veteran sailor, one who had spent long periods at sea. Some members of the group had once witnessed him stand up in class and defiantly counter a history teacher's assumption about an event that took place on Omaha Beach on D-Day. His refutation of what was stated was based on his having been a participant in that memorable event as a crew member aboard one of the many landing ships that had ferried troops and supplies that day.

"Where did everyone go today?" he asked without any show of emotion.

"Search me," Jim answered, masking any genuine concern.

Nick shrugged and inhaled languidly from his cigarette. A brooding spirit fueled his inner strength, making him respond to good or bad situations with the same countenance. In his case, it was a perennial look of shyness.

Jim watched as he thumbed open a textbook and then hastily snapped it shut. Obviously unsure of himself, Nick made a roundabout inquiry as to what Jim was planning to do after graduation.

The question released some latent aggressiveness in Jim. "What's there to plan? The future will take care of itself. There's no need to nurse it along."

Nick's head dropped in an expression of hurt feelings. "Sorry…sorry, I didn't mean to butt into your business."

"Hell, Nick, I didn't mean to sound off that way. After all, the university is the only excuse I've got for not having to scrimmage with the real world outside. Anyway, there's still time before this honeymoon with freedom ends. And when it does, there'll be no other choice but to make the future my concern."

Nick looked up and nodded his head in understanding. "You're right, Jim. Maybe we'll talk about it then."

"You name the place. I'll be there."

"That's good enough for me," Nick said, his face still void of any feelings.

Several others straggled up to the table and seated themselves, their bantering exchanges forestalling any further conversation between Nick and Jim. One of the newcomers, Frank Colucci, pushed back in his chair and quizzically eyed Nick and Jim. The look on their faces, he noted, gave the impression that he, along with the others, had intruded upon a discussion of a matter that both wanted kept to themselves.

"Are you two plotting a revolt or something?" Frank asked with a false display of seriousness.

Before they could reply, Hector Palofax, another one of the late arrivals, began to scold them in his usual caustic manner. "Quit holding out on us. What's the big secret?"

Jim held up an open palm. "Peace, brothers, the two of us were just putting off for tomorrow what everyone else is concerned about today."

"Hell, that could only be about the days after tomorrow. The future!" Frank exclaimed and pushed his eyeglasses back onto the bridge of his nose. Of all of those who customarily met at this cafeteria table, his sensitivity to words spoken by the others registered openly and without any attempt on his part to mask his feelings. He was the only one who would speak without restraint, or shame, of what he had done during his wartime years as a sailor in the U.S. Navy. The manner in which he belittled his duties as a seaman aboard a freighter operating in the Pacific was always comical, his words having the ability to transform scowls into smiles. Frank Colucci called himself a "bean counter," his shipboard responsibility having been to maintain an inventory of his ship's cargo destined for delivery to ports throughout the Pacific, where, at times, battles still raged. He made light of his duties, but his words and features took on a glow of a childish wonder when he touched on the subject of the ocean's power to thwart the planned actions of his commanding officers.

Hector's angular features twisted into a scowl. "Let's not discuss that subject of tomorrow today," he said. "I'm not in the mood."

"Agreed," Frank replied with a nod.

"I'm glad to hear that both of you agree on something for a change." Bessie Siegal laughed at her own remark as she dragged over a chair from a nearby table. She sat down, still holding her books pressed against her bosom. While most of the others displayed the gruff maturity evolved from having spent their teenage years in the wartime military, Bessie retained the bold sprightliness and exuberant gaiety of untroubled youth. The streetwise older students treated her with the humorous sarcasm reserved for the harmless naive. She made known to the rest of them that she had spent the entire war years attending high school. Her contribution to the war effort was the collection of scrap material for use in the production of military equipment. To some, she confided that her working-class parents had invested a great deal of their savings to finance her education. She did not begrudge the fact that the college expenses of all the others, with the exception of Hector Palofax, were being paid by the federal government. As an ex-merchant seaman, he was not entitled to the financial benefits offered military veterans under the G.I. Bill of Rights.

A loud bell signaled the end of another classroom session, and a few minutes later, Peggy Troy strode over to the group, followed by the girl who had recently moved into her apartment.

"I want you to meet Gennie Connors, my new roommate."

The introduction was hurried and informal. Quickly turning to her companion, she added, "You've met Jim Stahr before. The others you'll get to know soon enough." Her tone suggested that Gennie take heed in dealing with any of them. "By the way," Peggy added, "she's also an ex-army nurse who served in Italy." The words and the manner in which they were stated, warned her listeners that Gennie's feelings were not to be toyed with.

22

The group welcomed the newcomer with nods, smiles, and stares of appraisal, but they would learn little more about her this day other than her disposition to speak her mind even to strangers like themselves.

Hector Palofax glanced around at all of them and for no apparent reason exclaimed, "What a motley crew! How in God's name did this mess ever get together?" There was a snarling emphasis in the way he enunciated the word "mess."

Gennie Connors looked at him sharply, surprised and offended by his remark. His harsh words were unexpected, especially coming from someone in the group who Peggy had praised so often as being exceptionally independent and bright. She had anticipated their being snobbish, even haughty, but still refined.

Frank Colucci, on the other hand, was too sensitive to allow such a spiteful remark to pass unnoticed. "Perhaps it's beyond your comprehension, Hector, but we're all here because we share one thing in common. Nothing more."

"Okay, poet, tell me, what's that special thing?" Hector retorted heatedly. Frank's suavity, as always, had undermined his self-assurance.

"It's simple, friend. We owe each other nothing," Frank said.

Hector's features took on a disgruntled look. The habitual cutting manner in which he spoke was taken for granted by all the others. Collectively, they reasoned that the years he had spent aboard merchant ships left him burdened with coarseness in his speech as well as his demeanor. It was an unfounded bias but served as a sufficient reason for forgiving the brusqueness of his actions and way of speaking. Hector never socialized with the others. He claimed to be living alone in Spanish Harlem, which had become the neighborhood populated by newly arrived Puerto Rican immigrants.

He never made reference to family or friends. In their eyes, he was considered a real loner. If there was any obvious single-mindedness to his lifestyle, it was his habit of smoking dark, pencil-thin Di Nobli cigars costing five cents each.

Peggy was quick to note Hector's expression taking on a worried look, his cockiness having fled. She decided to intercede on his behalf. "Frank," she started, "your argument that we owe each other nothing may be true, but you've got to admit that our discussions have given us a better understanding of who we are as individuals, even though it didn't put us in debt to one another in any way." She stopped speaking and gave Hector a wink before turning back to address Frank directly. "You'd be hard-pressed to put a dollar figure on such an intrinsic value no matter how hard you try." After taking a deep breath, she declared with a self-confidence that bordered on smugness, "Is there anything wrong in my thinking this way?"

"I'd be a damn fool to deny an obvious truth, wouldn't I?" Frank responded quickly with an articulateness that took Peggy Troy by surprise. "It'd be pure madness on my part if I claimed that any wrong was committed by the informal way we've been meeting here. On the contrary," he went on, "our gatherings here allowed me to say what I felt and thought without having to pull any punches." He allowed a broad grin to cross his face before adding, "And I feel that I still have a steadfast rapport with all of you."

Gennie Connors looked across the table at Frank, the open sincerity of his statement making her regret having judged all by the words uttered by one.

Frank again addressed Peggy directly. "If you're looking for the reason that binds us together, it could be our irresistible need to voice our ideas and feelings free of restraints."

"That's too ambiguous a tie for me," Peggy said.

"Don't you agree," Frank argued further, "that perhaps there's a real need for some of us to lay bare our beliefs and emotions since all of us are guilty of being overly responsive to most things that touch us, even indirectly?"

"Maybe…just maybe," Peggy answered, still unconvinced.

Jim Stahr had paid close attention to the ongoing exchange of thoughts and opinions, thinking that it was not a craving for togetherness that had made him take part in the dialogues of this gathering of diverse personalities. Rather, for him, these verbal confrontations had primarily served as a sounding board for judgments derived from his reflections The presence of others had been essential to satisfy his compulsion to test his ideas, his observations and his convictions. It now dawned on him that maybe these verbal exchanges were nothing more than a means for boosting his ego. If this was truly the case, he wanted no revelation of such blatant self-centeredness. He suppressed the urge to openly propose that this same reason had driven the others to join in these impromptu polemics.

"Look around you," he began. "Do you see any habitual joiners in this crowd?"

Since no one seemed ready to hazard a response, he took the initiative to elucidate further. "Yet, here we are jammed together like some blood brotherhood. There has to be a reason why."

"But there's nothing deliberate in our coming together like this," Frank objected. "You've got to admit that our gatherings here in the cafeteria have always been spontaneous."

"What's so bad about that?" Peggy interjected.

"Nothing. Really nothing," Frank admitted lamely.

Caution made Jim Stahr shrink from the idea of intimating that ego satisfaction was the primary reason for their having formed such a tightly knit group. Instead, he shifted direction in search of a more plausible reason for their having stayed together all these years.

"Perhaps we're here because it's the only means we have for thumbing our noses at the Establishment. And who of us hasn't enjoyed doing that?" Jim stopped speaking and smiled before going on to inquire, "Could we have maintained our integrity any other way?"

Jim observed the expressions on the faces around him change from personal irritation to shared pleasure. The urge to express his initial rationale for their undeclared loyalty to one another withered and died before it took root. He felt relief for not having allowed whimsy to lead him astray. Any attempt at making such an unproven claim, especially one that concerned the touchy subject of ego, would only have created a disruptive turmoil among the others.

"It's too bad that we'll not be able to have such spontaneous meetings after we graduate," Bessie Siegal stated with a sigh.

"That's impossible, Bessie. There's no way of teaching the man in the street that to think and say is more important than to earn and buy," Nick said, his words exhibiting displeasure.

"He's right, kid," Hector added in a voice strangely free of its normal blatancy. "Just stick your head out the door and you'll hear that land-locked siren called 'dollar' enticing everyone to hound after her."

"Being able to do on the outside what we've been doing on the inside would be a miracle." Frank reached over to pat Bessie gently on the shoulder.

"Well, man has produced miracles before," Bessie declared. "Remember the bomb?" Her persistence brimmed with the rancor of the untried young who view life as their exclusive avenue for self-imposed change.

"Maybe it's time for a miracle all right," Frank proposed with weary solemnity.

"Maybe a revolution is more like it," Hector added defiantly.

"Fine, but no bloodshed," Nick cautioned.

"A revolution of values is more like it," Jim recommended.

Peggy Troy pushed her books nervously to one side and said, "How can there ever be such a radical change without someone getting hurt?" Her wartime experience had stripped clean all doubts she may have entertained about people's propensity to harm one another.

"I'm for changing values through poetic persuasion, not fiery rhetoric," Frank suggested.

"Hell," Hector burst forth disgustedly, "you can't change society with poetry. You've got to fight fire with fire!"

Frank did not bother to look at Hector Palofax when he responded to his taunting outburst.

"Hector, your friend Karl Marx did that—and all too well to suit me. As for fighting fire with fire, I think it is a gross scientific fallacy. May I suggest instead that urinating copiously would more likely put out your enemy's fire—that is, if your aim is good."

The others laughed.

Hector retorted flatly, "I'll keep it in mind, Frank."

"It might be worth your while to keep it in hand instead," Frank snapped out and quickly glanced up at the ceiling in a theatrical display of aloofness.

"Let's keep to the subject at hand instead of in hand, Frank," Bessie said with a grimace of annoyance. Turning to Jim Stahr, she pleaded, "Please, Jim, let's get back to your revolution."

Jim pursed his lips for a moment and said, "All kidding aside, there's got to be a basic driving force behind every revolt. And ours should be the unhampered criticism of society's values."

"That means having to consider ideas that oppose those of the majority," Nick started to object.

"Isn't that what democracy implies?" Hector asserted with mock naiveté. His witty remark brought chuckles of agreement, which helped restore some of his battered self-esteem.

"Yes, that would be the epitome of freedom," Jim concurred. "But it wouldn't work."

"Wait a second, friend, isn't that what we've been doing here all these years?" Frank's words poured forth stripped free of their customary pleasantry. "Here we've been able to think and say what we pleased, and without restraints. Now you're telling us that we won't be able to do the same thing once we leave here."

Jim Stahr pushed his chair away from the table. Lately, he had begun to indulge in the pastime of using his own words to ridicule his pretensions of possessing an abiding individualism. Even now, he found that he could not prevent a slight malicious belittling of self from seeping into his response.

He turned to look directly at Frank and said, "That's exactly what I'm saying." He shifted his gaze away and looked at no one in particular before saying, "None of us have the guts to remain free of society's demands once we have to earn our own way in the real world outside these walls."

His remarks did not trigger any vociferous objections, which had always been the expected response in the past. Somehow, this uncommon silence gave rise to feelings of embarrassment. It now seemed imperative to soften his accusation that all of them lacked the staying power to hold on to their free and independent spirit by explaining further.

"New ideas go against people's inherent grain, especially when their entrenched beliefs are threatened by them."

Frank merely mumbled in agreement.

Bessie, on the other hand, looked directly at Jim with a childish look of petulance. "You've been so damn negative lately. What's eating you, sweetheart?"

"Perhaps it's just a case of me harassing me," he answered, surprised by the forthright veracity of his reply.

"Welcome to the club," Peggy said.

Gennie Connors had listened to these exchanges, thinking that her entry into the discussion would have been an unwanted intrusion. Nevertheless, taking courage, she mildly interjected her own viewpoints.

"You're right, Jim. People fear change. Maybe that's how hate is born." All turned to her attentively. "The great men of the future will be those who can eradicate that kind of fear," she added without altering her expression. Her remarks met with respectful silence and some nods of approval.

"If and when such leaders do become a reality," Jim said with an unusual solemnity, "mankind will need to devise a new kind of God."

Gennie looked at him with apprehension, dreading that she was about to be made the target of his ridicule.

"You must agree," he turned a mischievous grin toward her, "those new prophets will certainly need a deity who would also be capable of doing away with people's fears and hatreds. Am I right?"

Bessie Siegal bent forward to stare at Jim quizzically. "Are you proposing some kind of mutation of God's mind?"

"In a way," Jim said. "I imagine that men who are able to do away with the fear that stems from new ideas would have to be wholly free of any bias. A compatible God would have to be just as objective when it comes to judging the worth of mankind's innovations."

Gennie suddenly stated with newfound boldness, "I see nothing wrong with that."

"There's none. How can anyone object?" Jim said.

"Go ahead, Jim, give us the rundown on your emancipated God," Bessie quipped, her hands flipping outward, palms open, in a gesture of submission.

There was a brief silence while Jim searched for a response that would be a source of delight and free of words that would reveal any self-condemnation.

"If this deity is to be free of bias then he will have to be color-blind and unlettered," Jim Stahr continued on with his revamping of a divine being, "so that he will only see people of all races as the same grayish figures and their written creeds as nothing more than mumbo jumbo. We'll make him an eternal sovereign without any singular loyalties and thus free him of the sin of favoritism." There was more to say, but he suspected that any further talk on this subject would be boring to his listeners. Jim stopped speaking and looked around to judge the reactions to what he had just said. His silence mingled with that of the others seated at the table.

Peggy Troy's thoughts surged back to the past, dredging up memories of wartime incidents that once threatened to do away with all the spiritual beliefs that were so much an integral part of her childhood. Now these memories gave vent to anger as her words crackled through the alien stillness that encompassed them.

"That's not enough! Your revitalized divine being should feel human suffering and be able to end it." Tears of anger brought a shine to her eyes.

Peggy's sharply worded criticism released ideas that Jim had locked away in fear of displeasing his listeners.

"Perhaps you're right, Peggy. So, if you'll allow me," he started, freeing his thoughts from all constraints, "I'll burden this new God with the ability to go astray. How else can he have insight of mankind's imperfections?"

Jim stopped speaking to study the expressions on the faces around him. They all appeared to be waiting for him to continue. He reacted by saying, "This God must be a moral spirit, mind you, one who'll reject homage being paid him by anyone setting out to maim and slaughter. Yes, he'll be the kind of God who is all-sensitive, not just almighty."

"I'll be God's man in the morning, if that's the case," Frank volunteered.

Jim's attempt at caustic humor had failed. His words did not generate either laughter or smiles.

Nick Grigoris broke the uneasy quiet by softly singing a lyric from a Dixieland classic: *"Count me in that number...count me in that number..."*

Frank picked up the tune and began to sing along with Nick, but somewhat louder. Some of the others joined in. *"And when the saints...and when the saints come marchin' in... count me in that number..."*

A hush passed through the cafeteria as the other students turned to stare at them with looks of aversion and astonishment. Only the sounding of the bell signaling a change of classes brought their spontaneous outburst to a halt. All who were huddled around the table grabbed their personal belongings and scrambled toward the exit doors.

Jim ambled off alone, reproaching himself for possessing a charlatan's wit. Inwardly, he knew that in today's troubled world his reconstructed God would be a prelude to chaos. There was no denying that humanity still hungered for the kind of God they presently possessed—one they believe exclusively favors them and whose blessings they self-righteously assume to be their divine right.

He was glad that there were no more classes to attend that day.

Chapter 4

Nick sat on a high stool with his heels hooked onto the metal bar bolted onto its two front legs. He sipped from his beer glass, awaiting Jim Stahr's arrival. A few minutes later, Jim entered, letting in a rush of cold air from the open door. He put his coat on a wall hook, slid onto an adjacent seat and asked how the week went for Nick.

Nick's puttylike features crinkled into a broad grin. "Okay," he said.

Rocky, the owner of the tavern served Jim a beer as they began exchanging small talk. A short while later, both of them lapsed into a moody silence. Nick broke the spell, asking, with muted bluntness, what Jim was planning to do after graduation. Jim sensed that the question was Nick's way of confronting the problem he himself was facing—trying to untangle his muddled speculations about his own future.

"Well?" Nick prompted. "A guy has to do something."

Jim shrugged. "Maybe."

"You've got to work sometime. That's how the game of eat and sleep is played," Nick persisted.

Jim fixed his gaze on the white foam cap in his beer glass. "Yes, no doubt I'll end up like all the rest. Somehow I'd like to float free for a while after we leave the not-so-hallowed halls of NYU."

As if trying to mask his embarrassment, he continued staring down at his glass instead of facing his friend. "Perhaps I'm undergoing a premature mid-age crisis. You know, that time in life when you have one more wild hair left, and it's making you itch to do something different. Well, it seems that's how I feel at this stage of the game." His tone conveyed a sense of defeat rather than optimism. "Anyway, I can't see myself joining the grand parade marching down the corporate glory road to retirement."

"Maybe what I want, Jim, is nothing more than a job," Nick said defensively.

"Then try an employment agency," Jim countered.

"Come on, quit pulling my leg. There're more cub reporters in New York than nickels in the subway. Besides my name isn't Sulzberger, and I don't believe in miracles."

"Then maybe it's time for you to get out of New York."

Nick sat deep in thought looking blankly at the mirror clamped to the wall behind the bar. Some minutes passed before he slowly rotated the seat of his stool to face Jim with a puzzled frown. When he did begin speaking, the words came forth slowly, as if he was unsure that what he was about to say would make sense.

"You know, that's an idea."

Jim kept his head down as he studied his beer and said nothing.

"Heck, we can go searching together," Nick continued. "I'll look for a job, and you can hunt for whatever is going to pacify that wild hair of yours. Well, what do you say?"

"You're not thinking of bumming around looking for a job, are you?" Jim stared at him in disbelief.

"Why not? Anyway, you're the one who came up with the idea. What's wrong with it?"

Jim swiveled from side to side on the rotating stool, stopping to survey his surroundings before placing his elbows on top of the bar. "Nothing…absolutely nothing."

He began seeking a way to fend off making any allusion to his participating in such a venture. The idea of wandering from city to city in search of a panacea that would temper his pervasive restlessness was not immediately appealing. Even the thought of such an undertaking failed to arouse the slightest hint of exhilaration.

"Why me, Nick? I've yet to make a single life-altering decision completely on my own. There's always been some other authority doing it for me, whether I liked it or not. Listen, I've talked a great deal about personal freedom, but to be honest with you, don't ask me what it's actually like. Anyway, what good would I be on such a trip?"

"You've got what I haven't—drive. Besides, you seem to know how to deal with problems when they come your way. It's just common sense that two is better than one when you're drifting around," Nick went on. "I want a job, and you want to experience something that will pacify that urge of yours. Well, here's our chance to satisfy both our needs. What do you say?"

Jim puckered his brow and said, "Let me think about it."

Never before had anyone challenged him to show that he himself possessed the independent spirit he extolled—that he could act solely in response to his own will, unaffected by the needs or desires of others. His constant espousal of the merits of this credo over the years had convinced fellow students by implication that he, too, possessed that inner dedication to self. Yet, deep down, Jim Stahr had always known that his constant glorification of individualism belied his feelings of inadequacy to act as the independent spirit he made out to be. Now, for the first time in memory, he had openly admitted that forces other than his own had shaped his life. Even so, this frank confession evidently failed to make any impression on his listener.

Nick's eagerness to secure a promise from Jim to join in his quest had made him indifferent to all words other than those of affirmation. This expectation remained unfulfilled as no reply was forthcoming. Instead, Jim sat studying the grainy surface of the bar as he pondered to shape an appropriate response. His past discourses on the need to maintain individual freedom in a society that demanded conformity were more pretense than truth. His inability to give even the slightest consideration to Nick's proposal was sufficient proof that he lacked the mettle to practice what he had been preaching to his classmates all these years. After all, he had to admit his words had been nothing more than lip service. At this moment, there was little more that he could say.

Jim looked up at the wall clock behind the bar. "It's getting late, Nick. We'd better get started if we're going to make Peggy's party tonight."

As they climbed up the stairs leading out into the street, both were aware that neither one of them had made any commitments to the other.

Chapter 5

Jim and Nick arrived late; the party had started an hour earlier. Peggy suppressed her displeasure with a welcoming grin, having quickly dismissed all thoughts of chiding them for their tardiness. Instead, she led them through the long corridor leading into the living room and hurriedly introduced them to a member of the university faculty, who was the honored guest of the gathering. She then excused herself and hurried into the kitchen while both Nick Grigoris and Jim Stahr answered the professor's questions concerning their studies. Frank Colucci strolled over to join them and gradually began to shift the subject matter under discussion to that of the mysticism of William Blake's poetry. Jim took this opportunity to tactfully remove himself from the group. He approached Peggy just as she exited the kitchen and removed one of the glasses of beer she was carrying on a metal tray. He thanked her and moved away to mingle with the other guests.

There were many people whom he had never met before. Those he did recognize seemed deeply immersed in discussions with others, and his entry into any one of these exchanges, he judged, would have been an unwelcome interruption. Seeking to smother a growing sense of isolation, he sought refuge by slipping into the kitchen where he switched off the light and positioned himself in front of the window that faced St. Marks. Shoving the curtain aside, he peered down at the street. People were scurrying by, heads bent as they struggled against the gusting wind.

There's a strange satisfaction about being alone in the middle of crowd, he thought. In his case, however, this situation stemmed from a personal shortcoming, one that made him feel more at ease by isolating himself from all those who wanted nothing more than to be deeply engaged in some discussion with others. Yet, here even amongst some of his closest friends, this same need for apartness had come to the fore, making him seek solace in the room's tranquilizing emptiness and silence. He stood alone in the dark observing the comings and goings on the street below.

A hand gently touched his shoulder, but he did not respond to its touch immediately. His mind was slow in shifting from its preoccupation with the world around him to that of the realm of physical sensation. What did break off his cogitation was Gennie Connors' whispered inquiry.

"Can one think in an unlit kitchen?"

The darkness of the empty room amplified her words. Jim continued to stare out the window without making any reply. Instead, he reached out and found her arm and gently drew her closer to the window until she stood parallel to him. "Look down into the street, Gennie," he urged as he pressed his own face closer to the windowpane, his breath spreading a vaporous cloud of moisture onto its cold surface.

"I was just thinking about the people down on the street. Theirs is not a bookish world like the one that we're in at this very moment. Look at them rushing to someplace or someone. Can you see?"

Gennie looked down and watched some pedestrians cross the street and disappear from view once they reached the curb fronting the apartment building. He released his hold of her arm. Lifting the glass he held in his other hand, Jim drank from it before setting it down on the windowsill.

"I'm hoping they're carrying some of that precious quality called spirit," he said softly. "And if they are, they'll probably end up squandering the little they have and hold on like misers to things they can count and store."

The light from the streetlamp commingled with that radiating from the full moon and flooded Gennie's features with a subdued luminosity. Jim turned and looked closely at her for the first time. Her features were soft and appealing, her blue eyes and crimson lips standing out sharply against the grayish pale light that shone down upon her. She had the look of a little girl in desperate need of being held, as if in want of assurance that she belonged and was unquestionably an inseparable part of the life of someone who truly cared. This time, he placed his arm around her waist and drew her closer to his side. Once more, they both stood wordlessly gazing into the street. Soon, it was empty of passersby. She reached up to stroke his cheek, hoping that her caress would turn his attention to her. Failing to get any kind of response, she slowly freed herself from his grasp, moved away from him, and walked back into the living room. Her abrupt parting left him with an uneasiness, which gave rise to unsettling feelings that extinguished the sense of contemplative well-being that he experienced when he first entered the kitchen. Minutes later, a hand reached in and switched on the kitchen light. Peggy Troy moved toward him, grasped his wrist, and propelled him out, commanding him to mingle with her other guests.

Chapter 6

The crispness of the wind was refreshing after the congestion and noise of the gathering in the apartment. Both Frank Colucci and Jim Stahr were now weary and emotionally drained. As they turned off Tenth Street and started walking on Second Avenue, Jim grumbled, "It was hotter than a Turkish bath up there."

Frank grimaced at Jim's joyless comment but shrugged it off thinking that his friend may have had too much to drink. Yet, his words deflated the good spirits generated by the evening's delightful repartee of humor and ideas. He felt an urgent need to sustain what he inwardly termed an intellectual high, convinced that the most effective stimulant for doing so was animating conversation. However, this motivating agent was not forthcoming from his companion. Jim Stahr's mood negated his willingness to take part in any verbal exchanges. The aftermath of the party had left him silent and uneasy. Frank decided to resort to another means to preserve his high spirits. Reaching into one of his coat pockets, he withdrew a thin, twisted cigarette and placed it between his lips. He stopped to light it.

Jim recognized the smell immediately. "You're not going to smoke that reefer on the street, are you?" he exclaimed, more in disbelief than alarm.

"Why not, amigo?" Frank replied. He blew a large cloud of smoke into the air.

They continued walking together without speaking.

Gradually, Frank's elation began to seep back. There was a growing determination on his part not to allow Jim's caustic words, or attitude, to squash the pleasure he had derived from the inspired conversations of these past hours. He drew heavily on the yellowish, misshapen cigarette. In time, his spirits rose further. Their words, which had been few and infrequent, had faded into total silence by the time they reached the Fourteenth Street subway station. It was well past midnight, and neither of them was looking forward to taking one of the slow, local trains that operated during the late evening hours. A police officer stood a short distance away, obviously watching them with a curiosity hidden behind a mask of indifference. Frank spotted him and slipped the cigarette into his other hand to hide it from the police officer's view before he turned away from the subway entrance and jaywalked across the street. Jim trailed behind. Frank threw a quick glance at Union Square Park before moving away in the direction of Irving Place. When he had gone a short distance, he turned back and beckoned to Jim.

"Come on! Come on! I'm going to show you one of the most aesthetically appealing doorways in the city."

A few quick steps and Jim caught up with his companion.

Frank chuckled aloud seemingly without reason, his feet lifting with a new kind of ease as if the earth's gravity had somewhat diminished. "Those subways," he mused aloud, his voice pitching higher than usual, "they can sometimes create some meaningful moments...even poetic ones."

"I doubt that," Jim said sarcastically. "Subways are nothing more than shaky metal containers on wheels that carry you from one concrete platform to another."

Frank showed no visible reaction to his companion's remark as he drew once more on the stub of his cigarette. A broad smile crossed his face with the realization that marijuana had once more raised a protective shield against his consistent fear of being ridiculed by others less sensitive than himself. Liberated from this apprehension, his self-confidence rose to a level whereby he held all of his convictions to be of incontestable validity. Now Frank felt dauntless against another's criticism or scorn.

They turned left at Irving Place and strolled past Washington Irving High School until they reached the edge of Gramercy Park. Frank stopped in front of one of the houses that stood on the corner. The structure was of Georgian design with an ebony door, and whose trimmings of polished brass were highlighted by a town crier's lamp that hung overhead.

"Here is the perfect balance of line and light. Here's a doorway that welcomes with dignity—a pragmatic masterpiece with a near perfect balance between strength and grace," Frank went on pedantically, his aesthetic sense now intensified and heightened.

Leaving Frank standing in place, Jim shuffled backward in an effort to get a better perspective. Yes, he admitted to himself, Frank was right. The doorway did produce an unusual welcoming serenity he had rarely noted from the many other doorways he had seen in his travels. Truly, it was a gem embedded in a city dwelling, he conceded silently.

Frank stood gazing straight ahead, judging that it would not serve any beneficial purpose to voice any further acclaim about the entryway knowing that beauty was a quality derived from feelings, not persuasion. Frank broke off his reflections, crossed the street and started toward Broadway with Jim following at his heels, their footsteps echoing through the vacant streets with a faultless consistency. Frank suddenly felt the need to disrupt the pervading quiet with words.

"Listen, amigo, if you want to find beauty in this city, you can even discover it in the subway," he proclaimed as he thrust a pointed finger into the air.

"Here we go again with the damn subways! Tell me, Frank, did you ever have an aesthetic experience in the subway?" Jim asked his friend, more to poke fun at him rather than to contest the veracity of what he said.

"Let me think." Frank put his hand to his chin and stroked it, then let it fall to his side and smiled. "No, not in the true sense. But I did learn about the hurt that comes from missed chances."

"On the subway?"

"Yes, on the subway."

Jim blew on his hands and slipped them into his coat pockets before urging Frank to go ahead and tell his story. The words conveyed the kind of indulgence one uses to humor an inebriated friend.

Frank did not respond until they reached Broadway, the lightness of his step beginning to increase as they turned onto this street.

"Well, go ahead, Frank, tell me."

"Tell you what?"

"How you failed to take advantage of something that happened on the subway."

"Yes…yes, I remember," Frank's stated absentmindedly as he again drew deeply from the shortened stub of his cigarette.

"Go ahead. I'm listening."

There was not a single trace of joviality in his speech, nor in his expression, when Frank began to recount his story about a lost opportunity in the subway. On the contrary, a shade of melancholy clouded his words.

"It was one of those days when I had those lonely blues, and I couldn't shake them. To be honest with you, I just felt like a motherless child. So instead of taking the subway home, I walked over to Third Avenue and took the El. Don't ask me why." He reached up to scratch his head before saying, "When I pushed the turnstile, it wouldn't budge. With my head turned down, I didn't notice that a girl was standing on the other side trying to push her way out. She waited for me to back away, with the most beautiful smile you've ever seen. We both stood there like fools gaping at one another, both of us wanting to reach out, touch our hands in greeting, and become more than friends. The message was in her eyes, and, surely, in my thoughts."

Frank's flow of words ceased when an ambulance sped past them. They stood and watched as it charged down the empty street, its wailing siren shattering the city's late-hour tranquility with a morbid fury. When the din had fully retreated into silence, Jim pulled a hand out of his coat, reached over and put it on Frank's shoulder, saying, "Well, what happened?"

Frank looked at him with a puzzled expression. Then his eyes flashed with recognition of what he had been saying. "Nothing. Nothing. The train was pulling into the station and she stepped back to let me pass so that I could catch it. Ha! Like an idiot I ran for it and got on the train just before the doors closed shut behind me. When I did look back, she was standing there smiling at me more with regret than joy, or so it seemed to me. I missed a chance to get to know someone who obviously wanted to get to know me."

"It sounds like a missed opportunity, all right," Jim said without any show of enthusiasm.

"Yes, it seemed like she was yearning to reach out…to know someone who could bring new hopes into her life. At least, that's the way it appeared to me. When the train pulled away from the station, I felt sort of empty, foolish and a little hurt. Simply, I wasn't happy with myself." He broke into a smile and announced loudly, "But, Jim, I'm an optimist. Did you hear me? I'm an optimist! Someday, I'll see that kind of look again, and next time I'll respond to its call. Just wait and see."

"I don't believe you'll ever get another chance," was Jim's gruff judgment. "The odds of that happening again, especially on a subway, are far too great."

"Why do you say that?" Frank blurted out, obviously hurt by Jim's acerbic pessimism.

"What happened to you that day can only be considered a long shot at best, that's why. And when you muff such an opportunity, all you're left with are unrealistic expectations." Apparently, the scorn that permeated his reply seemed directed more to himself than to anyone else. He realized that he, too, harbored some wish whose fulfillment also seemed unachievable—the ability to act free of any constraints set by others.

Frank's lightheartedness slipped away. "Hell," he began, his tone lacking its normal suavity, "a good dosage of dreams wouldn't hurt you rationalists. You might even find it a challenge when one plus one does not always equal two. Anyway," he fumed, "who wants to live in a world where every human response is predictable?" Disgustedly, he tossed the thumb-width stub of his cigarette onto the sidewalk and ground it vigorously with the sole of his shoe.

Jim, taken aback by his friend's anger, thought it best to refrain from making any other derisive comments.

They reached Herald Square and shuffled their way toward the subway entrance. Whatever elation Frank may have derived from smoking the marijuana cigarette was now beginning to wear off; melancholy apprehension now seemed fixed on taking its place. He shambled down the steps, his movements somewhat droopy and graceless. Halfway down, he stopped to look back at his friend, who stood observing him with a look of concern. This prompted him to give vent to his disquieting thoughts.

"Jim," he began, "maybe I'm just a wishful thinker. But I'd rather chase after fantasies than live in a world without them." He stood gazing up at Jim inwardly debating whether to give voice to his feelings, his hesitation arising from an intuitive awareness that his poetic sense might color his words in a way that could be mistakenly deemed to be derisive. Quickly falling victim to ego's urging, however, he allowed himself free rein over how and what he felt compelled to say. "If I had the power to choose how to live my life," he started, "I'd choose to be a mystic with the ability to establish a rapport with aesthetic realms beyond our earthly confines. Can you imagine the kind of poetry I could write?" He hurried down the steps without waiting for a reply. When he reached the bottom landing, he turned to shout up at Jim tauntingly, "Hey, Jim, how do you want to live?"

Jim walked down a few steps before he answered. "Me? Like a realist, that's how!"

"How's that?" Frank responded sharply, a slight feeling of uneasiness creeping in for having attempted to ridicule his friend.

"I'm going to try to bed down Mister Reason with a lady called Experience," he shouted back, "so they can bring to life a newborn named Convictions. That's how!"

Instead of the expected quick response, silence permeated the dark void that separated them. When it did come, Frank's words brought forth joyful pleasure, not resentment. "It's worth a try, amigo, it's worth a try." He waved a hand, turned and vanished, leaving in his wake an austere, empty and dank stairway.

Jim crossed the street and entered the downtown entrance of the subway, content in the knowledge that their candid exchanges had not marred their comradely relationship. Frank Colucci was too valuable a friend to lose over such marked differences of opinion.

Chapter 7

Jim raised the collar of his coat with a gloved hand as he stood before the glass door. Looking through it, he saw that the night's heavy snowfall had left the city's perennial somber hues buried under a blanket of thick white crystals. Just as he reached for the doorknob, the mail carrier shoved his way through and began pounding his mustard-colored galoshes on the hallway mat. After they had exchanged some terse greetings, Jim stepped toward the open doorway leading out of the building only to be halted in midstride by the mailman's upraised hand.

"Hold it, scholar, I think I've got a letter for you."

With his free hand, the letter carrier threw one end of a dangling scarf over his shoulder and reached into the leather bag that hung over the other shoulder. He extracted an envelope and handed it to Jim, who thrust it between the pages of a textbook without bothering to look at it. With a hurried word of thanks, he squeezed his way past the postman and made his way onto the street.

Standing alone on the sidewalk, he took note of the strange and awesome silence that surrounded him. It appeared as if nature had waved a magic wand at the city's hurly-burly, stilling its usual strident clamor to an unearthly calm. The intensity of the night's snowfall had locked automobiles into their curbside spaces, keeping them jailed in place by unbroken banks of thick snow piles. There were no other pedestrians in sight, for it was well past the time in which the hordes of students, factory, and office personnel crowded into public conveyances of one kind or another, their varied facial expressions displaying a gamut of human emotions. For him, the complete stoppage of the city's life-pumping motion left him suspended in a spatial vacuum where the cognizance of reality ceased and illusion took its place. His imagination projected him into an empty wasteland where each step forward seemed to bring him closer to the end of a bold journey. This state of mind persisted until he entered the subway station where the snapping crash of turnstiles sent his mind slipping back to an awareness of his everyday surroundings.

Jim pushed his way through one of them and hurried up the steps that led to the station's elevated platform. As soon as he reached it, a train rushed past, leaving in its wake a flurry of agitated snowflakes. The dull slapping sound of the train's doors slamming shut finally brought a conclusive end to his mind's immersion in a fantasy brought on by the city's alien stillness.

Signs of the early morning's tumultuous rush hour were evident in the twisted newspapers left atop the seats. Jim settled into an unoccupied one. He opened his textbook and removed the letter the postman had handed him. What immediately caught his attention was the return address—Walter Reed Army Hospital. The train halted at the next station, and the routine sequencing of opening and closing of doors was in process when he began opening the envelope. Quickly, the lifeless eyes of the nearby passengers registered interest as they began to observe his movements. Other riders, however, had pushed through the open doors of the subway car and blocked from view the curious stares of the passengers that were seated across from him. The looks of inquisitiveness of those who had begun the game of watching quickly reverted to that of impassivity.

The letter was formal, short, and regretful. The contents coldly stated that Lacy Hutchins was dead. No explanation as to why it was sent to him, nor was there any details as to the cause of his death or any information concerning burial arrangements. The signature was from an official of the Veteran's Administration. Jim folded the single sheet of paper and put it back into the envelope before slipping it back between the pages of his book. He felt a wetness seeping into his eyes. Why him? Why him? Just as the train rolled onto the Brooklyn Bridge, Jim stood up and turned to stare out the train window through tear-moistened eyes. The roofs of the industrial buildings below him were still whitewashed by last night's heavy snowfall.

"Poor Lacy...God!" thought Jim. "I hope there's no Jim Crow in Valhalla." This silent entreaty flitted through his mind and vanished. As the train made its way across the East River, Jim shifted his attention to the skyscrapers that lined the shoreline of lower Manhattan in an effort to rein in the burgeoning shock of his friend's demise. After the train finished rattling its way across the bridge, it picked up speed and plunged into an underground tunnel, obliterating from view all that helped diminish his feelings of shock and hurt.

Chapter 8

A record snowfall buried cars and left others stalled at odd angles along the city's main arteries, marring hopes for those who needed to drive to their Thanksgiving Day festivities. But the harsh weather had not hampered Jim Stahr's family from coming together for a turkey dinner. The food and drink had left him satisfied for a time. As the afternoon progressed, however, he felt a persistent desire to leave. Humorously persuading his family that study took precedence over gluttony, he grabbed some books off his desk and slipped out.

There were only a few passengers on the subway car that took him to Washington Square Station. The NYU Law Library never closed, not even during holiday seasons. He was convinced its environment would be conducive to writing the term paper that had left him mired in confusion in all of his past attempts to finalize it. As he entered the library, he saw that its only occupant was the security guard, who sat engrossed in reading a copy of the New York Daily News. The room was bathed in the kind of congenial silence that unleashes the mind from all its constraints, allowing it to probe freely into those realms most dread delving into because of a fear that their newly discovered insights could be interpreted as radical or disturbing.

Perhaps today he would be able to unravel the entangled notions that had stymied the completion of his term paper for a class taught by Sidney Hook, the famed political philosopher. Now that the course was nearing completion, the only students remaining were a stalwart few still willing to accept the challenge of determining what a citizen could do to reorder the governing forces currently shaping national policies. His past attempts to address this issue had left him with the feeling that he was incapable of formulating into words a course of action that seemed feasible. All of his previous efforts had led to the harsh reality that economic survival for most people left no other route open to them than that of participating in the national race for monetary security. The majority—especially those without special talents—were compelled to seek a livelihood by conforming to workplace rules and regulations determined by others. Like being hopelessly lost in a maze, he could not find any path that individualists could take that would allow them to hold fast to their unconventional ideals and still achieve economic self-sufficiency. For him, the resolution of this enigma had become a near fetish. Compounding this situation was the belief that the outcome of this endeavor would help resolve his own internal feuding and would put an end to his search for a workable synthesis between society's restrictive demands and his personal desire to retain control over his own thoughts and actions once he left the protective walls of the university.

Jim chose a table a good distance away from the solitary guard. He sat sorting through the many options that confronted him for a long while before he bent over and started writing.

As the process of origination in art, there is a similar course in the labors of scholarship, whereby the mind must work through an anxiety generated by the fear that inspirational ideas may slip out of its grasp before being fully explored. This same force now goaded him on, as his thoughts began to evolve into a logical pattern. Still, his physiological and intellectual forces had yet to attune to one another, as his mood kept fluctuating between self-confidence, when conviction surfaced that his assumptions were applicable and valid, and despondency every time his reflections appeared to be flawed and indefensible. However, in time, from his exploratory incursions into the domains of intuition and reason, there materialized the soothing balm of relief, as perplexity diminished and discovery emerged. After Jim completed writing his final words into a notebook, he felt a sense of gratification at having resolved a taxing problem that now could be banished to the clutter that constitutes the past.

The afternoon's efforts had conveyed him through the full cycle essential for fashioning a creative work, from the anguish of trying to bring order to muddled ideas, through to the delight that comes with the assurance of actually having done so. The aftermath of these exertions left him emotionally spent, but happy. He leaned back in his chair to peer out a nearby window. The afternoon's light had dimmed. Jim pushed his chair back, raised himself, and moved quietly toward a marble bust of Benjamin Franklin, its lifeless gaze fixed on the vista below. He positioned himself next to it and stared down at the leafless trees that stood in a disorganized fashion throughout Washington Square Park.

"I think I've got it, Ben. Yes, this time, I think I've got it," he silently confided to the frozen-faced sculpture at his side.

The library was still free of other visitors. There was a strange delight in this solitude. In time, however, the fading light began to dispel this feeling. Returning to his worktable, Jim retrieved his belongings from the table and made for the exit. The uniformed guard looked up from the newspaper he was reading and winked his goodbye.

Once he was on the street, there seemed only one way to go. This had been an eventful day, and he was in no mood to end it without first sharing his self-declared triumph with someone. Jim started trudging through the deep snow in the direction of the apartment house near St. Marks-in-the-Bowery but found that lumbering into a cold headwind turned what was normally a pleasure into a disconcerting task.

He pressed the buzzer with the index finger of his gloved hand, but there was no immediate answer

"Who'd be home on Thanksgiving, anyway?" he asked himself. He pressed the button again. Still not getting any reply, he removed his gloves, blew on his hands and began rubbing them together. Without replacing his gloves, he impatiently pushed down on the button in three short bursts, his thoughts already filled with loathing at having to fight the cold wind once again. For a moment, he was startled, then surprised, when words issued forth from the intercom's speaker.

"Who is it?" It was Gennie Connors' voice.

"It's Jim Stahr."

"Come on up." The invitation had an insipid ring to it.

A buzzer rang. He pushed open the heavy door leading into the building's foyer and started up the stairs, too impatient to wait for the elevator. The door to the apartment was ajar. When knocking on it brought no response, he cautiously pushed it opened and stepped into the long corridor that led to the living quarters in the rear. Once inside the living room, he removed his coat and placed it and his books on top of a vacant chair.

"Come into the kitchen," Gennie called out to him.

Sticking his hands into the pockets of his suit jacket, he entered as directed and greeted her with a joyful, "Happy Thanksgiving! And where's the other captain?" The question teasingly referred to their former military rank in the Army Nurse Corps.

"Peggy went home for the holidays. I'm here all alone today," she informed him with a slight break in her voice. What was most surprising to him was the formality of her attire. She was dressed as if she were about to leave for a formal party.

"I'm not interrupting anything, am I? It looks like you're ready to go out to some elegant gathering."

She shook her head negatively before hurrying to turn off the flames under a pot of coffee that stood boiling on the stove.

"Gennie, maybe I'm interfering with your plans. It looks like you're waiting for a visitor. I think it would be best if I left. Sorry to have troubled you."

Without waiting for a reply, he briskly moved back into the living room and picked up his coat and books. He had entered the apartment with high spirits, but feelings of embarrassment now took their place. Apparently, the only option left open to him was to leave. His confusion grew when she hurried to his side, placed a hand on his arm as if to restrain him, saying, "Please don't go, Jim, I'm sorry. Please forgive me...but please don't go." Her words resonated more with despair than apology.

"But it seems like you're expecting company. I'd better get going."

"Believe me, I wasn't going anywhere, nor was I expecting any visitors." Gennie smiled and repeated her regrets for having been so inhospitable.

He replaced his coat and books on a nearby chair.

"How about some of that coffee that you've got boiling on the stove?" he suggested with a noiseless clap of his hands.

Walking away, she turned to say, "Just give me a chance to hide my freckles."

Feeling more relieved than elated, he ambled over to a wall shelf that held records and began sifting through them in search of music that would suit his mood. Bypassing all the classical recordings, his fingers pulled out one that promised the smooth sounds that could help soothe his weary mind and jarred emotions. The record cover listed the songs, which turned out to be old standbys—"Tenderly," "Body and Soul," "What a Difference a Day Makes." He slipped the record out of its jacket and placed it with great care on the turntable of the record player that stood a few feet away. By the time the music began, Gennie had returned and had started pouring coffee into cups that were already on the table Only when he had seated himself did he become aware of the meticulous care in which every item on it was set in place in expectation of a single visitor. Surprised by the formality of the table setting, he inquired again whether she had been expecting someone, already convinced that it was another man and that his failure to show up was the cause for her dejection.

"Maybe the one I've been expecting has already arrived," she implied.

The expression on her face took on a worried look, as if her answer may have revealed something that she desperately wanted kept to herself. This was not the first time that she had spent this holiday alone. Early on, she had come to accept the idea that aloneness was to be an integral part of her life. There had been no other choice after her parents were killed in an auto accident on an ice-covered highway, not far from the farm they owned in upstate New York. She was only seventeen when it happened, but with the help of some distant neighbors and family friends, she managed to stay on at the farm, finish high school, and enter a nursing college in Albany, the state's capital. Nursing, she knew, would thrust her into a world that would never be empty of people—even on holidays. While others could gather with their families to celebrate such events, she was left to resort to her own means in dealing with her social isolation. And it was during these intermittent holiday vacations that she had begun to use her imagination as a tool for creating situations that fictitiously peopled her empty homes. For the time that she was engrossed in such games of make-believe, her feelings of aloneness fled, imagination always taking hold to fill the void with people and events. Yet, there was never any need to indulge in such fantasies during the years she spent in the military. Her world then was never empty of the presence of others. The medical staff and the wounded were ever-present. But today, for reasons that were not clear to her, she had felt compelled to resort to this odd pastime. Having done so was sufficient proof that her decision to move in with Peggy Troy, in order to avoid being apart from others during the holidays, had come to naught. She had failed to take into account that her new roommate had family and friends in nearby Westchester County. And to this day, an invitation to partake in that social sphere had failed to materialize. Shame now replaced any feelings of aloneness.

Jim was too caught up in the lyrics of "Moonlight in Vermont" to give any thought to her offhand remark that he may have been the one she was waiting for today. The music eased away all the emotional residue of the arduous hours he had just spent in the pursuit of ideas. Then, without any warning, Gennie's words broke into his thoughts and brought an abrupt end to the inner harmony that had put to rest all of his pestering concerns. What disconcerted him the most was his perception that disparagement dominated the tone of her intrusive query—"Do you like that kind of music?" The question not only destroyed this rare concord between mind and spirit, but inadvertently revealed a facet of his character that he wanted kept hidden from others. Instinctively, there seemed to be no other choice than to resort to his foremost weapon—rational explanation, which he found equally cogent whether used offensively or defensively.

"Yes, I do," he told her, a slight aggressiveness showing through. "And why not?" he went on defensively. "Can anyone survive on a strict diet of pure reason? Even I enjoy letting my emotions run free once in awhile. Doing so is what makes us human."

Jim lifted his cup and drank from it.

"I'll let you in on a secret."

"What kind?" Gennie's expression brightened.

"My imagination runs rampant when I see those Hollywood musicals. You see," he added with a grin, "I'm not just an ambulatory stack of equations."

Instead of getting the expected joyful response, she threw him a look of embarrassment. "I guess we all have our little hang-ups." Her words sounded like a weak excuse for some wrongdoing.

"You're right about that," he told her. "After all, some of the things we do or say would be considered downright foolish by others, even unforgivable at times." He stopped and took a deep breath before adding, "Who would want to tell people anything that would lay them open to ridicule? Anyway, even I have my share of hang-ups." His last words ended with a sigh of regret.

"That doesn't make you any different from the rest of us," she commented weakly.

He stirred restlessly in his chair, chuckled aloud and then stood up, shoving his hands into his pant pockets. "The hardest thing about these hang-ups is trying to hide them."

"That's not a problem when you're alone," she gloomily informed him.

Jim began pacing.

Without turning to look at her, he replied, "You're probably right. It does take some cunning to pursue one's own kind of madness far from the eyes of any bystanders."

"Where's your hiding place, Jim?"

"In the movies."

"You're kidding!" There was a slight trace of humor in her exclamation of disbelief.

Jim ceased pacing and turned to look directly at her.

"You can find privacy in the midst of the multitude, and the best place to do so is inside a movie theater."

He pulled a hand out of his pocket and pointed his forefinger toward his head, saying, "Well, if your eccentricity is purely the subjective kind, and if the only action it generates is played out only in your head, then it hardly matters where you go when you're doing your own thing."

"But of all places... in the movies?" she questioned.

"Remember, it's hard to read faces in the dark."

"True. But, it still lets me out."

She paused, picked up her empty cup, and started for the kitchen. Before going into it, she stopped and looked back. "I'm afraid my kind of kookiness needs a private stage. What drives me on the inside wants to exhibit itself on the outside, if you get what I mean."

"Well, if there's nothing hurtful in what you do openly, there's no need to be concerned about what others think."

Jim tried once more to boost her spirits. "Listen, Gennie, our quirks are nothing more than our private recipes for spicing up the dull moments in our lives—nothing more." She stood for a moment beaming with delight before disappearing into the kitchen.

The record had stopped playing sometime ago, their spoken words having sublimated the melody and lyrics to nothing more than an unobtrusive background for their thoughts. Jim walked over to the phonograph, lifted the tone arm, and gingerly set it upon its support mount.

Their conversation dispelled all the tension that had greeted him when he first entered the apartment. Once again, he kneeled down to survey the titles of the records stacked on the shelves. Tiring, he seated himself on the floor with his legs crossed, befuddled by his having gone to such lengths to vindicate his deriving pleasure from music that evokes whimsical desires. There was no denying that he had practiced the suppression of any outward display of his feelings with a rigorous discipline. Since returning home from the war, he tended to camouflage all expressions of tenderness with terms that were masculine in their fervor and their character. Yet, he conceded, there were moments in the past when a particular situation, or person, liberated his emotions from these self-imposed restrictive bonds. Nevertheless, in every such circumstance, self-will came into play and held back the unbridled expression of his innermost feelings. Now that the nostalgia generated by the music had come to an end, he no longer felt any need to justify his fondness for what he presumed his more intellectually inclined acquaintances would consider trivial.

When Gennie reentered the room, she found him seated on the floor, apparently deep in thought. Reacting to some instinctive maternal urge, she went to him, bent down and kissed the back of his neck. Jim turned and looked up at her with surprise and delight. Some wordless signal made him get to his feet, slip his arms around her waist, and kiss her.

The warmth that satisfies the need for affection, not passion, swept over Gennie, which helped ease her unvoiced pain of loneliness. There was no further need for words. Their emotions having fused harmoniously; conversation would have been nothing more than a detriment to feeling. They clung to one another for a time until Gennie pushed herself free.

As she started to move away from him, Jim reached out and took hold of her arm.

"Music later. Right now, let's go out for some pizza and beer," he said as his hand slid down to grasp hers.

Instead of immediately responding to his invitation, she pivoted around to survey the formal table setting, her features displaying signs of displeasure. However, she replied brightly, "Let's go. That would certainly be a great way of celebrating Thanksgiving."

When Gennie shook free of his hand to go retrieve her coat, Jim entered the bathroom. He was astonished to find a whiskey bottle lying in the sink. Lifting it with his fingertips, he checked to see if it was empty before placing it into the wastebasket. There had been so many surprises in the apartment this day, but Jim thought them inconsequential and not worthy of any second thought. By the time they exited the apartment building, all of these unusual situations had ebbed away to faded memories.

They said little as they plodded through deep snow until they reached a small combination bar and restaurant on Third Avenue. Holding hands, they entered, bypassed the cocktail lounge and walked through an open doorway that led into a large room with booths located on both sides. A jukebox stood in the center of the far wall, soundless and unlit, facing a vacant dance floor. The fact that the place was devoid of other people only enhanced their feelings of elation. They hung their coats on some wall hooks and slid into one of the empty booths.

The waiter came, took their order, and quietly left.

"It's just like having your own private ballroom," Gennie exclaimed.

"I like the idea of it being empty," Jim said, delighted with the unexpected privacy.

"I bet I know why."

"Go ahead. Tell me."

"This place...well, it's like the movies for you, only with the lights on." Then, as an afterthought, she explained, "You're not afraid to show your feelings in a place where no one can see you. Am I right?"

Gennie reached across to hold his hand when her comment failed to elicit a reply. She pulled her hand away when the waiter arrived with their food and drinks. Lifting a slice of pizza from the circular metal tray, she playfully sliced several long threads of cheese using her forefinger.

"This makes me feel like a kid again." Unsuppressed joy accompanied her words.

"You're right, Gennie, come to think of it, eating pizza with your hands is sort of childish. Anyway, when kids are left to do things their own way, they can be experts in reshaping reality into worlds of their own making."

"True. So true." Her comment was drained of her former vivacity.

"Anyway, make-believe is a kid's game."

"What's wrong with grown-ups playing it?" There was an attitude of defensiveness in the way Gennie asked the question.

"Just one thing—reality has a way of bringing a quick end to it."

"True. So true," she repeated in a sluggish and uninspired manner.

She looked directly at him, tilted her head slightly, and let a smile creep into view before offering her insights as to the benefits adults could derive from what Jim had termed a pastime of children.

"Life would be wonderful if people could be spendthrifts in the use of their imagination. You know…" she hesitated, having to take time to rethink what she intended to say. "Without our imagination, we'd be left with nothing more than empty dreams."

Jim quickly set about trying to restore the spirit of elation that she had been experiencing when they first arrived. "I'm in complete agreement with you. After all, dreams and hopes are the few things still left to our own making, although I have to admit, there're times that they're influenced by others."

He emptied his beer glass and placed it back on the table.

"Dreams...games. We all have them. By the way, Gennie, what are the games you play?" There was a playful humor in his question.

"My game?" A slight blush spread across her face. "In my imaginary world, I'm capable of giving and doing what I cannot do or give in reality."

"If that's truly the case, then your imagination ought to become your reality."

She laughed aloud. "There are times when it seems that it does." Gennie took a few small sips of beer while she thought about how much she should tell him. The blush had fully receded before she resumed speaking. "In a way, I was waiting for someone special when you came into the apartment today."

Now he was the one taken by surprise. He was about to offer an apology for his intrusion, when she held up her hand to stop him having anticipated his reaction. She hurriedly went on to say,

"No...no, not a real person. I was just pretending." Reaching across the table, she placed her hand on top of his.

* * *

...Gennie drew her hand back.

She stopped waving goodbye as Peggy's cab pulled away from the snow-laden curb, its wheel spinning as it sought traction. The final hours before her roommate's departure, she had displayed an unrestrained gaiety. Only after the cab had moved cautiously down the street and disappeared from sight did tears begin to flow. Even before she had reached the bathroom, she began to whimper aloud a demand to stop feeling sorry for herself. Impatient with her futile attempts to stem her tears, Gennie bolted into the kitchen and removed a partially filled whiskey bottle from one of the cupboards. She unscrewed the cap and began to swallow its contents in short, uneven gulps. The whiskey left a searing path as it slid down her throat and cauterized shut her flow of tears.

Placing the bottle on the table, she began wiping her eyes with the back of her hand before wandering listlessly toward the bathroom. Perhaps a tub would help drown her self-pity, if whiskey alone could not do it. As if impulse had given rise to second thoughts, she picked up the nearly empty whiskey bottle and carried it with her. Inside the bathroom, she looked around for a place to put it. Finding none, she placed it in the sink. Gennie gazed down indecisively into the bathtub, then slid to her knees, leaned over and opened the water faucets.

The air felt cold as she stood waiting for the water to rise after having thrust all her clothes in a disorderly pile in one corner of the room. Today, being alone, Gennie allowed herself to be careless, instead of her normal meticulous self. Now, it was the lack of warmth rather than the need to suppress her enervating despondency that made her stand erect and reach for the bottle lying in the sink. As she pulled it toward her, she caught sight of her reflection in the medicine chest mirror. She leaned forward to scrutinize the tear tracks on her cheeks. "Stupid!" she hissed back at her image before placing the bottle to her lips. Only a weak stream trickled down her throat, which gave rise to an expression of surprise followed by that of disgust. Holding the bottle against the ceiling lamp, she saw that it was now empty. Grumbling with dissatisfaction, she let it slide into the basin of the sink where it clattered its way to the bottom.

She bent down to test the water's warmth. Cupping her hands together, she scooped up some water and dashed it onto her face. Satisfied, she stood up as the droplets on her cheeks began their downward slide in winding rivulets, their twisting flow ceasing after they dropped onto the tiled floor in noiseless splashes. As she turned to close the bathroom door, she noticed her image in the full-length mirror mounted on the back of the door. She looked at herself admiringly, pleased by her trim figure, now partly hidden behind a screen of hair that hung down thickly from one side of her head. For a moment, she brimmed with that special ecstasy that stems from narcissistic self-adoration. Someone ought to love me, her mind kept repeating, the phrase sounding increasingly like a proclamation heralded by some resolute craving...

* * *

Gennie took her hand away from his. Jim sat mulling over her perplexing assertion that she had been awaiting an imaginary visitor when he first entered the apartment. The only reasonable explanation for her having said that may have been nothing more than an attempt to hide her disappointment over the failure of her real visitor to appear. After all, he surmised, it did not seem probable that she would have gone to so much trouble to set the table unless she was certain that the one she had invited would come as promised.

"Frankly, I think that you're pulling my leg, Gennie. Weren't you actually waiting for someone to show up when I came in?" He finished his inquiry with a grin.

"Yes, perhaps I was."

"Can you tell me who?"

She smiled at him and said, "For somebody who could not possibly come. But," she hesitated for a moment before adding, "having a real visitor show up was certainly better than waiting for an imaginary one."

"Thanks for the nice words, but I'm a little confused."

"Don't be. I meant what I said." Not caring to discuss the subject any further, Gennie took hold of her nearly empty beer glass noting that it was no longer cold. It felt warm to her touch.

* * *

…Gennie drew her hand back.

The water was now hot enough. She slid into the bathtub and lay soaking, the warmth of the water helping to stifle her antipathy for having to spend this holiday by herself. Afterward, feeling exhausted, she slipped into bed and eventually eased into a troubled slumber, sleep being the surest route away from the kind of dismal loneliness engendered by this holiday's solitude.

When Gennie awoke, the room's darkness left her with a false impression of the hour. She reached over to pull downward on the cloth-covered ring that hung from a yellowing window shade at the side of her bed. It slipped free of her grasp, sending the shade curling upward, its motion terminating with a short hollow thud. She pushed aside the curtain blocking her view of the street and held it in place, allowing a gray-white light to fill the room, disorienting her as to the time of day. Confused, she inched her way to the side of the bed, raised herself into a sitting position and peered out the window. Since the time she had last gazed through it, more snow had fallen, adding girth and stature to the mounds that had clustered in graceless patterns at the curbsides earlier that day. It must still be daytime, she presumed, and pulled the blanket up and over her shoulders.

The street below was empty except for a little boy who was engaged in extracting a cast-off broom jutting out from a snow pile. She watched the little gloved hands vigorously brush the snow aside to free this childish treasure. Once in his possession, the boy struck the worn bristles against the railings surrounding St. Marks-in-the-Bowery, the blows spraying the air with short bursts of accelerated white particles, like clouds of dust. Satisfied, he began to examine his precious find, apparently pondering what to do with it. A solution twisted his face into a mask of bravado. Placing the broomstick between his legs, he galloped off, his boots pummeling the soft snow leaving a trail of footprints as he raced away. Gennie smiled as she inwardly acknowledged that children were the only real masters of the art of self-deception. "That's one kid's game I've never forgotten how to play," she mused, letting a smile cross her face…

* * *

The warmth of the glass made her decide not to drink from it anymore. She pushed it aside and let her hand drop into her lap. Jim's words sifted into her stream of thoughts and thwarted any further reminiscing.

"You confuse me at times. Why would you go to such much trouble to set the table as nicely as you did, if you were not expecting anyone to come?" Jim shook his head slowly from side to side obviously befuddled by what she had told him.

Gennie stiffened before replying with a trace of self-mockery, "I guess I wasn't myself this morning." She hesitated for a moment, and then added as an afterthought, "Perhaps I was playing a child's game. And as you said earlier, that means disengaging from reality somewhat."

From the tone of her response, Jim surmised that his question might have been taken as a captious insinuation, rather than a means to unravel his own confusion. However, he still found it difficult to discern whether she was telling the truth or indulging in some sportive fiction. This time he addressed her with deliberate caution hoping to right whatever imperceptible hurt he may have inflicted inadvertently.

"Don't get me wrong. There was no ridicule intended by my question." He stopped speaking and waited to see a change in her facial expression. There was none. "Listen, I have to admit that anyone who can diverge off the beaten track has to be resourceful. In today's society, that would make them one of the chosen few."

A smile wiped away her frown.

Jim reached across and took her hand in his.

* * *

…Gennie drew her hand back.

The curtain she had pulled aside to gaze out the window fell back into place. "Be creative, girl, be creative." Like a mantra, this phrase had the ring of coercion to do something that would free her from the grip of despondency. Yet no response seemed forthcoming from within her as she continued sitting at the edge of the bed. The whole idea of resorting to child's play as a means of squandering the lonely hours away may well have been a diversion that bordered on absurdity. Nevertheless, she gave in to the idea by concluding that it was a harmless means of expending time painlessly. After all, she reasoned, it may well prove a way of shunting aside the depressive thoughts that had troubled her all day long, even though its implementation was sheer folly. For her, this was sufficient justification to vindicate her carrying out her proposed endeavor to prepare for the arrival of a fictitious dinner guest, one whose attributes would be characterized by wish-fulfillment in collusion with desire.

The game she eventfully chose to play was a prosaic one. Gennie intended to busy herself preparing for a candlelight dinner with a nonexistent inamorato, one who would magically free her from the grip of aloneness that had persisted with a troubling regularity these past years. In the hours that followed, she had risen from her bed, dressed, and eventually went about setting the table and grooming herself for her imaginary lover. These tasks took a good part of the afternoon to complete, once she had succeeded in tossing aside the unreality of the situation. The signs that foreshadow the approach of an oncoming winter night had already begun to appear by the time she was able to stand back and survey her handiwork. Satisfied, Gennie walked to the window and stood watching as several families carefully made their way through the deep snow. Streetlamps flicked on, their brightness making those same darkly clad figures appear in sharp contrast to the newly fallen snow. It was only then that she realized that the game was over. Once more, she was alone; the pretense of waiting for someone had ended. A hint of despondency surfaced and set about wearing away the thin veneer of contentment that had been generated these last hours. To quell this assault upon her spirits, she held fast to the conviction that her fictional pastime had made for a gratifying afternoon, and most important of all, this game of make-believe had masterfully precluded the gnawing agitations of self-pity. In a deceptive way, it had been a victory over self. Yet, this reasoning only had a trivial affect in bolstering her sagging spirits.

Seeking some means to halt any further erosion of her equanimity, she strode over to the radio and switched it on. Instead of the hoped-for music, only words blared forth. There was a moment when she thought she heard the door buzzer ring, but she immediately dismissed this as some ingenious expedient of wishful thinking. She did not bother to lower the radio's volume. When the buzzer sounded again, she underwent a moment of disbelief, fearing that her mind had begun to resort to trickery and deception. This time, however, her arm shot out to shut the radio. There was a short delay before she heard clearly three short, quick rings. She rushed over to the interphone, lifted the receiver, placed it against her ear and dubiously inquired, "Who is it?"

"It's Jim Stahr."

"Come on up," she responded, her excitement rising as she hung up the intercom…

* * *

Jim let her hand slip free from his grasp allowing her to push back a thick tangle of hair that had fallen over one side of her face, revealing a broad smile of self-satisfaction. Her joyful expression acted to allay all of Jim's qualms that he may have hurt her feelings by some remarks he should not have made. Then, for some unknown reason, she burst into loud laughter for the first time since he had known her.

"You been talking about children's games, Jim, and I just realized that the real Walter Mittys of the world are children." Her laughter morphed into a giggle. "Kids have an advantage that's been lost to adults. When they stop playing, they know that the game is over. But we so-called grown-ups sometimes have trouble putting an end to some of our pastimes, especially those that tend to delude us in one form or another."

Jim moved the pizza tray to one side before asserting that there was something wrong when one uses imagination to deceive oneself into believing what is obviously false. He leaned against the wooden back of the booth and folded his arms before declaring, "That would be a fraudulent use of imagination."

Gennie stirred uneasily. "And as far as I'm concerned, its imagination that helps breed hope. So who of us has not been guilty of using hope to lift our spirits when they were very low?"

"I guess that's truly the case, especially if you believe as you do."

This last statement left him feeling that there was nothing more to say. His thoughts turned inward, which brought to mind the recognition of his own self-deceit—that of portraying to others that he was a committed nonconformist. Jim sat thinking for a moment whether to openly admit that this was not the case, but pride prevented him from doing so. This was not the time, he speculated, for confessions that would alter how others viewed him. He retreated to the less damaging use of generalizations instead.

"Who of us is not guilty of self-deception?"

"What about you?" she teased.

"Yes, even me," he admitted. "Sooner or later, we're all forced to recognize who we truly are—realists or dreamers. Some dreamers could easily end up never getting close to achieving what they set out to do or be."

The disconcerting frankness of his words did not jar her feelings as he had expected. "You're probably right," she said with a self-confidence that assumed she was not destined for such an appalling end.

"The hardest part for some of us will be knowing what direction to take in the first place." His words came forth sounding more like a confession than a statement of fact.

"I guess that's not going to be a problem for you, Jim. You seem to know just where you're headed. I'm sure that you'll end up being the master of your own destiny." There was admiration, not envy, in what she said.

Her prediction left him immersed in feelings of self-reproach. He knew that his lack of commitment concerning what he proposed doing with his life disqualified him as a dreamer, for he did not possess their impractical ambitions. In reality, his lack of fixity of purpose made him nothing more than a perennial fence-sitter. Self-condemnatory feelings accompanied the realization that all he could foresee ahead of him was uncertainty. Any response to her judgment that he was a self-directed individual would have been maudlin, wasted, and conspicuous by its hypocrisy. He chose to remain silent.

Jim wiggled his way to the edge of the bench, got to his feet, and sauntered toward the jukebox. One hand fumbled through a pocket of his jacket and withdrew a quarter. Slipping the coin into the slot, he depressed several selector buttons with deliberation. Without walking back to the booth, he asked, "Let's dance while we've got the whole place to ourselves."

She stiffly got to her feet, went toward him and murmured, "Why not, inamorato?"

"What did you call me?"

"Oh, nothing—nothing that's real." Her words, spoken softly, were hardly audible.

He shrugged, then reached out and gently pressed her to him.

They danced well together, both delighting in discovering that their movements were well coordinated and smooth. Their bodies touched lightly, in a commingling of tenderness and desire. The musical mixture of strings and brass rendered the mood that fed their evolving passion. Only when the jukebox stilled, and they stood apart, did this sensation pause in its spiraling ascent. Hand in hand, they strolled back to the booth, and as if in tacit agreement, began to put on their winter garments. After Jim had paid the bill, they walked out into the street, where a swirling, snow-flecked wind greeted them. Arms interlocked, they began their trek back to Gennie's apartment. For them, this Thanksgiving Day had not ended; it was the start of a new beginning.

Chapter 9

The Thanksgiving holiday provided the group that habitually met in the university's cafeteria with a much-needed respite from their scholastic routine. Refreshed, they began to apply themselves with greater vigor to their studies. The fact that only two months remained before their scheduled graduation helped raise their earnest dedication to bring a successful close to their studies. Nevertheless, this same course of action did have a visibly deleterious effect, for their daily gatherings at the lunchroom table became less frequent as each of them began to spend more time in the university's libraries and study halls, their energies now channeled into distinct endeavors that would ensure a successful end to their undergraduate studies. The discussions at these sporadic gatherings consisted of short, nervous exchanges about their respective problems, as well as the progress being made as to their resolution. No doubt, each of them was aware of the progressive decay of the group's solidarity and that the disintegration of this long-standing relationship was entering its final stages.

The recognition of this pending dissolution brought with it feelings of insecurity and loss for some in the group. This was especially the case with Hector Palofax. Now sitting in the cafeteria with only Nick Grigoris in attendance, he voiced his concerns in his usual stinging manner, declaring that the group's do-or-die vow to ensure graduation was dismembering the unity of the group.

Nick listened sympathetically to Hector's dismal prophecy but suppressed the realization that he, too, had also become fully committed to satisfying the academic requirements needed for graduation. He realized that the frequency of such gatherings would surely taper off, and undoubtedly, more so in the few months remaining in the semester. In addition, the vehemence of their discussions would wither and probably become nothing more than reports of the progress being made toward completing their undergraduate studies. Nick listened to Hector's utterances of displeasure about the direction each of them was taking, fully aware of the truth of his prediction. However, he was realistic enough to know that there could be no turning back from their commitment to achieve the satisfactory consummation of their studies or of its detrimental impact upon the group's viability.

Hector finally brought an end to his disparaging criticisms and sat sulking, while Nick struggled with a sense of uneasiness. He desired nothing more than to get up and leave. At the same time, he did not want to appear so openly as one of the participants who were guilty of furthering the decline and fall of the group, although inwardly he was finding it difficult to appease an anxiety about the need to finish a report due that week. The craving to withdraw was compelling, but he sat cowed, fearing possible censure for what Hector would see as an uncalled-for departure.

Bessie Siegal approached the table, not caring to disguise her joyful exuberance in either her stride or appearance. A few minutes ago, she had cleared another hurdle on her way to fulfilling the academic requirements for graduation. One of the final exams, which had held such poignant foreboding, was now finished, and the certainty that her performance had exceeded expectations obliterated all former premonitions of impending failure. The completion of this exam had acted like a pressure release valve, permitting her to bleed off tensions without incurring any ill effects.

After greeting Hector and Nick, she dropped her books carelessly on the table and then hurried off to buy a cup of coffee. Bessie wanted nothing more than to relax and take a break from the routine of studying and test taking.

She returned carrying a tray that held a single cup. Hector was quick to surmise that she was happy and free of any troubling concern. Seeing her in such a felicitous frame of mind elevated his flagging spirits. He was content that she had thought to join them here in the cafeteria. Throughout the time that he had known her, he had felt an irresistible impulse to tease her affectionately. This compulsion had evolved from Hector's arbitrarily presuming that Bessie lacked the street-smarts of most of the women whom he had met while serving in the wartime merchant marine, thus making her susceptible to his masculine harassment. Regardless of all that, her usual response to his bantering was a shy grin, as well as a consistent pattern of taunting him with audacious personal questions.

Nick also was elated at her arrival, but for another reason. Her presence would somehow make his leave-taking a normal occurrence, and, therefore, would not expose him to Hector's mocking judgments After she settled into her chair, Nick inquired in the humorous manner that most of the men in the group employed when addressing her, "Bessie, what are you going to do after you leave this place?"

She glanced up at Nick, her expression changing from unbridled gaiety to questioning suspicion. As she had done many times in the past, however, she reverted to her defensive, roguish grin before replying, "What do I want to do? That's a laugh. Tell me, Nick, what does any girl want in the graduating class of 1950?"

The one lesson that she had learned from all the joshing over the years was that her best defense was an interrogative offense.

Hector pulled a half-smoked cigar from his shirt pocket and lit it, while observing Bessie's practiced circumvention of the question. Discerning that Nick was apparently perplexed as to how best to respond to her wary reply, he stepped in to bridge the conversational gap.

"What do you mean by that question, Bessie? You know as well as I do that every chick wants one thing, and that's to marry, marry, marry," Hector gruffly enlightened her.

Having just won a victory in the classroom, Bessie was resolved not to lose possession of her self-control. There was a noticeable change in her composure as she looked away from Nick to face Hector.

"Dear Hector, what you're saying may hold a particle of truth. What you're forgetting is that women want to have a romantic notion as regards to whom they sleep with. By the way, lover, you're not volunteering, are you?"

Hector shifted the cigar from one side of his mouth to the other, sensing a piercing sting to her derisive challenge. Yet he could not help but admire the steadfast way in which she had deflected his blunt assumption. Where there was once meekness now dwelled defiance, he concluded pensively.

"Ah! I see that you've learned something from this motley gang of bumbling mandarins." His praise came forth with direct candor and without a trace of resentment.

Nick glanced at his watch with agitation. There was still another twenty minutes before the bell would sound to signal a change of classes. The urge to leave suddenly turned to near panic. He lunged upright from his chair, grabbed his books from atop the table and bolted away without voicing any excuse for his abrupt departure. Only after reaching the exit door did he look back. Hector and Bessie were bent forward regarding each other intently; their lips curled upward in what appeared to him as forced smiles. He watched them for a moment before pushing his way through the swinging doors, glad that he was free to go about his tasks but somewhat troubled by their indifference to his unseemly departure.

Both of them, too immersed in their brewing encounter, failed to take note of Nick's hasty leave-taking. Time and event had lost their significance, as their interest fixed firmly on their heated discussion.

"Yes, I'm a big girl now," Bessie told Hector testily. "Come March, I'll be of age to vote and play around as much as I like. How's that, sailor boy?" Her voice pitched high with scorn when she referred to his wartime occupation.

He removed the cigar from his mouth, flipped its ashes onto the floor, and began pointing it at her as he spoke. "Me volunteer?" came the answer to her earlier question. "Romance is not even in my vocabulary."

"You're my pal," she began, "and the very fact that you're my buddy makes it impossible for you to be my lover. So that leaves you out in the cold." Not having any others at the table seemed to give her free rein over the exercise of her bravado.

Hector frowned and asked, "I'm curious. What are you looking for in a guy anyway?"

"Wait." She took several sips of coffee before looking at him with an impish smile. "Frankly, I don't know what I want. I only know what I don't want."

He thrust the cigar back in his mouth in a gesture of annoyance, which he was unable to conceal. "Come on," he pleaded, "just give me one clue as to what you want in a stud— just one lousy hint, that's all."

"Listen, friend," her response came back sharp and bitter, "what does any East Bronx girl want in a guy? Money...loot... hay...all those terms you war-weary stallions have taught me. If you need to start with something, start with that."

Making wealth the prime requisite for romance, she felt, would stir some anger in him. For years, Bessie had listened to him philosophize on the evils of money. His political views leaned far to the left, and, at times, he alluded to a past affiliation with the Socialist Party. One of the basic tenets of his personal beliefs was that people's perennial chase for the accumulation of wealth was the main obstruction to humanity's efforts to achieve peace and stability in the world.

His constant teasing of her these past years had reached a point that she now deemed intolerable and belittling. Her caustic reply to his question heralded a radical change from her former defensive posture when responding to his biting remarks. Today, and at this very moment, was the time to quash his habitual needling of her.

"Ha!" he sang out, hiding his dismay at her remark with newborn cockiness. "Do you think that money will make it more pleasurable to bed down with a man?"

"No, but it's a sure guarantee that the bed will be wide, soft, and clean." The derisiveness of her words gave the impression that she had reversed roles in playing the same mocking game that he had engaged in these past years.

Bessie inclined forward and curled the forefinger of her right hand, motioning him to come closer, as children do when they are preparing to divulge a secret. With his cigar still in the corner of his mouth, he leaned toward her, his features overshadowed by a suspicious leer.

"I'll let you in on a female secret. We prefer to fornicate in luxury rather than in poverty. I'm sure you're not capable of knowing that." She whispered the words to him while trying to avoid the smoke funneling upward from the end of his cigar.

Hector repositioned himself in his chair, screening his scowl of exasperation behind a series of rapid exhalations of smoke from his cigar. This was a new and different Bessie Siegal, he told himself. Apparently, he mused, she had refined the use of her wit, whereby she was able to tantalize with a cleverness that did not offend openly. He sat contemplating a new personality, whom he could no longer categorize as a callow kid. Fanning away the smoke that had drifted between them, Hector again tried to rile her.

"Why put the burden on the man to make the money? Why don't you make it yourself? Do I have to say more?"

As in the past, she reverted to her strategy of responding to his question with a question, but she changed her tactics by preceding her query with a declaration. "Look, friend, if you're implying what I think, then I have to tell you flat-out that I'm not shacking up with just anybody to make a buck."

"Well, honey, it's not so difficult." Hector grinned victoriously and began slapping the air in front of him so as to provide greater visibility for her to see the look of triumph on his face.

"You think it's easy?"

"It's a snap, Bessie. All you need is balls."

"That, I can assure you, I haven't got," she said coolly. "Neither physically, nor morally. So that kills that idea."

"Well, sleep on it. It's only an idea," he answered quietly, having noted that she was not responding to his crudity with any outward sign of annoyance.

"Since there is nothing else to sleep on, you leave me with me with no other choice."

"I'm trying, Bessie, I'm trying," he said, spreading his arms wide in an apologetic sign of his inadequacy.

"Hector, you're a girl's best friend. That's what I love about you." She winked at him and without another word, took her books and left.

Whatever joy she had been feeling when she first sat down had become twofold. Today was a day of dual victories. Perhaps it may have been a greater achievement, she reflected, to be able to stand up to Hector's chaffing and to have parried his ridicule than to have passed the examination that had held so many fears for her. As she walked away from the table, she intuitively became aware that he was staring at her. Impulsively, she deliberately began to wiggle her posterior sensuously, hoping to inform him as to where he could stick his ideas. Hector was quick to see the change from her normal walk, and he found it stimulating to observe. However, he was attentive enough to interpret the message she was intending to impart.

Nick's abrupt departure never once entered his thoughts.

Chapter 10

Gennie Connors was grateful to Jim Stahr for extracting her from the limbo of abandonment on Thanksgiving. Since the time of the accidental death of her parents, she had come to know the sufferings of the lonely, especially during those celebratory seasons when the holiday spirit calls for the close fellowship of family. And at such times, she had felt the unvoiced pain of those forsaken souls who are left adrift in a social void, powerless to distinguish between their being noteworthy individuals or paltry nonentities. All the same, when such times of togetherness had ended, Gennie, like other forlorn migrants, had always journeyed back to the domain where habit regulates human actions and emotional interdependency with others is no longer a necessity. Such submission to routine had proven to be a panacea for aloneness, ever since the loss of fellowship she had known while in the military. For her, this protective cloak of stability had proven satisfactory, although it never truly became a source of contentment. The time she had spent alone with Jim, however, had created a yearning to step out from behind the insular shield of habit and join with him in the warmth of shared isolation. This was not to be.

On the first Sunday in December, Jim had gone to the Law Library and had spent several hours refining a term paper. He was more weary than elated by the time he had closed his books, shuffled his papers into a neat pile, and prepared to descend to the building's main floor.

A short distance away from the elevator doors was a number of telephone booths. Exhausted, but not dispirited, he shuffled slowly to one of them, slid onto the seat, and dialed the number to Peggy Troy's apartment. Gennie Connors answered the phone. Without a moment's hesitation, she invited him to come to the apartment, informing him that Peggy was at home. His reply to her invitation was an affirmation that lacked enthusiasm. After hanging up the phone, he sat in the booth for a period of time holding closed its folding door, hoping that some time away from his studies would help shed his sluggishness. The fact that Peggy was at home was not troubling. Anyway, as of late, stress had become an integral by-product of his one-on-one conversations with others. He was hoping that her presence would prevent another such occurrence.

The snow on the city streets had started to melt after a series of warm days followed on the heels of the Thanksgiving vacation. Even so, the concrete sidewalks still glistened with wetness, while swift rivulets of water continued to course along the curbsides, eventually spilling into wide-mouthed sewers. When these flows ended their long plunge at the drainpipe's bottom, their impact echoed back with an ominous splash. Jim stopped next to one of them and stood listening to the fearsome sound of liquid striking liquid. Standing there, the warmth of the afternoon sun acted as a soothing balm. For the first time this day, he could find no reason to hurry. Only when he realized that others awaiting his arrival did he take the initiative to shuffle away. Before entering the building, he resolved to stay only for a short while and then start for home.

After climbing up the stairs, he found Peggy Troy holding open the door to her apartment. They exchanged some effortless greetings and started down the long hallway. Jim deposited his books and coat on a chair situated in the far corner of the living room. Gennie Connors strode in from her bedroom with a joyful look. Peggy took the initiative to ask him to join them in sharing some sandwiches and coffee. They seemed delighted by his visit, and not wanting to dampen their mood, he resolved not to allude to his weariness. Peggy set a cup of coffee before him and inquired, "Have you been working on that paper of yours again?"

"Yes, even on weekends." His words could not mask his lassitude.

"How did the rest of the week go?" Gennie asked.

"I can't complain. Sometimes I feel optimistic about making it through the end of this term."

"Making it!" Peggy grinned, "You'll probably end up walking away with honors of one kind or another."

He smiled at the absurdity of her remark, although it sounded with conviction. "Rest assured, that's not going to happen. I can't restrain expressing my curiosity, which some teachers find a disrupting influence in the classroom."

They all began eating their sandwiches quietly, with only a few inconsequential comments exchanged. The room darkened as the sun gradually passed out of view. Peggy got up to switch on the kitchen light and then reseated herself. Even after emptying the sandwich platter and coffee cups, their verbal exchanges remained scattered, few and lacking in spirit. Their collective frame of mind seemed mired in the common malaise that afflicts so many city dwellers on winter Sundays, when flagging spirits force some residents to remain indoors. It can give rise to a frame of mind that stills both reflection and movement. All of them seemed caught up in this state of apathy. The sounds coming from the street occasionally muffled the steady ticking of the wall clock. They sat in silence. Such a condition, however, lacks persistence. In time, the need for change seeps surreptitiously in and brings an end to this mood of indifference.

Finally, Peggy Troy gave voice to her feelings. "How about going somewhere—anyplace, just for a short while?" she appealed to the others.

"I don't know if we should." Gennie's statement failed to hide her unwillingness to do so, the desire to depart as a threesome held back by her wish to be alone with Jim. "Anyway, where could we go?" Her question did not project an iota of enthusiasm.

"It doesn't matter. Just out—somewhere! It's no fun being cooped up all day. Well, what do you say?" Peggy got to her feet without waiting for a reply.

Jim looked up at her thinking that the cause for his indifference to the idea of leaving was more apt to be his amatory desires rather than lassitude. Gennie and Jim quickly exchanged troubled looks that communicated a wordless agreement that this state of affairs did not leave open a single means for satisfying their personal wishes. The only option left them was to give in to Peggy's request.

"Get your coats," Jim suggested. "I'll think of a place that will satisfy your whims, Peggy, if you can tell me what kind of place you're looking for."

"Find me a busy one that makes you feel welcome," Peggy instructed him as she went into her bedroom.

Gennie stood up but did not leave the room. Instead, she walked over to Jim and gently stroked his face.

"Do you think we'll ever be alone again?" Jim asked softly.

"Peggy is going home for Christmas," she whispered back.

"That would give us some privacy packaged like a Christmas gift. Right?"

"Right." A wink accompanied her smile before she hurried away to fetch her coat.

Chapter 11

Jim had already decided their destination—Julius' Bar and Grill—before they started making their way through the wet streets. They walked along Eighth Street in the direction of Sixth Avenue, stopping occasionally to examine the decorated store windows. It was still early evening, and none of them felt any compulsion to hurry.

Paintings of Paris street scenes displayed in a window of an art gallery caught the interest of Gennie. "Let's go in. What do you say?"

"I'm all for it," Peggy agreed.

Gennie clapped her gloved hands and moved quickly to gallery's doorway and let herself in. Peggy and Jim followed behind her. They loosened their outer garments and responded to the store's welcoming warmth with grateful sighs.

A well-groomed young woman sat at desk reading a magazine. She looked up and welcomed them with a nod of her head. "Come on in. The place is all yours," she told them. She watched them enter the gallery's viewing area, where paintings hung from two opposite walls, before abandoning her interest in them and going back to perusing the glossy pages of the magazine on her desk.

"Gennie," Peggy asked, "is that how people with degrees in art end up?" She pointed back to the girl at the desk with the outstretched thumb of a balled fist.

"No, not always."

They started moving in a single file observing with care the many same genre oil paintings as those displayed in the store's window.

Gennie stopped in front of one depicting the Sacré Coeur, its church towers glistening under a summer's sun, before turning to address her roommate.

"I'd rather work in the quiet of a museum."

Peggy moved closer and carefully examined the painting that held Gennie's attention. It showed people seated on the steps leading into the church, absorbed in lounging, talking, eating or reading.

"Why would you want to spend your time in the back rooms of some airless museum?" she demanded to know. "Look at this picture. Isn't art supposed to be about people and places? They're so intertwined that one can't exist without the other."

"I agree," Jim added and stepped closer to them.

Gennie shifted around to face them. "You're both right." She hesitated as if thinking of what to say, but she said nothing more. Her irresoluteness was clearly visible. She moved away from them and stood scrutinizing the painting hanging from the wall directly in front of her.

Peggy and Jim looked at each other questioningly before edging closer to her. Jim reached out and touched Gennie's shoulder and asked, "If you agree with us, why would you want to isolate yourself in a museum when you can teach art to people who are anxious to learn?"

"I guess its because my interest in it started as a form of escapism. And, as you well know, that's the one human activity that does not compel anyone else to tag along."

Peggy gave her a puzzled look.

Gennie moved on to the next painting, stopped, and bent over slightly to get a closer look at it. Her two companions strolled over to where she stood, their interest centering on the painting that now held her interest.

"Gennie," Jim said. "Tell me how those solitary ventures of yours got you so interested in art."

She twisted around to face them and said, "Yes, what I said needs explaining." She pulled off the warm hat she was wearing and held onto it with both hands. "When I was stationed in Naples," she began "most of my days were spent in operating rooms at the army hospital. And when things got too much for me, I would slip away by myself to the Galleria Umberto. It's a unique glass-covered passageway with a good number of art galleries." She stopped speaking, as if searching for words that could turn feelings from the past into expressions free of mawkish sentiment in the present.

"I got caught up in studying works of art in a setting that never failed to lift my spirits. To start with, the structure was an artistic gem, which never failed to separate me from the pain and suffering inside those hospital operating rooms." She twisted her woolen hat back onto her head and declared, "And for the first time in my life, I felt content without the need for the company of others."

There was a moment of hesitation on her part, as if she was afraid to reveal anything more about herself. But her indecision quickly took flight, for she readily confessed that she was hoping to rekindle that same mood and spirit by studying art history.

"But I don't believe I could in a crowded classroom," she concluded before turning to cross over to the opposite side of the gallery. Peggy and Jim did not follow.

Peggy touched Jim's arm affectionately to get his attention. "Strange, Jim," she started, "how many different ways there are to deal with human tragedy."

"Is your means of doing so any different from hers?" There was an unexpected brusqueness in the way he put the question to her. Gennie's account of how she came to find her purpose in life had left him with the stinging realization that he alone in their group was still uncommitted as to what he proposed doing in the future. All the others had bona fide careers in mind, while he still remained without direction or goals. He had to admit to himself that the knowledge he had absorbed at the university offered a number of academic disciplines that held his interest, but he found himself unable to commit to any one of them. Perhaps he suspected that his quest for knowledge itself had overridden all practical concerns essential for making ones own way in the world. He quickly realized that the harshness of his words may have exposed his well-disguised but irksome frustration over his indecisiveness, which had begun to plague him these past weeks.

Peggy was taken aback momentarily by the disparaging tone embedded in her question. Her retort came back with its own form of curtness.

"I'm not going back to being a nurse again. That's for sure! And for the same damn reasons as Gennie." She stopped to let her anger cool. A weak grin crossed her face before she went on to say, "You can never tell, but I could end up doing research for a lab that discovers a cure for some disease. That's what lots of chemistry majors end up doing." She shrugged and crossed the room to where Gennie now stood gazing intently at an oil painting of another picturesque Paris street scene. Jim Stahr followed after her, his gait more of a shuffle than a stride. When the two of them stood at Gennie's side, Jim asked Gennie whether she was warm enough to leave.

"I'm ready. Let's go!" Gennie replied and started for the door with a newfound eagerness. On the street, the three joined gloved hands and started walking cross-town.

Chapter 12

They entered through an old speakeasy door, its peephole still intact. A thick layer of sawdust lay on the floor, and clinging from the overhead lamps and ceiling were assorted dust-covered artifacts from the war that ended in 1918. There were several polished spittoons along the base of the long wooden bar that were now used as receptacles for gum wrappings and cigarette butts. What held the most appeal for Jim was the charcoal grill opposite the bar. He had spent many late evenings eating the hamburgers that were prepared on it after having listened to music at Nick's, a citadel of Dixieland jazz just a short distance away. Frank Colucci and Nick Grigoris had joined him in this routine many times, especially when Muggsy Spanier or Pee Wee Russell was on stage. This was the first time that he had ever brought women to this place.

There was an exceptionally large crowd this evening, which forced newcomers to wiggle their way forward in order to get served at the bar. The three of them managed to do so after pushing and squirming through the crowd that stood in their way. Just as Jim caught the attention of one of the bartenders, a man backed off the stool nearest them and motioned Peggy to take it, his identity hidden by a barricade of people surrounding him Only after Peggy had seated herself did Jim recognize the person who had relinquished his seat.

"Hey, Frank! What're you doing here?" Jim asked raising his voice in order to be heard above the animated speakers that encircled him.

Frank saluted him by raising his glass above his head, before twisting his way through the press of bodies around him. The first thing he did when he finally joined them at the bar was point an accusing finger at Jim in mock anger.

"Here I'm alone in the midst of this noisy mob of guys, and you have two women all to yourself." Placing his glass on the bar, he reached up to tidy his hair and straighten his tie. After having done so, he addressed Peggy and Gennie, saying, "He's probably the kind of guy who believes in the fair distribution of wealth. How's that for hypocrisy?"

Their collective response was laughter and smiles.

"What are you doing here alone, anyway?" Jim asked in a near shout in order to make himself heard above the din.

Frank pushed his glasses back onto the bridge of his nose with the edge of his whiskey glass. The news that the Partisan Review had accepted one of his poems for publication was sufficient cause for his jubilation. He described effusively how he had spent the day celebrating the event, without giving them a chance to offer their congratulations. A boyish enthusiasm flavored his recitation. To his listeners, it was apparent that Frank desired nothing more than to share his triumph with them. It was only after he finished talking that they were they able to interject their praises. Whatever aversion any of them had experienced earlier concerning the next day's burdens was now gone. Frank's delight had bolstered their optimism in facing whatever tomorrow would bring, and like a salutary agent, his cheerfulness had swept them up and elevated their spirits. The time they spent together was filled with lively chatter, all of which bore profound import for them, although for those who clustered about them, this same discourse would have been void of any significance or meaning.

They returned to the apartment building strolling in pairs. Jim walked arm in arm with Gennie, both saying little. The last few hours had exhausted their zest for further frivolity or heart-to-heart talk. Frank and Peggy, on the other hand, were engrossed in those exploratory conversations that build bridges, which once crossed would enable them to reach the common destination known as rapport.

Chapter 13

The agreed-upon time he was to meet Nick Grigoris and Frank Colucci left him with no other choice but to board the subway during the evening rush hour. The densely packed riders held him pressed against the support pole in the center of the car, the pressure easing only when the train entered a curve and centrifugal force sent those around him swaying away with the slowness of a sluggish pendulum. It did not take long, however, for the bulky deadweight to swing back and pin him to the upright metal pole one more time. Whenever the train righted itself, it began a steady rhythmic swaying. And when it did, any physical movement on his part was no longer possible. Thinking was the only unfettered activity left him. What surfaced in his thoughts was the fact that his search of today's newspaper failed to uncover a single article that addressed the wasteful ravages of war that had taken place on this seventh day of December not so many years ago. All he found was a single report of a patriotic speech given by a politician, his words filled with a righteous air and lacking true sentiment. And what sent his spirits sinking even further was the memory of the recent death of his friend Lacy Hutchins, another casualty of that war.

The heavy pressure against his body gradually eased. The train had reached Queens Plaza, where many of the riders scrambled onto the platform and rushed toward the stairway that led out of the subway. Jim found himself locked in and carried along by the other passengers exiting the station. Freedom from the crowd's grasp came when his fellow passengers began to disperse upon reaching the uncrowded street.

The home of Nick Grigoris was still five blocks away. The winter air had a biting edge, making him walk close to the protective warmth emanating out of the many small retail businesses strung out along the street, their neon window lights daubing multicolored splotches onto the monotone gray concrete. He turned his coat collar up and pulled his hat down tightly. This day was going to be free of the pressures of study, leaving him eager to participate in the banter that flowed spontaneously whenever they met to listen to Dixieland jazz. His spirits rose as he walked hunched up, casting quick glances into store windows as he strode by them. A few blocks farther, row after row of two-storied buildings, each with a concrete stairway leading into them, replaced the stretch of stores. These structures held no interest for him as he hustled past without bothering to look in their direction.

On the corner of Nick's street, a well-lit bakery emitted an aroma that always evoked feelings of warmth and security. He stopped to breathe it in deeply before curiosity made him amble to the store's window and peer inside. He observed a black man in a baker's hat placing a tray of cakes into a glass display case. After completing this task, the man looked up and caught sight of Jim staring at him through the window. He raised his hand and threw a salute in his direction. Jim instinctively returned it. When the baker dropped his hand to his side, Jim recognized the army quartermaster patch sewn on the brim of his hat.

The sight of the military insignia jolted him, making him step back and hurry away. Perhaps the man in the store, like Lacy Hutchins, had driven a supply truck in support of the advancing troops in Europe. He now recalled Lacy telling him that on one of those trips, his truck suffered a near hit by a shell and that a piece of shrapnel ripped into the side of his head. Strange, he mused, how Lacy's absence from the gatherings in the school cafeteria had elicited only a few passing inquiries as to his whereabouts. To his way of thinking, these same questions failed to manifest any show of sincere concern. His response had always been a wordless shrug and nothing more. Such an apparent indifference was uncharacteristic of this group. Jim reasoned that it was probably due to the exigency of having to satisfy their respective academic goals. Self-interest now consumed everyone, which decided him to withhold the painful news about Lacy Hutchins. The prevailing mood amongst his friends now, he judged, was not fit for the telling of his friend's demise.

The stairs leading up to the doorway of Nick's house still showed traces of yesterday's snowfall. Moments after pressing the doorbell, Jim heard footsteps descending a flight of stairs, followed by the click of a hall light. Nick opened the door and without a word of greeting, turned and started up a long wooden stairway. Before Jim had a chance to follow, Frank Colucci called down to him. "What held you up?"

"I got caught in the rush hour."

All three entered Nick's room; its location blocked out the sounds of all the ongoing household activities elsewhere in the building.

Frank looked closely at Jim and was quick to note the pained expression in his eyes.

"You look grim, friend. Are the problems worth telling?"

"No," Jim assured him, "it's nothing a drink and some music couldn't cure."

Frank turned to Nick and suggested that the drinks come first.

As if responding to a command, Nick marched over to his desk, withdrew a bottle of Scotch whiskey from a drawer and placed it on a nearby coffee table where three glasses already stood, along with a pitcher of water and a bowl filled with ice cubes.

"There's water and ice, if you want them," Nick said, and started pouring the whiskey into each glass. Then, assuming his role of host, inquired, "What's it going to be tonight?"

"It's your choice, Jim," Frank suggested. "It seems that you're carrying the heaviest load."

Without saying another word, Jim walked to the wall where a series of shelves stood, each filled with records. As he kneeled down to study the titles, he marveled at the orderly fashion in which the records were grouped and labeled.

"Let's stick with the blues," Jim declared without bothering to turn his head as he pulled a record free. He handed it to Nick, who removed it from its jacket and placed it carefully on the turntable.

As soon as the music began, Frank grinned at Jim, obviously pleased with the choice.

Each of them picked up a glass from the coffee table and found a place to sit.

Intensive listening had become their habitual prelude to any subsequent exchange of views in their previous gatherings. Also their introspective concentration on the freewheeling music and its folk-bred lyrics acted to liberate the forces that left each of them lost in their own thoughts, while the subsequent give-and-take exchanges that followed led to a better understanding of their respective opinions and values. As in the past, they spent the first hours in this same fashion, alternately taking turns to pour generous amounts of whiskey into their glasses or selecting records and placing them onto the turntable. Their verbal exchanges were limited to comments about the merits of the music, or the lack of them, after each record finished playing.

When Bessie Smith's voice stormed into the room, uprooting the quiet with a growling rendition of "Careless Love," Jim sank lower on the sofa, the song's lyrics making him think back to some freshly minted memories. *Careless love...careless love.* The song's lyrics were certainly appropriate for what took place that Thanksgiving Day after he had taken Gennie Connors back to her apartment. Their lovemaking had been a fusion of frenzy and compulsion, an act where need was fulfilled by gorging on abandoned restraint. Nevertheless, in the end, when the peace of exhaustion had replaced the avidity of desire, a bridge of pervasive tenderness was formed, which both had crossed. Yet, he now acknowledged, each of them had failed to voice their self-indulgent feelings of gratification, mindful of having taken generously from the pleasures of love and having given little of themselves in return. It had been a classic example of careless love. *Careless love...careless love.* This musical refrain drifted repeatedly into his thoughts.

A single banjo note sounded, followed by a solemn hush that seemed to fill the room with a prophetic threat of everlasting silence. The stillness ceased only when the same vibrant banjo note permeated the room once again, before it was engulfed by the high-pitched wail of a clarinet, the sweetness of its tone drawing the listener's attention away from the singular sound that had preceded it. Jim had followed the rise and fall of the banjo's moment of splendor, before he, too, yielded to the lyricism proffered by the clarinet. Then a trombone's throbbing crescendo replaced the clarinet's sedulous cry.

"Two Jim Blues," Jim announced, his foot keeping time with the beat of the music.

"You're right," Nick confirmed. "I got that record when my ship docked in New Orleans way back when. Jim Robinson is on the trombone." Nick perceived with a learned clarity the manner in which the trombone pumped music into the air, converting what in most cases were considered leaden and harsh sounds into those that were buoyant and mollifying. He had never played this record in the company of others, for whenever he listened to this particular solo, it never failed to bring to mind an incident in the distant past, which even to this day still haunted him. Now, even in the presence of others, he found that he could not restrain those memories from invading his thoughts. He drank from his glass, acknowledging to himself that if there were two sides to Jim Robinson's personality, he knew only the good one.

* * *

"...Hey! Are you a nigger lover?"

Nick could not drown these words into the oblivion of forgetfulness. The scornful question still pained him even after so many years. This remark meant to ridicule, after he took a fellow navy recruit into his confidence by telling him that he was a devotee of Dixieland jazz. Ever since then, Nick had taken measures to avoid the recurrence of such a confrontation. Today, he put these same precautions into practice. He departed his ship alone, knowing that he was going to visit a dance hall situated in an impoverished Negro area well beyond the French Quarter. There was no doubt in his mind that none of his shipmates would dare venture so far off the beaten track

After the bus departed, he started walking through an unlit dirt field guided by the sound of music coming from a building hidden in the dark. His excitement rose as he drew closer, the music gradually drowning out the clicking sound of crickets. Even before he entered, he knew that he would be the only white person to attend such a jazz session. Once inside, a quick survey of the hall proved the accuracy of his prediction. He found a dark corner to stand in at the back of the room before turning to study the wooden dance floor, its surface scratched and unpolished. A smile crossed his face when he spotted George Lewis, the bandleader, standing at the opposite end of the room behind a wooden railing with a large metal can nailed to its center. He watched individuals place coins into it before requesting that he play a particular song. George Lewis always responded with a nod and a grin. Once the music started, Nick shifted his concentration to the dancers, who rhythmically shuffled and stomped, their clothes stained with wetness as they gyrated under the dim overhead lights.

No one bothered to take notice of him. He took comfort in his isolation and made the passage of time a trifling matter; that is, until an urge rose up to participate in this carnival of joy. Like an internal seesaw, he swung between restraint and compulsion. An impulse to act dueled with his ingrained shyness, the former gaining victory when reinforced by the memory of the taunt thrust at him just months before: "Are you a nigger lover?" This time, however, there were no biased witnesses to censure his actions. Perhaps this factor shelved his hesitancy and gave him the boldness to step onto the dance floor. He crossed it, taking caution to avoid bumping into the dancers, who now stood waiting for the sounds that would again trigger them into cadenced motion. When he reached the makeshift bandstand, he extracted some change from his pocket and dropped it into the tin can, the clatter muffling a nervous sigh.

"Two Jim Blues," Nick said, his words enunciated just above a whisper.

Jim Robinson removed the trombone from his lips and leaned over to nod at Nick, exclaiming loud enough for the dancers to hear, "You can smile, sailor, because I'm going to blow this one just for you."

Nick heard laughter break out around him as he started back to the shelter of the darkened corner, aware that his timidity was again coming to the fore. When he had reached the outer edge of the dance floor, a ripple of applause broke out, which sent a flush of redness rushing to his face. He was unsure how to respond, for it was the applause of esteem rather than what could have been hisses of scorn.

The music started before he could reach his shadowy niche. When he turned to face the band, Jim Robinson was the only musician in the group standing. He lifted his trombone and began to play. The beauty of the music swept over the dancers, shifting their attention away from themselves to the soloist. Their movements gradually slowed, eventually ceasing with the halting motions of mechanical toys whose spring motors have begun to unwind. Robinson pointed his trombone toward him, making all heads turn and stare in his direction, his uneasiness somewhat diminished by the realization that he was cut off from view by the protective darkness that engulfed him. The music flowed forth with obvious feeling, its magic sweeping all into a bond of togetherness whose covenant was shared joy. Shouts and a loud clapping of hands ricocheted through the hall as soon as Jim Robinson completed his solo. For Nick, it was a rare coupling of the many and the few, a union fostered out of the recognition that all had shared a common mania—Dixieland. Who could forget "Two Jim Blues"?

* * *

A metallic click of the turntable closed off the flow of music, as well as memories. Nick took a long drink from his glass and absentmindedly wiped his mouth with the palm of his hand. Without looking at anyone in particular, he suggested that Frank Colucci choose the next record.

Uncoiling from his twisted position on the sofa, Frank ambled over to the shelves of records, pushing upward on his metal-rimmed glasses in order to position them more securely. He bent down to scan the titles, his finger cutting a wavy trail as its touch swept clear the thin veneer of dust that magnetically clung to the outer edges of the record jackets. He pulled one out of the stack, and after removing the record from its protective cover, he stood up, placed it on the turntable, and read aloud the title of the song: "That's How I Feel Today."

Frank became absorbed in watching the preciseness of the words inscribed on the record label gradually transform into fuzzy circular lines once it began spinning. Arms crossed, he stood fixedly staring down on the revolving disc. A troubled look crossed his face but remained unseen by the others.

"That's How I Feel Today." The title of song mentally reshaped itself into an inner-directed query. His response came forth in a disjointed drift of thoughts.

> *Mentally shiftless, that's how...can't even think straight today...I'm just aimlessly seeking...it's like trying to straightjacket clouds...everything seems to be changing...dissolving...nothing seems stable or consistent...the world around me is in a state of flux...*

The wail of a saxophone broke into his string of ruminations.

"Now that's music!" Frank exclaimed, his words failing to elicit a response from either of the others. He drifted back to the laconic candidness of his own musings.

> *That music sounds right, it's satisfying...perhaps that's what I've been searching for...a feeling...not a thing...an impression...some novelty for dormant senses...one that hasn't been tossed into the dustbin of spent sensations...something different....unique...*

"This sound has it all—melody, harmony, rhythm. It's the Mona Lisa of sound. Listen...just listen." Frank eagerly wanted to persuade the others of his own convictions. They, in turn, sat tapping their feet to the beat of the music without saying a word.

> *It's the kind of music that can free the soul when it gets bogged down by warnings of don't and can't...if only we could ride the loop-the-loop of illusion by paying ten cents for the ride...just slip a dime into the slot...good-bye reality.*

The music stopped and as Frank was about to lift the tone arm, Nick asked him to play the other side of the record.

"None of you have probably ever heard this next tune. It's called 'Old Folks.' It'll change your mood. Trust me." Nick's words offered new promise.

"It's Pee Wee Russell's best clarinet solo," he said, confident that his opinion would soon be proven correct.

The music started up again with the introduction of a clarinet solo that put an end to Frank's flow of fragmented thoughts, his excitement now quelled by the melodic tenderness of this new and soothing sound. With his back still turned to the others, he heard Jim ask Nick to repeat the name of the song. The reply set in motion another stream of reflections.

> *It's sad, but gentle, like the sweet sadness of lost friendship...old folks would be mindful of that kind of loss...that's for sure...from the peaks of illusion to the depths of reality...thanks for the ride, Nick.*

Frank listened intently to the music's tender cry, goading him to put aside all introspection in response to it. But that was not to be. Aversion took possession of his thoughts.

> *Old...old...when the senses begin to falter...that's reality, all right...it has the stench of a musty tomb...take a deep breath and you'll smother ...time...that everlasting mistress of reality...it may rob my senses, but not my memories.*

When the clarinet solo ended, Frank commented to no one in particular, "That's how I feel today." The others ignored what he said.

All three sat quietly. None of them took the initiative to remove the record from the turntable.

Nick leaned back in his rocking chair, debating whether to put aside his ever-present wariness about voicing controversial opinions of any kind.

"I have been sitting here thinking," he started, "that the jazz idiom might be as good a way as any to try and convince people that they're all truly one. After all, it does give everyone a chance to have his or her say. And I mean everyone—the musicians and the listeners." He lifted his glass in a salute before taking a swallow from it.

Jim and Frank looked at each other and smiled. Both knew of how Nick disliked starting any conversation with a proposition that could lead to contentious debate. They recognized that he was beginning to free himself from this self-imposed constraint. They judged that the whiskey, the music, and no doubt his memories had combined to overthrow his reticence. Nick's flimsy gambit nonetheless opened a door that easily led to the exchange of diverse viewpoints. Jim took the initiative to pass through that portal where one was free to propose and defend concepts and beliefs. This time, he resorted to humor as the messenger for his opening pronouncement.

"You've got a point there, Nick. Can you imagine the impact a horn-blowing Saint Paul would have on some cotton-belt rednecks if he was out to convert them to the brotherhood of jazz?"

The laughter that followed cleared away all preoccupations with self and shifted their concerns to that of others.

"Let's go one step further," Nick countered. "I'm ready for a Second Reformation. Can you see Louis Armstrong pounding the tenets of jazz onto the front door of the United Nations?"

Jim and Frank laughed, but Nick's features remained unsmiling and placid.

"That's not a bad idea, Nick, not bad at all," Frank said. He rose to his feet and placed his empty glass next to the whiskey bottle on the tray. Then he balled up a fist and slammed it into his open palm, saying, "But remember—jazz doesn't have any inflexible dogma. There aren't any good books to memorize, or quote. You can't preach lyrics."

"But we can sing them," Nick growled.

Frank responded by breaking out with a Bessie Smith lyric: "Gimme a pigfoot and a bottle of beer."

A smile crossed Nick's face. "What's wrong with that?" he asked, his words full of contentiousness.

The question triggered laughter.

"Friend," Frank responded to Nick's harsh sounding query, "there's nothing wrong with it, as long as the worshipers have equal say, be it in word or song."

Jim had been listening to their discourse without any real show of interest, but Frank's last remark caught his attention. "You're right, Frank," he started. "I'm for two-sided telling, not one-sided listening. You have to admit that the big difference between the call and response of jazz, and that of the usual religious service, is spontaneity. How many times have we seen crowds erupt in mass ecstasy in the give-and-take sessions between jazz and its listeners? Now that's what I call collective agreement."

"That's because everyone was rooting for the same team," Nick said, his words somewhat slurred and indistinct.

"That's the kind of spirit that's as earthy as sin," Frank added.

Frank's words cut through the last remnants of Jim's lethargy.

"Right again. Let's get jazz out of halls and back into the streets again. After all," Jim summed up his feelings in a way that made apparent a waning interest in the subject at hand. "Jazz is about people, and the street is where it belongs." He stood up and placed his empty glass onto the tray, wanting nothing more than to retreat from the speculative.

"It's the booze, Jim. It has a way of letting you kid yourself." Frank's tone was almost apologetic.

"Wouldn't it be great if jazz could do the same thing and not leave you with a hangover," Jim said, tongue in cheek. "That'd be a real high." His rejoinder was an attempt to rise above the unrealistic claims fueled by the exaggerations of those on the periphery of sobriety. "But if you're a realist," he continued, "it'd still fizzle down to a real low once you got back to your day after day routine."

Nick's silence made Jim look turn to look at him. He smiled when he observed Nick's head bobbing, the glass in his hand dangling loosely from his fingers. Jim walked over, removed the glass and placed it next to the others on the tray. All three glasses now stood empty, as well as the whiskey bottle.

"I think it's time to go, Frank," Jim said.

They reached for their coats and slipped them on before they descended the worn wooden stairs and walked out of the house. A penetrating cold wind persisted as they strode toward the nearest subway station.

Chapter 14

Jim Stahr spent the entire morning at home complying with the demands of study, but as the afternoon wore on he found himself struggling to stifle an urge to get up and leave. The destination did not seem to matter. Yet, a sense of discipline kept this longing in check and he continued working on his assigned tasks. As the afternoon progressed, however, it became increasingly difficult to suppress this yearning, and it began taking a toll on his ability to think clearly. Perhaps the underlying cause for this dilemma was an unexpected call from Gennie Connors earlier that day. She phoned to tell him that Peggy Troy planned to see a movie that evening. She did not invite him to come visit, which he thought was the purpose of her call, but the tone of her voice hinted that he do so. In the end, he decided that his assumption was right and started for the apartment house on Tenth Street.

As he was about to cross the street and make his way into the building, he spotted Peggy Troy and Frank Colucci exiting onto the street, hand in hand and in deep conversation. The night they all had spent in Greenwich Village apparently had forged a new alliance within their small clique. He watched as they walked briskly to the corner of Second Avenue, where they turned and disappeared from view. He jogged across the street and headed directly for the entrance of the apartment house. Out of habit, he went up the stairs instead of taking the elevator. Jim knocked on the door. While waiting for a response, he realized that this was the first opportunity to be alone with Gennie since that eventful Thanksgiving Day. It did not take long before he heard footsteps hurrying toward him. When Gennie opened the door, she stood staring at him with a mixture of astonishment and pleasure.

"I thought Peggy may have forgotten something and was coming back to get it. She only left about a minute ago," she said, her initial bewilderment quickly fading.

"Come on in! I didn't think you'd be coming." The words mirrored a change from delight to out-and-out joy.

Jim crossed the threshold and started walking behind Gennie as she hurried through the long corridor.

"It sounded like you needed some company when you called." His words made her stop in the middle of the hallway and reverse direction. She walked back to meet him, slipped her arms around his neck and held him closely. The warmth of his response aroused in Gennie a feeling of gratification, one that shelved the quiet pain that aloneness habitually generated.

Placing her hands on his shoulders, she looked up at him, saying, "I'm glad that you came. But I didn't want to interrupt your studying." A look of indecision crossed her face. A moment later, it changed to that of resolve, as if she had suddenly decided to reveal some troubling matter.

"Lately, I can't stand being by myself. It makes me want to do things that are unreal," she announced mournfully.

Instead of responding with words of consolation, he took her hand in his and guided her into the living room. Once inside, they parted to allow Jim to remove his heavy winter jacket and toss it on one of the chairs. Approaching him, Gennie pulled the scarf from around his neck, threw it atop his jacket, and once more slid her arms around him. She raised her lips to his, her kiss expressing gratefulness more than passion. Without any parting words, she slipped free of him and started for the kitchen. He followed.

"I just saw Peggy and Frank leaving together," he informed her. "Now that was an eye-opener."

"Something was in the air the night we walked home from Julius.' They seemed to take to each other right away. Today, when they were here, they hardly took notice of me." Gennie hesitated for a moment and then continued talking. "Now I know what they mean when they say three's a crowd. But no one ever talks about how the odd one out feels when they've been shut out of things."

Jim sensed the note of chagrin in her words. In an effort to soothe any hurt she may have experienced by her roommate's failure to invite her to accompany them, he began to justify their having done so.

"When two people's feelings get wrapped up in each other, they have to pair off from the crowd. Anyway, it's probably the only time in their lives that the world becomes a microcosm and the two of them are at its center." Jim stopped, thought a moment, and then added, "No one likes being alone. At least they're doing something about it. Anyway, aren't we trying to do the same thing?"

His words brought a smile to her face, but she remained silent.

Perhaps, she admitted to herself, the fault lies with her. She always demanded more from her relationships with men than most women might consider appropriate. She sought not just love, but a partner to share in a never-ending search for experiences that would enrich her life. Moreover, if this was truly so, intuition forewarned her that aloneness would be a deep-rooted factor in her future. Tonight, however, she wanted to prove this prophecy wrong by bringing Jim Stahr's intelligence and sensitivity into play, in order to engender the kind of intellectual stimulation she yearned for as foreplay to physical love.

"For the little time we have tonight, Jim," she started, "why can't we build our own little cocoon, just for the two of us?" The suggestion hovered close to pleading.

Jim reached out and drew Gennie tightly to him, his ardor pushing constraint aside.

This response was not the one she had sought. She wanted this evening to begin on a different note, one that would not start in the way she wished it to end.

She twisted free of him in order to try once again to bring to the fore what had now turned into a real need for her. "Make me want to follow you into some private hideaway, Jim. Entice me with words that arouse desire, as a prelude to passion. Make the usual unusual, even if it's for a little while."

Restlessly, she moved to the wall opposite the window, sensing her own inadequacy to bring about the very thing she wanted him to do. As Gennie stood with her back to him she began to suspect that romance may have a set pattern, a matter of man and woman giving and taking, every action performed according to some standardized routine, repetitious and with little or no originality. She wondered what role intelligence played in the involvement called love. Perhaps, she told herself, what I want can't be; therefore, I can't have what I want. Nevertheless, one ought to still keep trying she chided herself. She turned to face Jim, her mind already probing for verbal means to filter the ordinary so that it could emerge noteworthy.

"Jim, would you mind if we talked for a little while?"

"Sure, why not?" His optimism was suddenly clouded with a foreboding that warned of a disastrous end to what he thought had been a promising beginning.

"I know very little about men who create beauty. Do you have any idea what makes them tick?"

Gennie's efforts to initiate an exchange of ideas and feelings seemed to Jim a tactful way of dissipating his pent-up emotions. If this was a game, it left him with no other choice but to play it.

Anyway, he surmised, there was no quick answer to her query, nor was he willing to offer any response that could end up as a debatable theory. He decided to embark on a different tack.

"As a dyed-in-the-wool rationalist, I don't know what drives such men. But surely you must have some ideas regarding their character, even if you've derived them from your wishful thinking." Getting no answer, and hoping to steer the conversation in a direction that would lead to the satisfaction of his physical cravings, he feigned a show of interest in what she was attempting to do.

"Anyway," he said, "if your perceptions of creative men are out of the ordinary—and I'm guessing yours are—then no one man could ever meet all of your expectations."

But his lame effort did not achieve its desired end. Gennie spun on her heels and started for the kitchen. Her wish for stimulating conversation remained unrealized.

The look of dejection on Gennie's face told him what he had already begun to suspect. Today was not going to be a replay of what had taken place on Thanksgiving Day. He might as well participate in whatever diversion she may have decided upon, although from her expression, she probably considered it a lost cause. Jim wanted his time spent in an atmosphere that cheered, not one in which the prevailing mood could impose a harmful burden on their relationship. This was a time, he decided, for making pragmatic compromises.

He tried to revive the discussion. "But I know of one man who created poetry and had all the traits that you could wish for."

His words brought her to a sudden halt. Gennie stopped and stood immersed in thought for a while before turning to look back at him. "Who?"

"He's not real. Nevertheless, he has all the qualities that you can conceive of in a man dedicated to creating beauty in any form. He's also very courageous, sensitive, inspired, romantic and adventurous."

She smiled back at him, displaying a puzzled look of interest in what he said.

"Imagination allows us to invent people who rarely, if ever, become part of our lives," he continued, hoping that she would accept a fictitious figure, instead of a real and proven one, in response to her query as to what are the attributes of an artistically inclined male.

There was no hiding her curiosity as she stood before him, arms folded across her chest, and again asked, "Who?"

"How can any man, or woman, not see Cyrano de Bergerac as the ideal man?"

Her face lit up with happy surprise. "Yes, he'd be a good choice."

"But," Jim went on to caution her, "let me tell you that real ecstasy is better than anything imagination can furnish."

"I'm not so sure," she said teasingly, "but I'd be willing to find out."

"It'll take lots of homework. You'll need time," he warned her, affecting a look of concern.

"I'll have plenty of that before you know it." She took a step away from him before saying, "Are you trying to lead me astray?"

"No. I'm hoping to lead you to reality. You know…to the other end of imagination's pole—where what you feel is real."

"Later." She looked at him with a puzzled expression. "Right now, you've only stirred up my curiosity."

"Where was this taking them?" Jim wondered. Intellectual arousal was not the kind he was attempting to effect. He sensed his ardor starting to wane.

Gennie threw him a questioning look. "What made you think that Cyrano could satisfy what you imply are my illusions?"

Again, her question made him retreat into the past, hoping to extract from memory some viewpoints formed years ago and bolstered by his recent viewing of a film version of the play. It was this combination of poignant impressions that he drew from in the hope of making Gennie redirect her interest to his emotional needs, and, perhaps, to her own. The mental effort expended in playing this game was beginning to take its toll.

Jim made his opening gambit. "Men admire dogmatic will and courage, and he had both." He hesitated a moment before adding, "Yet, he was capable of forming tender attachments. He could be aggressive in defense of his own dignity but still able and willing to give compassionate support to others. Most humans lack those qualities."

"If that's the case, then it truly makes him a figment of the imagination...and not just mine," Gennie declared with a look of regret.

"Yes, he's pure invention," Jim affirmed, inwardly wishing that it was not truly the case. "He's just a rare offspring of fancy. Nothing more."

Suddenly, and without any noticeable reason, Jim started for the kitchen and took up his usual position by the window that faced onto Tenth Street. Gennie did not follow.

He drew the curtains apart, allowing the streetlamp to thrust a shaft of dim light into the room, making any additional illumination unnecessary. He found a quiet pleasure in being a solitary observer of the movements taking place below him. This pastime now acted to diminish his disappointment at having his amorous intentions so neatly subverted. If emotions were not to be the source of tonight's pleasure, then the mind's introspection would have to suffice, he told himself.

His eyes fixed on the two statues of American Indians standing guard in the St. Marks churchyard. These stone monuments, as well the leafless trees around them, were free of snow. For some reason he felt a twinge of loneliness. Winter, he ruminated, is man's season for solitary vigil. Nature's furies intensify isolation, and wintertime makes us what we truly are—animals in search of warm cover. He never heard Gennie enter the kitchen. Her probing words broke his cogitative spell.

"Jim, do you truly believe that the spirit of a soldier and that of a poet can't form harmoniously in a single human being?"

She waited for a response and, not receiving one, let out a sigh of frustration before answering her own question.

"You're probably right. I have to agree. It's not in the genetic cards—at least, not yet."

Although he failed to react to what Gennie said, he silently concurred with her. Yet, he reflected, another aspect of that particular French drama, which he left unspoken, was that in today's world, Cyrano would not be extolled as a hero. Nowadays, the audience only cheers winners. Those who attempt to deliberately undertake a unique approach to living but fail to achieve their professed goals—for whatever reason—can expect to find themselves tossed aside without an iota of recognition for their efforts. After all, in the end, Cyrano de Bergerac did not win the lady's hand. In today's competitive world, such an outcome might have left him judged a loser. The possibility that any attempt on his part to live within a world of his own making gave rise to a troubling apprehension that he, too, could one day be labeled as one.

Jim glanced at his reflection framed in the window, aware that introspection had captured his interest with enough force to thrust aside his longings to hold and possess. Gennie's desire for intellectual stimulus to be the innovative start to lovemaking had inadvertently made him a captive of his own impulses. There was no constraining the urgency to voice views held so intensely in the past, now demanding release from the archival bins of memory. Still maintaining a steady gaze on the activities outside the window, he began to speak more to himself than to his listener, who now stood by his shoulder bathed in the early evening's fading light.

"Many of us hide behind false images to give our peers the impression that we have the attributes essential for success. If we lack such qualities, we're tempted to resort to guile to falsely portray that we possess them. Apparently, our friend Cyrano got himself caught in such a dilemma." Jim raised his hands and placed them against the top edge of the lower window frame.

Gennie moved behind him, encircling her arms around his waist. She rested her head on his shoulder, troubled by her contrivance to bring spontaneity to a situation she falsely assumed followed an unvarying routine. She deposited a soft kiss on the side of his neck, wanting him to turn and take hold of her. This he failed to do. His hands remained fixed to the window frame. Her efforts to bring about a stimulating prelude to what she eventually wanted to take place had set him adrift in a sea of rationalization.

"Cyrano had to resort to subterfuge to portray the good looks he didn't possess if he was to be the winner of the fair maiden's heart," he said thoughtfully.

Gennie listened, saying nothing, no longer expecting him to display the same intensity of feelings that he exhibited when he first entered. She now found herself trapped into listening to matters that held no interest for her. Perceiving that this one-sided conversation was no longer leading toward the gratifying end she had set out to achieve, she backed away from him, resigned to the fact that her efforts to create an atmosphere of shared mental stimulation had resulted in failure.

The sudden absence of her body's pressure against his made him thrust aside his ruminations and begin looking for her. Through the open doorway, he could barely make out Gennie in the partially darkened living room, as she now stood outside the perimeter of weak light that came through the kitchen window.

Her words came out of the darkness with a quiet urgency. "There's so little time left before Peggy returns. Let's not waste it discussing the merits of some unreal character," she said in a final effort to steer the conversation away from the hypothetical and back toward the rapturous.

"You're absolutely right," he asserted.

Jim went to Gennie, drew her close, and began stroking her hair before hugging her tightly. "I guess we've been trying to find our way to where we wanted to go to in the first place. It's too bad that we had to take such a time-consuming detour to get there," Jim declared, a sense of relief apparent in his words.

"Maybe love has a way of getting people to move in the same direction. It's truly a one-way street," she remarked, her words affirming the restoration of a wish that she had discarded just a short while ago but whose fulfillment now seemed possible.

"But it's best traveled in the dark," he countered.

Without another word, Jim released her, strode back into the kitchen, and pulled down the shade, throwing the entire apartment into total darkness. She waited for him to come back, having resolved that analytical discussion would best serve as an epilogue to passion rather than a prologue.

Chapter 15

For two others in the city, the switching on of overhead lights inside a movie theater prefaced the start of a revelation of their innermost thoughts and feelings. The relay of lights embedded in the ceiling of the cinema came to life as soon as the film had ended, sequentially shedding the darkness of the cinema's interior. Peggy Troy and Frank Colucci found themselves locked into a slow-moving crowd inching its way toward the theater's exit doors. Once outside, Frank grabbed Peggy's hand and began to lead the way. He skillfully treaded around some isolated clusters of bodies, whose momentum had ceased but were now alive with cross fires of bubbling commentary. His zigzagging continued until he reached the curb, where a throng of men and women formed a crooked line waiting for the traffic to ease. When it did, the solidity of the crush of moviegoers disintegrated as they all scrambled forth in a disorderly array. Peggy and Frank raced along with the others heading for the other side of Fifth Avenue.

They started walking crosstown along Fifty-Seventh Street, each engrossed in their own thoughts. To any attentive observer, they seemed physically together but spiritually apart.

"Would you like to have some coffee, Peggy?"

"I could use some," she replied, slightly out of breath.

Frank Colucci felt the kind of rapture that comes from viewing a masterpiece. Nevertheless, this experience created ambivalent feelings within him. A strange form of melancholia had lodged its way into his thoughts seemingly bent on undermining his elation, brought on by the realization that another such elevating experience was not likely to come his way in the near future or perhaps ever again. Laurence Olivier's performance of *Hamlet* had lifted Shakespeare's poetic phrases to heights of admiration that Frank had never scaled before. Yet, this same exhilarating experience left him with a troubling doubt about his potential as a poet. In his mind, the artistry of what he just heard and seen made all his creative efforts mere trivia by comparison.

The movie also affected Peggy. The initial high spirits that the film produced were now eclipsed by a gnawing sense of disquietude. During the war, she had been an intimate witness to tragedy too many times, as well as to its consequences. That experience had instilled in her an unalterable belief that life brings relatively few and mostly superficial gains when compared with the number and profundity of its losses. Shakespeare, she knew, had the prodigious gift of making human misfortune palatable to his audiences. But for her, human adversity in any form always proved unhinging and left her at times overwhelmed by an abject despondency that sometimes chronically lingered. How could anyone forget the human afflictions brought on by war? She had asked herself this question so many times in the past because of one particular memory that had haunted her waking and sleeping hours with a disquieting regularity.

They had gone the entire distance between the movie house and the Automat without any exchange of words. Frank pushed the heavy revolving door to allow Peggy to precede him into the restaurant.

They bought coffee and sandwiches, seated themselves, and indicated their wish for privacy by hanging their coats on the backs of the two empty chairs at their table. At this hour, no one thought to challenge their unvoiced request.

Peggy decided to bring their awkward silence to an end. "Well, Frank, did the picture move you in any way? You've got to admit the acting was beyond compare."

Frank bent over and sipped his coffee with meticulous care, seemingly oblivious to the question. Before responding, he felt the need to deal with the dread that the film had spawned, one that had given credence to the possibility that he may lack the natural qualities to write the kind of poetry that would receive some measure of recognition by his peers. The merits of the motion picture were now a secondary consideration to that of an urgent need to rid himself of this demoralizing negativism. This effort left him momentarily too preoccupied to form any response to her question.

At first, she experienced a sting of rejection, for she assumed that Frank's failure to reply to her query was his way of ignoring her. She threw him an angry look before giving vent to her pride by again asking him the same question, more out of obstinacy than her original intent of starting a friendly discussion.

"Don't you have any opinion about the film?" she pressed him for a reply, a muted anger showing in the manner in which she posed the question.

Frank glanced up, surprised by the biting tone of irritability in what she had said.

"Oh, I'm sorry, Peggy, very sorry. I guess I got lost for awhile in my mind's preoccupation about myself." His features remained impassive as he voiced his apology. "Certainly, I've an opinion. I can't remember the last time a movie affected me so much."

He cupped a hand over his eyeglasses, pushed them back in place and looked directly at Peggy.

"In all honesty," he began, "after seeing that movie, I just can't seem to get rid of the feelings of inadequacy it brought on concerning my ability to write poetry. Frankly, I'm just about ready to give up on the whole idea." There was a low-keyed finality couched in this declaration. "When I compare what I've done to what I've just heard…" He shook his head slowly and said nothing more.

"That's a large dose of self-criticism. Remember, someone like Shakespeare appears with less frequency than do miracles." Her sudden upsurge of wrath faded as quickly as it had risen.

His ego rebelled against her unintended implication that his creative prowess had limitations. Yet, there was no denying that what he had seen on the screen tonight had given rise to a premonition that his poetic ambitions might well be beyond his ability to attain them.

Peggy now understood the reason for Frank's unwillingness to respond to her question. Without giving it a second thought, she undertook her habitual role of easing the pain of others. If this evening was to end on a joyful note, she had to find a way of stopping Frank's dismal harping on the limitations of his competency.

"Poetry didn't die after Shakespeare. There will always be radical changes in form, language and content. Am I right?"

Frank listened, inwardly admitting the truth of her assertion. A smile crossed his face for the first time since they left the movie theater.

"There's a great deal of truth in what you said. I should have known better," he conceded, his words bolstering his crestfallen spirits.

Shaking off his feelings of despondency, he turned his attention to Peggy. He realized that he had been less than a considerate companion this evening. He thought that a show of interest in drawing out her reactions to the movie would be a means for remedying this indiscretion.

"What feelings did *Hamlet* produce in you this evening?"

"The picture almost destroyed me," she found herself saying earnestly.

Frank's interest took hold. "In what way?"

"It's my Achilles heel. Whenever I am a witness to tragedy—human tragedy—so explicitly, a bit of me is torn apart in the process."

Her response aroused his curiosity.

"But why?"

"The reasons are obvious, even trite."

"It's not because of some bad love affair?" He tried to sound as if he was only joking.

Peggy shook her head, indicating that was not the case. She puckered her brow in a way that warned he had edged close to the unmarked limit where inquiry about personal matters begins to skirt on the fringes of impertinence.

Frank read the meaning of her frown and quickly concluded that it would be best to suspend further questioning about her personal life, even if he was doing so in jest. He lit a cigarette, took a deep puff from it, tilted his head back and started blowing smoke rings. It struck him that of the entire noisy bunch at the university, she should have been the one least afflicted by the dread of human suffering. After all, Peggy was the only one in the group who displayed any attributes of wealth. Even as he tapped the ashes of his cigarette into an ash try, his mind continued its self-interrogation—what could have caused such a vehement reaction to what she had seen in the movie? After all, he told himself, human misfortune is an everyday affair. Besides, she certainly must be intimately aware of the human misery brought on by the war...war...war!

"Or maybe it was the war?" Frank asserted, giving voice to the assumption that resulted from his speculative meanderings as to the cause for Peggy's profound feelings of melancholy generated by the film.

When she did reply she appeared unruffled, but the signs of cheerfulness she had displayed earlier were no longer visible.

"Well, it was a different kind of love—and the war," she admitted without any show of emotion.

"Both?"

"Both."

Frank leaned over to sip from his coffee, his thoughts filling with self-criticism for lacking the ability to utilize the information he gleaned by his usual keen sense of observation. Structuring elements of a situation together in a meaningful way was not one of his inherent qualities. In his mind, that was the function of the scientist, not the poet. Thinking back, he could not remember Peggy ever saying anything in the past that could provide a clue as to the meaning of what she had just said. Asking her outright was out of the question, of course. If he continued the discussion, he reasoned, and took care not to appear to be probing, a clearer understanding of what her words had intended to convey might result.

"Peggy," he started, "I don't believe you can live life without getting a taste of that bitter herb called calamity." He realized that sweeping statement sounded trite.

"True." A bitter smile crossed her face. "But I find its flavor caustic and its aftereffects harmful. To sense its presence and escape its reach that…" She broke off, as if her own words were a cause for pain.

Frank did not react to what she had said. He finished drinking his coffee. Their mutual silence decided him to suggest that they leave.

They stood up, put on their coats, and pushed their way out through the revolving door.

The overhead streetlamps provided not only visibility, but also a sense of security against the unfamiliar stillness that pervaded everything around them. Frank glanced at his wristwatch. It was well past midnight.

Chapter 16

The time they had spent together had proven agreeable. An evening he expected to spend in a routine exchange of facts about one another became instead a time of withdrawal in which his spirits had risen and fallen to levels beyond those he had ever experienced in the past. His agitation had finally sifted away, and he now felt a pressing need to make up for his earlier moodiness. A solution occurred to him, one that he had resorted to in the past and had proven effective.

"You've heard of people talking about their favorite spots in the city. Come on, Peggy, and I'll show you one of mine." Frank led her in the direction of Carnegie Hall without waiting for her to agree.

From the secretive tone of his voice, Peggy Troy suspected that he wanted to take her into his confidence by revealing something that he judged a very private matter, one that he had never shared with anyone else. Her present mood, on the other hand, dampened her desire to play a part in any such revelations be they either secretive or confessional in nature. Frank's earlier inquisitiveness as to the cause for her unsettling response to the film production of *Hamlet* had pierced the psychological retaining wall that she had built to keep irksome memories in check, but like an open wound, they now hemorrhaged forth with a perturbing effect. Her mind lacked the coagulating self-will to inhibit its flow. She took her hand away and looped her arm around his, letting him lead the way. They walked arm in arm without any exchange of words. The silence opened the gates, allowing recall to take command of her thoughts by fetching the past and depositing it into the present, bringing with it the memory of the kind of love that never demanded any reciprocity from her. Unlike this moment, however, the stillness around her at that time was shattered by a sudden, but not unexpected, outburst of abrasive male voices.

* * *

…As soon as the doctors had completed their morning rounds, the respectful silence in the ward broke into a noisy outburst of shouting.

Lieutenant Peggy Troy did not smile. Pandemonium of this kind was a daily occurrence. As she went about her duties, she responded glibly to each soldier's particular brand of jesting, ranging from outright vulgarism to lofty flattery. As usual, the kid said nothing. He was too busy reading. From the day he arrived in her ward, she noticed that a book was always sticking out from under his pillow. The first time she had raised his head off of it, she spotted the title of the book that lay partially hidden underneath—*Uncle Tom's Cabin.*

"Are you a Yankee?" she kidded him, her features screwed up in a mask of mock seriousness.

"Not exactly. I'm more like a beginning reader," he replied.

"When did you begin?" She resettled his head on the pillow and furtively shoved the book under it.

"Only about two years ago. The army taught me how."

"Two years ago? Come on, soldier, you wouldn't kid an officer," she joshed.

"In a way, I'm still learning. Reading is better than medicine, at least for me."

She bent over him and whispered, "Listen, kid, if you've got to have a vice, it's the best one you could have chosen." With a quick wink, she moved to the adjacent bed.

For the month that he was in her ward, he read most of the day, while others participated in their bedridden rowdiness. The day he was to return to his unit, she found him waiting outside her barracks. When he saw her approaching, he came forward quickly, obviously embarrassed.

"Look, Lieutenant, I hope you don't mind my coming around to say goodbye."

"No, not at all," was all she could manage to say.

"Well, I dropped by to thank you," he started haltingly.

"There's no need for thanks." It took some effort to effect the brisk manner that she was instructed to use in distancing herself from enlisted personnel.

"Anyway, I wanted to thank you for getting me all those books." His features tightened in a frown and his face reddened. She silently scolded herself, thinking that the tone of her voice may have been overly harsh. She saw that the last paperback book she had given him was in his hand.

"Still reading?" she asked, pointing to it, hoping the question would make up for the curtness of her previous remark.

"Can you think of anything better to do?" he snapped back, before turning and trotting away without bothering to salute, the North African sun blurring her view of his retreating figure...

* * *

Peggy Troy turned up the collar of her coat. A chilling wind greeted them as soon as they turned onto Central Park South. They instinctively quickened their pace. Conversation was out of the question. When she turned to look at him, he had the look of a little boy who just realized that he can never get what he prized the most. Peggy stifled a maternal desire to soothe and touch. There were many times in the past when she found great difficulty in restraining the need to reach out in an attempt to restore the self-confidence of men whose lives would never be the same because of their injuries. Now, as she had always done in such situations, she looked away.

Frank's expression, that of wounded pride, she remembered, was registered on the face of the teenage soldier on the day he arrived as a patient in her ward for the second time. Her attempts to quash the memory of that day ended in failure. Her face, now hidden behind her upturned collar, concealed from Frank her growing sense of apartness, one that held out the promise that the privacy of her mental wanderings into the past would be safeguarded against any intrusion from the present.

* * *

…The essence of war is chaos, yet from out of it people and events are sometimes linked in ways that are life-altering, but cannot be easily understood.

One day, the same young infantryman was back in her ward again, with shrapnel embedded in both legs. This time the hospital was in England, and the invasion into France had only recently begun. The sunken cheeks, glazed eyes and sallow coloring of his skin no longer warranted the childish appellation of "kid." This time she greeted him with a guarded, "Hello, bookworm."

When she prepared his belongings for storage, she found a blood-speckled copy of *Look Homeward, Angel*. She placed it under his pillow and allowed herself to be more open and friendly, especially if the kind of books he was reading was any measure of his growing maturity. For this reason, she began to refer to him as her budding scholar. He had become a patient warranting more than normal care. It was the first leeway she had made since promising herself not to get emotionally involved with any of the wounded who filled her ward.

Treatment and time soon overcame pain, freeing the soldier to once again become an insatiable reader. During his period of recuperation, Peggy would push his wheelchair through the long corridors and out of the building onto the hospital lawn. Once settled outdoors, a routine began whereby he asked questions that demanded insights about people and events that she could not provide, forcefully making her aware of her own inadequacies concerning the meanings and values of her own life's experiences. Apparently, his was the desperation of the imaginative young, who respond to the events in books they read with an unrestrained eagerness to derive some significance out of them. In his case, she noted, his earnestness seemed coupled with a fear that there might not be enough time left him to explore these newfound worlds. These sessions with his pertinent questions, and her inadequate answers, provided her with new insights about the true value of learning. The daily exchanges helped influence the direction her life would take once the war ended. Before long, the boy scholar was gone.

After Cherbourg, strategic towns and cities spelled out the route that eventually brought a successful end to the war for the Allies—Avranches...Caen....LeMans...Paris...Metz. This forward motion was brought to a sudden and unexpected halt, however, when the German Army unleashed a powerful attack near a Belgium town named Bastogne. Impatience drove her to volunteer for special assignments, one of which was removing wounded infantrymen from a building that had taken a direct hit from enemy artillery. Peggy accompanied a doctor and several medics in the ambulance delegated to carry out this unpleasant duty.

A russet sun was descending, and the interior of the battered farmhouse was awash with a reddish-yellow light that gleamed through jagged openings in the walls and roof. Bodies lay bent and disjointed, flung into their various positions by an indiscriminate violence. The medics began retrieving the wounded without any command to do so. The only human sound was the frenzied shout of one of the corpsmen: "Let's get a move on, damn it...move your asses!" Courtesy died with the dead.

The few found that were found alive were loaded onto stretchers and carried to the ambulance parked outside. The dead were turned, prodded and checked with a minimum of caution. Enemy artillery again began pounding the area around them, creating the kind of fear that made attentive handling of the living and the dead an inconceivable nicety, beyond thought or reason.

"Get the lead out! Move! Damn it, move!" another harsh male voice commanded. "Have we got them all?" The inquiry was more like a shouted demand.

In answer, all scattered to touch and feel once more, clawing and stumbling over the rubbish and debris.

"Hey! Troy, did you check up there? Behind you! Behind you! Get a move on, will ya?"

She did not recognize the voice but obeyed by scrambling up a broken stairway that led into a small attic. The ache of exhausted muscles turned to pain when she stumbled, slipped, and fell at the top of the stairs. In front of her, a soldier was kneeling with his back toward her, his head resting at a strange angle atop his rifle, which protruded downward out of a smashed window. He had not turned to look at her, although the sound of her fall had created enough noise to alert him of her clumsy entry into the room. The fact that he took no notice of her, but continued to sit rigid and indifferent to what was taking place around him, brought on a flash of anger.

"Move, soldier, move!" she screamed, driven more by fury than by any concern for his well-being. Edging forward on all fours, she managed to grab hold of the shoulder strap of his backpack and began tugging it as hard as she could. Relief washed away her annoyance as the body responded to her furious pulling. The soldier leaned backward, hesitated for a moment, then changed direction and fell sideways, this latter motion sending his helmet spinning away. Peggy quickly got to her feet and moved closer to the soldier, fending off a strong desire to run. She kneeled down next to him and carefully lifted his head. He was dead. The soldier's head struck the wooden floor with a dull thud when she spontaneously thrust both of her hands up to her mouth to muffle a cry of shock. The face was one she knew well. It was the kid—the boy scholar—the bookworm. These phrases darted through her mind, filling her with rage and disgust, and for some reason she failed to grasp, a feeling of shame.

"Troy! What in the hell are you doing up there?" The question had the ring of an impatient command.

She heard someone comment harshly, "I wish she'd move her butt. We ain't got all day." A shell struck a short distance away with enough force to reposition the living and the dead.

"Troy! Let's go!" someone shouted sounding more like a plea than a command.

Peggy got to her feet and rushed over to retrieve a small, tattered paperback book that had dropped out of the dead soldier's helmet when it had fallen off his head. She reached down, took hold of it, thrust it into one of the pockets of her field jacket. "I'm on my way," she called out before starting to go down the wooden stairway.

"Snap it up, will ya? Let's get a move on! We ain't got all day," the same angry voice responded.

Only after she reached the waiting ambulance did the image of the dead soldier's contorted features take precedence over fear, for it refused to be obliterated from memory. Etched in her mind's eye was a face that was no longer boyish, like that of a punk kid, nor thoughtful, like that of a scholar. Her inability to rid herself of it brought on a sickening queasiness that sent her reeling against the side of the ambulance for support. One of the medics took hold of her arm and unceremoniously pulled her into the waiting vehicle.

The enemy artillery ceased firing. Peggy found herself swept up by some alien stillness. Someone tapped her on the shoulder, pointed to a moaning soldier lying on a stretcher and harshly commanded her to lend a hand.

She removed the paperback book from her field jacket as soon as she returned to her tent. The title of it was *Walden Pond*. On the inside of the cover was written: "To learn is to live, and I live to learn." The handwriting was crude, but clear. War, she conjectured, creates more than one kind of love. She wiped away some tears before closing the book and placing it under her pillow...

* * *

The sharp crosswind lessened just as Frank and Peggy approached one of the street benches that abutted the stone wall marking the southern boundary of Central Park. The bench faced the Park Plaza and the St. Moritz hotels. They seated themselves close to one another in an effort to share each other's warmth.

"This is my favorite bench, and I use it only at night. Do you like the view?" His speech was awash with the conspiratorial excitement of revelation.

Peggy glanced up at the assorted and irregular-shaped buildings across the street, bewildered by Frank's presumption that what she saw before her could possibly offer any kind of stimulus.

"I'm sorry, Frank, but all I can see are buildings of irregular shapes, with lights on in some windows and not in others. It doesn't bring on any special feelings. Should it?"

"That's it! It's all about windows! You've got it!"

"What've I got?" She grinned, still not fully cognizant of what he was trying to tell her.

"Well, then I'd better explain," he said, with the resignation of one left with no choice but that of carrying out the frustrating task of translating feelings into words. Underlying this statement, one sensed an internal exuberance that suggested this form of labor was neither imposition nor drudgery.

"Maybe the whole idea is foolish, but when I'm sitting here in the park at night, it's easy to let my fancy run free." He removed one hand from his coat pocket and pointed at the buildings across the street. "Behind those lighted windows, people are involved in doing things with their lives even at this late hour. But it's best when I let my imagination invent the people who live in those rooms. Sitting here, I'm free to concoct all kinds of situations that they may be involved in. This bench may be anchored down, but it's my flying carpet."

Bemused by his explanation, she quickly asked, "What about the windows without lights? Those must tax the full limits of your imagination." Her upturned collar hid the smug look of one sure of victory for having outwitted another.

"It's true. Sometimes my visionary resources fail me," Frank began, "especially when I try to conjure up what's possibly happening behind those darkened windows—the unlit ones. Perhaps they're empty. Anyway, if anyone is in them and awake, then their involvements with themselves, as well as with others, could prove deeply moving. After all," he went on to explain, "darkness provides us with the isolation to gather up the courage to judge ourselves, as people."

He drew Peggy closer to him and sighed, as if faced with no other choice but to disclose some secreted truth. "I have to admit that withdrawal into this self-imposed isolation can bring on intense feelings of loneliness. But, then again," he said, allowing a mischievous smile to light up his face, "the absence of light can release lovers from their bonds of prudery."

Although moved by his words, Peggy found that in response to his theoretical explanation, she could only manage to utter just a questioning word: "Love?"

"Yes, love. But in the dark," he went on, "the rapture of each lover is exclusively his own—solitary and unspoken."

He stopped speaking and pushed his glasses back in place. "You're right, Peggy, those unlit windows can be a real tough challenge."

Frank sat staring up at the buildings, engrossed in his own thoughts and seemingly no longer aware of her presence. He had the look of an oversensitive little boy, waiting for his fanciful wish to become a reality. She wanted to reach out to touch him but decided not to. This gesture of affection, she felt, would disturb more than please. To push aside this last pessimistic reflection, Peggy made an inquiry that begged a direct comparison between his ideology and that of another. "What do you think your buddy Jim Stahr would say about your free-wheeling imagination?" She immediately regretted having said what she did.

He looked at her coldly for a moment and did not reply. Peggy sensed an obvious effort on his part to muffle disappointment, or even displeasure. When his inner turmoil subsided, he responded without any show of emotion. "I suppose that the difference between the two of us is a matter of dreaming and doing."

Shifting to a lighter vein, he added, "No doubt, he'd want to experience the very things I dream up. That's what I think he'd say."

"You're probably right. No doubt, he'd feel that your fantasies would just be happy ones. Anyway, he's too much of a pessimist to place much value on that part of your mental wanderings, whether they were poetic or not."

"But that's not so!" Frank objected. "You mentioned tragedy earlier tonight. Well, don't you think that I can visualize tragedy—especially behind those unlit windows?"

"What pleasure could you possibly derive from your devising predicaments about people faced with pain and loss?" she probed gingerly.

"Because tragedy is part of the human dilemma that none of us can escape."

"Even when we try," she agreed. "And I can attest to that."

Frank slouched back on the bench and gazed blankly at the buildings on the other side of the street, their windows set in a crossword pattern of light and dark rectangles, his thoughts immersed in a losing battle to stifle saying what he was thinking.

"As long as people try to overcome ignorance with viciousness, we'll just keep on doing the same cruel things. For me, that's tragedy."

Then, without any warning, Frank took his arm from around hers and got to his feet. Peggy also rose and took his hand in hers. They started walking toward the nearest subway station, neither of them harboring any further need to say more, finding gratification instead in having shared time together that proved neither dull nor wasted.

Chapter 17

Hector Palofax and Nick Grigoris sat with their elbows resting atop Rocky's bar. Both of them had spent the last hour belaboring the dissolution of the group's former solidarity. Now that their exchange of misgivings was finished, both sat warding off the apprehension of those fearing an impending loss. Neither had found, nor sought, a substitute for the stimulating polemics that the group had enjoyed most of their days at the university.

Bessie Siegal used her shoulder to help push open the heavy door leading into the tavern. Once inside she waited a moment until her vision adjusted to the partial darkness of its interior. Before long, she was able to catch sight of Nick and Hector, their backs bent forward, heads together, as if exchanging secrets. She walked over to them and with her free hand lightly tapped each of them on the head. They turned aggressively to face the intruder, their expressions of displeasure promptly annulled by recognition. They got down from their high stools and greeted her with a gusto that she instinctively felt was suspiciously excessive. They helped her onto a stool, and Nick took her books and placed them on one of the empty tables next to the silent jukebox.

Rocky, the owner of the tavern, brought her a Coke, and an exchange of criticism and gossip began, especially about those who no longer showed up in the university's cafeteria. In the discourse that followed, censure for the gradual disintegration of the group followed on the heels of a heated exchange as to the causes that brought it about; this, in turn, was countered by vindications of themselves, the whole discussion finally ending in disagreement and eventually silence. It was then that Bessie changed the subject by telling them that she had received a firm teaching offer from the school system in Newburgh, north of New York City. This news resulted in a burst of congratulations and best wishes. She was the first in the group whose postgraduate future seemed firmly assured. Now they all sat quietly, a sense of dejection pervading the air.

Nick decided to leave. He was in no mood to participate in any further discussions. Without bothering to empty his glass, he slid off his stool.

Bessie did the same.

Mumbling good-byes, both walked away to retrieve their belongings, leaving Hector sitting facedown, examining the contents of his glass.

Nick helped Bessie into her coat. Hector spun around on his swivel-topped stool and observed Bessie leaning down to place her arms into the sleeves.

"That's my girl!" he thought admiringly. Leaning back against the bar, he watched them walk off, admiring how gracefully Bessie moved. In his mind, the female form was an aesthetic structure in which every movement was a subconscious ritual for enticement that soon led to lust. This, to Hector, was not a theoretical matter; it was a conviction. He spun around, looked into his beer glass, and began to rub the frost off its surface with his index finger. Yes, he confided to himself, she has it, all right—that natural, robust lure of the untried young.

As they walked to the subway, Nick proposed that they go to a movie. Bessie declined the offer. Undaunted, he asked if she would like to have some spaghetti at Romeo's on Fourteenth Street. This invitation she accepted.

By the time they had finished eating, she agreed to attend a jazz concert, so that Nick could introduce her to the fine points of its musical form. Both knew, however, that their need for fellowship mattered more than listening to jazz. Their failure to meet a single person from their group in the cafeteria these last few days left both of them with the depressing awareness that their separation from friends, with whom they had shared so much these last years, had already begun. They could all promise to stay in touch with one another, but common sense advised them that the deep ties that had bound them together would eventually wither away with the passage of time. Their agreement to attend a jazz concert may well have been nothing more than a feeble attempt at preserving the status quo that both had cherished in the past.

Hector Palofax, on the other hand, had found no one to reach out to who could help rid him of a growing sense of despair. He ordered a second beer and began drinking it directly from the bottle. His gloominess persisted. Once an orphan, always an orphan, he reasoned. Impulsively, Hector spun around on the stool, let his feet drop to the floor, walked slowly to the jukebox, and deposited a coin. A loud, thumping rendition of "The Beer Barrel Polka" overpowered the stillness of the room. Perhaps the song's robust gaiety would dispel his low spirits, which were beginning to show definite signs of self-pity. He glanced up at the clock behind the long bar. It was nearly four o'clock.

"I've got to stop this pissing and moaning," he told himself. He strode back to his seat, sat down, and took a long swig from the bottle. As he placed it back atop the bar, a woman in her mid-twenties seated herself on one of the adjacent bar stools. The scent of perfume made him turn to look at her. He recognized her immediately. She was the wife of an ex-merchant seaman with whom he had sailed during the war years.

"Hi." Her greeting was not a warm one and sounded close to tears.

"How's my old buddy Al doing these days?" Hector inquired without any show of real interest.

"How should I know? He took off on me a week ago," she spat out, trying to muffle a sob.

Hector sought to fend off any further verbal onslaughts by reaching for a partially smoked cigar that lay stuffed in his shirt pocket. Hastily extracting it, he placed it into the corner of his mouth, lighted it quickly and turned to study the young woman sitting next to him.

Her hair was blonde and hung in long, uncombed tresses that were haphazardly flung across her back and shoulders. From Hector's viewpoint, her body was not altogether shapeless. Yet, he was unwilling to classify it as voluptuous, for it lacked the enticing, youthful curves of Bessie Siegal. Yet her face had the aristocratic air of the women who he would see shopping in John Wanamaker or Bloomingdales whenever he went into such stores to use the men's room. Her rounded lips, however, gave off more than a hint of sensuality. Under her unbuttoned white sweater, she wore an oversized blouse. Several strands of colored wooden beads hung in large loops around her neck. Hector saw her features suddenly twist into an uncontrollable rage, her eyes welling up with tears, as grunts and whimpers escaped from her lips. The combination of looks and sounds made her appear punch-drunk with fury.

Hector, now recovered from receiving such shocking news instinctively gave expression to his disbelief. "You're kidding! Al wouldn't leave someone like you."

"No, it's true," she whined, wiping away tears with the sleeve of her sweater. "Believe it or not, he took off on me."

Experience warned him not to burden himself with someone else's problems. Nevertheless, his conscience urged that he show interest in her predicament, and warned him that to turn away from her at this time would be a sign of cruel indifference.

"What're you going to do about it?" he asked with a show of concern. "You've got to do something, I guess."

She smiled, although tears were still visible on her cheeks. Whatever anger showed in her eyes began to quickly dissolve into an unequivocal firmness.

"What do you take me for? Some kind of dummy? I'll get even with him, if it's the last thing I do." She jutted her jaw forward pugnaciously. "You don't think so?" she challenged.

"No! Hell, no! I know you can handle yourself. Remember, girl, I know you."

"Come on, Hector, I'll show you what I mean. What do you say? Huh?" She began to button her sweater, taking for granted an affirmative reply.

He sensed a kind of helplessness, thinking this must be what it feels like to sink into a pool of quicksand. Wordlessly, he eased himself off his stool and started after her. He grabbed his leather jacket off a wall peg and walked through the door, which she held open for him.

"Man. Oh, man," he said aloud as he pushed his arms through the sleeves of his jacket while walking up the stairs.

"Just follow me!" she commanded as she sped by him taking two stairs at a time.

Once out on the street, she skipped and hopped ahead of him like a child at play, winding her way through the crowd of students crossing the street. She sped through Washington Square Park, periodically stopping to turn and see whether he was still following her. Assured that he was, she trotted past the circular fountain in the center of the park, where she again paused to look back at him. She stood waiting for Hector to close the gap that she had made wider by her sprightly pace, motioning him to hurry by a vigorous wave of her hand. She slowed down to a brisk walk when she reached MacDougal Street, crossed Waverly Place, and entered an apartment house a short distance away. Hector had been in this building several times before as a guest of his former shipmate. Now as he started lumbering up the stairs to the top floor, whatever feelings of compassion he had experienced a short while ago were laid aside as he began to consider whether he was letting himself get into a predicament whose outcome he would later regret. What he expected to encounter, however, were tears, pictures, letters, and undoubtedly, in the end, an indignant censure of her husband's adulterous behavior. Hector had been through this kind of experience before, at other times and in other places. He thrust the cigar into his mouth that had been clamped between his thumb and forefinger as he raced after her, tilted it upward, twisting his features into a know-it-all smugness.

The woman withdrew a key from a sweater pocket, opened the door with a quick twist of her wrist, and pushed it open with a kick of her foot.

Hector followed her in and took a seat on the solitary couch.

"Wait right there for a minute, Hector. I want to show you something," she instructed him before hustling into another room.

"Here come the pictures. Or will it be letters?" he mumbled to himself.

Removing the cigar from his mouth, he cast a final longing look at it before squashing the lit end in a nearby ashtray. He stared down longingly at the discarded stub, as if he had just rid himself of the one thing he could cling to for support in this questionable situation. Hector removed his jacket and placed it beside him. Not having to hide his agitation, he stood up and started pacing the floor and cursing himself for lacking the resolve to ignore this kind of unmanageable involvement.

Hector was not aware that his friend's wife had silently returned to the room and stood waiting for him to turn and face her. As he put one foot in front of the other, he methodically added up the number of repetitious patterns that ran, chain-linked, for the full length of the carpet. An awareness of another's presence made him look up. What came into view made him instinctively reach for a cigar in his shirt pocket, but his fingers ended up twisting empty air.

He made an effort to keep his gaze on her face, noting that her oval lips now formed a malicious smirk. She stood facing him with her right hand clenched and pressed tightly against her hip at an angle that implied a threat. In her left hand, she held a face towel. Otherwise, she was nude.

They stood like two fighting cocks, indecisive as to which of them would attempt the first ripping thrust. She struck first.

"I'm going to bed down with you, Hector," she stated in a voice seething with rancor.

Momentarily taken aback by this form of feminine aggression, Hector stepped away from her, unable to think of anything to say. Only after his shock and surprise began to recede was he able to sputter, "Why me?"

"It's not just you. You're not the first, and you won't be the last." With several quick steps, she pressed close to him and started removing his tie. Working against the impulse to turn and storm down the stairs was a counter stimulus generated by the sight of her nudeness, as she clumsily set about unbuttoning his shirt. Flustered, he allowed her to continue undressing him with an awkwardness that reflected impatience rather than passion.

"I'll get even with him, I'm telling you. I'm going to spend lots of time with all his friends, one by one. I'll show him," she repeated a number of times.

Like an incapacitated invalid, Hector allowed himself to be wrestled to the floor, where he gave in to her energetic tugging and pulling of his trouser legs. This was not the rule he had observed in the past concerning adultery. This was a situation that he knew would leave him contrite and filled with self-disgust. He wanted no part of it.

Most of his clothes now lay scattered in various parts of the room, as if someone beset with an uncontrollable frenzy had flung them. The fact that he was still clothed in his underwear, however, gave him the assurance that he still held the upper hand in deciding whether to act in accordance with the woman's wishes or not. He got up and rested on his haunches; the ineptness of what was taking place suddenly struck him as funny, which resulted in a series of badly suppressed giggles that soon cascaded into uncontrollable guffaws. He got down on his knees, and putting his hands protectively against his face, pressed his head to the floor, his upper body shaking with a new series of uncontrollable giggles. A stupid, sophomoric joke had come into his thoughts and took an unyielding hold of him. His chuckles gradually lapsed into barely audible sniggers. This whole proceeding was turning into a fiasco as far as he was concerned. He wanted no part of it anymore.

With his face still leaning heavily against the carpeted floor, and his underwear-covered rump pointing upward, he let out a string of barely coherent words, none of which were understood by the woman who sat at his side, legs outstretched, obviously flustered as to what to do next in light of this unexpected situation. Hector's uncooperative behavior had a mitigating effect on her fierce determination—but only for an instant. She drew a deep breath before attempting to kindle his ardor by getting on to her knees in order to reach out and stroke his back. Even so, it was to no avail. His intermittent seizures of an irrepressible cackling defeated all her earnest attempts to arouse him. With the same abruptness with which she had begun, she broke off her fruitless efforts. Disgusted, she seated herself next to him, drew her legs back and locked them in place with her arms. Chagrin, coupled with humiliation, clouded her eyes and tightened her lips so that they lost their lascivious curve.

Hector still lay facedown, exhaustion having gagged his outbursts so that they could be easily mistaken for whimpers.

Lifting his head off the floor, he threw a glance at the woman now sitting at his side with an expression of wrathful indignation. It stifled him into silence. Tears of frustration were streaking down her face in irregular patterns. A feeling of unpleasantness emerged within him, stemming from the interplay of varied emotions. He now regarded her with pity rather than passion. Yet, if he were to comply with her wishes, he would have to resort to a false display of satyriasis. He wanted no part in such a fallacious undertaking. Left with the choice of either acting in accordance with her wishes or getting up and leaving, he chose the latter path. Hector dispensed with any feelings of commiseration for her, his decision to depart having crystallized his proposed course of action. This whole episode had become so ludicrous in his opinion, that all thought of letting passion rule this situation vaporized. It was time to go.

As he started to lift himself up from the floor, his upward movement came to a sudden and unexpected halt. A pained look of shock registered on his face, causing his eyes to squint shut. Some heavy-weighted object had pounced on his rump, its sharp metallic-like prongs seemingly intent on ripping through the protective cover of his boxer shorts. It forced him to cry out with pain and surprise. He stayed frozen in place, too afraid to move.

Looking sharply at the woman who was sitting at his side, he yelled at her, "Something…something fell on my backside! Oh! Oh! Get it off! Oh God, get it off!" The last phrase was a yell of command commingled with that of pleading.

In response, a look of alarm registered on the woman's face, which brought a halt to her flow of tears. Perched atop Hector's bottom was her Persian cat, its whiskers flung upward in a feline smirk. With an effort marked by impatience, she twisted sideways and reached up to grab the cat by the scruff of the neck. Cursing, she flipped it away as if she were tossing aside a dirty towel. Hector sighed, then groaned with relief as the painful burden lifted free of him.

"What in God's name was that?" he whined.

"My cat. Just my cat."

"Your cat!" he shouted, not caring whether her neighbors heard him or not. "A lousy cat! Can you imagine? A lousy cat," he spat out angrily, reaching back with his hand to gingerly pat the injured area.

"Gee, I hope that my cat didn't frighten you," she said, an awareness creeping into her apology that her plan was doomed to fail. She reached over to soothe the scratches raised by the cat's paws. He reacted by quickly rolling away from her, his back striking the floor with one of his hands still glued to his bottom.

"Wait a minute," she instructed him as she got up and made her way to the medicine chest in the bathroom. Grabbing a bottle from one of the shelves, she rushed back. "Come here and let me put some of this on it," she baby-talked in an effort to soothe him.

"Hell, no!" he burst out indignantly and clumsily got to his feet and began collecting his clothes. His reaction to this offer brought an end to what she set out to do. Her day had ended in the late afternoon.

Fully clothed and still grumbling under his breath, Hector slung his jacket over his shoulder and without saying a word, started for the door.

"Wait, Hector, what do you want to leave for?" she appealed to him.

"Baby, I owe you nothing. That's why!" He strode out the door, ignoring the forces of temptation by not glancing back at her nakedness. Using both hands to hold onto the banister, he painfully sidestepped his way down the stairs.

"Why? Oh, why do I always stick my nose into other people's business?" he reproached himself. "I should know better. Nice guys always get it in the end." This latter conviction activated a physiological link between mind and body, advising him to gingerly touch the areas where pain persisted.

Chapter 18

It was morning.

Jim Stahr had never had a stable and continuing relationship with a woman. Perhaps his entry into the wartime military as a teenager had bred a wariness of abiding friendships, as well as an unrelenting conviction that chance, not he, was the factor that determined their longevity. In the years that followed, all ties with others were mostly of a transient nature. This guardedness had become as entrenched as a root buried deep in the ground. The collective light of all succeeding experiences, even those that proved his inability for commitment to be an adverse shortcoming, could not penetrate the dark surroundings of this disposition.

As he plodded his way toward the apartment, he began to think that it might have been a mistake to have committed to spending the entire day with Gennie Connors. On this second Saturday in December, certain academic tasks should have taken priority. This development of constancy to one woman was starting to try his patience. Yet, he could not deny that he and Gennie had begun to forge a strong attachment to one another, although not the kind one associates with the promise of a long-term commitment. When off by himself, Jim understood that his role in their physical indulgence in this game of romance was nothing more than a form of sensual self-deception. He now suspected that this pastime had its snares. It was easy to be a player in this kind of diversion and unwittingly become ensnared by promises bred by passion, which somehow can turn into obligations that are real and morally irreversible. Before entering the building, he resolved that this time he would not be trapped into participating in any of her game playing. He was in no mood to dabble with reality. He was determined that the day's events should occur naturally.

As soon as he entered the apartment, Gennie Connors informed him that Peggy Troy had left for the day with Frank Colucci. He reacted to this news with a look of surprise that quickly changed to a smile and, moments later, a frown.

"Look," he said, pointing to a window, "the sun is shining and the streets are free of snow. Let's get out for a change. We still have the whole day ahead of us. What do you say?" He knew what staying indoors could possibly lead to, but he had made up his mind not to let it happen.

She ran to the window, looked out to survey the street below, and exclaimed, "What a beautiful day! One could almost believe it's springtime. Shall we go out, hold hands, and skip through the streets like a pair of Hollywood lovers?" Her question stressed the invitation to feel, think, and do what was untrue.

"No, Gennie, it's still winter, and there're no green leaves sprouting out of those naked limbs across the street. Anyway, I'm not willing to restructure the real into the unreal today. Why don't you just get your coat?" A tone of impatience dominated his request, which sounded more like an order than a good-natured suggestion.

The sharpness of his response startled her. She had not meant her remark to be taken seriously, for it was nothing more than an effusive expression of good feelings. She left the room masking her hurt.

Jim led the way out of the apartment and told her of his plans for the afternoon, trying to alleviate whatever mortification might have arisen by his testy response to her earlier suggestion. She smiled at him, but not warmly.

As they made their way toward the Washington Arch, Jim made a try at idle chatter but soon came to the realization that his endeavors to do so with any degree of skill revealed an obvious ineptness on his part. Small talk was for small minds, he reasoned, and not worth the effort required to develop this skill. He broke off utilizing this means for passing the time.

Once on the bus and heading uptown on Fifth Avenue, Jim held Gennie's hand as they sat staring out the window. Their subsequent conversation dealt with their respective opinions about the value of the course work they were taking this semester. Only when Jim touched on the subject of his forthcoming class paper that he was to deliver did he exhibit any fervor in his speech and mannerisms.

At Sixty-Fifth Street, they got off the bus and strolled along Fifth Avenue to the Frick Museum. Once inside, they separated and drifted apart whenever some object caught their respective attention. Like driftwood floating in a narrow stream of slow-running water, they would occasionally meet and clasp hands until some other work of art captured the interest of one of them, causing them to part.

While the frigid beauty of the marble interior made Jim think of robber barons and their manipulative powers, Gennie found herself rejecting the crushing strength of the building's entirety. The individual works that she did find appealing for their warmth and grace helped offset her unfavorable impression of the edifice itself.

Out on the street, she told him of the uneasiness she felt inside the museum. "A place of art," she explained, "should make us feel at ease with ourselves. Inside that building, I felt like a person stranded on an iceberg drifting in some unmapped Arctic sea."

He stopped to glance back at the museum and smiled. "Perhaps, you're right. It does have a sterile look about it."

Gennie nodded in agreement and they resumed walking, saying little more until they passed a row of stately buildings that lined the street. Jim stared up at the ornate designs that fronted each of them. "There are times," he began, "when ostentation seems to be used for no other purpose than to capture one's attention. It makes me think of women who are gifted with rare beauty but appear haughty or aloof—and frigid."

"There was nothing fancy about the farmhouse I grew up in," Gennie informed him. "All the same, it glowed with friendliness and welcome. I always felt comfortable and secure there."

Noting that she had caught and held Jim's interest, she decided to continue expressing her thoughts and feelings.

"Everyone who lived inside it left some kind of mark on me. Maybe," she hesitated, slowly shaking her head from side to side, "it's nothing more than wish fulfillment on my part. I've been guilty of changing fantasy into reality before. But, I firmly believe that I derived a sense of belonging—of being somebody with an identity—when I lived there with my family." She took her hand away from his, hurried a short distance ahead, then stopped and turned to face him with a childish smile. "Now that the house is empty, I can't possibly feel the same way about it anymore."

At first, Jim doubted the sincerity of what she said, thinking that her words might be just another subterfuge of some kind. On second thought, however, he decided not to make an issue over beliefs that he considered questionable.

"Perhaps you ought to go back there at the year-end break," he suggested, puzzled by his inability to suppress an emerging sense of loss, especially in light of his disconcerting concern that this relationship was imposing on the personal use of his time.

"Maybe I ought to." She sounded unconvinced. "By the way, what're your plans for the holidays?"

"I haven't given it a thought," he answered indifferently.

"But you've got a family, Jim. There'll be plenty of things for you to do, I'm sure."

Jim Stahr shrugged his shoulders.

"I've got an idea," Gennie said. "If I go up to that empty house, it's not going to be much fun. I could take it for a few days, but I know that I'll come running back to the apartment in a matter of days. I'm wondering whether you could find some time to come up for a visit? That way, we could see the New Year in together." She tried to coax him by gently pulling on both ends of his coat collar.

Impulse and desire combined to decide that such a trip deserved some thought. A number of years had passed since he last traveled beyond the immediate environs of the city. Maybe a change of scenery, he reflected, would be a welcome break from the routine of study. This invitation made him give some careful consideration to her idea, although he still entertained some strong doubts about taking such a trip.

"Are you sure that you would want me to?" he asked, as if seeking further inducement to strengthen a faltering conviction.

"Silly fool! Your coming would be like bringing light into a dark cave. If you only knew how lonely that house gets during the holidays, you'd understand that I'm not merely asking you to come, I'm begging you to do so."

Jim looked down at her upturned face, her eyes beginning to glaze over with a veneer of moisture. How could he say no? He gave in to her wish without giving any thought as to what such a journey would entail.

"I'll get there sometime before the New Year begins—that is, if nothing comes up to prevent me from doing so. Please remember that." This promise left room for ways in which it could justifiably remain unfilled without dashing her hopes.

She stood up on her toes and pecked at his lips.

Arm in arm once more, they walked toward Third Avenue in search of a restaurant that could offer a stimulating ambience and good food.

That evening, during the subway ride home, a suspicion began to form that perhaps he had erred in establishing a new basis for their future ties, from that of fiction hatched from make-believe, to fact based on reality. In the final analysis, he judged, if and when honesty becomes the criterion for forming bonds with others, then it is essential that all promises have integrity, or the basis of the relationship becomes as fallacious as tales woven by imposters.

Chapter 19

It was noon.

The Third Avenue El offered the most potentially interesting means to get to the Battery in lower Manhattan. Frank Colucci and Peggy Troy had boarded the train at Fourteenth Street and found seats on the hard wooden benches of the well-used train. They seated themselves side by side, necks twisted, facing each other as they gazed out at the houses that flashed by. Their observations ceased only when the train screeched to a halt and the platform's advertising billboards blocked their view. They had agreed to go through with Frank's plan to leave their familiar surroundings and go someplace where their environment would be unfamiliar, but could possibly prove animating.

During these last weeks, what had begun in a chance meeting at a tavern had changed from a respectful acquaintanceship to that of mutual admiration, which grew with their discreet probing to uncover each other's insights and attitudes. This afternoon would be the longest time they had spent together since the beginning of this newfound relationship. Instead of continuing their exploratory exchanges within the confines of Manhattan, Frank had suggested a change of locale.

When the train reached the last stop, they descended the stairway that led to the Staten Island Ferry. The winter sun peeped from behind an assemblage of clouds, and thrust effulgent lances of warmth at them as it slid slowly from behind this barrier.

After boarding the ferry, they stationed themselves at the stern. They watched as the boat propelled itself away from the wharf, leaving in its trail a gushing turbulence. The sun finally broke free of its cloud cover, diffusing its clement strength across the open deck. Basking in the sun's warming light, they watched the land recede, the buildings gradually diminishing in size.

Frank gazed past the Narrows toward the open sea. "Peggy," Frank started, "even after sailing all those wartime years in the Pacific, I still can't fully comprehend the ocean's vastness. And when I can't visualize something in its entirety, it leaves me with a feeling of inadequacy, as if my mind's eye has only partial vision. Yet, the ocean's immensity has the power to do away with my anxieties. It's an enchanting enigma. I'm glad that I can look at it as a source of tranquility rather than material wealth."

She mentally concurred with his assumption about the mind's limited capacity to comprehend the totality of the sea. But she discerned a smug inference that the works of literary creators were superior to those of scientific researchers. Having just completed her studies in the field of chemistry, Peggy could not tolerate this viewpoint. It implied that poetry was somehow worthier—of more importance to people—than was science. Still keeping an eye on the skyline, she could not resist voicing her objection to his remark, which she took to be a form of intellectual snobbery.

"Don't knock the doers, Frank. In comparison to them, the rest of us are merely history's onlookers. That includes the fearful ones like me, and the interpreters like you. All we're really good for is to applaud their accomplishments when they prove beneficial to the rest of us." She wanted to say more but stopped, alarmed at her own outburst, mindful that whatever mood Frank had intended to create had died stillborn. Regret for having been critical of what he had said soon turned to self-reproach.

The sharpness of her words sounded with resentment and caught Frank by surprise. The impact had the effect of thwarting his ability to respond. When he turned to face her, he was quick to see that she was having misgivings for having spoken so boldly. He admonished himself for not having learned to strip conceit from his words.

The glare of the sun made them turn and lean back against the boat's railing. They now stood facing the passengers peering out at them through the ferry's glassed-in enclosure. Frank moved closer to her. He reached over to stroke her arm.

"You're absolutely right…so right. What you've said is true."

Responding to his touch, she looked up at him with an expression of remorse, alarmed that her words may have been needlessly abusive. Sensing her concern, he smiled in a way that assured her that he was once again on good terms with her, and he supplemented it with words intended to rid her of any misgivings for what she had said.

"You'll have to excuse me, Peggy. I didn't mean to imply that any artistic endeavor could ever affect the world the same way as those generated by scientists. I have to confess," Frank began, "there're times when I realize that the poet's greatest creations can never receive the same recognition as that afforded scientists, especially since scientific discoveries change the way we live. Sometimes envy breaks through and I lack the fortitude to disguise the sarcasm it breeds."

"Well, Frank, when it comes to spite, we're all part of the same gigantic brotherhood." She laughed, confident that Frank had forgiven her for her curt outburst.

"You can say that again. Nevertheless, you're right about the real doers. There are times when I have my doubts whether it's worth dedicating myself to writing poetry. The financial rewards for doing so are not enough to live on."

This was the first time that he had ever openly hinted that his creative efforts might not generate the wherewithal needed to meet his basic economic needs. She instinctively felt the urge to proffer words that would give a boost to his determination to succeed in what he most wanted to do—write poetry. What held her back from doing so was her sincerity. Any voicing on her part that such an undertaking, even if successful, could ever generate anything other than meager monetary gains would be an out-in-out falsehood.

The Statue of Liberty drifted into sight. They turned to stare at it.

"Frank, why do we always end up quarreling? I've always thought that I was like that iron lady out there." She motioned toward the monument with a sharp movement of her head. "I'm an advocate of peace, not strife."

"Peggy, you provide nourishment for the hungry."

She turned toward him with a look of surprise, but one that begged a compliment. "What do you mean by that?"

"You have ideas," he told her, "and you express them very well. And by doing so, you manage to arouse my opinions out of their lethargy. Ours is a friendly war of words that has no winners or losers. Our differences are a source of inspiration for me. Shall we leave it at that?"

"I hope that's truly the case," she replied and fixed her gaze on the seagulls as they swirled around the Statue of Liberty, their cavorting not unlike those of children gamboling in some sunlit playground on a summer's day.

Chapter 20

It was night.

Nick Grigoris and Bessie Siegal pushed past the swinging doors leading out of the Village Vanguard. This had been the first time that Bessie had attended a jazz concert with someone who knew the structure and history of this musical idiom and who was willing to help solve some of its rhythmic complexities. Aside from having learned some new insights about this musical form, the hours spent listening to it had provided her with a respite from her scholastic preoccupations. Once on the street, they made their way toward the Greenwich Delicatessen. They both commented on the marked change of the temperature, as it had dropped sharply from the daytime's warming sunlight.

Inside the restaurant, they began to remove hats, coats and scarves, draping all of them atop one of the vacant chairs. They sat down and ordered sandwiches and coffee. When they finally began talking to each other, they did not mention the music at all. Instead, they embarked on a discussion of what remained for them to complete their requirements for graduation. The subject may have been a humdrum matter for any eavesdropping diners, but for them, the details of academic life were the critical minutiae that dominated their every judgment and action. For the present, no other pursuit could merit an equivalent effort on their part. Goading Bessie's eagerness to finish her schooling was the fact that a teaching job awaited her soon after she finished. For her, the seven weeks remaining before she faced her last exam would be the final test of her fortitude, both physical and mental. Already she was informing Nick that as soon as she earned some money, she wanted to get a master's degree at Columbia. What Bessie craved most right now was for the future to be absorbed by the present. Some feminine intuitive sense made her break off her onrush of words and take notice of Nick's expressionless face.

"Silly of me to have said so much about myself. I'm sorry."

He lifted his cup in a wordless toast as a sign that all was forgiven.

"Seriously, Nick, what're you going to do after you finish?"

"Look for a job...nothing radical. Just look for a job, that's all."

Bessie waited a short while before asking, "Are you going to be looking in the city?"

He perked up this time before replying. "No, Jim Stahr and I are planning to leave New York and hunt for work."

"If I were a man, that's just what I'd do. I'd pull a Horace Greeley and head west," she stated with a childish eagerness.

"I'm going to hunt for a newspaper job, and it doesn't matter where. I just want a chance to get started."

"But what's Jim going to do?" she asked with a look of concern.

"I don't know what he's trying to find, but he's planning to tag along with me." Nick was mindful that Jim had yet to inform him in any specific terms as to what he would be searching for on this trip.

They finished eating their sandwiches and dawdled over their coffee, both aware that much more still remained to be said concerning the paths each of their friends would take after graduation.

"Do you know who puzzles me most of all?" she remarked. "It's Hector. He's truly a loner."

"Yes," Nick agreed with a grin, "that guy is a hard nut to crack. I find it difficult to communicate with him, especially when he gets moody."

Nick waved to the waiter and gestured for him to refill the cups. Turning back to face Bessie, he started to tell her about Hector's recent activities.

"You know, he doesn't go to the school cafeteria anymore. The day you met us in Rocky's, he was scraping bottom. Our little group suddenly falling apart like it has put a dent in his morale."

"Somehow I can't visualize him being sullen for very long. It just doesn't go with that wise-guy image of his," she said with a shrug of her shoulders.

"Perhaps he kids you in a rough sort of way, Bessie. But maybe that's his way of showing affection, especially to someone like yourself, as if you were his kid sister."

The waiter came by to pour their coffee, his arm suddenly blocking them from seeing each other. Before he had finished filling their cups, Bessie began speaking again.

"Sure, I can sense his feelings behind that barrage of tough-guy words. Maybe he thinks that I can't see through him. But I'm not that naive."

"Oh, he has his reasons for teasing you so much. You're young and pretty. No doubt that's what he wants most in a woman. Maybe it's his way of telling the world that he'll never be able to find one with those qualities for himself."

Nick stopped, lifted his cup and took a sip from it. "He's the kind of guy who can easily get into trouble, one way or another." He started to censure himself the moment he finished talking. The discussion of other people's personalities was an odious pastime for him. So far as he was concerned, any further discussion about Hector Palofax had just come to an end.

Bessie responded to this snide comment with a blunt statement of her own. "You don't like him, do you?"

"I guess there's some truth in what you say, Bessie."

"Did you ever try to figure out why?"

He drank from his cup before answering. To his surprise, he could not find any specific reasons for feeling like he did about him. Yet when he did manage a reply, his emotions dominated more than did sound judgment.

"I guess part of the reason may have something to do with some shortcoming on my part rather than his."

He stopped to give himself time for his multitude of thoughts to arrange themselves into some reasonable order. "I like the idea of sticking to accepted rules and principles. Hector tends to thumb his nose at them. Without them, I'd be at a loss. Maybe that's my Achilles heel."

"Don't tell me that you always follow the crowd. I know you better than that," she said good-naturedly.

"Not always. But if and when I do, you can bet that the crowd will be heading in the same direction that I want to go." Nick hesitated, searching for the words that could express the sense of well-being he derived whenever he found himself an unobtrusive figure in the midst of many. Finding none, he made up his mind to discontinue any further conversation about his feelings toward Hector Palofax. He sat waiting for her to say something.

Bessie began to tire and wanted to end all these exploratory incursions into self. Her response to his fragmented admission was silence. Both sat quietly, allowing their thoughts to meander through the intricate labyrinth formed by the combination of conjecture and inference.

They finished their coffee and Nick asked for the check.

After leaving the restaurant, they began walking in the direction of Union Square, where both could board their respective subways home.

"Doesn't this city make you feel lonely?" Nick asked, hoping the question would shift the conversation away from him to her. He was now uneasy about having spoken of his own inadequacies with such candor.

She seemed taken aback by the question.

"Lonely? Manhattan is the one city that can never become dull for me. Just the opposite—I find it the most exciting place on earth."

She knew that what she was about to say would make her sound like an overly romantic kid. But if Nick could speak so freely about himself tonight, why couldn't she? With an open determination, Bessie declared guilelessly what had always been an integral part of her wishful thinking.

"Nick, if I ever fall in love, I want it to be here in this vivacious city of ours."

He was unprepared for her unaffected openness. Confidence was not a virtue he easily inspired in others.

"But, why of all places, in this concrete madhouse?" he prodded. Nick gave her a big-brother smile, feeling gratification for her trust in speaking to him so frankly about such an intimate wish.

"Can't you see why?" she gushed with joyous innocence. "Look around you. Don't you see people? They are the catalytic agents of love. Don't you know?" Bessie scolded him gently.

He shrugged. "I'm not too bright tonight. I can't see what you're getting at."

"Nick," she kidded him, "you'll never make a great lover."

"Oh! You can bet your life on that," he confirmed, his smile stretching to its full limits. "To me, love is a private matter between a man and a woman. What do people in the street have to do with it?"

"Okay, okay—I'll tell you," she said impatiently. "The only kind of man that I could love would have to be an observer—a people watcher, like me. In a city like this, we could never run out of the basic material needed for our shared adventures with others. There are so many places where we could go and eavesdrop or even talk openly to a myriad of people. This would be the secret of our love, for we would have a common interest outside of ourselves."

Her speech took on a new kind of enthusiasm, one that she had never exhibited before. Nick felt the need to say something, more to encourage rather than to disrupt her zestful flow of ideas.

"I suspect that lovers can get weary of each other in time. Is that what you're trying to tell me?" Nick asked.

He felt that there was no need to reply. It was obvious that he understood what she had implied. Nevertheless, she continued to elaborated further.

"In this city, the odds of meeting interesting people are very high compared to Dudsville, U.S.A., right? Besides, if we start to drift apart, maybe our shared memories will help keep us together. Now wouldn't that be grand?"

Nick pressed his lips together hard and shook his head.

"Bessie, for once I agree with Hector. You're still a kid. Your theory is delightful, but as for the possibility of it happening, no matter what odds I'd give you, I'd end up being accused of stealing your money." There was no evidence of disdain in his remark; rather it had the insipidness of a weather report.

"Maybe you're both right. Maybe I'm still a kid. After all, kids are guilty of wishful thinking, so you'll have to let me believe in mine."

"Go on dreaming, Bessie, go on! I'm not going to rip them apart."

"We all have to have our daydreams, and there's nothing wrong with the ones I have," she said in self-defense.

"Bessie, yours have a unique twist. It'd be a front-page story if you could make it come true." He reached out and placed his arm around her shoulder. "I wish I could just wave a magic wand and smash-boom-bang, make your dream a reality."

"Nick, you're a true Greek cynic."

His laugh echoed its message of hilarity through the empty street.

"You're right. You're so right," he said, his words were free of any signs of pleasure. "You're young and an optimist. I'm old and a pessimist. Yet," he went on matter-of-factly, "there's not that many years separating us."

While walking toward Fourteenth Street, he noticed that she kept smiling, apparently unruffled by his criticism of her love wish. Perhaps he may have been too disparaging in his criticism of her harmless concept about people and love. Nick thought it best to try and make up for any hurt resulting from what he had said by acknowledging the likelihood that her daydream may one day become a reality.

"Bessie, should it ever happen—I mean you finding a guy who's hooked on people—would you let me know? He'll have to be someone special."

Bessie turned to him, her laugh lyrical and free, her eyes alight with absolute joy.

"If it ever happens, Nick, I'll tell it to the world, to all the people, and especially to you, old man."

At the entrance to the subway station, they shook hands and parted, she mentally visualizing her dreams, he trying to palliate his uncertainties.

Chapter 21

Early Sunday morning, Jim Stahr rose from his bed and started dressing himself, although his joints ached and his movements responded to his commands with a disturbing sluggishness. By the time he had finished shaving, he felt so weak that he was forced to lie down again. When he did, he felt the onset of perspiration that soon left the top of his body wet and sticky. Only by closing his eyes did his illness seem to lessen. He gave no thought to removing his clothes, for that would have been an admission that he was truly sick. When his mother called to him, he felt too exhausted to respond. His silence caused her to hurry into the room. Seeing the perspiration stains on his shirt, she went over to him and pressed her hand to his forehead. She left the room and soon returned holding the paraphernalia she judged would help relieve his symptoms. She opened the front of his shirt and started swabbing him with alcohol.

His awareness of time became somewhat disoriented. Nausea had made hours and minutes nothing more than a vague muddle without any meaning. Before dozing off into a feverish slumber, he had begun to accept his mother's practical diagnosis that he was suffering from a bad case of the flu.

When he awoke, the sky cover of cumulus gray clouds screened the sun's rays, leaving the room draped in an impalpable lifelessness. His first waking concern was to know the hour. Not finding his watch within reach, he called out to his mother demanding to know the time.

She came into the room drying her wet hands with a dishtowel.

"It's early," she told him. "It's only about ten."

He struggled to push himself erect using the bed's headboard to support his back, and stared perplexedly out the window.

"Did you say it was ten o'clock in the morning?" he asked incredulously.

His mother checked her wristwatch and informed him once again, "It's a little after ten."

"What day is it? What day is it?" Mustering whatever strength he had at his command, he attempted to get out of bed fearing that he may have been ill for several days and missed attending classes.

"It's Sunday, Jim. Sunday morning," she answered hastily, startled by his sudden movement.

Jim groaned in recognition of his own helplessness and inwardly conceded that he was physically unable to leave the house this day. He fell back heavily onto his cushion. His mother pulled off his unlaced shoes and slipped his blanket over him.

"Yes, I'd better rest. Sick or not, I have to read my term paper on Thursday," he informed her with the assuredness of someone setting an arbitrary date for terminating his illness. The day progressed with a dispirited languidness, as did the others that followed. Throughout this period, his physical activity was limited to making changes to his term paper.

On Thursday morning, his strength now only partially restored, Jim slid out of bed and started a slow and poorly coordinated process of getting himself dressed. His mother watched silently as he struggled stiffly into his clothes. That morning, Jim decided that it would be best to drive to Washington Square using his brother's Chevy instead of taking the subway during the early morning rush hour. After shoving the car keys into a coat pocket, he walked unsteadily out the door.

"Watch the way you drive, Jim," his mother cautioned him.

He closed the door behind him before responding. "Yeah, yeah, yeah," he muttered, his words linked together by a heedless impatience. Weakness made him take hold of the wooden banister, his right hand clutching and slipping along its polished surface as he descended the stairs.

The black Chevy stood on the corner, the dullness of its paint displaying the poverty of its condition. As unserviceable as it looked, he felt assured that it could afford him greater protection against the inclement weather than would the subway, with its cold winds gusting in every time the train's doors were flung open. He got into the car and with a twist of the ignition key, the engine started running with a rhythmic clattering of its worn-out valves. As he started away from the curb, he spotted a can of oil lying on the floor next to a combination opener and spout. His brother had warned him that he would need to add a quart of engine oil before the day was out. Aware of the poor operating condition of the car, and fearful of not arriving punctually for his class, Jim had left home early to allow time to deal with any mishaps that might occur along the way.

The heavy traffic slowed his progress and created an unfounded concern that he would be late for his class. His confidence returned only after he reached the entry ramp leading onto the Brooklyn Bridge. This feeling of optimism, however, was of short duration. When he reached the far end of the bridge, the engine produced a single tubercular cough and stilled itself into total inactivity.

"Damn!" he hissed with displeasure, pounding his hand on the steering wheel. Cautiously, he pushed the door open, walked to the front of the car, and lifted the hood. A check of the oil level indicated that it was already a quart low. A cold wind stung his face and brought tears to his eyes. He stood staring down at the engine in dismay, convinced that his chance of getting to his class on time was now nil. Although fully aware that it would not serve any useful purpose, he went back to retrieve the quart of oil and punctured the can with the opener. Taking care to avoid passing vehicles, he returned to the front of the car and inserted the spout into the filler-neck, the unsteadiness of his hands resulting in some oil spilling onto the sleeves of his coat and exposed shirt cuffs.

"Damn!" he shouted angrily. When the can was completely drained of its contents, he removed it and lowered the hood. He made his way back to the car, opened the door, slid behind the wheel, and slammed the door shut. Without turning to look, he tossed the empty can behind him with the spout still stuck into it.

All of his attempts to start the engine resulted in failure. It barely turned over. Apparently, he judged, the battery was weak, but not completely dead. The only option left open to him was for someone to push his vehicle. He banged an open palm against the rim of the steering wheel, cursing with the rage of those who are bereft of all hope. Perspiration moistened his armpits, his chest, and the back of his neck. Sick at heart, he rested his head sideways on the steering wheel, tension making him lift his arm every few minutes to look at his wristwatch.

Ten minutes passed with no one coming to his aid. Most drivers looked guiltily away as they drove past his stalled vehicle. He lifted his head from its resting place and stared ahead of him, thinking that all the time and energy he had expended in preparing for today's talk had come to naught. Another five minutes passed before he felt someone attempting to push his car forward. A small truck had driven behind his vehicle and tapped his rear bumper. Jim glanced up at his rearview mirror and saw the driver gesturing that he was going to push his car. Without any show of feelings, Jim pressed down hard on the clutch pedal, shifted into first gear, and thrust his hand out the window to signal that he was ready. The first attempts to get the engine running again failed, but as they neared the exit ramp of the bridge, the engine sputtered and zoomed into a working tempo. Jim gave a thumbs-up salute when the truck driver moved into the adjacent lane and passed him.

He made his way through the heavy traffic on Canal Street before turning onto lower Broadway. All concern about being late for his class left him as soon as the Cooper Union Building came into view. Squeezing the car into a tight parking space on Tenth Street left him drained of energy. Even the weight of his books seemed to add to the tiring heaviness of his legs as he plodded his way toward Washington Square.

The heavy door that opened into the large hallway of the university's main building failed to respond to his weak push. Fearing that he lacked the strength to open it, he used his shoulder to shove against its glass face. It gave way throwing him off balance and making him stumble through the open doorway. Regaining his footing, he made for the bank of elevators at the opposite end of the hallway.

The classroom door was open. He entered and headed straight for the clothing hooks on the sidewall and hung up his coat and hat. Jim slid into an adjacent empty seat. Professor Sidney Hook began speaking to the students, but Jim's attention was fixed on the oil stains that now smudged the top page of his lecture notes. Taking his handkerchief from a jacket pocket, he began to wipe the pages dry. He stopped doing it as soon as Professor Hook looked at him and asked, "Are you ready, Mr. Stahr?"

The class size now stood at a mere dozen having been reduced from the initial thirty due to the amount of reading demanded by this course of study. Their final assignment was to come up with some hypothetical, but potentially troubling, political or economic condition and evolve ways to resolve it by democratic means. Although such a task left a great deal to the imagination as to what form such problematic situations could take, the resolution of them was sharply constrained by the demand for practicality as to their solution. Adding to this challenge, the talks would be limited to no more than fifteen minutes, the timing of which was personally monitored by Professor Hook using an old-fashioned pocket watch that he kept in one of his vest pockets.

Wearily, Jim got to his feet and walked slowly down the aisle that separated two rows of desks, wishing that he had more time to regain his composure. After placing his term paper on top of the lectern, he lined the pages up so they lay neatly one atop the other. While doing so, he noted somewhat shamefully that there was an oil smudge on the palm of one hand. He used his handkerchief to wipe it away and then shoved it back into his jacket pocket before starting to speak.

"In a democracy like ours, when government threatens to rob us of what we deem to be rightfully ours, we as a people can become the progenitor for change," he began. "The experience of war should have strengthened our determination to contest and do away with such situations whenever they arose."

Jim stopped speaking and stared out at the faces before him, searching for some clues as to whether the subject matter had caught the interest of his listeners. Their sober facial expressions failed to ease his concern.

"The need to revamp such state of affairs," he continued, "is given impetus by the awareness that one's dignity is being injured or that our rights or freedoms are being denied. In a free society, both the affronted and the disavowed lay cause for their condition on the existing political establishment, its agencies, and its operating systems. From this singular perception, the seeds of defiance can sprout into unbending resolve. This process, if utilized constructively, can be a compelling force for reform. For as long as we can think and sense, we will have aspirations; and as long as we can analyze and originate, we will invoke change."

He hesitated and then stopped speaking. Droplets of sweat had begun to run down his forehead and slip into his eyes, blurring the words on the page that lay in front of him. Jim again removed the dirty handkerchief from his jacket pocket and wiped away the blinding moisture. The weakness of his body cried out for a quick termination of his talk, but his mind pressed him to do otherwise. Much of what had taken so much of his thoughtful labor had yet to be read. Jim glanced up at the clock affixed to the wall opposite him, and just above where Professor Hook now stood. There was still plenty of time to finish reading his term paper. He placed the handkerchief, now smeared with oil stains and perspiration, alongside his stack of papers.

"The keynote of any rebellion is to have a reasonable cause. Without a definitive objective in mind, all efforts to transform values become as inconsequential as anarchy in a vacuum, for any social struggle calls for pragmatic and realistic goals. Our aims, therefore, must be based on reason and not uncontrolled passion."

He put forward the suggestion that his generation's wartime experience provided them the maturity to recognize when the need for such a political restructuring comes to the fore, as a good number of them had been eyewitness to the injustices inflicted on the citizenry of dictatorial governments, as well as others, under the guise of preserving its national interests.

An all-consuming feebleness made Jim stop speaking and grasp the edge of the lectern with both hands in order to steady himself. His anxiety now centered on whether he would be able to continue speaking with clarity and passion. He stubbornly brushed aside these troublesome fears.

"There are two basic paths we must shun in trying to remodel society," he started, the pace of his speech slowing and losing some of its former intensity. "First, any group action taken must not resort to disorderly behavior. The basic ingredients needed for reforming policies in a democracy must resort to the use of reason, experience, and knowledge, not greed or one-sided politics. Thus, we cannot deny the past. On the contrary, we must learn how to use it for our own benefit, and for our own time."

Doubts began forming about his listeners' willingness to accept his ideas as feasible. His classmates may have been a select group intellectually, but not one of them ever displayed any signs of a rebellious spirit in his presence. Fatigue added to his uncertainty, deciding him not to look up at his audience again but to keep his eyes centered on the pile of papers in front of him. He began reading once more, hoping that the strength of his convictions would help persuade his audience of the reasonableness of his ideas.

"Secondly, our use of reason should not be thwarted by the pernicious myth of conformity, which acclaims as righteous the obligation to accept the existing state of affairs. Such a belief can easily become compelling when a nation's leaders promise that stability and security for all is achievable, just as long as every individual voluntarily surrenders his impulse for change and commits to the status quo. This century has given birth to a good number of such imposing dictators, whose creeds outlawed protest, raised subservience to the highest of virtues, and condemned criticism of the existing conditions as the cardinal sin. They were leaders who sought to do away with freethinkers; their aim having been to shape a conforming populace—slaves in mind if not in body, having been denied the use of their self-will. Such a populace cannot contribute to social reform."

Jim's legs began to wobble. Fearing that he might fall, he desperately grasped at the sides of the lectern with both hands and leaned forward, his head almost touching the top of it, which brought an abrupt halt to his talk. His initial confusion changed to bewilderment, as an onrush of dizziness threatened to throw him off balance. His listeners stared at him in stunned silence. They sat puzzled not knowing how to respond to what was taking place in front of them. Their attention was riveted on Jim's efforts to steady himself, the knuckles of his hands turning white as he slowly pushed himself upright. His equilibrium now barely restored, Jim released his grip on the lectern, reached for the crumpled handkerchief with one hand, and wiped away the beads of moisture that had formed on his face and neck. The pages now lay in disarray in front of him. His hands shook as he rearranged them into a neat pile. His classmates waited with expressions of bafflement and surprise, unsure whether he would be able to continue. When he did begin, embarrassment over what had just taken place strengthened his resolve not to look up and face his audience. Anxiety made him take a quick look at the wall clock. The time remaining left him wondering whether his failing energy would necessitate cutting short what had taken so much time and effort to prepare.

"What dissuades most individuals from taking appropriate action to bring about change in their lives is the fundamental need for economic survival." His words now issued forth without any emotion. "To earn your way in today's world, one has no other choice but to accept current social values. This makes conformity to the status quo the order of the day and compromise the norm. There are no rebels on the assembly line.

"From such an essential need to comply, there could arise governmental leaderships that join industry and politics in a common cause—that of securing inequitable rewards for themselves, at the expense of those whose interests they had been elected to uphold and protect. Such an alliance could bring about an economy driven by an insatiable greed for the accumulation of wealth on the part of those legislators allied with corporate officers of such politicized business entities. Thoughtless compliance to the policies of such new authoritarians would limit the opportunities for the economic betterment of its general population. We, the people, have the responsibility for preventing the emergence of such a body of self-serving political leaders and corporations."

Earnestness about the ideas that he was advocating boosted his resolve to continue, regardless of the humiliating effects of his illness. This determination, coupled with a rising sense of elation, gave new life to his diminished spirits. In spite of this, he could not push aside his feelings of self-disgust for his inability to provide an energetic delivery of what he had so studiously written. He brushed away the perspiration on his forehead with the sleeve of his suit jacket and began to read.

"There is a real possibility that a body of appointed officials representing the world's most powerful industrial nations could one day come together for the purpose of implementing such a self-centered economic policy. Such a situation would raise the specter of the emergence of a worldwide industrial power that could set the economic policy for all of the largest industrial nations. This would have a catastrophic effect on the livelihoods of the working public throughout the globe."

Jim went on to give his listeners the various reasons for the decline of independent thinkers in the postwar society. While doing so, one of the students shifted carelessly in his seat and sent a textbook slamming to the floor with a resounding bang, causing ripples of laughter as well as grunts of annoyance. The explosive thud sent Jim's adrenalin racing. He waited for calm to return before proceeding. A nervous glance at the wall clock indicated that only two minutes remained for him to finish his presentation. He grasped the dirty handkerchief that lay in a crumbled heap next to the thin stack of papers and squeezed it.

"The heroes of the future," he said putting as much emotion as he could muster into what he was saying, "will be those undaunted individuals who will stand in opposition to the flagrant inequities that permit great wealth to be accumulated by those who constitute the oligarchies of greed. They will possess the social courage to stand in open opposition to such one-sided practices."

His awareness of the room's persistent silence that followed the completion of his talk made him assume that his presentation had been an outright failure. He gathered up his paperwork and the crumpled handkerchief from the lectern before shuffling back to his desk. Taking his textbooks that lay on top of it, he walked uneasily to the back of the room and removed his coat and hat from the wall hook. Turning to Professor Hook, who stood nearby,

Jim informed him that he was ill and needed to leave. Without waiting for any reply, he started out the door. Just before passing through it, the students began to applaud. Exhaustion and self-disgust mitigated his emotional response to it. A droplet of sweat slid into the corner of his mouth. He did not bother to wipe it away.

Out on the street, he crossed over to the Chock Full O' Nuts and slid wearily onto an empty stool. When the counterman asked if he wanted coffee, he nodded his agreement. As soon as the cup was set before him, he lifted it to his mouth with shaking hands and gulped from it several times. The hot liquid acted as a stimulant to his worn senses.

"I've just got through trying to solve the world's problems," he thought, "and now I've no idea how I'm going to drive that junk heap of a car back to Brooklyn." This concern injected a touch of weak humor into his growing despair. After the cup was empty, he ordered another. Drinking it, however, did nothing to alleviate his weariness.

Without any warning, a hand slapped him on the back, and before he could look up, he saw Hector Palofax seating himself next to him.

"How's it going?" Hector greeted him.

"Not too good. Not good at all," he answered weakly.

Hector studied Jim closely. He was quick to note that his face was unnaturally pale. Beads of sweat glistened on his forehead, the light emanating from an overhead lamp giving them an added luster.

"Hey, are you sick?" Hector's question was full of concern.

"I'm afraid so. Can you do me a favor?"

"Sure. What do you need?"

"Just get me home to Brooklyn. That's all."

"What subway?" Hector asked briskly.

"Not the subway. I've got my brother's old Chevy parked on Tenth Street."

"Let's go," Hector responded and stood up. Jim wearily got to his feet, went to the cash register and paid the bill. They exited and headed for the car.

Hector was able to take the subway back to Spanish Harlem by early evening. The time and energy expended in getting his friend home left him in high spirits. Today had been a day that altered a routine that had become increasingly demoralizing for him these past weeks. Besides, he commended himself for having the skill and patience to drive that dilapidated car back to Brooklyn without it breaking down along the way. As a reward for having done so, Hector purchased a Di Nobli cigar at the corner candy store, lit it, and swaggered back to his apartment.

Chapter 22

The train slowed as it started to cross the trestle spanning the river. Outside of its warm interior, the signs of winter were evident in the leafless oak trees whose branches twisted in untraceable patterns against a sky colored a lifeless blue. In contrast, patches of snow, still preserving the purity of its whiteness, clung to the evergreens that stood stolid, proudly impervious to the ravages of the season's frost.

Jim Stahr leaned his forehead against the train window and stared down at the river, its height raised by the continuous flow of water seeping into it from the melting snow that ran down its banks. He watched as the unending rush of water dashed against an island of obstructive rocks, which churned its limpid surface into a dizzying froth before it plunged onward with a surging violence. A meek sun dimly illuminated the thrashing foam, which gradually regained its transparency as it shot past the obtrusive formation and commenced flowing once more on an unimpeded journey downstream. He twisted his head in a wasted effort to retain a view of the river as the train rolled off the trestle and began to pick up speed.

Inside the train, there was the special silence created when humans assemble but all remain speechless. The passengers, few in number, sat scattered throughout the car, each apart and alone, some undoubtedly engrossed in their own thoughts about things desired but never achieved. For Christmas could be a depressing time, the gaiety of others weighing heavily on the spirits of the lonely and cheerless. Jim thought about Gennie. The awareness that she was going to spend the holiday season by herself was the primary factor that made him decide to undertake this journey.

His thoughts drifted back to the time when, as a teenage soldier, he had experienced the excitement of being on his way to new destinations, believing that each of them held the promise of the discovery of something new and exciting that could be secreted away and treasured. Smiling at his boyish folly, he slouched in his seat and closed his eyes, speculating that only the young and inexperienced can believe that the future is always going to be a rewarding adventure filled with unique experiences, nothing jaded or repetitive. Those reminiscences created a sense of euphoria that remained unbroken until the train blew its whistle and began swaying vigorously as it swung onto a curving stretch of track.

Jim roused himself from his dozing, annoyed at having missed viewing the passing scenery. He placed both open palms against his face, sealing his eyes from the sun's light, which reflected sharply off the unblemished snow packed against what seemed an endless stretch of rolling hills. After rubbing his eyes with the balls of his fists, he took his hands from his face and stared out at the landscape flashing by with a speed that did not allow a full comprehension of its beauty. Gennie Connors came into his thoughts.

A strange girl, he conjectured, but in her eccentric fashion, game playing may well be her way of holding on to the only form of solace she had known as a youngster. In her case, that was understandable. Perhaps, he surmised, her resorting to the use of imagination was the most reliable means of filling the emptiness created by the loss of both her parents while still a teenager. In all probability, in her fairy-tale world of make-believe, everything turns out for the best in the end, because imagination has the facility to provide virtuous protagonists willing and able to overcome all sorts of misfortunes. Nevertheless, he had no doubt that playing with illusion in this strange way could result in detrimental repercussions, especially if it became a habitual means of escaping reality. Anyway, the whole reason for doing so was foolish, and it did not merit consideration Yet, he could not refrain from his analytical probing.

The sun began to slip behind the row of hills that ran parallel to the tracks, its fading light beginning to mar the snow's whiteness with irregular blotches of dark shadows. He leaned back and rested his legs on the empty seat across from him. His recent illness had left him drained of energy. He closed his eyes, his mind no longer responding to his sense of sight but to the train's steady beat and swaying motion. He drifted into a deep sleep.

The moon had risen by the time he awoke. Its light illuminated the tops of the high piles of snow that lay open and unprotected from the densely packed pine trees situated a good distance behind them. He soon lost interest in the passing scenery and turned to survey the few passengers seated near him. Apparently, their attention was turned inward; their features were immobile and expressionless. The train's interior lights came on, flooding their faces with a whiteness that washed away all color from them. Their frozen looks of concentration led him to assume that all of them were caught up in wandering through inner realms of their own making, in which memories were filled with regrets over things done or those left undone. On the other hand, he speculated, perhaps each of them, in their own way, were like the Knights of the Round Table, embroidering their victories with heroics and their losses with deceits. Perhaps, he went on guessing, they will flaunt their lifetime of deeds, some real, most contrived, as proof that they were too much an integral part of their time to have been nonentities. However, in the end, he told himself, they, like the rest of us will take to the grave the unbiased truth about who they truly were in life. These thoughts pushed aside his former mood of placidity. He gave up staring at his fellow passengers and again turned to gaze out the window.

The moon had risen higher, providing enough light to give colorless form to the objects that flitted by. In a short while, his absorption with these fleeting shapes helped rid him of his gloomy introspection.

Chapter 23

The first thing that he became aware of as he stepped off the train was the air, its freshness completely free of those ever-present city smells. His glance down the empty platform revealed only a tiny brick building, its interior light made dimmer by the ominous blackness that enshrouded it. Lifting his suitcase in one of his gloved hands, he started toward the solitary structure. A hand took hold of the sleeve of his overcoat before he could enter. He stopped and looked behind him. His initial surprise quickly turned to joy.

"Hello, Jim!" Gennie greeted him, her words shattering the night's pervasive stillness.

He placed his suitcase onto the snow-covered platform, took her in his arms, and gently kissed her. She took a step backward and said, "It's getting late, we better get going. I've got supper waiting for us." He lifted his suitcase and followed Gennie as she led the way to her car parked a short distance away. Jim slid the suitcase onto the back seat and sat down beside her. They sat awhile, quietly looking at one another. Gennie broke the silence by informing him that Christmas had been empty of any meaning for her.

"It was like having a birthday cake without candles," she said, her flow of words ending in a giggle. Her hand reached out to touch his face, caressing it with the hesitant movements of a child longing for affection.

He responded by moving closer to embrace her. Entwined in each other's arms, they kissed—first cheek, then lips—her passion springing loose from the grasp of loneliness with a silent cry for intimate tenderness. For a short while, they remained sheltered within a world of their own making, one that set them apart from people, time and place. Then, and without any warning, she pulled herself free and moved back behind the wheel to look at him.

"Nick told me that you've been sick."

"Nothing to worry about," Jim assured her as he attempted once more to hold her close to him.

Eluding his grasp with a disarming smile, she turned and started the car. It moved slowly on the bumpy, unpaved roadway that led out of the station.

"What did Nick tell you?" he asked.

"He told me that you went to school and delivered that paper of yours, even though you were down with the flu. You've got all the makings of a silly fool."

Gennie drove onto an unlit paved road, fully absorbed in maneuvering safely through its many winding curves. The car's headlights revealed nothing that caught Jim's interest. As was the case for most of this afternoon's train ride, his mind prompted him to search for meaningful perceptions about people; it did not matter whether they were friends or strangers, as long these reflections could provide constructive insights. However, the intrusion of her words into his thoughts terminated his musings.

"The house, it's old, built more than a hundred years ago; it has warmth unlike that of city homes," he heard her say, "and it's a good way off the main road."

"Well, isolation is the universal domain of lovers," Jim commented, hoping to affect a show of interest, although what he truly wanted to do was to just sit quietly and allow his thoughts to wander undirected and free.

"I want you to enjoy your stay. You can do what you like here and whenever you like. There's lots of space to wander around in, with hills and a small forest. There's even a little brook on the farm, but it's difficult to find. You can have all the isolation and quiet you want. And if you'll be happy, so will I."

Reaching into the pocket of his coat, Jim withdrew a pack of cigarettes and removed one, along with a book of matches wedged under its cellophane wrapper. The burning match sent a flare of light in all directions, expunging the darkness for the short time it remained lit. The transitory brightness revealed Gennie staring straight ahead, alert and fully engrossed in her driving. When the match's flame was extinguished, the dimness of the car's interior and the steady hum of the engine combined to lull him back into the world dominated by his own thoughts. This preoccupation took precedence over any obligation to be attentive to the woman at his side. He sat quietly, his eyes fixed on the road, not fully mindful of the words being directed at him. An approaching truck blew its horn just as they started up a spiraling slope. The car shook as the heavy vehicle drove past them. The noise and movement it created did away with his wish to just sit and think. Instead, he began to pay closer attention to her animated description of her home.

"My house is eight miles from the train station. We'll be there soon. I hope you're not getting restless."

"I've got all the time in the world right now," he assured her.

Twenty minutes elapsed before the tires grated loudly as they bit into the hard-packed gravel of a roadway that led to a large house standing at its far end.

"We're just about there now," Gennie informed him. The car slowed as it moved onto a concrete driveway before stopping in front of the house. Its interior was brightly lit, the light projecting a warm welcome in sharp contrast to the dispiriting darkness that hemmed it in. Before exiting the car, Jim ground the lit end of his cigarette in the car's ashtray and dropped it inside.

Sparks popped and burst off the surface of the burning logs in a miniature display of fireworks. Jim lay on the floor, his head resting against a cushion, letting the heat from the fireplace warm his feet. His attention focused on the erratic patterns of the flames formed by the unyielding suction of the chimney's draft. Gennie sat cross-legged next to him, content also to just silently stare into the fire. Jim ended this contemplative stillness with a trite remark about rural life being less stressful than that of city dwellers.

"For me, it'd be going backward. I have to admit that I get lonely in the city, but I never feel completely cut off from people like I do here." Her words reflected a forceful conviction.

"You're changing, Gennie," he declared, taking note of the decisive firmness in the way she expressed herself.

"You're guilty of helping me to do that."

"Well, there comes a time when each of us has to do what's best for ourselves. That's what makes dreamers into realists." A touch of scorn filled his words.

"Maybe I'm only in the process of learning. I don't have any dogmatic convictions about tomorrow." Her words conveyed no emotion.

"Probably just as well. Maybe there's a greater reward in formulating convictions than living them."

"Maybe...just maybe." Again, her response was one of indifference.

Jim slowly reached up and pulled her down toward him. "Just a kiss, that's all."

"What kind of kiss?"

"A simple good-night kiss. I'm shot...used up. But happy."

She bent down to kiss him, lingering in the process before sliding down to place her head next to his on the cushion.

He whispered apologetically, "I haven't got it in me tonight. I'm washed up."

"You're stealing my line, sweetheart," Gennie teased, and rolled away from him.

An all-consuming need to sleep forced him to curl up and close his eyes.

"Go ahead," she soothed, "shut your eyes. We still have a lifetime of tomorrows ahead of us."

Her suggestion washed away all desire to remain awake. Moments later, he drifted off into a dreamless slumber.

Chapter 24

The high-pitched whistling of a boiling kettle awakened him. Once he emerged from sleep to wakefulness, his attention centered on the flickering light in the fireplace. He looked down and saw that Gennie had covered him with a heavy blanket. Pushing it aside, he sat up and began rubbing the nape of his neck. His initial reaction to the realization that he had fallen asleep on the floor was one of self-disgust.

"Gennie!" Jim shouted. "Where are you?" Not getting any response, he let his voice drop to just above a whisper and began making an apology to no one in particular. "I'm sorry, very sorry. I was completely worn out last night...damned tired."

Gennie Connors walked into the room and heard Jim muttering to himself, his words indistinct and barely audible.

"Good morning, Jim," she greeted him. "Do you always get up talking to yourself?"

He got to his feet clumsily, ran a hand through his hair and said, "I was talking to you and myself at the same time. Can you understand that? I was apologizing about my being so damned tired last night. I'm sorry. I thought I'd kicked this bug of mine, but…" His apology ended with a shake of the head that conveyed his feelings of self-disgust.

Gennie smiled, walked over to him, and slipped her arms around his waist. "Sorry about what? You've been sick. Who do you think you are? Indestructible like John Wayne or ever ready like Clark Gable?"

The scent of perfumed shampoo wafted upward from her hair. He drew her close to him and held her tightly.

It was still early morning when they entered the barn. Jim took note of the rusting hand tools and mechanized equipment stored within it. Like any productive object, decaying from lack of use, they made a forlorn sight. A dormant farm was so symbolic of waste, he told himself. Under the present circumstances, caution advised him to keep his views to himself. This was not the appropriate time to express in words what he was thinking.

"A barn can be a solitary hideaway when you are growing up. It's a place to read, to think, even to dream," she explained.

Jim put his hands in the pockets of his heavy corduroy jacket. "Children in the city have a difficult time finding such a hideout. As kids, we never tired of looking for a place that would isolate us from the hustle and bustle out on the streets. We were lucky if we could find an empty lot, or even a haunted house nearby."

"Haunted house?" Gennie questioned with a grimace.

"That's the name we gave to any abandoned store, factory, or any other deserted building that served our purpose. Broken windows, filth, human or any other kind, did not deter us from entering. That's where we could hide from the adult world in order to share our secrets."

Jim sauntered out of the barn without any explanation. Gennie ambled behind him.

"Hey, is there anything wrong?" she asked.

"No. Nothing," he replied impassively. "It's just that I don't want to get caught in any whirlpool of old memories—anyway, not today. What I do want is to get involved in something new…something vital. What do you say?"

They started back to the house holding hands with the artless trust of small children.

The only heat in the bedroom came from a coal-burning stove in the far corner. Nevertheless, the warmth was sufficient to allow them to lie next to each other without the use of blankets. Their winter-bleached bodies provided a weak contrast against the white bed sheet. Entwined, they lay luxuriating in their ebbing passion. Their lovemaking had been unrestrained, each giving to the other their emotional outpourings with the consideration and patience of mature lovers. Now they wordlessly hungered to sustain this reciprocal submission to cravings for each other's touch. Only after the coals in the stove began to lose their glow did they feel a chill seep into the room, causing them to part out of necessity rather than desire.

Jim Stahr shoveled more coal into the open mouth of the small stove, using a short metal shovel. He fanned the flames with it until they sprang high enough to fill the room with pervasive warmth. Gennie lay on her stomach watching and inwardly applauding his efforts. When the lumps of coal were finally glowing brightly again, she slid off the bed and went to him. Taking his hand, she led him to the window where they stood gazing out at the snow-covered landscape, the sun enveloping them in a yellowish warming light that fused their spirits in an uncommon bond of compatibility. They stood with arms around each other, their sense of touch transmitting feelings of sensual joy. For them, it was a spiritual union stumbled upon by chance, and once having found it, they reveled in its marvels, even though both were mindful that it soon must end.

A cloud drifted ponderously across the face of the sun, progressively snuffing out its warming rays and leaving in its place a graceless, uninspiring shadow that eventually enveloped them in a chill that wrestled them apart.

Chapter 25

It was the last day in December and both of them were determined to use the day in some energetic pursuit. Last night, Gennie had mentioned that there was a forest thick with evergreens along the northern edge of her property. They decided to hike there for a winter picnic. They ransacked the barn, the glove compartment of the car and the kitchen, collecting the items they would need and stuffing them into several worn backpacks they had found in a tool shed. At the last minute, they decided to carry a tent for protection against any radical change in the weather. They were quick to note that the wind had strengthened as they were making preparations to leave. With Gennie taking the lead, they reached the far edge of land that once had been under cultivation and was therefore level and free of trees. The cold wind racing across the open field had left parts of it blanketed with irregular shaped islands of lusterless ice. From where they stood, the terrain changed radically, gradually sloping upward for a considerable distance before it leveled off at the top. Jim pressed his gloved thumbs under the straps of his backpack and followed Gennie as she started up the hill. She deliberately paused several times to allow him to catch his breath, fully aware that his recent illness had taken a damaging toll on his energy.

He fixed his gaze on the spruce trees that clustered more thickly on one side of the hill, thinking that a painter's motionless depiction of the outside world tends to soothe and reassure, but that in reality, nature's only constancy is change, mostly peaceful, but at times violent. He broke off his mind's interplay with the surroundings and glanced upward. She stood waiting for him to close the gap that had widened between them when he had paused to take in the view of the aesthetically pleasing aggregation of the snow-draped trees.

Nearing the top, Jim tired and had to stop and rest. When he looked up, he saw Gennie beckoning him to come join her with a wave of her hand. He took a deep breath and started plodding toward where she stood waiting for him. When he finally arrived at her side, they exchanged smiles and both resumed clambering toward the crest of the hill, which now lay a short distance away. When they finally did reach it, they stopped and looked back to where they had started. The hill appeared to Jim much longer, but not as steep, as he had judged when he first looked up at it. They turned and began trudging toward a dense expanse of evergreen trees that lay ahead of them. Gennie guided Jim through it, stopping only after they had reached a rectangular clearing, where tall spruce trees formed a protective wall around them. An eerie silence left Jim feeling as if he had unwittingly stumbled into an empty and roofless cathedral.

Gennie removed her backpack, let it slip to the ground, and began dragging it to where several large boulders stood grouped together a short distance away. "These will protect us from the wind," she informed him and nodded her head in their direction. "Can you hand me the part of the tent you're carrying, and I'll get started setting it up next to them."

Jim removed his backpack before kneeling down to remove the tent half that was strapped to the top of it.

Still bent over, Gennie twisted around to look at him and said, "I can set this tent up by myself. Be good enough to go look for some firewood. I always keep some stacked nearby, but we'll probably end up needing more."

Moving into the surrounding circle of trees, Jim began to search for branches and twigs that lay free of snow under the protective cover of the trees. It turned out to be a time-consuming task. By the time he had gathered an armful and returned to the campsite, he found the tent standing upright. Gennie had driven the corner pegs into the ground with a large rock that still lay near the tent. She told him to put the firewood next to a shallow pit ringed by stones, the interior of which she had cleared of snow in his absence. They pooled their efforts in getting a fire started inside of it. Before long, the smoke from the burning wood rose up accompanied by intermittent showers of short-lived sparks.

Finished with all the requisite preparations for a short stay, they slipped into the tent, leaving the flap open to allow the fire's warmth to enter. They lay atop the single blanket Jim had carried up in his backpack, the inflow of heat infusing them with a newfound tranquility.

Gennie thought back to the many times that she had come to this place as a teenager, dreaming about building a house someday in this very clearing. How simple are the wishes of children, she mused. They never leave any room for doubt. The thought brought a wry smile to her face.

By the time they finished eating their lunch, the fire had consumed the last of the firewood, leaving smoldering white ashes scattered within the ring of stones. Gennie tossed the coffee remaining in her cup into it and suggested that they start back.

"Wait a minute!" Jim burst out. "I've got an idea." His voice sounded with an exaggerated stridency in the hushed emptiness of the clearing.

She threw him a questioning look.

"Don't you remember? Tonight is New Year's Eve," he reminded her.

"We can have a party at the house," she responded eagerly.

"Why not have it here?" he suggested with a grin.

No longer smiling, she looked up at him and asked, "Will it be a party that ends the way we want it to...here?"

"How can the party end any other way?" The manner in which this question was asked sounded with an assertion that made any reply superfluous.

"We'll have to go back to the house first, if we're going to spend the night outdoors." As she spoke, her thoughts suddenly centered on all the things that they would need for such a venture.

"We can come back after supper. Do you know your way at night?" Jim asked, suddenly unsure that his idea may not have been a sound one because of the unpredictability of the weather.

"As well as by day," she assured him.

"Then let's get started back!" His words overflowed with a boyish excitement.

"No, not yet, city boy. We have to gather plenty of firewood while there's still light. Now, let's get started," she mimicked him. They burst out laughing.

The trek back to the house was less burdensome, as they had left behind practically everything they had carried up with them.

Chapter 26

Frank Colucci and Peggy Troy had spent the holiday season with their respective families. This year, the celebratory activities left him unsatisfied. For each day, he tried and failed to appease a persistent yearning to spend more of his time during the holidays with Peggy. Moreover, he viewed his family's ongoing festivities with an uneasiness that he could not suppress. Frank feared losing his normal complacency if impelled to attend another gathering of his parents' friends and relatives. On the last day of December, he gave in to the urge to call Peggy, hoping to persuade her to return to the city and spend New Year's Day with him. Thus far, he had avoided making a commitment to attend a party at the home of his father's longtime crony, who had accumulated a good deal of money constructing houses. Besides, the man had a marriageable daughter, leading Frank's mother to make subtle hints that he take an active interest in her—with a frequency that took a toll on his patience.

The corner drugstore had several phone booths, which allowed the privacy that his home could not offer. It took the aid of the telephone operator to track down Peggy's phone number. After being connected to her home, he was told that she was not in, the words of the woman who answered the phone sounding sharp and clear, her tone cool and superior. When he asked at what time she was due back, the woman informed him that she expected Peggy to return home by six that evening. Suspecting that he was speaking to her mother, he told her that he would call back later and hung up. There was an element of foreboding in the woman's manner, her conceit evident in the tone of her voice, her words communicating a not-so-subtle snobbishness. He felt that he had won some kind of nondescript victory by not having left his name.

The hours passed with just a single objective in mind—to call Peggy again. He spent his time strolling through the neighborhood streets and peering into store windows with the sole intention of avoiding an early return to his parents' home. He wanted nothing more than to avoid meeting the people they had invited to welcome in the New Year over glasses of Chianti. He censured himself for not having planned to meet with Peggy during the holidays. His failure for not having done so had become for him a disconcerting and inexcusable blunder.

Feeling that it would be more discreet, he waited five minutes after the hour of six before placing his call again. The same woman, whom he was now sure was Peggy's mother, answered the phone. The pitch of her voice gave off the kind of confidence of those who are free of any self-doubts.

"No, Peggy came home early and went out for the evening," she announced haughtily, the only subtlety being the caution that she employed to ward off revealing Peggy's destination.

"Tell her that a friend from school called to wish her a Happy New Year."

"Oh, she will be pleased!" The woman's voice dropped its iciness for the first time. Frank hung up before she could ask him the expected and practiced phrase: "Who shall I say called?" All hope of meeting Peggy Troy on New Year's Day fizzled away.

Chapter 27

Enough snow had fallen after their return from their morning exploration to make use of a sled that was stored in the barn, its metal skids still encased in heavy grease. They packed and tied to it all the things they thought would be needed for an overnight stay atop the hill. To celebrate the arrival of the New Year, they wrapped a half-filled flask of whiskey in a blanket and placed it in one of Gennie's old army barracks bags.

By the time they started on their way, less than three hours remained before the arrival of the New Year. Just as they approached the foot of the hill they had climbed earlier that day, a thick shower of snowflakes began to fall. The sudden change in the weather left Jim with second thoughts about having undertaken this venture, but he decided to keep his misgivings to himself.

After they had traversed a third of the way up the hill, the wind started blowing harder, sending the descending flakes whirling around them in an agitated flurry, diminishing visibility and making the pulling of the sled more arduous. The buffeting wind soon took its toll, sapping their strength and slowing their progress. Before long, Gennie signaled Jim to stop, exhaustion having forced her to rest. They sat on their haunches with their backs resting against the side of the sled, inwardly hoping that the wind would die down.

The prevailing silence began to trouble Jim. When the shower of descending snowflakes began to block out his immediate surroundings, he became concerned about their safety. He glanced over at Gennie. There were no signs of any unease on her part. Unlike him, she appeared unworried by the increase in the intensity and volume of the falling snow or their inability to see the top of the hill. The darkness and isolation in which he now found himself, infused life into a wartime event that he had long ago buried so deep in his memory that it had proven to be well beyond recall's reach. Now, however, it threatened to break through this self-imposed constraint in order to bring it to light. He closed his eyes in a futile attempt to prevent it from infiltrating his thoughts. Nevertheless, the accumulative fatigue of these past weeks left him too feeble to cap the inrush of the circumstances that had given birth to thoughts and feelings he so desperately tried to eradicate. Weariness finally gave way to his mind's demand to allow the past to charge unchecked into the present. And when it did, it made him tremble.

* * *

...The partial moon's weak light failed to penetrate the curtain of large snowflakes that fell thickly around them, which hampered their ability to locate the enemy's positions.

The all-encompassing darkness filled Army Private Jim Stahr with an uneasiness that bordered on dread. This was his first nighttime combat patrol. Aside from its leader, he was in the company of six other newly arrived replacements, mostly eighteen and nineteen-year-olds like him, without any frontline experience.

They had started out from the far side of a bridge that spanned a swift running river in eastern Belgium, staying on a path that paralleled it, taking care to skirt the edges of the thick coniferous forest situated on their right. They were loosely strung out one behind the other with Jim Stahr being the last in line. As soon as they entered a clearing that fronted the forest, a volley of rifle and machine-gun fire sent several men staggering backward, some of them crying out in surprise and pain, while others collapsed into twisted heaps without uttering a sound. Jim flattened himself on the frost-covered ground and started to creep toward the heavily wooded area on his right, the piercing crackle of gunfire hastening his pace. Once inside the protective cover of the trees, he got to his feet and scooted his way around the obstacles that stymied his forward progress. He gave no thought as to the direction he was taking.

When the sound of weapons firing finally ceased, a pervading silence again dominated his surroundings. Feelings of guilt arose, goading him to go back and see if he could be of help to those who had been struck down by enemy gunfire. But fear suppressed that impulse without giving him a chance to entertain any second thoughts about doing so. As he stumbled his way through the dark, his rifle held tightly to him, he felt shame for his lack of courage. He had broken and run, as surely would have any of the others had they been lucky enough to escape being hit. His feelings of remorse grew, which made him stop and look around for anyone else who may have escaped unharmed. No one was in sight. He impulsively tried to retrace his steps, hoping to find some other member of his patrol. Unsure of what to do next, he turned around to survey his surroundings. There were no paths in sight. He found himself in the dark, his visibility obscured by the moon's inability to thrust its light through the cluster of tall trees that encircled him. Alone and puzzled as to what direction to take, he was instilled with a sense of fear he had never experienced before—one that grew out of the realization that he lacked the skills to find his way out of this predicament. Simply, he had to acknowledge the fact that he had never been in a forest before, no less lost in one. This thought made him spring to his feet, grip his rifle in one hand, and hurry away, unsure that he was heading toward the forest's edge.

He continued wending his way through the densely wooded area. After a time, he tired and was forced to sit and rest with his back against a tree, his rifle resting between his legs. A growing sense of hopelessness threatened to overwhelm his thoughts and actions. In order to quell this feeling, he forced himself to redirect his thinking in a disciplined search for ways and means that he could employ to find his way out of this predicament. It eventually dawned on him that the only logical solution was to find his way back to the river. He got to his feet, slung his rifle onto his shoulder, and set off in the direction he reasoned would lead him to it. His confidence rose with the realization that the patrol leader had never strayed too far from it, or for that matter, from the forest's outer boundary that abutted it.

Time passed with a slowness that tested his patience and endurance as he plodded his way forward. The moon began to edge its way above the obstructive trees allowing its weak light to thin the nightmarish darkness. Frightened, and still unsure that he was making progress in reaching his destination, he tried to fend off a growing sense of despair but failed. Doubt and weariness made him stop and sink down on one knee, his rifle positioned upright at his side, in order to rest and restore a waning self-assurance that he was truly heading in the right direction.

Muffled sounds that he could not immediately identify intruded upon the fearful stillness that held him captive by its threat of never-ending isolation. It quickly dawned on him that what he was hearing was many booted feet tramping toward him. Recognition that enemy infantry were approaching brought with it outright panic. All procrastination fled. He took a firm hold of his rifle and started running, anxiety making him inadvertently charge into obstacles that stood in his path, sending him slipping and falling at times. Abject fear impelled him to distance himself as far away as possible from the advancing German infantry. Time was of the essence; the direction he was taking no longer mattered. Once out of earshot of the sound of their movement, he stopped to catch his breath and wipe away perspiration with the damp sleeve of his field jacket. His breathing slowed and the forest's eerie stillness encompassed him once more, but this time it was accompanied by a constant sound he did not recognize at first. He listened intently for a moment before racing toward its source. His elation grew as did his recognition that what he was hearing was the sound of running water—the river was directly ahead of him. The enemy had been his compass; the thought diminished his dread of being captured by them. The assuredness that he would soon be free of the forest's frightening confinement sent him racing toward the river.

The sound of the running water grew stronger, making him speed up his pace as he continued making his way through the thinning stand of firs, the decline in their numbers allowing the quarter-moon to project its faint light unhindered onto the open space ahead of him. When the same path that the patrol had previously used came into view, he rushed onto it and began jogging in the direction of the bridge, where the rest of his infantry company was now encamped. As the path followed a sharp bend in the river, the tall girders of the bridge rose above the horizon. Exhaustion forced him to stop and rest.

The serenity of his surroundings beguiled him into thinking that in such a setting no harm could come his way. His ability to have a clear view of the bridge only reinforced this belief. This peaceful hiatus was quickly ended, however, by the thud of many feet tramping on the cold ground behind him. He sprinted away to warn his fellow soldiers of the whereabouts of the approaching enemy. He knew that they, like himself, would soon be engaged in a battle to retain possession of the bridge. He felt less fearful in having to do so now, although how he had acted just a short while ago left him with feelings that he wanted never to experience again, no less remember. He felt himself begin to tremble. Shameful words now forced their way into his thoughts, which kept cadence with the striking of each shoe on the snow topped path—*Run...coward...run!...Run...coward...run!*

* * *

Gennie and Jim said nothing to each other for some time as they sat with their backs supported by the fully loaded sled, both seemingly entranced by the moonlit shower of snowflakes. When Gennie wanted to break their silence, she reached over to touch him fondly. She was surprised to find him shivering. "You're trembling. You better put on some warmer clothes as soon as we get back to the tent," she advised him with a look of concern.

"How far do we still have to go?"

Desperation filled his words. It startled her. She stared upward, but the dense curtain of swirling snow blocked from view the top of the hill, which she felt confident was just a short distance away. "Don't worry. I'm sure that we're almost there." To placate his anxiety, she quickly suggested that it would be best if they started making their way up the hill before the weather deteriorated any further.

They got to their feet, took hold of the sled's guide rope, and started dragging it again.

They plodded on for another ten minutes before the snowfall began to lessen, thinning the obscuring curtain of falling snow, allowing the moonlight to reveal the crest of the hill. When they stopped and looked up, they exchanged smiles of relief. From where they stood, the end of their tiresome trek seemed within easy reach.

Soon after the sled slid onto level ground on top of the hill, the gusty wind faded away, as did the downfall of snowflakes, revealing their surroundings bathed in a chalky light tinged with a bluish hue. They made their way to where they had camped earlier that day. The tent stood upright in its protected corner, its sloped roof now heavily flecked with freshly fallen snow. Irregular mounds of snow were lumped atop the encircling mixture of spruce and firs trees, which added girth to their contours and imparted a touch of eeriness to the entire setting. The charcoal-colored sky embedded with glinting stars added color and strength to the full moon's light. The hypnotic beauty that encompassed Jim left him feeling that some mythical artist had made this morning's halcyon setting reverential by enveloping it in a rare celestial radiance.

Jim tramped through deep snow to the center of the clearing and gazed upward, transfixed by the moonlit vastness above him.

"If humanity wants to worship God, then it should be in holy places like this," he said, expressing his thoughts aloud although they were addressed to no one in particular. The unearthly stillness amplified the sound of his words, which echoed through the dark before gradually fading, leaving him once again immersed in an unfamiliar hush.

Gennie stared at Jim with a look of perplexity and surprise, before her own curiosity made her look up at the dark sky in an effort to discern what held his attention so fixedly. Not perceiving anything unusual, she turned to study him. His face, now tinged with the same blue-whiteness that glowed around them, remained tilted skyward. Without lowering his gaze, he beckoned for her to join him. Jim became aware of Gennie's footsteps as she crunched her way through the snow. As soon as she reached him, he pointed toward the sky. "Have you ever seen this place as awe-inspiring as this before?"

She looked up and let her eyes roam over the sky's immensity. Yes, she had to admit to herself, there was something unique about it tonight, although she did not give any thought as to the reasons why. She lowered her head and took in the unbroken ring of trees around her; the heaven's light illuminated them in a way she had never seen before. The majestic setting filled her with feelings of solemnity. She now understood what had captivated him.

Gennie finally responded to his query in a near whisper. "Not ever in the past, and probably never again in the future."

"This is truly a spectacle, and not a single human hand went into its making."

"It's more like a miracle that the two of us can experience it together," Gennie said as she looked around her.

"Too bad it's so fleeting. The morning's sun will destroy it."

"That's a sad fact," she replied, unable to hide her look of melancholy. "It's a pity that in a lifetime we get only a handful of opportunities to share extraordinary experiences."

"Then we ought not to set any limits on our emotions when such situations occur." Jim's mood was too buoyant to allow any gloomy thoughts to alter it.

"It's too bad some of us are never satisfied with ordinary pleasures, like the lucky ones who've learned how. I wonder what makes some people demand more out of life than the rest us are willing to accept as gratifying?"

Her question melted away Jim's feelings of pleasure. He left off gazing at the sky and looked at her. Any honest response to her question would have necessitated the disclosure of the driving force that had given direction to his thoughts and actions from the day he returned home at the war's end. There was never an occasion, however, where there was any need to openly discuss this subject with anyone. For him, it had become a deeply held and private matter. Nevertheless, he felt a strong desire to do so now in light of their growing interdependency. He was convinced that such an explanation was long overdue. Yet, he wanted to do so in a way that would not leave him open to any spiteful criticism.

"Maybe," he started, "the war inflicted some of us with such an insatiable craving. Perhaps," he paused for a moment before going on to say, "there may be a handful of us who want to live life in a way that tries to make up for all those who never had the chance to live theirs, the war having robbed them of that opportunity."

"But not everyone has the drive, or the courage, to take on that kind of a challenge—especially people like me," she said forcefully before turning to make her way back to the sled.

Jim watched her stomp away, but waited awhile before following in her footsteps, relieved that his response to her query did not result in any controversial discussion, no doubt because of his failure to make clear that he was one of those driven by such a longing, which he had begun to suspect of late was an end that was beyond reach. At such times, when deeply perturbed by his inability to be specific as to what goals would satisfy this need, he thought of himself as one of the many unaccounted for wartime casualties, his wound being an insatiable desire to live life to the fullest, which was still left untreated because he lacked the know-how of how best to go about doing so. These disquieting musings ended the moment he began helping Gennie unload the sled.

After Jim succeeded in starting the campfire, Gennie poured some coffee from a Thermos bottle into a paper cup and offered it to him.

"Thanks. That's just what I needed."

She nodded and seated herself atop a log that she had rolled in place that undoubtedly had been used for this same purpose in the past. She stared into the fire with an expression that could easily have been mistaken for apathy instead of contemplation.

"Nature had something very special up her sleeve tonight that even overshadows its everyday magic," he stated aloud, not bothering to look at her.

His words come forth with an uncommon slowness, but they still managed to disrupt her ruminations and set her mind thinking of something appropriate to say. For a time, she had been content to be wholly absorbed in musings about herself. She leaned over to extract a long branch from the pile of firewood that lay nearby and used it to reposition the hot embers at the base of the fire.

"You probably have to wait for some unnatural set of events to occur," she said, "before the usual can become the phenomenal. I go a step further. I let my imagination convert the ordinary into the remarkable." She turned to look at him before saying, "I can't wait for Mother Nature, or even fate, to do it for me. Yes, it's only just a game and no doubt I've probably overplayed it. That is, until I met you."

She tossed the remains of her coffee to one side, staining the unblemished surface of the freshly fallen snow. Jim waited silently for her to continue, as if what she had said needed some clarification.

"You've convinced me that reality can be more fulfilling than anything my vivid imagination can ever conceive," she continued. "Lately, I've been finding it very difficult to concoct what's untrue." A crooked smile trailed after her last words. Jim did not see it. His attention had become fixed on the sparks popping upward from the fire.

"You've been my undoing, Jim."

This time he merely nodded in response to what seemed like a grateful accusation. Jim glanced up at her, but he could not see her face clearly through the flames and smoke. Yet, from the tone of her voice, he surmised that despite her words, she was not ready to truly put an end to what he had come to believe was her way of seeking refuge from troublesome reality.

"Gennie, which do you prefer—my chance occurrences of the extraordinary, or your changing life's drabness at the beck and call of your imagination?" Jim supposed that a predictable response could not be taken for granted

"Right now?" Feelings of uneasiness arose from a fear that a candid reply might alienate him. At this moment, however, she felt no need to resort to deception in order to please. "To be perfectly honest, I haven't the fortitude, or the patience, to be waiting around for some unusual event to happen." A cold resoluteness was evident in what she had said.

"At least you know what you want. I wish I could say that about myself," he commented, a note of defeat embedded in his words.

Gennie felt that his admittance of being undirected in his plans for dealing with the future sounded fallacious. "Somehow what you've said about yourself doesn't ring true," she told him. Then, as an after-thought added, "Yet, I don't mind being deceived by you."

He remained poker-faced and said nothing more. Both of them sat quietly observing their surroundings, free of any concerns but those that were deeply personal and never revealed to anyone else.

Chapter 28

Midnight was still more than an hour away when Gennie suggested hiking to the brook that ran through her property. They moved deftly through a heavily wooded area with Jim carrying the partially filled pint bottle of whiskey in his backpack. When they got within hearing distance of the water's flowing movement, a flurry of snowflakes began to fall, causing Gennie to quicken her pace. The first thing she did when she reached the brook was to seek protection from the falling snow. She strode over to a tall pine tree and sat herself under the protective shelter of its overhead branches thick with needles. Jim joined her and hurriedly removed a small canvas tarp that served as protection for the whiskey bottle. He handed the bottle to Gennie and spread the tarp on the ground. They seated themselves on it and watched the snowflakes glide on to the surface of the brook's shallow water, where they quickly dissolved and vanished. They felt relaxed and secure in this protective niche, both wanting nothing more than to rest.

Gennie removed the cap from the bottle she was holding and took several sips from it before handing it over to Jim. "Here, take it. I've had enough."

Jim took hold of the bottle, drank from it, and screwed the cap back on to it before setting it atop the tarp next to him.

"Hey, Jim, aren't you wondering what the rest of our friends are doing tonight?"

"I haven't given it much thought until you just brought it up." He looked away from her and said, "Now you've got me thinking about the people who spend New Year's Eve by themselves—like Hector."

"Please pass me the bottle," she said, trying to suppress a feeling that their ensuing conversation would not be free of any controversial or disturbing matters.

Without a word, he handed it to her.

"But what about the ones who have dates, Jim?"

He turned to look at her questioningly.

"I'd bet they are going to parties, or maybe to Times Square, or even Rocky's, just to be with other people." She paused to see if there was any reaction to what she had said. His features did not change; he just looked at her curiously. She decided to express her own feelings concerning their being alone to welcome in the New Year, one that marked the beginning of the second half of the century. "Yet, here we are isolated from everyone. Doesn't this bother you?" She took a quick gulp from the bottle but did not hand it back to him.

"Why should it? Why would I want to be in the midst of all those bellicose bastards shoving and pushing, trying to squeeze a whole year's worth of joy into one herd-stampeding evening? I couldn't ask for anything more than to be alone with you right here."

She smiled in silent recognition of his flattery.

"I feel a kind of ambivalence right now," she confessed. "I love being here with you alone," she started. "Nevertheless, I'm also fighting off the yearning to be part of a crowd, to look for people, lights, music, even if it's just plain noise. Is there something wrong with me?"

"The same thing happens to a lot of us on New Year's Eve," he said, sarcasm showing in his words and expression. "It's a time for fellowship with the multitude, with everyone trying to purge reality of all its hurtful truths, at least for a few hours. It's make-believe time for everyone from the rich to the poor." Reaching over, he took the bottle from her hand. "But I have to admit," he continued, "New Year's Eve can also be the loneliest night of the year, especially if you're by yourself in the midst of a mob of loud and rowdy strangers." A smirk crossed his face before he said, "Under those conditions, even a hermit could feel left out."

Raising the bottle to his lips, he took another drink and then held it up to check the remaining contents by the light of the moon. There was just enough left to welcome in the New Year, he told himself. He placed the bottle back into his backpack with great care.

"Sure, I know the kind of tug-of-war that's going on inside you, Gennie."

"So you don't have any regrets about ushering in the New Year here instead of in the city?" Her question seemed filled with the skepticism of one fearful that any reply to it might turn out to be a bold lie.

"I'm just a freak in a crowd. Mobs always strip away my identity. In the midst of many, I feel like someone who doesn't belong." He got to his feet and, without a word, started to walk away.

"Where're you going?" she called after him.

"Nowhere special," he answered listlessly.

Gennie watched as he walked along the edge of the brook, until she lost sight of him in the dark. She was about to get up and join him, but on second thought decided that it would be best not to do so. The suddenness of his departure had the effect of altering her mood. She began to entertain doubts about the wisdom of having spent the greater part of the holiday at the farm. Yet, at the same time, some pervasive feeling of guilt accompanied these thoughts, for she felt that it was an unforgivable wrong to be dispirited about spending New Year's Eve alone with the only man she had ever known so intimately.

She got to her feet and called out to him, "Jim, we've got to get back to the tent. It's getting close to midnight."

For what seemed the longest time, she waited for him to respond, his silence giving rise to a fear for his safety. Relief flooded over her when she heard him coming back, his steps audible as he crunched his way through deep snow. When he finally drew close to her, she reached out to take hold of his outstretched hand, pulled herself erect, and they started back to their campsite. She led him along the same path they had used to reach the brook and again made their way through the densely wooded area where the snow-laden trees intermittently shut out the moon's light.

Chapter 29

As soon as they reached their campsite, they immediately began to pile more firewood atop the still-glowing embers making the blaze reach higher than in all their previous efforts. The light from the flames projected a transparent russet coloring onto the lower branches of nearby trees. The large fire lessened their feelings of solitude and added to their delight as the flames leaped upward, accompanied by the sputter and crackle of burning wood. They entered the tent, leaving the flap pinned open, removed their outer garments and lay down next to each other. The jittering flames filled the tent's interior with their warmth, accompanied by the fire's sizzling sounds. Their interest soon shifted from the fire to themselves as the prelude of lovemaking began with touches and whispers, these secretive exchanges meaningless in light of their seclusion. The only sounds they heard were those emanating from the campfire.

Midnight came and went without their notice. The New Year arrived in the throes of the amatory transport lovers yearn to prolong. While the outside world cheered, or was saddened, by the beginning of a new decade, they lay together indifferent to its entry, the ecstasy of the moment having thrust aside the cares of worldly time and event.

The sleep that followed was a restless one. The cold forced them to get up and dress hurriedly several times in order to place more firewood atop the languishing flames. Dispirited by her inability to fall asleep, Gennie nudged Jim awake and suggested a predawn march back to the house. He concurred immediately, as he, too, found it impossible to fall into a restful slumber.

As soon as they were fully clothed, they stepped out of the tent and started loading all the things they had brought with them onto the sled. Gennie's army bag, with the disassembled tent and blankets inside it, as well as both of their backpacks, which were now filled with a disorderly array of camping accessories, were eventually roped to it in a haphazard manner. They started on their way back just as the sun crept its way into view, bathing the sky with a faint light. By the time they reached the house, it had cleared the horizon, its rays glinting off the recently fallen snow. They pulled the sled to one side of the house. Unloading it would have to wait, exhaustion having coerced them to satisfy their urgent need to sleep.

Chapter 30

The first thing Gennie did after preparing breakfast was to call a neighbor to make arrangements for her car to be picked up at the railroad station and driven back to her home. Afterwards, she hurried into the bedroom and began packing. They wanted to leave on the late afternoon train, as there were classes to attend the next day. The end of their getaway from the hectic routine of these last few months now generated mixed feelings. Circumstance, nonetheless, left them no other choice but to return to the city, rather than give in to their mutual longing to continue in their isolation without having to cater to the wishes of anyone but themselves. What was mutually understood, but left unspoken, was the fact that nothing held higher priority for them at this time than the completion of their undergraduate studies. Whatever intense feelings they had for each other took second place to that of satisfying this unrelenting need.

After they had eaten lunch, and with their luggage deposited near the door, they decided that a New Year's toast was in order. Jim emptied the contents of the small flask of whiskey he had brought back from their nocturnal campout into some drinking glasses. They wished each other good luck and took several sips from their glasses. At this very moment, Gennie thought this was a humdrum way to end an adventure of shared pleasures—she felt a need to say more.

"I'm looking forward to doing something new and exciting after graduation. There may not be many opportunities for an ex-army nurse who majored in art history, but I know one thing—I never want to earn my way ever again trying to ease human suffering. I want to live with beauty, not pain. Can you understand that?"

"Well, it won't be long before you'll have the freedom to try and do whatever you like," he replied in a tone of resignation. "Anyway," he added with a grin, "we're going to have to earn our own way without any more handouts from Uncle Sam."

She drank from her glass and looked away from him in order to conceal any telltale signs of anxiety. The pressure of economic need, she recognized, could easily thrust her back into a work world not to her liking, one absent of art and in which imagination could not play any beneficial role. There was no doubt in her mind that monetary concerns would have to be taken into consideration if one was unwavering in their demand to be selective in the job market.

Gennie turned back to face him and said, "Some of us may not be in a position to be too choosy in the kind of work we end up doing."

"But without that ability, you'll never be able to convert your dreams into realities," he replied, and put his empty glass on a nearby table. The candor of what she had just said, nevertheless, undermined his steadfastness to make his own way in the work place. Determination had resonated in his previous declarations concerning this singular goal. What habitually remained hidden was the knowledge that making such a self-directed decision required a certain amount of wherewithal in order to be able to do so.

"What I'm trying to achieve is not going to be easy." Never before had he set forth in words any doubt concerning the likelihood of his finding what he wanted most to do with his life.

Gennie did not bother taking a swallow from her glass before setting it down. "Have you any ideas how you're going to use your freedom?" she asked.

"Right now, I haven't even a clue." He picked up his heavy winter jacket from off a wooden folding chair and put it on.

An expression of perplexity crossed her face. His open admission about being so completely undirected took her by surprise. Ever since she had known him, his obsession to think, choose, and act as he saw fit implied that he had a resolute purpose in mind. Apparently, his admission that this was not the case left her berating herself for having been taken in by a fallacious assumption of her own making. When she did speak, her words sounded with muffled anger directed more to herself than to Jim Stahr.

"It seems that the independence that you want so badly is something you don't know what to do with once you have it."

"Hopefully, it won't always be that way."

"Strange, I never knew anyone so set on going nowhere, and so committed to getting there in such a hurry."

"It doesn't matter where I'm heading, as long as I find what I'm looking for along the way."

"Freedom must have a purpose, if it's to be meaningful."

"I'm still looking for it. But, so far I'm just about one step ahead of confusion."

"Then you must begin to make plans," she suggested, her words offering a way out of what seemed to her a self-created enigma.

"The only plan I've got is to go looking for something I want to do with the rest of my life that will satisfy needs that I have yet to fully make clear, even to myself. But if and when I do, I will call it work…my job... my career."

"You better find a practical one soon. It'd be a great waste of your talents if you ended up searching for something you could never find."

This conversation had brought to the surface feelings Jim thought best left hidden. Saying nothing more, he picked up their luggage and started out the door.

Gennie put her coat on, grabbed the car keys off the kitchen table, and started after him, thinking that all her recent efforts to alter situations for the better seemed to bring about opposite results. The high spirits that had filled her these past days were thrust into oblivion by their exchange of words.

The city had its own greeting. The intermingling of sounds generated by people and machinery in motion created an atonality that jarred their senses. Jim had to shout in order to be heard above the noise around him. He insisted on accompanying Gennie to her apartment before he started home via the subway.

The taxi deposited them directly across the street from where she lived. They stood on the street surrounded by their luggage, both troubled by the thought of having to part and go their separate ways. The short time they had spent together resulted in fusing an emotional bond, and its impending rupture could only produce feelings of hurt and loss. Gennie, not wanting to prolong this parting, lifted her suitcase and hurriedly placed a wet kiss on Jim's mouth. She winked and carefully crossed the street, taking short steps as a precaution against slipping on the ice-covered street.

Jim watched her enter the building. He felt thankful that she had not drawn out her leave-taking. He stood staring up at the kitchen window that faced the street, thinking that the aftertaste of pleasure could be bitter at times. As soon as he saw the kitchen light flick on, he picked up his suitcase and started for Second Avenue. Before he reached the corner, he turned and looked up. Gennie stood observing him from the kitchen window. There was a smile on her face as she waved. Unseen by him, however, were the tears that glided down her face. She vanished from view as soon as he turned the corner.

Chapter 31

Hector Palofax was in jail. Nick uncovered this information after his habitual perusal of the back pages of the morning edition of the New York Times while riding on the subway on the second day of the New Year, 1950. The article had scantily informed the reader that his arrest and incarceration resulted from his striking a man in a subway toilet on the last day of December. For most readers, this was an inconsequential news item considering the time of year. Fracases were not unusual during the festivities that welcomed in the New Year.

When informed of this news by Nick Grigoris, Jim Stahr took it upon himself to try to unravel the mystery of what truly took place in this dispute by having a face-to-face talk with Hector at the Raymond Street lockup. Nick insisted in joining him in this investigation. They planned to meet as soon as their classes ended that day.

During the subway to Lower Manhattan, Nick remarked that any extended stay in jail would eliminate Hector's chance of finishing the course work necessary to graduate at the end of the semester. Jim reacted to this information by shaking his head in the affirmative, just as the train made a screeching entry into a darkened tunnel, his thoughts already searching for ways and means to raise bail should it become necessary.

Jim let Nick attend to all the formalities required to gain entry into the prison wing of the police station. Eventually they were led by a police officer to the cell where Hector stood gripping the bars. At their appearance, his worried look quickly turned into a joyous grin.

"Welcome to the Raymond Street jail," he greeted them, his words sounding harsh and throaty.

"What did you do to get into this kind of a mess?" Jim fired back.

In response to Jim's question, Hector simply shrugged, the expression on his face reverting to its earlier troubled look.

Nick moved closer to the bars of the cell, removed some Di Nobli cigars from his pocket, and quickly offered them to Hector, saying, "Look, we came down here to lend a hand, but you've got to tell us what this is all about."

Hector reached out from between the bars and took the cigars without thanking him, his face expressing the defiant conviction of someone caught committing a wrong in defense of a cause that could only be viewed as irrefutably just and free of bias.

"Come on, Hector, spill it! What did you do?" Jim exhorted.

More wretched than annoyed, Hector strode away from them to place the newly acquired cigars atop his solitary bunk. When he next spoke, it was only to inquire whether they had brought some matches with them.

Nick searched through his pockets and found a book of matches, its cardboard cover bent and stained. He shoved his arm between the bars and handed it to Hector. This time, Hector muttered some words of gratitude and placed the matches on top of his bed next to the cigars, his conscience pressing him to offer some response to their questions in return for their concern and kindness.

"Oh, you'd think I'm some kind of nut if I told you what really happened," he began shamefacedly.

"What's the big secret?" Nick pressed him, his words evincing growing impatience.

"It's not worth telling—that's what!" Hector snapped back.

"Look," Jim began, in an effort to soothe rising tensions, "if we're going to be of any help to you, then we'll need to know what happened to you yesterday."

"Well, right now I'm up the creek without a paddle," Hector declared. Clasping his hands behind him, he began pacing from side to side. "You'll never believe me. Never…" Hector declared, the last word dropping off to a near whisper.

"Give us a try," Nick prompted.

"Okay, okay, okay," he spit out rapidly. "Do you want it right from the beginning?"

"Come on! Before you know it, the cops are going to kick us out of here," Nick egged him on, displaying an aggressiveness that even took Jim by surprise.

"Well, it was like this, you see," he started. "There was no one around to help me welcome in the New Year so I got to feeling blue—but real blue, understand?" He stopped to rub a hand across his mouth. "I couldn't stand looking at those grease-stained walls in that room of mine so I got up and I got out. All I wanted to see was a familiar face—nothing more."

Jim and Nick stood waiting for him to continue.

"Before leaving home," he started to explain once again, "I did put away a few jolts to drown the blues, but it didn't do me any good. I was feeling so low that I was beginning to think that being born was the worst thing that happened to me. Yep, that's how bad I was feeling."

Hector's hands began to flail about aimlessly, as if in search of something steady to hold on to. Overcome by feelings of self-disgust, he slowly made his way to the bed and settled onto it, both hands gripping the edge of the iron bed frame beneath him.

"I'm beat," he muttered. "Truly beat."

"Go on, Hector," Jim prompted cautiously.

"Things got a lot worse when I got on the subway. You know, seeing all those people—mostly couples—heading somewhere, all dressed up in their fancy party clothes." His voice trailed off, as if his reminiscences seemingly had enervated the power of speech. After a short while, he looked up at his visitors.

"To be honest with you, I was jealous of everyone who had a place to go to that day. Those New Year's blues! They can get you down."

What formerly may have been a troubling matter appeared to have degenerated into outright bitterness. For no visible reason, he released his grip of the metal bed frame, stood up, and started ambling diagonally from one corner of the cell to the other, immersed in his own thoughts, this involvement with self seemingly having set aside any awareness of the presence of others. Anyone who has ever been subjected to it firsthand, he reasoned, would certainly be familiar with those feelings of aloneness and dejection that envelop people shut out from those celebratory events that give rise to a need to be with others. Perhaps his friends, who now stood waiting for him to speak, could try to imagine this form of social exclusion, but they would never truly know the stinging sense of isolation it engenders.

"Well, what happened after you got on the subway?" Nick urged, his question cutting into Hector's contemplations and forcing him to address them directly.

He stopped pacing and turned to face his visitors. "Yeah, as I was saying," he began, "between the drinks and the blues, I wasn't exactly in the mood for extending any goodwill to anyone." His tone assumed its normal defensive gruffness. "Anyway, there was only one thing left for me to do—just can the blues and head for Rocky's. I was hoping that there'd be some other free-swinging loners like myself there. Well, with that in mind, I got off the train at Fourteenth Street feeling more like my old self again." He stopped talking and shook his head in disbelief of what he had done.

"Yeah, all you have to believe is that somebody is waiting for you with a good word, and life becomes sunny again. That's what I was thinking when I started skipping up the subway steps, dead sure that once I got to Rocky's, there'd be someone there to bat the breeze with."

He walked to the wall opposite the bed and leaned his back against it, his right hand slipping down to fumble with the zipper on his pants.

"That's when I got the urge. So, I slipped into the bathroom on the upper platform and started doing my thing and whistling."

Nick glanced down at his watch and saw that there was not much time left before they would be ushered out of the cellblock. "Well, then what happened?" he demanded.

"Yeah," Hector growled, "yeah, I did what I thought was right, and here I am in the cooler and with my case backlogged until tomorrow because the judges are taking their time coming back to work."

"What in the hell did you do?" Nick shouted, no longer taking care to hide his exasperation.

"Okay, okay—don't rush me!" Hector brushed his lips with his hairy arm and began telling them what had happened. "I never took any notice of the guy standing next to me. It was only when I got around to zipping up did I see that he was one of those old rabbis with the long black coats."

Hector stopped, shook his head several times, as if trying to shake loose the memory of what took place.

"Well?" prompted Jim, his curiosity intensifying.

"Well, in comes this Bowery bum, mind you, a real stinking tramp, who spots the old man and starts cursing him out for no damn reason. Well, the old guy kept his cool. He just stood there saying nothing. The filthy insults didn't seem to bother him at all. But in the mood I was in, they sure got to me in a hurry."

"It would have been best had you stayed out of it," Nick said, his words expressing criticism and censure.

"If I did, I wouldn't be in here," Hector replied angrily and walked to the center of the cell, stopped, and spun around to face them.

"Everything was fine until the bum tried to get me to agree with what he was saying. Well, the rest is history."

"What do you mean by that?" Nick asked.

Hector took a step toward them before answering. "Don't ask me why I did it, but I belted him." Hector curled his right fist up and slammed it into his left palm several times, lamenting aloud, "What made me do it? Oh God, what made me do it?" His strode to the far wall, banged the side of his fist against it and again spat out, "What made me do it? What made me do it?"

When this short-lived frenzy passed, Hector walked over to his bed, picked up one of the fresh cigars that he had tossed atop it, stripped off its cellophane wrapper, and lighted it. After some frenzied puffing, he removed the cigar from his mouth and let escape an audible sigh of relief, as if his mind had just freed itself of some lingering anxiety. When he looked at his friends, all signs of his outburst of self-incrimination had fully receded. In its place was a self-contesting ego, which prodded him to express what common sense counseled to restrain and smother. The resolution of this inner conflict resulted in his jerkily removing the cigar from his mouth and bursting into cackling laughter, which took them by surprise.

"What's so funny?" Nick asked, not understanding why a feeling of shame had swept over him.

Hector's laughter stopped as quickly as it had started. "Well, when I didn't make any move to leave, the old man came up to me and told me that I shouldn't have hit the guy. Maybe the bum was just trying to be somebody, he went to explain, and abusing people was the only way he knew how. I just stood there like a damn fool and said nothing." Hector broke off recounting what had taken place that day and backed away from his visitors. A sly grin wrinkled his features. He looked directly at them and then continued with his story. "After advising me not to feel bad about what I did, he told me, 'After all, the poor fellow didn't know the meaning of sweetness until he tasted the bitter.' He wished me a Happy New Year and walked out the door humming a spooky tune."

Hector stopped talking and took a few nervous puffs on his cigar before shuffling back to his bed to snuff it out by tapping the lit end against its metal frame. He blew on it to make sure that it was fully extinguished before stuffing it into his shirt pocket. "It was stupid of me not to have hurried out of that place when I had the chance. Someone must have seen what happened and called the cops because they were waiting for me when I tried to leave the station. It's a holiday story not worth telling," he ended up saying.

"That was a crazy thing to do," Nick censured him.

"Look, damn you," Hector snapped back, "I've got feelings. I'm not a machine."

The sharp rejoinder brought a blush to Nick's face, sending his former self-assurance fleeing.

Jim quickly interceded to put a halt to their petty quarreling. "Look, Hector, we've got to get you out of here and quick if you're going to graduate at the end of this semester." He stood immersed in his own thoughts for a moment and then asked in a commanding tone, "Who's your student advisor, anyway?"

"His name is Peter Hendricks. He teaches history," Hector informed him, his temper cooling as quickly as it had flared.

"Well, I've got an idea, but I don't know if I can swing it. Let me try," Jim told him.

"Go ahead, Jim. Do anything you can to get me out of this cracker barrel."

Hector noted that Nick had retreated from him, obviously perturbed by his harsh retort. Feeling guilty, he offered his apologies.

"Sorry, Nick, I didn't mean to fly off the handle. It's just that I don't like being cooped up in this cage."

Nick smiled and dismissed the matter with a wave of the hand saying, "Who would? No hard feelings. Forget it."

"No...no," Hector insisted. "You've got a good point. I've been sitting here thinking why I did it. All that comes out is that I'm hooked on helping the underdog. That's all that comes out—that's all." His last words again trailed off into inaudibility.

An awkward silence followed, as each of them stood wordless waiting for the other to speak. Hector breached the stillness by asking with false enthusiasm, "Hey, what's this rumor about you two guys hitting the road after you graduate?"

"Yes," Jim answered, trying to mask his waning resolve to do so by the manner in which he responded to Hector's inquisitive query. "We're going west after graduation. Maybe not too far, but west."

"I'd surely like to tag along." It was apparent to both of them that his wish lacked any real hankering to join them.

Nick stole a glance at Jim before turning to Hector and said, "Maybe you can make it. What do you say?" He prayed that the response would be a negative one. Hector, he surmised, would surely be a burden on such a venture.

"Hell, it's not up to me. I'll have to be going before the judge tomorrow. I would hate losing the whole package as far as school is concerned, especially at this late stage of the game."

"Look, Hector," Jim said, "I've got an idea. I'll give it a go tomorrow, but right now I'd advise you to tell the judge what you told us, only leave out all four-letter words. He might be a minister's son."

"Yeah, Jim, I'll remember that."

Jim slipped his hand through the bars and shook hands with Hector. Nick did the same. As they were making their way out, Hector bellowed after them, "Hey, guys! Keep your fingers crossed for me."

"Will do," Jim yelled back just as they neared the prison guard who stood next to the locked exit door.

There was no need for Jim to talk to Hector's student advisor to discuss the possibility of letting him take his final examinations in prison. After listening to his account of what had taken place in the subway toilet, the judge declared that Hector was guilty of a misdemeanor and placed him on a month's probation. The man, whom he had punched, however, never appeared in court to press charges, leaving the judge with no other choice but to drop the sentence of probation. Hector was set free the day after Jim Stahr and Nick Grigoris had visited him at the Raymond Street jail.

The news about Hector Palofax's brush with the law soon circulated amongst the group that had habitually met in the university's cafeteria. All agreed that his release from jail was reason enough to close ranks in order to celebrate his escape from academic disaster. The date for this reunion was set for the following weekend. Moreover, and to everyone's surprise, the entire group showed up to participate in the evening's festivities, although there was an obvious decline in the vivacity of their discussions. Yet, under this semblance of gaiety, their exchanges reflected the sad realization that their ties to one another were soon to end. Not one of them ever made mention of this impending dissolution in their subsequent and sporadic encounters.

The days that followed this last full gathering of the group, all of them began to apply their time and energy to ensuring a successful end to their undergraduate studies. This final academic commitment eroded whatever remnants of group loyalty that had prevailed during the welcome-home party given Hector Palofax. That get-together marked the beginning of the end of their long-standing and unorthodox relationship.

Chapter 32

Less than a month remained before graduation. This gave rise to dialogues that forewarned of disunions between the most devoted of friends.

All the way through the first two weeks in January, Gennie Connors and Jim Stahr met infrequently, their personal time fully committed to their respective demands for study and test taking. Their anxiety to assure the timely completion of their course work stood in silent conflict with their wish to build upon the affections fostered during their stay in the country. They spent their time together whenever they had occasion to meet, exchanging brief commentaries on the status of their respective activities. There were moments, though, when their conversation touched on their aspirations for the future, which cycled through mood swings ranging from the lyrical highs of enthusiasm to those that echoed with irksome self-doubt.

Throughout these hurried but intense discussions, it became evident that Jim remained undecided as to what he proposed to do once free to make his own way. Even the trip he was planning to take with Nick Grigoris lacked real commitment. And as far as Gennie was concerned, the impending liberty that would allow him to make independent decisions left him in a quandary. Without a positive course of action, he anticipated that their relationship would have to be put on hold, while he searched for a viable direction to take, one that he determined would give real meaning to his life's endeavors. On the other hand, a growing awareness of his inability to find some means to make effective use of his freedom had left him confused and indecisive.

After the successful termination of each of his final tests, his restlessness became more apparent, his words echoing with the heedless bravery bred from the intermingling of chagrin and desperation. Fueling these sentiments was the fear that he could end up being just another nondescript cog in a mechanistic society, one in which he considered himself to be intellectually alien. Yet, left unsaid was the troubling recognition that his quest to be free from the influence of others not only lacked direction, but it was a search for something that he was still unable to define in specific terms. The one aspect of such an undertaking that remained unyielding was his refusal to enter a work world that would compel compliance to rules not of his own making. He had to admit that the reasons he gave others as grounds for his proposed venture smacked of bravado.

The activity behind the store front of Romeo's Spaghetti House on Fourteenth Street was a showplace for the curious. Even the bustling train-catchers would turn to peer through the large window facing the street whenever the chef lifted free a dripping load of spaghetti from a very large pot of boiling water with a long, oar-shaped paddle.

Inside the restaurant, Gennie Connors and Jim Stahr sat in one of the booths, the stress of exam-taking apparent in the listless manner in which they poked and rolled their forks in their plates of spaghetti while fitfully sipping from their glasses of Chianti. After they finished eating, they sat facing each other, taking infrequent sips from their wine glasses. Their conversation thus far had bordered on the insipid.

"Hector told me last Friday that you and Nick are going to leave town and go job hunting when the term ends."

Jim did not look up when he began telling her what he intended to do after graduation.

"Yes, we've been discussing it for months. But I'm still not fully committed to doing so as yet. And that being the case, I didn't think it was worth talking about right now. Anyway, I don't even know where we'll be going. I'm leaving the details up to him."

"If you do go, have you decided what you'll be looking for?" The question, or so it seemed to him, was asked in a manner that was meant to ridicule.

Jim had an urge to color his response with vehemence, but on second thought, he smothered this impulse.

"Not yet, but I know what I don't want to be doing the rest of my life," he said, his words exposing a tinge of repressed anger.

"And what, may I ask, is that?" The look in his eyes decided her to refrain from any further belittling insinuations.

"All I've ever done was to comply with the wishes and rules of others and with routines I didn't have a hand in devising. I want no more of that." A look of indecision crossed his face, as if he was weighing the consequences of expressing what his emotions were prodding him to put into words. Tossing aside discretion, he impulsively blurted out, "Maybe it's in opposition to your craving for security, but I'm willing to take my chances with the outcome of the risks I take, as long as they result from decisions made exclusively by me."

She reacted with a hurt look, one that confirmed what prudence had forewarned.

To conceal a mounting feeling of compunction, he went through the mechanics of draining his glass and refilling it from the bottle of wine that stood on the table, his gaze avoiding hers in the process.

233

Gennie, startled by his angry eruption, now felt taut and resentful. She persisted in seeking some sort of commitment from him that their relationship would continue after they had completed their studies by suggesting, "Don't you think that holding down a job that's rewarding is worthwhile?" For a moment, the fear that she may have phrased the question in a way that condoned conformity filled her with dismay. Instead of the expected tirade, and much to her surprise, Jim replied politely, still feeling self-reproach for his own caustic outburst.

"What you say is fine for the majority, but I want to do things my own way, and I'm willing to take the consequences of my actions. The one thing I don't want is to get into a lifetime rut that I can't get out of. I want no part of that."

Gennie did not want to interrupt him. It was obvious that Jim was unbending in his commitment to go ahead with his plans once the semester ended. Trying to steer him in a direction that was not exclusively his own, she surmised, would be a form of feminine guile that he could easily perceive and deem as one-sided.

His words took on a more soothing tone when he tried to provide some understanding of what he was hoping to achieve in the future. Somehow his idea—to look for some endeavor that was devoid of any tangible end—was proving incomprehensible to everyone but himself.

"Look, I've given the whole business of the future a great deal of thought. Thus far, my solutions are as vague as my goals. The only thing that I have going for me is my rejection of blindly accepting the status quo. I want and need change."

"Jim, love," she said in a conciliatory tone, "that's the very point that I'm driving at—you must find some aim in life. Your inability to do so puzzles me. You're going to be running hard and fast with no real objective in mind. Yet, all your friends are pushing toward practical goals. That's the way it's always been. Can't you see?"

"How well I see. What you say is true. I guess it makes me one of those mutants who choose to swim upstream while all the rest are content to be swept downstream by the existing current." He paused to drink from his glass, mopping up the spillage at the corner of his mouth with his crumpled napkin. "But you've got to admit that I'm highly motivated to find something that I'm still unable to define in any concise terms."

"If you can apply that same commitment to achieve a specific goal, you'll end up one of the best in whatever you end up doing."

Her expression of confidence in his ability to accomplish whatever practical aims he set for himself was intended to bring an end to any discord that may have arisen between them. The attempt proved successful, for Jim decided to let the discussion rest there.

His thoughts disengaged from any effort to devise any further explanations or justifications for what he proposed doing in the future. He stared ahead, his features exhibiting the signs of one faced with a distressing inner conflict. Then a remorseful smile appeared. The thought that his quest might possibly end in failure had crossed his mind. There was no denying that such an outcome would leave him an incomplete person, someone in constant pursuit of a lifetime commitment that would give meaning to his life and make him whole. In all honesty, there was no denying that some impractical facet of his personality had mired him in a vocational vacuum, his future seemingly empty of any means to achieve down-to-earth goals. Even this self-recognition of the truthfulness of his situation could not stifle his resolve to enter the work world free of the demands and vicissitudes of the market place.

It was now clear to Gennie there would be no dissuading him. Though she failed to accept his reasoning, she knew that any hope of changing his mind at this time would be merely fantasizing. Strange, that he had been the one who helped wean her away from that habit. Perhaps her assumption that he cared enough for her to alter his plans was proof enough that she was still unable to hold back the urge to turn reality into fantasy.

In an effort to stimulate conversation rather than to seek further clarification for the reason he was leaving, she asked apathetically, "What will you do while Nick is hunting for a newspaper job?"

The simple question jarred him. He had yet to give any thought as to how he was going to utilize his time on their journey. The only idea that he had entertained thus far was simply to improvise. Now, her question made him scurry mentally in search for a straightforward reply.

"This trip of ours..." he began, his uncertainty showing. "Nick and I—well, he's planning to look for a job. Well, as for myself..." He stopped, unsure of what more to say.

"Well, what about yourself?" Gennie probed.

His response was slow in coming, but when it did come, it gave her the first inkling of what Jim was hoping to find on this journey.

"I'll be looking for something that is important enough to make me want to stop and live with it a while. It's not so much a person as an activity—something to do, to build, and to bring into being. I believe there's a little spark of creativity in me that needs kindling by some dedicated commitment if it is ever to burst into flames. And, if I'm lucky, I'll find it along the way."

The enthusiasm that filled his words masked his recognition that such a haphazard search for meaningful direction was likely to be as farfetched as that of seeking new worlds by sailing under starless skies without a compass. For those willing to accept the current means for achieving personal security, there was no need to venture out of their safe havens in search of unique pursuits. Yet, some strange impulse was thrusting him onto such an indeterminate path.

His response to Gennie's inquiry satisfied neither of them and brought to a close all further give-and-take exchanges concerning their viewpoints and opinions about the future. Their discussion, which began for Gennie with the prospect of forging longings into commitments, concluded in a void that was empty of fidelity. For while one longed for union, the other rejected it out of a craving for self-direction.

They whiled away the time drinking wine and saying little more of any consequence.

Chapter 33

Peggy Troy and Frank Colucci met daily during the first weeks in January, arranging their free time to share a cup of coffee at a small luncheonette that did not cater to students. At such times, they displayed genuine concern about each other's progress in overcoming the academic obstacles still facing them. Their solicitude for each other in this endeavor was both sincere and wholehearted. Tonight, Peggy had arrived earlier than the agreed-upon hour and sat drinking her coffee while casually studying pages of handwritten notes. When Frank did enter, it was with the unrestrained glee of one who had pulled off some unbelievable athletic achievement and was now possessed by the cheers of the crowd. He seated himself opposite her, his grin ecstatic with the joy of a youngster who has accidentally stumbled upon a trove of comic books. He pulled an envelope from between the covers of a notebook and began waving it in front of her.

"Remember? Just a few weeks ago, I told you that there was nothing ahead of me but a blank wall. Don't you remember?"

The loudness of his voice caused the other customers to turn and gape at him.

"What's it all about?" she asked softly, hoping that the manner in which she spoke would make him take notice of the loudness of his speech. She glanced around her in an effort to make him aware that people were staring at them.

Her gesture made him look at the other diners sitting nearby. When he started talking again, it was in a more subdued manner, but this had little impact toward diminishing his outward jubilation.

"A few weeks ago, there was nothing ahead of me but a dream. Well, that's all changed now."

Holding the envelope by its edges with both hands, he placed it in front of Peggy with the exaggerated grace of one handling a holy relic.

Peggy began to grin; his joy had become contagious.

"Tell me, Frank, what magic did you use to solve tomorrow's problems? Did you find Aladdin's lamp in Klein's basement?"

"So, you're still laughing at me. Still thinking I'm going down that fool's road to poetic extinction?"

He picked up the envelope off the table and began to slap it against the palm of his left hand.

"Well, Peggy, you're wrong...completely misinformed. I'm on a road leading somewhere, one that offers hope and opportunity."

Joining in this conspiracy of humorous intrigue, Peggy leaned over and, with a secretive twist of her head, inquired in a near whisper, "Does this road lead to some hidden paradise?" Then, straightening up again, she inquired seriously, "Frank, please be a darling and tell me what this radical change of heart is all about."

"So you want to know what it's all about?" He leaned back to display an air of self-satisfaction, not unlike that of a gambler who knows he holds the trump card.

"Please tell me your little secret," she cooed in supplication. "Or would you prefer that I get down on my knees and beg?" she added, her voice suddenly filling with histrionic threat.

"Oh, you'd make a great hit with the manager if you did that little thing," he warned her with an I-dare-you smirk on his face.

Leaning her elbows on top of the table, she rested her head in her cupped hands, looked at him blankly, and waited for him to speak.

Finally, Frank offered her the letter, saying, "Okay. You win. Peg, here's the letter. Read it and cheer. Go ahead, read it!"

Peggy took the envelope and started removing its contents without bothering to look at the return address. When she unfolded the single sheet of paper, she read a statement informing Frank of his acceptance for graduate study in English poetry at London University. Peggy's reaction was an initial surge of delight that soon dissolved into dejection. The latter emotion, however, lay hidden behind a broad smile and a jubilant outburst of congratulations.

"How did you manage it?"

"Well, after months of letter writing and submitting all kinds of paperwork, including some of my poems, I finally got this letter in yesterday's mail."

"I'm very happy for you, Frank. You'll be doing something that you want to do. That's something to be envied."

She folded the letter and carefully placed it back into the envelope before handing it back to him. Frank, in turn, shoved it between the pages of one of his textbooks.

Although her joy was undoubtedly genuine, Frank sensed an underlying tinge of sadness in the way she expressed her best wishes. "It's not going to be very easy, Peg," he informed her, solemnity evident in his expression and speech for the first time since he had entered. "I haven't the money for a ferryboat ride to New Jersey, no less a trip to England."

"You'll manage somehow, I'm confident that you will," she encouraged him. "I'm going to miss our little talks. It's difficult to describe. Just thinking about you leaving the city makes me feel as if I'm being robbed of something of great value," she said, her disappointment obvious and deeply felt.

Frank tried to humor her by asking, "Look, why not come along? That's if you won't mind sailing on a freighter."

She smiled a sad smile. "I wish you could've asked me that in earnest, rather than in jest."

The idea sounded delightful to Frank, and without giving it further thought, he blurted out, "What's holding you back?"

Peggy's smile vanished.

"I've a puritanical streak in me," she began. "I'd be a lousy mistress even in the most romantic setting. Anyway, I'm too old-fashioned to want love without the rest of the things that come with it." She ended by stirring her coffee with her spoon.

"Are you proposing to me, Peggy?" Frank teased good-naturedly.

"No. I wish I could be that aggressive. In fact, it's not even a proposition," she said, her eyes narrowing defensively.

Frank frowned and pushed back on his metal-framed eyeglasses, out of habit rather than any need to set them back in place.

"You know, I like the idea, Peggy," he began seriously. "Yes, I like the idea."

"What idea?" Peggy asked, afraid that she may have slipped up in her use of the word "proposition."

"Well, what do you know? I'm suddenly at a loss for words. I ought to be spouting beautiful phrases to convince you to come with me. Yet, in this neon-lit eatery, I can't even get stimulated enough to utter a single lyrical sentiment. Strange, so strange." He shook his head slowly from side to side, as if chiding himself for his inability to do what he deemed essential. "Most of us only daydream about what we crave to do and hear in reality. I guess I'm no different from all the rest. I have to confess that my greatest joy comes when I put words on paper, although I can't deny that putting my hands on you also sends my spirits soaring.

Hopefully you'll be able to tolerate sharing my love for you with that I have for poetry."

Frank looked at Peggy, unable to hide his feelings of inadequacy. "If that's okay with you, then I'll ask again, what's holding you back?"

She reached over to him and placed her hand over his and asked, "Is that a proposal?"

"Yes, Peggy, unromantic and indirect. I'm asking you to come with me on your terms. Well, what do you say?"

She beamed with pleasure, staring at him with an expression of love whose dominant characteristic was deep affection rather than passion.

"I'll go with you to England, Frank, if you promise never to tell me that you're sorry that you asked me."

"I would never have invited you along in the first place if I had any doubts," he told her, certainty evident in what he said.

They sat quietly sipping their coffee, celebrating in silent communion the blissful irrationality of love.

The meditative silence ended abruptly when Frank got to his feet and said, "Come on, Peg. We've got to go."

Frank paid the bill at the cash register before they exited onto the poorly lit street. No one would have suspected that they were more than casual friends as they walked slightly apart, their hands holding fast to their books, along a street lined with brownstone houses. Without any reason or warning, Frank stopped, took both their books, placed them atop the stairs of one of the buildings, and reached out to take Peggy in his arms. They embraced, kissing with the clumsy passion of novice lovers, their hands beginning the initial explorations of each other, both harboring an unspoken hope that the delight derived from these prefatory revelations would endure forever.

Chapter 34

Each student sat surrounded on all four sides by empty desks. This arrangement was not the result of any instructions given by the class instructor, but arose out of a self-imposed and unspoken agreement amongst the students themselves. To the small number who had managed to complete this demanding course of study, the separation provided intellectual elbow room that diminished the awareness of one another's presence, stimulating thought and expression for those inclined to do their most creative work in isolation. This atmosphere gave added impetus to Jim Stahr's proven ability to diagnose and interpret. These same skills were essential for this particular exam, since it did not call so much for the recall of facts, but demanded instead the full use of each student's aptitude to analyze a situation and alter it to bring about an explicit end. For those with such capabilities, outright failure seemed unlikely. For this reason, there was no air of tension in the room. The students went about developing their concepts in light of the analytical techniques that they had been taught, each seemingly responding to the questions with a great deal of self-assurance. Outside in the hallway, Professor Sidney Hook leaned against the wall, absorbed in his own cogitations about life and all its delusions.

Jim wrote his answers with methodical precision, feeling no intimidation in responding to the test problems. This was what he had expected to be the intellectual climate of a university. How different the academic milieu was, he discovered, with its constant demand for the memorization of viewpoints and particulars.

More than an hour passed. The only sounds in the room were those of pages being turned and bodies shifting on wooden seats. Jim stretched his arms upward before beginning to answer the final question. No one took notice of him, as the others were too fully absorbed in their own efforts to originate innovative ideas.

Twenty minutes later, he closed the test booklet. When he looked up, he found the room empty. His immediate reaction was panic. The thought that he may not have finished on time suddenly seemed like a reality. He sprang to his feet and sped out of the room in search of Professor Hook. His fears were quelled when he spotted him outside the door, leaning against the wall, unperturbed and puffing on a cigarette. A sense of relief rose up in both student and instructor.

"Are you finished, Mr. Stahr?" The question took for granted an affirmative reply.

Still somewhat ruffled, Jim instinctively snapped back, "Yes sir," and handed him his test paper. The professor, in turn, put it together with the thin stack he held in his hands. Both reentered the classroom to collect their coats and put them on before leaving.

As they started toward the nearest stairwell, Professor Hook casually inquired, "Stahr, when's your next exam?"

It dawned on Jim that he had just finished the last test needed to complete his undergraduate studies. This realization left him not with a sense of elation but rather with a sense of loss. There was a moment of hesitation before he said quietly, "This was my last one."

Dr. Hook turned to congratulate him. "Well, Stahr, what are your plans now?" Without waiting for a reply, he started down the stairs with Jim trailing after him.

Jim's reply was a bland, "I guess I'll go hunting for a job."

They reached the main floor and walked together toward the exit doors.

"Why don't you go to graduate school?"

The suggestion caught Jim by surprise.

"Most faculties could use an infusion of young blood. You see," Professor Hook went on to explain, "universities also had their wartime casualties. We lost a good number of our young staff members to the military. Many never came back, for one reason or another."

Jim responded with a false note of enthusiasm, indicating that he would give it some serious thought.

They made their way to the Eighth Street station of the BMT subway exchanging banal pleasantries, both avoiding the start of any subject that would require airing judgments and predictions. Without quite knowing why he did it, Jim followed Professor Hook into the train going uptown instead of waiting for the one going in the opposite direction to Brooklyn.

Their conversation ceased completely after the train left the station. The screech of iron wheels against steel rails would have necessitated their having to converse in a near shout in order to be heard. Neither of them had the energy, nor the will, to make the effort, especially if their exchanges were going to be nothing more than small talk. When the train came to a jarring halt at Penn Station, the renowned philosopher managed a hurried "Good luck!" With a wave of his hand, he merged into a mass of exiting passengers, most of them striding toward the Long Island Railroad to catch trains to suburbia. The loud thud of the subway doors slamming shut cut short Jim's words of farewell. The train moved swiftly to its next destination—Times Square. Jim grabbed a leather hand strap and hung on to it as he watched the subway pillars flash by with a ceaseless regularity.

There was no reason for his going uptown. The perception that he was free of all commitments had left him wandering aimlessly in the subway. And much to his surprise, this drifting about without any purpose or direction failed to imbue him with any feelings of self-reproach for wasting time in such an unintelligible diversion. Caprice had taken command, making him act without the stimulus of need, desire or purpose, and free of solicitude about the past, the present, or the future. The world around him now seemed radically altered, this change having come about without any clamor and leaving in its wake tranquility, whose cornerstone was the total absence of concern.

At the Times Square station, Jim stepped out of the subway and started up the concrete incline that led to the cross-town shuttle, still undecided whether to take it or to exit the subway and ramble through the busy streets. Still without any specific end in view, he let himself be carried along by the closely packed crowd pressing into the train. It was just a matter of minutes before it whistled its way into Grand Central Station and rolled to a stop. The directing force of the multitude hurrying out of the subway station propelled him toward a stairway leading out of the subway. There was a pleasurable release from the pressure of body against body once the crowd splintered apart upon reaching the street. He sighed with relief and hurried eastward in order to distance himself from the crowd.

"Strange," he told himself, "I should feel overjoyed, like a kid out of school."

Chortling at the irony of the expression that had come to mind, he gave in to a sudden urge to celebrate the successful end of his undergraduate studies in some self-rewarding way. The first thing that flitted into his thoughts was to call Gennie Connors. Some inexplicable will, however, sent this short-lived notion spiraling down into the realm of oblivion. What proved more influential was a state of mind that prodded aloneness, to be apart and free of the company of others. Self-centeredness mandated that he should cater only to the satisfaction of his own wants, although he was unsure of what they truly were. He began searching for something to do that would satisfy an unrelenting desire to trumpet this day's accomplishment. Any action taken by him that was not strictly his own would have marred this unmatched pleasure of independence.

He wandered along Forty-Second Street, drinking in the sights and smells of all that caught his interest. Engrossed in these observations, he reached Third Avenue just as an antiquated elevated train came to a screeching halt at the nearby station. The resulting cacophony put an end to his indecisiveness about what he should do. He removed his wallet from his back trouser pocket and counted his money. There was just enough to cover the cost of doing something to celebrate the end of one personal epoch and, hopefully, the entry into another. When the overhead train finally moved out of earshot, the street became winter-quiet again. It was only then that he moved closer to the buildings lining the street and began searching for a place that would suit him. Peering into the windows of restaurants and taverns, he made snap decisions about each establishment after first having dreamt up reasons for not entering. When he reached Manny Wolf's Steak House, he stopped and scanned the prices on the menu posted outside. Jim watched customers enter and leave as he debated whether treating himself to an expensive dinner was truly a worthwhile way to celebrate the end of his college days.

"Hell, I'm scot-free of everything for the first time that I can remember. Yet here I stand unable to make a simple decision of what to do. Damn it!"

Walking away in disgust at the idea of eating in that restaurant, he strode downtown, his hands sunk deep into his coat pockets, a victim of his self-generated tug-of-war.

He began to tire after walking a good number of blocks. He slowed down, debating where to go, then hesitantly turned and headed back with the intention of eating at Manny Wolf's Steak House. The manner in which he retraced his steps was much more lackadaisical than his initial retreat from the restaurant. It seemed that the closer he got to his objective, the more debilitated became his resolve. When the restaurant came into view, he shuffled toward it, still undecided whether to enter or not. Then, for no apparent reason, he twisted around and hurried away, this time displaying a sense of finality in the firm determination that marked his stride.

His pace speeded up when he spotted Tim Healy's Saloon. If there was a spot to commemorate this day's event, this would be as good as any, he decided. The bartender's lusty greeting was sufficient proof that his decision had been the correct one. Instead of ordering the usual beer, he asked for a scotch and soda. He lingered over the drink before regret, if not conscience, released him from his normal compulsion to act only as compelled by his own volition. Using the phone booth in the rear of the tavern, he telephoned Gennie Connors and related the events that led to this day's academic achievement. The length of this conversation necessitated a repetitious insertion of nickels and dimes into the telephone coin slot.

Chapter 35

Students were bunched together and pressing forward to reach a glass-encased bulletin board upon which hung strips of graph paper listing end-term grades for various courses. Jim Stahr stood on the edge of the agitated mass, while others shoved past him in an effort to get close enough to decipher the coded results, each student having been given a personal identification number next to which their respective grades were to be posted. Jim backed away from the crowd without attempting to enter the melee. He watched some of the grade seekers push free of the scuffling mass, their findings registered in expressions of delight, despondency, or indignation. Jim was in no mood to scrimmage with this tangle of arm-flailing bodies and decided to walk away without bothering to check his final grades. He ambled out of the building, confident that he had done well in all his courses.

The sun's rays could not diminish the biting cold. After turning up the collar of his coat, he glanced down at his wristwatch. There was still another half-hour before he was to meet Gennie Connors at Joe's Tavern, where the author William Sydney Porter, known as 0. Henry, had habitually come to pass his evenings so many years ago. The tavern always generated warm feelings whenever

Jim spent time in this remaining icon so reminiscent of another era.

The elevated spirits that had persisted this past week did not leave him until his thoughts turned to the forthcoming trip with Nick Grigoris.

The possibility now crossed his mind that this journey could turn out to be more a detriment to his unbridled spirit than an adjunct to it. Now the pestering thought that he might be better served if he did things by himself, and only when his impulse moved him, left him troubled. This negative reflection put a damper on his mood, slowing his movement as he made his way toward his rendezvous with Gennie Connors.

The wall of the building provided a protective shield against the wind as Gennie leaned against it, waiting for Jim Stahr to arrive. Soon, she noticed him striding toward her, his head tilted downward in order to avoid the wind's impact. How stubborn he looks, even in the way he walks, she thought, bemused by his cumbersome movement. He came up to her, took her by the arm just as a blast of cold wind forced them to dash inside, making it impossible for him to greet her with either a word or a kiss. When they were within the tavern's interior, his salutation was a query as to why she had waited for him outside in the cold.

"Don't ask me why. I don't know," she answered, her response sluggish and lacking spirit.

They hung up their coats and seated themselves in one of the booths. When the waiter arrived, they decided to order wine to toast their new status as college graduates.

Jim rubbed his hands together to restore their warmth before inquiring, "Well, how does it feel to be finished with school?"

"To be honest with you, it's left me confused. I can't seem to make any kind of judgment lately. I've been sitting on an emotional seesaw. One minute I'm thrilled that it's over and done with, and the next minute, depressed for the same reason." Her tone of voice reflected the latter aspect of these dual sentiments.

"Maybe your mixed feelings are like those combat blues—glad that it's over, but dejected by the petty gains of victory. Except in this case, what we've probably won is only a skirmish. The real fight is still ahead."

The waiter arrived to deposit their drinks on the table and departed with a nod of his head.

Gennie lifted her wine glass to make a toast. "Well, here's to our futures...may they be happy ones." They touched glasses and drank.

She placed her drink onto the table and leaned her head against the cushioned back of her seat, her words drifting upward and not toward him. "Right this minute, I don't care to think about what's ahead of me. Today there's no need to hurry for anyone or anything."

"Well said," he replied facetiously. "Instead, we can spin tall tales of scholarly valor like some egghead troubadours draped in cap and gown."

"No." She laughed. "Why can't we talk about today and not about yesterday or tomorrow? For a change, I want to forget the past and not think about the future. No, let's talk about today...only about today," she insisted. The intensity of this wish predominated over the dejection that had filtered through her request.

"I not only like the idea, but I promise to abide by it. You'll see," he went on, "today, I'm going to be as cooperative as a bee in a hive."

"Then shall we talk about us?"

"What about us?" he replied quickly, sensing that she wanted to drop the casual banter.

"Well, Jim, I've replaced reality with wishful thinking for so long that there're times when I can't tell the difference between them. This relationship of ours, for instance, I'm not sure what to call it."

He smiled. "Well, call it what you may. You've been the best thing that's ever happened to me. I'll not deny that."

Gennie gripped her glass and began to move it in slow circles, taking care not to spill its contents.

"Yet, I'm certain that you'll be leaving soon," she said, taking pride in her ability to show no signs of disappointment in word or demeanor.

Jim readied himself to squelch any discussion concerning his plans to leave the city. He took the initiative to shift the conversation back to the subject she first addressed.

"I can't put a name on the experiences we've shared these last months," he started. "It doesn't matter to me. But it's been a relationship that didn't rob us of our independence. Isn't that a rare and enviable form of sharing mind and body?"

"Yes, but it has made me more emotionally dependent on you," she stated emphatically. "And it's true that our romance didn't inhibit us from doing and acting as we pleased." A new firmness was apparent when she went on to declare, "Whatever I've taken and given in our little secret exchanges was done without guilt or regret."

Jim reached across the table to pat the back of her hand before telling her, "Anyway, you've got to admit that we've had some memorable experiences together." Hoping to provide a lasting quality to what he had just said, he added, "In time, they'll create feelings of nostalgia that we'll both end up treasuring."

"For me, that'll be a long time in coming," she commented glumly.

"Perhaps you're right." He stopped to think of what more to say.

"After all," he went on, "nostalgia takes aging, like good wine, before it can bring a heady flavor to memory."

"That may well be the case as far as you're concerned." She took a quick sip from her glass, looked at him sternly and said, "My need is for more shared experiences, rather than for any nostalgia for the measly few that we've had thus far."

As far as she was concerned, his words had hinted at an impending separation rather than any desire to elevate their relationship to that of a long-term commitment. She pushed some loose hair back in place and stared at him questioningly before deciding to speak. "In my opinion, what makes our relationship different is the lack of steadfastness on your part to continue doing what we're doing." She stopped to assess his response to what she said. Observing no change in his demeanor, she declared, "If there's any element of uniqueness in our relationship, it would be my sticking by you in spite of the reasons you deem it enviable and exceptional."

The truth of what she said left him with a disquieting uneasiness, as if he had been caught in the act of toying with the truth in order to satisfy the emotional wants of another. They sat for a short while without any exchange of words, dawdling away the time fingering their wine glasses.

Growing uneasy, Gennie broke the silence by telling him that in the past, it would have been easy for her to conjure up an odd relationship like theirs when game playing but that she could not do it anymore. A profound look of sadness spread like a dark shadow across her face. Jim remembered seeing that same pained expression the day he first met her in Peggy Troy's apartment.

"This inability, however, hasn't stopped me from mourning the loss of those times when my imagination could turn my wildest dreams into believable realities, even though they weren't very long lasting," Gennie admitted, aware that such candor could possibly expose her to embarrassment and ridicule. However, Jim responded to her openness with a look that was free of scorn.

"You've changed for the better," he told her.

"How?"

"Well, it seems that you've learned the difference between reality and fantasy."

"It hasn't made me any happier." She sipped from her glass, troubled as to what more to say. After replacing it back onto the table, she looked directly at him and declared, "Realism can be hurtful. It doesn't leave much room for dreams."

Jim's features softened with understanding. "I guess one can get hooked on the unreal, especially when it comes to love."

"Yes, when it comes to that, it can deceive you into believing what is far from the truth." Her remark mirrored her self-reproach.

Gennie observed him pondering for a response, openly displaying an inability to reply with his customary quickness. This inadequacy, however, was of short duration. Jim began speaking with his usual self-confidence, the speed of his recovery having taken her by surprise and putting to flight all former feelings of complacency.

"Humans are not capable of enduring love," he said. "Hate is always just under the surface."

She stared back at him, new insights forming as to the cause for his unbending pessimism about things that held such great importance for her, as well as for most others.

"I'm afraid the war did something to you."

"I have to admit that it did make hate more real for me than love." He stared coldly at her making her look away. Jim's steely look quickly faded. Trying to make amends for his abrasive negativism, he set forth an apologetic form of compromise for his forceful declaration that people lacked the ability to retain long-term commitments. "Anyway, I believe it's a worthwhile endeavor to try to accomplish the undoable, even though reality keeps proving that such intentions can turn out to be costly failures most of the time."

Gennie looked up and met his gaze, her expression reflecting her apprehensiveness.

"Who of us has not been tempted to try and win on life's roulette wheel with its power to turn even our most outlandish wishes into reality?" he continued, the look in her eyes signaling that he may have lost her confidence and trust. His words apparently lacked the ability to restore them, for her countenance remained unchanged. Yet, his admittance that even exorbitant-desires had the possibility of being fulfilled made him pause to consider whether his plans to set out on a search for some lifetime endeavor could well turn out to be the same kind of chance taking. And if the outcome of that undertaking proved to be an event that did not accomplish its intended purpose, than it would make him just another dreamer, imbued with idealistic ambitions that are visionary, unrealistic, and possess an indisputable probability of remaining unfulfilled. The possibility that such an outcome could one day become a reality, made him backtrack into silence.

Gennie drank from her glass, her apprehension apparently beginning to recede. When she did begin speaking, it was evident that she was attempting to placate him by her acquiescence to the opinions he had expressed with such vehemence.

"Maybe you're right, Jim. Those who pursue preserving love are either naïve or fools. After listening to you, I'd have to classify myself as a fool."

"Which of us have not admitted being one or the other?" Jim intoned jocosely.

Her response was a forced grin.

"We humans are always chasing after what we can't have," he added in explanation.

"If that's truly the case, it makes us all naïve and fools."

"Well, at least we agree on something."

They chuckled, then touched glasses and drank from them in wordless acknowledgment that they were once again on the road that terminated at the state of harmony.

They passed the time exchanging stories about the people who they had met while serving in the military. Most of them were humorous.

Chapter 36

Peggy Troy and Frank Colucci were planning to attend a poetry reading at the Ninety-Second Street YMHA. They arrived at the box office early to secure seats close to the stage. After buying their tickets, they started walking to Yorkville, the German district, where most business activity took place along two city blocks on Eighty-Sixth Street.

"Well, have you told your folks the big news yet?" Frank asked.

"No, not yet. Did you tell yours?"

"No, I haven't. What's your excuse, Peg?"

"Oh, I guess I'll end up smashing some of their dreams when I do."

"What dreams?" A note of suspicion crept into his words.

"Oh, like having a big wedding at the country club. It's not something I want to do."

"You should've told them anyway. You're not getting cold feet, are you?" Frank responded hotly.

Her reaction to his question was to reach over to pinch his arm and wrinkle her brow in a sign of displeasure. "Don't be a damn fool!" she snapped at him. "Why should I be afraid of what brings me joy? For the first time in ages, I haven't any worries about the future. Just think—all those tomorrows to come, and you'll be there to share them with me," she went on, affection and concern peeking out from behind her wounded feelings.

After a moment's hesitation, she decided to ask him the same question. "How come you haven't informed your parents? Don't you realize that I've never even met them?"

"Well, I've never met yours either," Frank retorted.

"Oh, that can be remedied easily enough. Why don't you come up to meet them next Sunday?"

Frank recalled the chilling voice of her mother on the phone, and his courage took flight.

"I haven't got a tuxedo. Therefore, I'll have to decline your most gracious offer. Thanks just the same." He tilted his face upward, his lips curling downward, affecting an overly dramatic look of haughtiness.

"We're not that snobbish, Frank. You make it sound like a visit to my home would be an ordeal."

"I'm not much on convention, no matter how civilized it's supposed to be. I hate the fakery of formality, and for me all formality is fake," Frank pointed out, clothing his sarcasm with alliteration.

"My parents are not that way," she exclaimed, leaping to their defense. "But you'll get no argument from me about social conventions being a pretentious form of dishonesty—it's conceit of the worst kind."

They walked in silence. Frank reflected on the reason for his crude response to Peggy's request to meet her family. He had to admit that his immediate rejection of her invitation had been nothing more than the expedient use of his own standoffishness. Some deep-seated streak of integrity urged him to own up to this form of ghetto snootiness, even if he had to resort to a roundabout way of doing it.

"You realize that poverty also creates its own brand of self-centeredness," he began, choosing his words carefully. "If you're not wealthy, you tend to identify with the have-nots. It seems to me that all groups pride themselves in some way with an exaggerated sense of self-importance, even the most needy of us. I guess we all have our affectations no matter whether we're rich or poor. That's just the way it is."

Without looking directly at him, Peggy nodded silently to show him she understood.

"The shoemaker's son and the banker's daughter. God, I hope it can all work out!" Frank's words spilled out without any reference to anything that Peggy had said or done, his skepticism clearly apparent in his appearance and speech.

Peggy sensed Frank's self-consciousness over the obvious differences in the financial situations of their respective families. Concern made her stop and turn to examine the look in his eyes. What she saw crushed all of her feelings of contentment.

"If you have any doubts, Frank, we ought to discuss them now rather than later, when it'll be too late," Peggy said forcefully, doing her utmost to conceal her feelings of dismay.

"No, no." He waved his hand at her. "I was just thinking out loud about the Hollywood aspects of our intended marriage. That's all."

"I don't see what you mean by Hollywood aspects." She glared at him with a sharp look of annoyance. "Look, Frank, it's who we are that counts. Not what our parents do, think, or where they came from. I've had enough experience with fear to know when to be afraid. Right now, I'm not frightened about anything, especially when I know that I'm going to be with you." Her words did nothing to rid her of a growing sense of despair.

"Well, then why are we all so shook-up about telling them about our intentions?" he questioned her. "I wish I had the courage to shunt aside all concerns about their feelings. Somehow our parents have us tied to some umbilical cord of guilt, one that makes us committed to upholding their values. Maybe we're not as free as we think we are."

Peggy smiled. "I can't deny that," she said, eager to dismiss any doubts about their decision to marry but failing to crowd out some troubling misgivings brought on by Frank's premonitions. "You'd think that we certainly have done enough in our lives to have formed the maturity to handle this kind of a problem. Yet, here we are lingering like a bunch of kids at having to tell our parents something that they'll probably oppose anyway, for one reason or another."

Personal fears about confronting her parents with the news of their intended marriage slipped out, although she had promised herself not to allow it to happen.

Frank nodded in agreement before adding his own thoughts on the subject. "If I went and did what I truly wanted to, I'd end up feeling like I committed a crime."

"I guess that goes for both of us." She smiled pensively. "Throughout the war, we were all so bold. Now it seems that we've skipped some phase of emotional development. You'd think that we'd be able do as we damn well please, without fearing the opinions of anyone else. Yet, we're still afraid to upset them. What's the matter with us?"

"I believe we did miss some part of growing up. You know, I never took a girl to a drugstore fountain for a soda in my life. I was seventeen when I joined the navy."

"But doing so should've speeded up your maturity. You should be completely bullheaded by now," Peggy remarked, trying to inject a note of humor into their conversation.

"Maybe we started doing adult things before we had a chance to do what young kids normally do. I mean, we were learning to drink booze and kill when we should have been downing milkshakes and necking in the park."

"Yes, that does make you half adult and half child."

Frank grinned. "In a way, we're kind of emotional half-breeds—still undecided whether to take to the warpath called life or hurry back to the wigwam called home," Frank declared, thrusting his free arm upward into empty air.

She shook her head. "Let's be truthful. We're nothing more than social cowards, but with real, hard-earned medals to prove our courage."

"And if jesters had their own fools, we'd qualify," he summed up.

"Well, if that's the case, then let's tell our parents that we're going to get married. They'll be sure to back up your claim by calling us fools. What do we have to lose?" Peggy said with a sudden laugh. She beamed with newborn optimism. "Not telling them would annoy them even more. So no matter what we end up doing, Frank, we're going to hurt and be hurt. We're left no other choice but to tell them. So why don't you just come up to Westchester this weekend? What do you say?"

"That puts us right back to where we started," he replied, without agreeing to do what she suggested. A sense of defeatism took hold, wiping away any willingness on his part to comply with her wish. "It's not that I don't want to meet your family, it's just that I don't have the guts to do so. Maybe it's something I'm lacking."

Peggy decided to offer a new solution that would compensate for their ineptness in handling what should have been a happy occasion.

"There seems only one option left us if we can't put up with our parent's wishes."

"And what's that?"

"Run…run like hell!"

"You've got a point there, Peggy. Yes, you do have a point. After all, distance would certainly help stretch thin our guilt-ridden obligations."

"It's one way of getting out of the reach of this compulsive obedience to family," she assured him.

"The best thing that could happen to us is our going to England."

"You're right about that," she agreed, her joyfulness now entrenched and safe. "Let's be honest with each other, Frank. You and I know that it can't be any other way. It seems that neither one of us has the guts to erase a lifetime of inculcated values simply by saying the hell with them. We're going to have to run from here."

He stopped walking and stuck his hand out, saying, "Quitter, take this quitter's hand, we're both too cowardly to make a stand."

Peggy took hold of his outstretched hand and countered spontaneously, "Coward, take this coward's hand, and swear to be together in another land."

Laughing, they jogged down the street, leaving them panting for breath by the time they reached the Lorelei Restaurant.

They seated themselves at the bar, their order for glasses of dark beer quickly set before them by the attentive bartender They spoke of many things, but never once touched on the subject of their having successfully completed their undergraduate studies. Their forthcoming marriage made all such attainments fade into insignificance, their feelings so intertwined that the thought of all else was refused entry into their exclusive and shared domain of interest. They sat in quiet admiration of each other, indifferent to everything around them.

Some time passed before Frank looked up to check the time on the clock mounted on the wall behind the bar. As if responding to an alarm bell, he slid off the stool exclaiming that is was time to leave and started hurrying away. Peggy grabbed her purse from off the top of the bar, got to her feet, and trailed after him, a smile fixed on her face. The poetry reading was scheduled to begin in twenty minutes.

Chapter 37

Nick Grigoris called Jim Stahr the last Sunday in the month of January to tell him that he had completed all the planning for their trip. They agreed to meet that afternoon at the top of the stairway leading into Carnegie Hall. Jim did not look forward to spending time discussing details about a trip that had yet to capture and hold his interest. He would have preferred to be in the company of Gennie Connors instead.

He boarded a subway train early enough to assure that he would be on time for this planning session. Upon reaching his destination, he made his way out of the subway and onto the street. To his surprise, the weather had taken a radical turn. The early morning's sun was now hidden behind unwieldy darkish clouds. Frowning with disappointment, he stepped down from the curb and dashed across the street.

Nick was waiting for him, the walls of the building's entryway sheltering him from the cold and the wind. They greeted each other with a handshake, something they had not done since they first met at the university years ago. Nick suggested that they go to the Russian Tea Room a short distance away. Once inside, they hung up their coats and hats and made for the bar. They seated themselves and ordered whiskey and sodas. When the drinks were set before them, they tapped glasses in a silent toast.

"Well, Jim, I've got our trip all laid out for us."

"Are you ready to leave?" Jim inquired, with a fallacious show of enthusiasm.

"I'm just waiting to hear from some newspapers and wire services that I sent my resumes to." Nick began to fiddle with the plastic stirrer that projected out of his whiskey glass. "After I get back their rejection letters, there'll be nothing to hold me back." His downcast look, more than his words, conveyed the belief that this assumption was a foregone conclusion.

"Then you better fill me in on the details about the trip."

Nick pulled a map out of a jacket pocket, unfolded it, and placed it atop the bar. A dark red line zigzagged across its full length with circles drawn around towns and cities. "You see, this itinerary will take us through places that have either weeklies or daily newspapers," Nick explained. "I'm planning to check and see if any of them have any job openings."

Jim listened but did not make any comments. It mattered little to him where they were going. To his way of thinking, the trip for him was nothing more than a long-shot gamble, but one that seemed the only course left open to him at the moment. While Nick had a specific end in mind, his own goal still remained a mystery, for it still lacked a description, no less a name. In spite of the differences in their objectives, he made an effort to show an earnest interest in Nick's rationale for having mapped out the journey the way he did. Inwardly, he was fully aware that what he was searching for was something intangible—the means for self-fulfillment on his terms—and there was no telling where or how he could find it.

"Where's the first place that you'd like to go job hunting?" Jim inquired with a false show of eagerness.

"Pittsburgh."

Jim nodded in agreement.

After Nick finished outlining the proposed layovers on this trip, he asked Jim whether he was in agreement with what he had proposed doing on this trip.

"Nick," he answered dryly, "it's fine with me. If a town has a good newspaper, there's a good chance that it will have an intelligent readership. And if I can get to meet some of them, that'll suit me fine."

Nick smiled, folded the map, and put it back in his jacket pocket; Jim's acceptance of his travel plan boosted his spirits. This same feeling of elation freed him from his habitual reticence to discuss personal matters, for he began to describe to Jim the pleasures he had derived from his recent and burgeoning relationship with Bessie Siegal.

He told him that her easygoing and unaffected manner had been a boon to his flagging spirits. As Nick recounted some of the details of the experiences the two of them had shared, he repeatedly stressed that it was her sense of humor that helped siphon off some of his anxieties these past weeks. Moreover, what he found most gratifying of all was the optimistic and innocent, almost naïve, fashion in which she expressed her hopes for the future. He let it be known to Jim that that for him, it was a long-awaited and welcome change from the unsentimental attitudes and caustic speech of his ex-military fellow students.

Jim listened with a true show of interest, occasionally offering some perfunctory remark. Nick continued to do most of the talking, a role he rarely assumed as a participant in the crossfire discussions that constantly erupted whenever their group met in the university cafeteria. To all the others, his innate shyness was considered an immutable factor in his character, each of them acknowledging that he would always be the least outspoken participant in their daily exchanges.

They idled away the time maintaining their respective functions as storyteller and listener, the tedium of the past week's labors seemingly expunged from memory, while both held fast to an unspoken agreement not to touch on the difficulties that were bound to come their way in the days ahead. To the knowledgeable city observer, they appeared caught up in that special repose that descends on the emotionally spirited segment of the populace on winter weekends, which creates for them a respite from their everyday concerns. This was that kind of day.

Jim quickly put aside all thoughts about the forthcoming trip as soon as they had gone their separate ways. As he started down a side street, its many factories now Sunday silent and empty, this unusual setting brought with it feelings of melancholy, which made him reverse direction and stomp back to Seventh Avenue, where the traffic noise and hurrying pedestrians acted to forestall this depressive mood from taking hold. When he spotted a public telephone on the street corner, he rushed over to it and placed a call to Gennie Connors.

She quickly informed him that Peggy Troy had gone to her parents' house for the weekend. Their conversation ended with an invitation for him to come by and keep her company.

Chapter 38

Passengers twisted their way through the mass of bodies, trailed by friends and relatives as they anxiously made their way toward various departure gates. The terminal pulsed with disorder. The bustle of people burdened with packages and suitcases filled the bus station with an air of tension that grated nerve and fiber. Nick Grigoris dodged and swerved with great agility, heading in the direction of the information booth. Upon reaching there, he approached the woman who sat patiently behind a marble-topped counter. To his surprise, she was able to tell him from memory the departure gate for the next bus bound for Newburgh, New York.

He had hurried away from his meeting with Jim Stahr at the Russian Tea Room in order to witness Bessie Siegal's departure for the upstate city where she was to begin her teaching career. She had told Nick of her travel plans but had pleaded with him not to see her off for fear that her mother would make an embarrassing scene as soon as she boarded the bus.

Nick made his way through the crowded terminal to the departure gate designated by the clerk. A bus stood waiting in its angular bay, its destination inscribed in large white letters in the rectangular panel above the windshield.

Bessie Siegal was not in sight. To safeguard against any unwanted discovery of his presence, Nick positioned himself behind a pillar a short distance away. He waited for Bessie to appear along with her parents. The time for her departure was drawing near.

As he stood awaiting Bessie's arrival, it dawned on him that she would be the first one from their group at the university to leave the city. He was fully engrossed in watching the passengers form a line to board the bus, when a hand grasped his shoulder. The strength of its grip prevented him from twisting free. Still held tightly in place, he heard the person holding him issue a sneering demand.

"What in the hell are you doing here?"

Nick recognized the voice instantly: Hector Palofax. Anger gave added strength to his determination to break the grip that held him. He grabbed hold of Hector's hand and twisted free. Taking a step backward, he spun around to face Hector, his anger showing in his words and features, and spat out, "I guess for the same damn reason you're here!"

A scowl crossed Hector's features, but it faded as soon as he started to explain why he himself was at the bus station. "Bessie told me when she was leaving, but she didn't want me to see her off thinking her mother might cause a ruckus. But I couldn't resist trying to get a peek at her one more time."

"That's what I was also told," Nick responded curtly, his resentment beginning to ebb.

"Then what're you doing here?" Hector demanded.

"Keep your cool, dammit. I'm just getting a last look for old times' sake," Nick responded, his resentment aborted by the realization that both had come motivated by nothing more than a wish to see off someone they had treated like an unsophisticated kid sister these past years. Her fervor to learn about life had an artlessness that not only amused them, but also challenged their pessimistic view of the world. She had drifted into their everyday meetings by chance, neither one of them able to recall how this had come about. In the end, it didn't matter. She had injected a kind of vivacity into their discussions that had been stolen from them by the special circumstances of war. Although left unspoken, both shared the belief that the likelihood of their ever seeing her again was doubtful, at best.

"So you're also here to sneak one last look at the kid." Hector's tone had softened, and it was clear to Nick that he was making an attempt to forge a link between them, not unlike that shared by conspirators compelled to trust one another because they are left with no other choice.

Suddenly, and without any warning, Hector grabbed Nick by the arm and pulled him behind the square column where they had initially positioned themselves. "Get back, get back, will you! Here she comes," he muttered sharply.

They peered from behind the post and saw Bessie join the other passengers lining up to board the bus. A porter came by and hurriedly took her suitcases, placed them in the vehicle's cargo bay, and handed her several ticket stubs. As soon as the riders started to shuffle their way onto the bus, her mother rushed forward to hug and kiss her. However, there were no outbursts of cries and tears, as Bessie had feared. Her father stood to one side, staring at his wife and daughter. The self-control displayed by her parents made Hector and Nick look at each other and shrug. Without any words of agreement, they stepped out from behind their hiding place, walked toward the bus, and watched as Bessie boarded. She took a window seat and waved good-bye to her parents. Hector and Nick, in turn, began to impulsively wave at her. Had they moved any closer, they would have readily seen that the expression on her face was one of nervousness, as if overtaken by fears of what life in Newburgh held in store for her. A short while later, she spotted Nick and Hector. Bessie's smile broadened into one of sheer delight. She blew kisses at her classmates with both hands, and they moved closer to the bus. This exchange of silent farewells literally flew over the heads of her parents.

Nick and Hector did not wait for the bus to pull out. After hearing the final boarding call, they waved at her for the last time, backed away, and started for the nearest exit.

Once outside the bus terminal, they trudged down the street side by side, neither of them having any specific destination in mind.

"Let's go eat. I skipped lunch today. Well, what do you say?" Hector inquired, without any expectation of receiving a positive reply.

"Might as well, I'm hungry," Nick concurred, although feeling somewhat disinclined about having to spend an extended period of time with Hector Palofax.

"Follow me. I know just the place," Hector said, and started walking toward Penn Station, with Nick trying to keep up with his long-legged stride. After they entered the train terminal, he led the way into the Cannery Restaurant, its interior greeting them with the inharmonious sound of chattering voices, punctuated by the occasional clatter of heels as waitresses pounded the hard wooden floors scurrying to and from their assigned tables.

"We might as well eat in a place with some class. I think we deserve it." Hector chortled and winked at Nick.

"Sure. Why not? I'm for some class, especially in a woman." Nick's comment was a deliberate attempt to appear friendly, although he now felt the same exasperation he always experienced whenever he was alone with Hector.

Nick's remark brought a crooked grin to Hector's normally saturnine appearance, which helped subdue Nick's disquietude to some degree. In Nick's judgment, the probability of their ever meeting again was beyond measure, now that their college days had ended. This thought helped further diminish his edginess as they followed the hostess to their table.

They checked the menu and both decided to indulge in a steak dinner and a bottle of imported beer. The waitress came and took their orders.

As soon as the beer bottles arrived, they filled their glasses and took quick swallows. Neither of them made any effort to propose a toast.

Hector may have appeared to be outwardly crude, yet he was sensitive enough to be aware of Nick's uneasiness in his presence. When he started speaking, he took care to bridle the malevolence he habitually displayed when talking to others.

"Well, how does it feel to see our ship breaking apart at the seams, Nick?" he asked, resorting to naval parlance in a conscious effort to help bridge the gap in their uneasy relationship, as well to camouflage his wounded feelings. Hector did not wait for a reply. "Bessie's leaving town was like taking a torpedo in the side," he continued. "And I'm willing to wager that tight ship we knew as the USS Cafeteria is now so shattered that we'll never be able to spot its debris."

"Yes, the breakup is over and done with," Nick agreed. "But there's still a good chance that most of us will get together sometime in June, on Commencement Day," he predicted without any show of conviction.

"I wouldn't be putting any money on that if I were you!" Hector warned, challenging the soundness of Nick's belief with a belligerence that seemed to reflect an extreme aversion to the mere prospect of such a reunion. The pained look that registered on Nick's face made him resort once more to a more temperate manner of speech.

"I doubt it will happen," Hector rephrased his statement in an effort to eliminate any emotional vehemence from his remark, but it sounded out of place and insincere.

While waiting for the waitress to bring their food, they idled away the time discussing the influences some teachers had made on them. When she did appear, she placed the plates on the table, warning them to take care as they were still hot. A strained lull followed as soon as they started eating, with very little of any consequence being exchanged between them. As soon as they had finished, however, Hector again tried to establish some semblance of verbal rapport while waiting for their coffee. He was fully aware of Nick's reticence to talk openly about himself throughout their mealtime conversation.

"By the way, Nick, have you and Jim settled on any plans about going west?" he asked.

There was a new fervor in Nick's reply that had been noticeably absent before. "It's all been worked out. And Jim has agreed to go along with the plan I've come up with." A note of pride filtered through his bland affirmation.

Delighted to have succeeded in getting an animated response to an inquiry pointedly aimed at stimulating conversation, Hector continued probing for reasons for their leaving the city. The responses to his queries came quickly.

"I'm looking for a job on a newspaper, any kind of a job, as long as I can get started."

"But what about Jim? What's he got in mind?"

Nick looked somewhat puzzled. "Well," he managed to say, "I don't know—that is, he never told me...well, not exactly, anyway. He's just tagging along, I guess."

"Ha! I know this much about Jim. He must know what he's after, otherwise he wouldn't be going with you," Hector said, unconvinced by Nick's oversimplified speculation.

"To be honest with you, I don't know," Nick responded, a sense of ineptness overtaking him for his inability to provide a succinct answer to Hector's incisive questioning.

"Can't you even guess at why he's going? He must have given you some kind of hint," Hector pressed Nick, while taking care to curb any outbursts of aggression.

"Are you asking for me to tell you what I think?" Nick responded with indignation.

Chapter Thirty-Eight

"That's right," was the blunt retort.

"Don't get me wrong," Nick went on to say, "Jim's a great guy, but he doesn't let anyone get inside his head, if you know what I mean. If I had to come up with some kind of reason for his coming with me, I'd guess he's going to look for something that's missing within himself, something that'll help him find what he wants to do with his life. But, like I said, it's only a guess on my part."

Hector reached over and patted Nick on the arm. "Good boy, good boy...I agree with you. There's something stewing inside that restless brain of his. And the day that mixture comes to a boil, we'll end up hearing about it."

"If he gets started toward some down-to-earth objective, then I'll agree with you," Nick assented. "What puzzles me is why he'd want to leave Gennie Connors. She has a crush on him a mile wide. Yet, he's going to pick up and run. Now that's a mind-twister for you." Nick's discomfort about being in the company of Hector Palofax began to recede as he became more absorbed in trying to uncover the real reason for Jim Stahr's agreeing to accompany him.

"I'd chance a guess as to why he'd want to leave town, even if he was crazy about that girl." Hector directed his gaze at Nick, his eyes squinting with the slyness of a cat having cornered a mouse.

"You think you've got an answer. Go ahead, tell me...I'm listening." Nick returned Hector's steady look with a smirk that signified disbelief in his ability to do so. "You'll have a hard time trying to convince me why anyone would want to go off in search for something he can't even define, when he has a good thing going for him right here."

Still peering at Nick with eyes partly closed, Hector took up this challenge with guarded eagerness. "I don't claim to be a headshrinker, but there's nothing wrong with my eyes and ears. So I can make an intelligent guess, can't I?"

"I didn't say you couldn't, did I?" Nick responded.

Hector put his hand into a jacket pocket and withdrew one of his Di Nobli cigars. He bit off the tip and was about to spit it out on the floor, when he caught sight of the look of embarrassment that flooded into Nick's eyes. With the last three fingers of his right hand extended stiffly in an effort to indicate poise, style, or just a belligerent imparting of some unspoken condemnation, Hector removed the piece of tobacco from his mouth and deposited it neatly into an ashtray with a feminine twist of his wrist. After lighting the cigar, he tilted his head back and blew a stream of smoke into the air, his face alight with a look of savored joy, like that of a winner of some much sought after prize.

Nick, his patience beginning to wear thin, repeated his question in a manner that bordered on disdain. "Well, can you tell me why, or can't you?"

The mocking harshness embedded in the question startled Hector. His immediate defense was a blank-faced smile, one that masked his surprise and anger. As soon as calm returned, he began to formulate an explanation for Jim Stahr's decision that would sound well thought-out.

"You asked me why a man would leave a situation that makes him happy in order to begin a search for something that's so vague that he can't even describe it. Is that right?" Ideas quickly formed and fell into place, making Hector thrust aside any need for confirmation of his pointless query. "Jim's like a fighter in training," he started to explain, "who knows he still has a lot more bag pounding to do before he can go up against the toughest challenger of all—life. Maybe, in his case, to get more muscle, he needs the kind of conditioning that comes only from experience. Understand? Doing things in the real world is the best way of learning about yourself." He stopped speaking in order to puff at his cigar, before going on to say, "For those who want to be real doers, meeting reality head-on is their way of turning flabby, pot-bellied brains into mental muscle. Jim wants to be a doer, but he doesn't know how. At least, not yet."

Hector looked at Nick to see whether his theorizing had made any impression. Seeing a blank look on Nick's face left him feeling unsure whether he had the inherent ability to communicate with clarity what his mind concocted with ease. Caution, or a lapse in self-confidence, persuaded him to preface any further observations with an excuse for his ineptitude. "Look, what I'm telling you isn't something I learned from a textbook. There're some things you learn on the street that you never can in a classroom. So if what I'm saying is a little hazy…"

"Go ahead! Go ahead! I haven't said a word. You're doing fine," Nick assured him. "You've just about convinced me that your metaphorical muscle-building theory may be a plausible reason for Jim wanting to tag along with me." His statement was devoid of any ridicule.

Hector gulped some coffee from his cup and took several draws at his cigar. After expelling a large smoke ring, he fanned it away with a wave of his hand.

"Well," he said, starting on a new track in an effort to lend credence to his notions for Jim Stahr's decision to leave, "did you ever think that for some people, knowledge could be like a key to Pandora's Box? And once they open it, all that they find inside are questions, not answers, and most likely about themselves." He wiped his mouth with the back of his hand, looked at his cigar, and said, "Maybe Jim is like that. Education may have left him adrift in a sea of knowledge so vast that he's now lost and trying to find his way."

Nick shifted uneasily in his chair, trying to cope with a rising sense of guilt for having persuaded Jim to accompany him. In an effort to divert blame from himself, he suggested that perhaps Jim was looking for an excuse to distance himself from Gennie Connors. "If what you say is so, he wouldn't be ready to take on any long-term commitments. Don't you agree?"

"Nah! That's not it." Hector swung the cigar from side to side several times to emphasize his rejection of the idea.

Nick made another effort to ease a cloying sense of wrongdoing by asking another question.

"Perhaps he's running away from something he can't handle?"

Nick's suggestion irritated Hector. He took several quick draws at his cigar. "Did you say he's running away? Nuts! He's running toward some place—even if it means heading into the dark. Maybe, just maybe, there's some guiding light at the end of the tunnel. Who knows?" His words spilled out with open vexation. Hector reached out to bring an ashtray closer to him and twisted the lit end of his cigar into it. He checked to see that the cigar was completely out, and then slipped it into the handkerchief pocket of his worn suit jacket. When he resumed speaking, it was with a visible air of confidence.

"Doing things on your own is a form of weight lifting for the mind. It helps develop the psychological brawn called guts. I've been pumping that kind of iron ever since I was a kid. I had no other choice."

"What do you mean by that?" Nick asked.

"Well, when you've been living alone as long as I have, and you've no family, you either end up running with a pack of misfits, or you choose to be a loner. But if you do decide to go your own way, then you'll probably end up a tough-minded individual. That's for sure."

Nick nodded his head in agreement.

Hector slid back on his seat, looked away from Nick. "You know," sounding more sedate and thoughtful than usual, "it takes a certain kind of pluck to break away from the conventions of society in order to do things your own way. Not all of us are cut out of that cloth." He turned to look directly at Nick and declared, "I dislike the bastards who take pleasure in gloating over the failure of those who've gone off the beaten track and sooner or later lose their way."

Nick's reply, an unequivocal affirmation that he felt the same way, was delivered with a broad grin that replaced his former aloofness.

This unexpected assent of what he had said caught Hector by surprise. Throughout the time they had spent together this day, he had felt intimidated by Nick's disapproval of his habitual stridency in the way he spoke, which had cautioned him to employ a greater civility in what he said, as well as in his behavior. Now, with Nick appearing less standoffish, he surmised there was no longer any need to continue employing these self-imposed constraints.

"Yeah," Hector began, "this trip of yours will be nothing more than a nerve-tester for Jim, a self-check of his grit, spunk, or whatever you want to call it. As far as I'm concerned, you can sum it in one word—balls! For it's balls that make the man."

Nick felt more forgiving of Hector's vulgarisms. He confessed this newfound tolerance by telling him, "You may never be free of corrupting the language, Hector. Nevertheless, no matter how and what you say, your words can ring as true as those of the purists. Anyway," he added, "you're probably right about Jim's reasons for wanting to tag along with me."

Hector reached back into his jacket pocket to retrieve his partially smoked cigar. After lighting it, he emptied his cup of coffee. Nick did not bother drinking from his.

From the booth opposite them, two girls stood up and made ready to leave. Hector's attention fixed on their movements as they struggled into their heavy winter coats. The pleasure he derived from observing them was suddenly marred by the intrusive realization that he had deliberately omitted a highly detrimental aspect of being an individualist in lauding the reasons for Jim undertaking the journey with Nick. How well he knew that being a nonconformist can and does inflict the pain of ostracism. He had deliberately skirted discussing that aspect of going off on one's own in a society that nurtures compliance to certain accepted values. Nonetheless, Hector was wholly mindful that toiling to establish an individual identity in a world that upheld the sanctity of convention could inflict harsh stigmas. In the past, his voicing of far-left political ideology had exposed him to such onslaughts on his own character. These personal trials had proved to him that he did not have the essential dauntlessness to undertake such a solitary venture. Jim Stahr, he surmised, had a great deal more. In his mind's eye, he envisioned those few who rejected society's demand for conformity as disowned knights in a bold search for some new crusade to which they can append their allegiance. He knew he was not of that breed. His own gallantry was impulsive, not enduring. Verbalizing such thoughts at this late hour, he judged, would not serve any constructive purpose. Hector asked for the check and paid all of it.

Only when they were walking through the domed hall of Penn Station did Nick think to ask Hector about his plans for the future.

"What am I going to do?" Hector flicked the cigar, releasing ashes that paraded through the air in a descending line of flakes that eventually floated soundlessly onto the tiled floor. "I'm thinking about going to California, that's what."

"What are you going to do out there?" Nick inquired with renewed interest.

"Try to swing a job with the Teamsters Union."

"When do you think you'll be leaving?"

"I don't know yet."

"Maybe we'll meet out there," Nick ventured.

"I'll be at the Long Beach docks."

"We'll look you up if we ever get that far west."

"That'll be a surprise."

They shook hands uneasily and parted. Nick Grigoris walked away with feelings of misgivings for having underestimated Hector's moral strengths, as well as for having judged him only by the crudeness of his speech. He should have known better.

Hector had gone only a few paces when he suddenly wheeled around and scampered back to catch up with Nick, who was sauntering away from him. When he came within reach, he reached over to tap him on the shoulder. Nick stopped and turned with a look of embarrassment, as if Hector had managed somehow to read his thoughts.

"Hey, Nick, do me a favor, willya?" Hector asked in a loud voice.

Nick hastily replied, "Sure, name it."

"Tell Jim to grab the world by the tail and twist it just once for me."

Hector Palofax turned and walked away, his face empty of expression, his eyes revealing nothing.

Chapter 39

Hector felt pleased with himself, his conversation with Nick having proven that he was capable of convincing others of his beliefs. The ability to do so would be a prime requisite if he was going to earn his way as a union organizer. Yet, the moment he had entered his one-room apartment, all such lofty feelings of accomplishment fled. The slovenly bareness of it gave rise to feelings of self-disgust. His initial reaction was to reach for a bottle of rum that stood on his badly scratched table. After picking it up, however, he shook his head with distaste, and set it back in place. A pressing awareness that important matters still needed to be addressed took dominance over the impulse to use liquor as the means for keeping in check an emergent despondency, one that threatened to govern his thinking and actions.

From under his narrow metal bed, Hector removed a shoddy suitcase, which he lifted and tossed atop the mattress before flipping it open. One by one, he pulled open the drawers of his solitary dresser and started flinging his personal belongings into it. This was a good time to leave, he mused, the decision to do so having popped into his head as soon as he had entered the room.

He could not help thinking that too much time had been spent these past years in a friendless vacuum, this social isolation forced upon him not so much by the discipline of study, as by the critical need to conserve his limited monetary resources. There was no denying that this self-sacrifice, nevertheless, did make getting a college degree a reality, a goal he once thought to be nothing more than an inconceivable daydream. Now, the successful fulfillment of one aspiration gave rise to another—that of seeking the company of others who held the same kind of social and political aims. To satisfy this new endeavor would necessitate freeing himself from the limitations that poverty imposed upon his ability to do and see these past few years. Looking at the skimpy furnishings that cluttered the room spawned a thirst for change— for some close friendships. He hungered for an involvement with others in some concerted effort that would prove both revitalizing and engrossing, yet would be filled with enough opposition to provide him with the stimulus of challenge. The austerity of his surroundings now served to strengthen his conviction that in order to satisfy this desire, he would have to leave. He knew that staying here would no longer serve any useful purpose.

Although his personal belongings were few in number, the disorderly fashion in which they were packed did not leave any room for the few textbooks that he wanted to keep, the need for cash in the past having made it necessary to sell all the others. He removed the leather belt from around his waist and used it to tie these few books together. The expense of his university studies had exhausted almost all the savings he had accrued sailing as an able-bodied seaman. He harbored no complaints for having done so. It had been a better than fair exchange. Hector closed his suitcase and placed it and the bundle of books near the door. The day's events, along with his decision to depart the city, had taxed his emotions but left his mind overflowing with unconnected thoughts. And along with them, a strange lethargy had set in, making him put off his leave-taking. It demanded that he lie down instead and try to put his mind at ease before starting on his way.

Giving in to this silent counsel, he switched off the light and lowered himself onto the unmade bed. After removing his shoes, he stretched out full-length on it, using both hands to cradle his head. He liked the idea of resting in the darkened room, having long ago suppressed his awareness of the nearby streetlamp that sent its unwelcoming light streaming through the room's single, uncurtained window. Throughout the time he had lived there it had become a fixture, which was as integral a part of the room as the doorknob. Anyway, he was too taut to even think of sleep, much less desire it. He lay with his eyes open reflecting back to his conversation with Nick that afternoon. While lauding himself for having gained Nick's respect, he was unable to cast out the troublesome thought that he lacked the fluency of the others in the group he had befriended at the university. This shortcoming had nettled him from the very day he set foot in those not-so-hallowed halls. His mind now set itself awhirl with ideas, such as the other things he could have easily said, and with greater clarity, in his discussion with Nick Grigoris. Would he ever learn, he wondered, to be as eloquent as the others? When a simple yes or no answer to his mind's query was not forthcoming, he let his thinking address another inadequacy: the present lack of forcefulness to carry out what needed doing—to cut loose from all that anchored him to his present surroundings. This time, a response did spring forth in the form of phrases and words, uncoordinated, yet rhythmic, intent upon turning diffidence into relentless resolve.

> *Don't stall...go!...it's time to get off your duff and strut your stuff...you'll do what you want to do...so don't cry...get out there...give it a try...yep, it's time to leave...starting anew is no lark...it takes guts...yes...you can very brave in the dark...but nuts!...don't kid yourself...your Tough Guy Systems*

*won't work...TGS...all coded in acronyms...the
puritan's graffiti...not for toilet walls...but more
likely for military halls...go! So...get up...and
go!...but wait...what about tomorrow?...will it
bring sorrow?...no matter...I guess blues is better
than booze...get up and go!*

The light cast by the streetlamp that faced his window flickered
for a few moments. Then, with a sizzling sound, it switched off
throwing the room into total darkness. This had never happened
before in all the years he had spent in this cheerless room. Now
the night's array of stars was framed within the washed-out white
window panels. The sudden shift from the room's faint light to
that giving forth from a star-filled windswept sky blinded his
mind's eye to all consideration of errors made and opportunities
missed. He spotted the North Star and stared fixedly at it. He
recalled how night was made less fearful whenever the stars filled
the nighttime skies during his wartime voyages at sea. This
recollection of the past lifted his spirits. In time, optimism took
possession of his thoughts, beckoning him to start anew on a path
that would lead away from his present isolation. He knew that if
this was ever to become a reality, he was left with no other choice
but to take leave of his current surroundings and start afresh
elsewhere Nevertheless, lassitude urged him to linger on a bit
longer. Hector looked up at the ceiling, closed his eyes, and gave
in to his mind's entreaty to stay. A smile wrinkled the corners of
his mouth as his thoughts drifted back to a time when voices and
sounds gave meaning to everyday life.

*The smoking lamp is lit...the smoking lamp is
lit...it's time to rest a bit...life is good at sea... you
feel free...most tomorrows are routine...like a well-
oiled machine...it's not the same now...on land
there's nothing but change ...always leaving you on*

*some isolated strand…where you've got the
choice…cry or rejoice…but now you're free…so
start making tomorrows today…so let's get out of
here…you've got to head somewhere…someplace
where you can do your best…join the rest…that'll
be your test…so get up and go…blow!*

He became aware of the measured ticking of the cheap alarm
clock that lay on top of a wooden orange crate that stood upright
next to his bed, its steady cadence begetting a repetitious phrase
that muffled his mind's inducements to leave, the words keeping
time with the clock's pulsing beat.

*Tick-tock, join the flock…tick-tock, join the
flock…tick-tock, join the flock…break out…get
out…bug out…move, you've got to run…to another
crusade…this one's done…so now you've got it
made…you've got your degree…you're free…it's
time to blow…get up and go…hell, life without a
fight is like day without night…get free!…out of this
cell and into the street…don't be a creep…find
work…don't be a jerk…join the huddle…get into
the muddle…get up!…get out!…run!*

This time the mind's coaxing produced results. Swinging his
legs off the bed, he slowly got to his feet, flicked on a lamp, and
shuffled over to a small washbasin. He turned on the faucet,
scooped up some of the running water, and pressed his face into
his cupped hands. Reaching for a towel that hung from a nearby
plastic hook, he pulled it free and began to rub his face with it.
Finished, he flung the towel on top of the rumpled bed, removed
his jacket from the back of the only chair in the room, and slipped
his arms through its sleeves. Taking the key to the room from one
of its pockets, he slid it into the door lock. With slow, careful

movements, he hoisted the bundle of books by the loose end of the belt that bound them together and slid it over his shoulder. With his other hand, he took hold of his suitcase and walked out the door without bothering to close it. The half-empty rum bottle stood atop the room's solitary table, forgotten, a chance gift for the next exile from the multitude.

The successful termination of academic studies brought in its wake the expected dissolution of the eristic coterie of which he was an inveterate participant. Unlike the others, who were seeking new careers in which they could utilize their studies, Hector withdrew from the scholastic halls to begin treading the same vocational path that he had traversed before. In his case, the personal rigorousness of isolated living, along with his having successfully managed to subsist within self-imposed, but confining, spending limits, had helped form the kind of fortitude that made him impervious to those forces that threaten failure whenever adversity comes to the fore.

Hector Palofax went down the stairs and out of the building without taking the time or the trouble to look back.

Chapter 40

Several weeks had gone by since Jim Stahr's graduation. His family's elation over this event had begun to diminish, as he had yet to inform them of a single promising job offer that had come his way. They showed their concern by making worrisome inquiries as to what he had accomplished after his return home from his daily job searches in Manhattan. Propelled by a nervous need to do something, and in order to mask his true intentions, he would leave the house every morning with the classified ads of the New York Times folded under his arm without any intention of responding to any one of them. He hated this deceptive playacting. However, he told himself, a white lie would hurt his family less than telling them what he truly intended to do.

He would exit the subway each day and set off walking with whim leading the way. The weather these last few days could only be described as severe, the penetrating cold forcing him indoors before he could venture very far. When he needed to get out of the cold, he would seek the warmth of an inexpensive luncheonette and idle away his time over coffee and a doughnut. At these unscheduled stops, he would often try calling Gennie Connors. To his dismay, she had not been at home the entire week. No doubt, he reasoned, she was scurrying about the city seeking a starting position in some art museum or gallery. Each time she failed to respond to his call, he would place the phone back on its cradle feeling dejected, knowing that he was left with no other choice but to continue drifting through the city streets. What he found most disheartening of all was the realization that his discoveries and encounters throughout this period of aimless treks were few and inconsequential, and had yet to prove stimulating to either mind or senses.

His liberation from the academic discipline under which he had labored so long left him restless and agitated. He was no longer subject to any directive influence by others; he was free to do as he wished, when he wished. Yet, instead of the anticipated sense of release and high spirits, he felt chagrin, which stemmed from the realization that he lacked the innate capacity to use his newfound independence in a manner that would bring about a satisfying sense of accomplishment. This indecisiveness, he recognized, was a critical defect in his character. Things were not going his way, he judged, because he had not decided which way to go. His subjective probing, as he roamed the streets these past weeks, failed to provide a single clue as to how to resolve this predicament. However, it did give rise to the realization that he could one day become such a victim of self-entrapment, whereby his overwhelming desire for personal freedom, once achieved, had thrust him in a quandary as to how best to use it. Nevertheless, his introspective search for practical solutions to this enigma resulted in the recognition of the root cause of his need to be and do as he saw fit in dealing with the future.

There was no doubt in his mind that the cruelties of war had instilled in him an unswerving need to live life to the fullest, free of constraints that could prevent the realization of his full potential to immerse himself in the humanistic aspect of life's endeavors, rather than that of the purely materialistic. This, he believed, would be the driving force that would satisfy some psychological demands that he failed to fully comprehend at times. Yet, admittedly, it would be a challenge to which only the hardiest of innovators could respond. He had his doubts as to whether he had the attributes to be classified as such. All the same, the practical means for achieving this end still remained a mystery that he, and only he alone, could possibly solve. Frustration, rather than common sense, left him convinced that his decision to leave the city in search of a means to satisfy this unyielding demand was the right one.

It was a Friday morning when he called Gennie Connors from a Greek restaurant on a side street littered with empty cartons and wooden boxes. His spirits lifted only slightly when he heard her voice and the teasing playfulness in the way she spoke.

"What makes you sound so happy this morning?" Jim asked petulantly, unable to conceal his underlying mood of dejection.

"And what makes you sound so sweet and lovable so early in the day?" she retorted with biting sarcasm.

A guilty coloring spread across his face before he could reply. Realizing that he had spoken with an unprovoked harshness, he quickly apologized. "Sorry if I sounded abrupt just now, Gennie. Perhaps, I've been walking with my hands in my pockets for too long. I'm not used to it."

"You've got to keep calm," she advised him, her words taking on a sympathetic quality. "It's only been a couple of weeks since we walked away from our last exam."

He closed the door to the telephone booth out of a sudden desire for privacy. "I guess it's like coming off of drugs. The first few weeks are the hardest," he told her, his normal self-confidence apparently restored, giving a crisp edge to his words. "Yes, you're right. I've got to give it a little more time."

"Hold it a second," she instructed, "I want to light a cigarette."

"Sure, go ahead. Time is something I've got plenty of."

The sound of a match sliding across a rough surface ended with a muffled pop as it burst into flames.

"Okay, I'm back again," she announced. "And I've got a surprise for you."

What he expected to hear was news that she had landed a job.

"Tell me only if it's pleasant."

"Peggy told me that she and Frank are going to visit her parents today and that they'll be spending the night at her home. What do you think about that?"

"Maybe serious intentions are in the wind. Couldn't you get a whiff of it when she spoke to you?"

She giggled like an adolescent embarrassed by listening to an off-color joke for the first time. "Yes, come to think of it, there was a kind of I've-got-the-world-by-the tail lilt in her voice when she told me the news."

"Well, well, isn't that a surprise?"

"No, that's only part of it. She left early this morning, and I was thinking that you might like to come up after you get tired of walking the streets."

"I can't think of a better reason to get out of the cold. I'll be there, just tell me when."

"Please give me a call around noon. I've still got some chores to do this morning."

"I'll do that if you like."

"I'll be waiting. So long...I've got to run."

He sat on the curved seat in the telephone booth holding the receiver in his hand, surprised at Gennie's hasty termination of their conversation. His spirits rose knowing that there was something purposeful to do later in the day. Killing time, at least for the next few hours, should prove a less burdensome task than it had been these last few days.

What had passed between them in terms of conversation was of little consequence. Jim had come into the apartment with a frenzied passion that he could not contain. The anxieties of these last weeks now acted like a blast of air upon the warm embers of latent desire. At first, Gennie appeared to respond to his overtures out of obligation, rather than from any need to appease her own cravings. In a short while, nevertheless, an emotional undertow swept her up, leaving her awash in unrestrained desire.

They now lay spent, their faces turned to the ceiling, which was visible in the room's barely penetrable darkness. Their breathing was heavy, its rhythm slow and tinged with the exhaustion of lovers. Her words filled the room with the soft sounds that add to the feeling of isolated togetherness lovers experience when their emotions join harmoniously and for a time set them apart from the troubled world around them. Now, however, this moment of bliss had passed its emotional peak, for reality intruded and sent it into the quagmire of trivia, which is viewed by some through distorting lenses that give rise to misconceptions about themselves as well as others.

"You make love with the same fury that you live life," she whispered to him.

"Maybe you're right about that." His words gently ruffled the still air. Both had spoken with their heads lying straight back on their pillows, their words floating upward into empty space.

"For all your scientific reasoning, it seems you have all the makings of a romantic," Gennie said.

He was tempted to shout out his denial, but good sense prevailed. "How did you arrive at that opinion?" The sound of his voice rose noticeably.

The gripping emotions that had embraced both of them in their rare, spiritual communion now edged closer to the periphery of dissolution. She got up and sat herself on the edge of the bed, her feet wiggling in to her bedroom slippers before getting to her feet.

Jim looked up at her, noting the curvaceous blending of her hips with her narrow waist. He leaned back once more on the bed, his hands behind his head, thinking that since he had met Gennie Connors, their affection for one another had brought with it the greatest sense of contentment he had ever known. Yet some impelling force had already begun to drive a destructive wedge into this bond of shared experience, whose end result could only be the rupturing of it. He felt a sense of remorse at this foreboding.

On the other hand, there were no signs of uneasiness on her part as she twisted around to face him. She brushed aside some hair that had fallen down and partially blocked her vision. When she bent down to look at him, she noticed that he had the chagrined look of a small boy whose capricious demands had been rejected outright without any thought or consideration. A maternal protectiveness arose, making her impulsively bend over to kiss him. Kicking off her slippers, she slid down next to him.

"Jim, I've fallen in love with you in a way I can't understand. It's even a mystery to me because I know you're not ready for any lasting commitments." Her smile turned to a frown. "Now I know what it means when someone says they're between a rock and a hard place."

"Right now I couldn't take on any kind of commitment, no matter how much I wanted to. I still haven't the slightest idea of what kind of work I'll end up doing."

His assertion emitted a straightforwardness that detracted from the happy mood that had prevailed from the moment he had entered the apartment. This was the first time that he had candidly responded to what Gennie wished would result from their growing devotion for one another. The openness of his reply surprised her. She reacted with a pained look that was short-lived. The expression on his face changed to one of relief, which also proved transitory. Finally, Jim broke the silence that followed by attempting to appease any hurt feelings that may have arisen from their brief pillow talk.

"It seems that we've just reached a standoff, but I don't think it'll last forever. The odds are I'll be back from my trip sooner than you think." He put his arms around her and drew her tightly to him. She did not resist. Temporary as this situation was, she felt, it still afforded her a great deal more contentment than any generated by her past trespasses into the world of pointless fancies.

She kissed him before lifting her head to whisper, "Love is for now. Talk is for later." She positioned herself to undertake once more the spirited labors of physical love.

They sat next to each other on the sofa, now showered and fully dressed, revitalizing their dissipated energies with cups of strong coffee. Despite the intensity of their lovemaking, each was keenly aware that in the last hour, a gulf had formed between them. The consequences of things said, or left unsaid, had underpinned the likelihood of any binding course of action between them.

"What did you mean by calling me a romantic?" he pressured her.

"It's simple, can't you see? Isn't anyone who demands to take charge of his own destiny a romantic?" Her declaration emerged clothed in joyful triumph.

"I've never thought about it that way," he commented weakly.

"Anyway, it makes you a rare soul, in my mind. And it's one of the things that makes me love you." She leaned over to kiss his cheek.

"I admire the way you rationalize those generalizations of yours," he said convincingly.

"But does that make you love me...now?" Her question came forth with an uneven blend of jest and earnestness.

There was a moment of hesitation before he replied. "How can an incomplete man love a whole woman?" His question seemed a deliberate ploy to fend off an explicit answer. Nevertheless, there was an implicit note of sincerity in this indirect and noncommittal response. Under other circumstances, he may have reshaped reality in order to please her. Now content and free of any physical cravings, he saw no need to resort to adorning the truth with suspect words of adoration and flattery. Besides, no matter how strong his feelings were toward her, he was ill prepared to offer, no less promise, to satisfy her wishes in either the present or the future.

"Anyway," he went on to explain, "I couldn't handle the responsibilities of a domestic life right now, no matter how much I wanted to. I've got to find my way out of the maze I'm in. And to be honest with you, I haven't the slightest idea how."

This was not the first time that Jim had put into words what he knew would be an explicit indication of the course their relationship was destined to take in the near future. The decisiveness of his words quashed all hopes of eliciting any promises from him. She reacted with a hurt look and mocking commentary. "Well, you've got your precious freedom now, and all it's done is riddle you with anxiety."

Jim's composure frittered away, allowing aggression to burst forth.

"Yes, you're right," he erupted angrily. "I'm not proud of the way I've handled myself these last few weeks."

As soon as he stopped speaking, he experienced an inrush of shame for having said what he said, as well as the manner in which he had said it. There was no denying the truth of her disparaging criticism. Getting to his feet, he walked away from the sofa, making an effort to take control of his ruffled pride.

Gennie said nothing. His display of wrath was sufficient proof that she had erred by saying what she did.

After his equanimity was restored, Jim turned to face her and began offering excuses for the meaningless use of his time.

"I'm new at this business of doing nothing, and it seems I'm not very good at it." He stopped speaking and looked away from her.

"Waiting around with nothing to do hasn't been easy for me. But everything should fall in place as soon as Nick and I get started."

She raised herself from the couch, moved toward him, put her arms around his neck and said, "Maybe so…maybe so. We'll just have to wait and see."

"Women are trickery incarnate," he declared, exasperation permeating his words.

"No, sweetie, women can also be loving and damning," came her rejoinder. "And they are known to experience pangs of hunger."

"That also goes for men. So it seems best that I go out and get us some Chinese food."

The expansiveness of his grin reflected his feeling of relief at having their conversation come to an amicable end. He grabbed his jacket from where it lay and started toward the long hallway that led out of the apartment.

Their hunger appeased, they sat in the kitchen, fiddling with their cups of tea. Watching them, anyone would have concluded that they took great pleasure in each other's company. In reality, what bound them together at this moment was their having put out of comprehension's reach the fact that this union of body and spirit was soon to disintegrate. However, Gennie employed an insidious means for undoing this resolve by her casual mention of the likelihood of having to face boredom in the days ahead. It was her way of telling him what would result once they went their separate ways.

The painful recollection of the tedium brought on by his recent misuse of time and energy made Jim Stahr nod sympathetically in response to her prediction. "I've had my share of it these last few weeks. It makes you feel like you're living in a world whose only attribute is monotony."

"But you've always talked about freedom, especially the freedom to choose. Now that you have it, boredom should be the last thing in the world to trouble you." Disappointment showed in her voice and words.

"I'm still looking for a way to use my freedom."

"And how will you know when you find it?" There was no rancor in her question, just doubtful curiosity.

"Whatever it turns out to be, it'll have to meet my need for Cs."

"What are you talking about?" she questioned bitingly, her frustration showing.

"Whatever I finally end up doing, I want it to be constructive creative, contributive, and communicative…just for starters." Signs of weariness were evident in the slow and deliberate way he spoke.

Gennie sat debating whether to propose some actions that he could take that would satisfy both their wishes but quickly came to the conclusion that any suggestion on her part would only upset him. She decided instead to tactfully imply that what he was seeking was nothing more than an unrealistic obsession.

"You're like a pilgrim seeking some promised land," she told him. "And, in a way, that makes you just another dreamer."

He readily perceived that what she had said implied that his planned search harbored as much fantasy as any of her fanciful digressions from reality.

"Maybe." Jim got out of his chair and made straight for the kitchen window that faced the street. Gennie pushed her unfinished cup of tea to the center of the table, got to her feet and strode over to where he stood. By the time she was at his side, she was smiling, in spite of her strong belief that his proposed journey west with Nick Grigoris would not lead him out of his quandary, nor would it afford her any role in its resolution.

Jim reached out to her to press her to him. She showed no signs of displeasure at his having done so. When they kissed, it was absent of any passion. At this moment, their feelings toward each other were those of caring, with the unselfishness of givers devoid of any need for taking. Arms around each other's waists, they stared out the window as the sun gradually eased its way below the city's skyline, its dying light beginning to cast slow-creeping shadows onto the walls of St. Mark's. The wind strengthened and carried aloft some loose newspaper pages, plastering them against the fence that surrounded the church. They watched in silence as darkness edged its way into the world outside the window. The streetlamp turned on, its light bringing into sharper focus the movement on the street below. Jim's attention fixed on the activities of the pedestrians as he had done many times before from this same vantage point.

Gennie's voice jarred him out of his musing. "There's a chance I'll also be leaving New York."

He turned to face her with an incredulous look. "Why would you want to do that?"

"I'm sorry. I guess I forgot to tell you that I received an offer for an internship with the Walker Art Center in Minneapolis." She hesitated, making up her mind whether to say what she was thinking. "I wasn't sure about taking that job, but I've just decided that it would be the best thing for me to do now that you're getting ready to leave. I don't ever want to be alone in this city again."

She took her arm from around his waist, slipped free of his grasp and stepped back. Her eyes moistened. "I don't want to be in the midst of so much activity and not be part of it. More than ever before, I need to belong—to someplace, something or someone."

He left off his attentive watching of the activities on the street and looked at her. "Being alone in this city would make any sane person want to leave," he said, his words nothing more than an attempt to allay a rising feeling of guilt for his being somewhat to blame for her decision. "In a way, we're in the same boat, but for different reasons."

"At least I'll know where I'm going and what's ahead of me." She managed a pitiful smile, while retaining her resolve not to shed tears.

If her remark was meant to taunt him, it failed. However, it did give rise to a feeling of insecurity instead. To rid himself of it, he made a deliberate effort to center his attention on the actions of the pedestrians on the street. He moved his face closer to the cold windowpane, his interest focusing on the quivering shadows that trailed after those who passed under the shaky light of the wind-buffeted streetlamp.

Gennie shuffled closer to him and took hold of his hand. Grief had broken through her buttressed resolve not to cry. The headlights of a passing vehicle intensified the light entering through the window, which gave added luster to the teardrops that slid down her cheeks. Jim failed to take any notice of them.

"Perhaps we should make the most of whatever time we have together," he suggested in an effort to steer the conversation away from any further depressive talk.

"Yes," she answered without any show of resentment, having sealed the emotional breach in her resolution not to shed tears as quickly as the breakthrough had occurred. "Yes, but no matter what we do, it'll only hold out the same kind of promise as those imaginative games that I used to play. Anyway, I'm an old hand at doing that." She reached up and patted his face as he stood gazing out the window.

The noisy whipping of the wind came to a sudden halt. The mutative change from disruptive sound to a calming silence made Jim break off his observations and comply with an instinctive wish to bring Gennie closer to him. With their arms around each other, they turned to stare out at the nighttime panorama, the distance between them and it seeming so vast that it created feelings of isolation that enabled them to deal with their joys and sorrows without any regard for the needs and wishes of anyone but themselves.

Chapter 41

Their departure date was finally set. Just five days remained before Jim Stahr was to meet Nick Grigoris at the bus station in midtown Manhattan to begin their journey. They had come to this agreement a few days earlier in a hurried telephone conversation. Neither of them had taken note that they were to leave on Valentine's Day. Had Jim done so, he might have seen the irony of his severing his only continuous relationship with a woman on the very day that celebrated love.

Jim Stahr had met with Gennie Connors several times since their last rendezvous in her apartment. These meetings had been pleasant but unusually casual, as both had resigned themselves to the fact that they were soon to go their separate ways. It was during one of these last get-togethers that he discovered a clear-cut deficiency within himself. His habitual reliance on the use of reason to resolve issues of all sorts left him ill-prepared to articulate what he emotionally derived from his relationship with her, either by the use of rationalistic terminology or those absurd flatteries that at times some women seem to prize more than truth itself. This shortcoming placed him in a paradoxical situation, whereby he thought himself a sentient person but psychologically handicapped by his inability to express his true sentiments, and even more so, his passion. In the end, he fixed the blame on an attitude formed by his wartime experience as a teenage soldier. The first lesson he learned in surveying the aftermath of battle was the absolute necessity for reason to dominate emotion if one was to guard against sentiment of any kind, whether it was in relation to friend or foe. The suppression of feelings, even those of pain, had become for him the only badge of honor that warranted respect. Dominating his emotions had become a self-indoctrinated discipline, one that he seemed unable to alter, although he had made sporadic attempts to do so since his return home at the war's end. Conceivably, that may have been the reason for his inability to openly refer to those closest to him as friends.

The morning was an exceptionally cold one. It forced him to retreat indoors more frequently than in his previous meanderings through the city's streets. Walking along upper Broadway, he spotted a drugstore that had a small soda fountain. Jim went in and ordered coffee. He sat taking sips from his cup without bothering to remove his coat. Boredom and aloneness decided him to phone Gennie. He finished his coffee with several quick gulps, walked to the store's phone booth, and placed his call, hoping that she would still be at home. She had told him at one of their recent encounters that she had several job interviews slated for this week, and her curiosity about these job offers made her put off accepting the internship position at the art museum in Minneapolis. Much to Jim's surprise, it was Peggy Troy who answered the phone.

"Jim, is that you?" she blurted out. She did not give him a chance to reply before informing him that she had just gotten off the phone with his mother.

"She told me that you went job hunting. Boy, am I glad you called!" Relief was evident in the intensity of her speech.

"Why?" he asked anxiously. "Has something happened to Gennie?"

"No, no, she's fine. I wanted her to come with me, but she had an important job interview to go to." A moment of silence followed before Peggy implored him to meet her in a matter of hours. As if trying to appeal to his sense of loyalty, she informed him that Frank Colucci would also be there. "It's an important matter for both of us. Please!"

"Sure, why not? I've nothing else to do. Where and at what time?" Anything was better than walking the streets, he told himself. Jim listened as she asked Frank where would be an appropriate place to meet. He waited patiently.

"Can you be at city hall at eleven sharp? We'll wait for you on the steps in front of the building." Her question sounded more like a demand than a request.

"I'll be there, eleven on the nose." Inquisitiveness made him ask, "What's this all about?"

"Oh, you'll see," she crooned. "Please don't be late. As a favor to me," she begged.

After a quick glance at his wristwatch, he told her, "I'll be there! Don't you worry."

"We'll be waiting for you!" Peggy ended the conversation on a cheerful note, as if all of her former worries had magically vanished.

He put the phone back in place and remained seated. Even having a firm commitment to do something failed to raise his dampened spirits.

They were standing with hands clasped, on top of the steps leading into city hall, so absorbed in each other that they seemed immune to the raucous cacophony of the wing-flapping pigeons that circled above them. It was easy to discern that a strong emotional bond had formed between them. When Jim drew closer, the mutual look of adoration on their faces quickly verified his prediction. He stood a short distance away thinking that any interruption on his part would be a crude indiscretion, so he decided to wait until they took notice of him. When they finally did, they came bounding down the steps in a noisy greeting, which caused some passing pedestrians to lose their smug indifference and turn to stare at them, their faces coming alive with curiosity.

Taking positions on each side of him, they made their way around park benches, people, and trash baskets, pulling Jim along with them. They hurried across a narrow street that paralleled Broadway and began twisting their way through the crowd, the majority of whom were moving in the opposite direction. When they reached the municipal building, they entered and glanced around for the nearest elevators. Frank pointed to them before hurrying away to hold open one that had just opened its doors. Jim noticed that their conspiratorial humor began to fade as soon as the elevator started upward.

"What's this all about?" Jim asked with feigned innocence, his suspicions having turned to certainty.

"We need you to be a witness," Peggy stated stiffly.

"Do you want me to witness Frank writing poetry on toilet walls?" he continued with exaggerated sobriety.

"No! No! Nothing like that," Frank blurted out with an uncharacteristic display of vexation. The elevator door opened and he led them down a long hallway, its marble walls and floor reflecting a bureaucratic coldness. At the far end, they stopped. "This is it!" Frank announced, pointing up at a metal placard engraved with the words "Marriage Bureau."

"Are you definitely going to go through with this? Well, what do you know!" Jim exclaimed with a false look of surprise. He found himself gently eased through the door before he could make any further comments. Peggy sat down with him on a bench while Frank went over to a clerk seated behind a large desk and handed him several legal-sized papers. They were checked, stamped, shuffled by him and then inserted into a nondescript envelope and given back to Frank. The official employed gestures to direct

Frank to the wedding chapel. Peggy and Jim rose and followed him out of the office.

They had only proceeded a short distance down the long hallway when Peggy suddenly stopped and looked at Frank with an open display of nervousness. "The ring! Did you bring the ring?"

"I didn't forget it," he assured her, and handed her the large envelope containing the required marriage documents. He started searching his pockets, first calmly, then with a growing agitation.

Fighting to take control of her thoughts and emotions, she instructed Frank to stop and think. "You told me that you were going to hide it in a place where it couldn't possibly get lost. Your special place," she reminded him.

"Yes, it's so special that I can't even remember where it is," he whined, visibly flustered.

Both Peggy and Jim held back their immediate inclination to laugh, while Frank scowled with displeasure as he once again began a search of all his pockets. This second effort produced only a shrug.

"In twenty minutes, it'll be our turn to go before the judge," Frank declared, flinging his arms upward as if beseeching aid from one of fate's apostles. Disgusted with himself, he jammed his hands into his trouser pockets.

"I wish Hector was here," he said in a monotone of despair.

"Why do you say that?" Peggy demanded.

"At least he'd have a cigar band we could use. That's why," he snapped at her.

Peggy burst out in unrestrained laughter, taking no heed of his growing irritability.

"There's still one place you still haven't checked," Jim stated calmly.

"Where?" Frank muttered.

"Right there!" Jim pointed to the breast pocket of Frank's suit jacket.

Frank reached into it and withdrew the ring. "My secret hiding place," he exclaimed, and let out a sigh of relief. "Here, take it. Take it!" he pleaded, and handed it to Jim.

They walked briskly to the chapel's waiting room and entered. A thin-framed woman sat behind a desk situated on one side of a closed set of double doors. She stopped writing when they entered, peered up with a broad smile and motioned for them to approach.

"You're right on time. Can I have your paperwork, please?"

Peggy walked over to her and handed over the envelope Frank had given her. She then stepped back to stand next to him and clasped his hand.

The woman removed its contents and started entering information into a leather bound ledger. Without looking up, she politely informed them that they would need two witnesses to sign the marriage certificate that she would be preparing for the officiating judge's signature.

The expressions on their faces registered despair. They stood eyeing each without saying a word.

Their failure to respond made the woman look up. Observing their dismay, she told them, "Don't worry. I'll be your other witness. Take a seat, it won't be very long." She pointed to a wooden bench that ran along one wall of the room. All three retreated to it and sat down. The clerk resumed making entries into her ledger.

A short while later, the strains of Mendelssohn's "Wedding March" came from inside the chapel, signifying that the wedding service in progress had ended. Soon the doors swung open and the bride and groom exited followed by a boisterous group of men and women. This joyous bedlam swept away all the hallmarks of reverence. The raucous babble of excited voices gradually dwindled to absolute silence after the entire wedding party exited the room and unhurriedly made their way down the long hallway that led to the elevators.

The transition from the uproar of celebrants to that of an alien noiselessness left Peggy with a baffling sense of exclusion. She entwined her arms around those of the men on either side of her, hoping their closeness would help rid her of this troubling feeling. The clerk pointed out where they were supposed to sign their names on several documents. All of them approached her desk and nervously did so, the woman and Jim Stahr signing their names in places set aside for witnesses. Taking with her the marriage license and several other papers, she instructed them to follow her into the marriage chamber. The judge stood waiting for them, dressed in his black judicial robe. The clerk handed him a sheet of paper with their names printed in large letters on it and informed him that she was acting as the second witness. He nodded his approval and introduced himself. The woman moved back to stand next to Jim.

As soon as the proceedings started, the judge's voice took on a sonorous pitch. He read with self-confidence and ease from a thin pamphlet that lay in the center of a wide lectern that stood in front of him, his words coming forth in a practiced cadence, distinct and emotionless, the only hesitation occurring when he bent over to read the names of the bride and groom with exaggerated clarity. The constant flow of words ceased briefly, when he halted to ask Peggy and Frank the unchanging and proverbial questions as to their acceptance of the commitments they were making to one other. After enunciating some customary phrases, Jim stepped forward and passed the gold wedding band to Frank who, in turn, slipped it on Peggy's finger.

The ending words of the ceremony were terse and familiar: "and by the power vested in me by the state of New York, I pronounce you man and wife." After advising the groom to kiss the bride, the judge waited for the clerk to hand him the marriage license. He placed it next to the pamphlet that he had been reading from, which now lay closed atop the lectern, reached under his robe to remove a fountain pen, and signed it with a flourish, allowing the ink to dry before handing it back to her.

A recorded rendering of the "Wedding March" filled the austere interior as the newlyweds and their witnesses started toward the exit doors. The music ceased playing, however, before they had time to pass through them. Their return to the waiting room left them enveloped in a thought-provoking silence that promised auspicious expectations for tomorrow but did not afford the slightest inkling of what they would be.

The woman clerk discarded the original envelop that lay on top of her desk and inserted the marriage license into a new white envelope, embossed with the New York state seal and handed it to Frank. They thanked the friendly clerk for serving as a witness before making their way out the door. As they headed for the elevators, their collective mood was more subdued than when they first entered the building.

The aftermath of their civil wedding was radically different from the one that had preceded it. Once outside the confines of the municipal building, Jim felt duty-bound to turn their apathy into a festive frame of mind. He insisted that they accept his invitation to celebrate their marriage. Frank concurred with a nod of his head, took hold of Peggy's hand, and followed Jim as he zigzagged his way through the heavy traffic moving along lower Broadway to the Longchamps Restaurant across the street.

It would have been less troubling for him had they reacted to their marriage in the customary fashion. Now they sat wordlessly awaiting the arrival of their martinis, their only distraction being an occasional outburst of laughter from a nearby table. Husband and wife appeared lost in their own ruminations. Jim Stahr, nonetheless, thought it best to break the silence.

"Going to London for graduate work, Frank, will make for lots of new experiences for you." A prosaic comment at best, he judged, but it was at least a start, although a weak one, in his endeavor to fill the conversational void. He could have gone on enumerating specifically other things they might possibly encounter, but realized that doing so would not have added any substance to the dialogue he hoped would evolve between them.

"Yes, but we won't be sailing to England for another month, at least," Frank said eagerly.

"And with a new wife," added Peggy.

"Yes, of course, let's not forget a new wife," Jim said with a grin.

Frank reached over to touch her hand reassuringly. "It's not a grave error if Jim forgets, Peggy. You've got to start worrying when I do."

She turned to face him with a look of bemusement before saying dismissively, "That'll never happen, rest assured. Not if you love me as much as I love you." There was a guarded intimacy in her words, and both men understood that the statement carried a clear implication—a promise of sexual satisfaction that would leave little room for any competitive challenge. For a moment, her words made Jim feel like some eavesdropper who by chance overhears the extravagant praise and vows that lovers exchange in privacy without fear of ridicule. He hid his uneasiness by drinking from his nearly empty glass.

Frank broke the interlude of silence created by Peggy's words. Looking directly at Jim, he declared without his customary passion, "You know it hasn't been a completely happy beginning for us."

Jim glanced up, puzzled as to what Frank intended to convey. He waited for his friend to provide some further clarification of what was meant by what he had said.

Frank threw a precautionary glance at his bride before resuming. "Last week was like a foretaste of hell. Unfortunately, we went to visit our parents to tell them that we intended to marry. Well, as expected, it ended up in that tribal adult-child-versus-parent confrontation. I'm sure you would know what that's like."

Disappointment was evident in the shrug of his shoulders. "It was a scarring defeat for both of us."

More to stimulate conversation than from any real need to know, Jim asked Frank what had brought on this falling-out.

"There were too many differences—that's basically it," he declared."

Apparently, whatever conflicts may have arisen from their proposed marriage had offended Frank more than they had Peggy.

"Some individuals make more use of beliefs that separate people than those that unite them," Jim offered in reply. He waved a hand in the air in a sign of disgust Strangely enough, he felt that even talking about negative situations lent a more positive atmosphere to this postnuptial gathering than did their initial silence. The acceptance of this premise prodded him to resume his efforts to reverse the emotional climate that had bordered on despondency from the moment they had entered the restaurant.

Jim spied the look of hurt that flickered across Frank's face even before he had finished speaking and intuitively surmised that his friend may have been treated in a condescending manner by some affluent member of Peggy's family. His reference to there being too many differences had inferred that such an occurrence may have taken place. Hoping to allay his friend's anguish if this was truly so, he intoned in a prideful manner.

"For me, snobbery is the weapon of the fainthearted." Jim paused in order to remove the olive from his martini. "And when you get down to the nitty-gritty," he pressed on, "it's society's weaklings, those who are so lacking in self-confidence that they have to resort to arrogance to hide their shortcomings." Peggy glanced at him with a look that showed her uneasiness, if not outright hurt, by the direction the conversation was taking. Her look made him stop talking and sip from his glass. Nevertheless, some uncontrollable impulse compelled him to say something— words, he knew, could only trouble Peggy Troy even more. "Snobbery is just a ploy used by those trying to inculcate their biases into the mainstream of people's thinking. Like propaganda, it's just another cultural power play." Satisfying this compulsion left him with feelings of shame and regret.

"Maybe you have the ability to fend it off with logic, but I react to it emotionally," Frank commented, a weak smile shedding his look of melancholia.

"Hurt feelings can make you forget that ignorance is the prime motivator of prejudice," Jim countered, "and snobbery is nothing more than ignorance's shield."

"Then you know that there's no way of fighting it," Frank argued.

"To be honest, I could never tackle snobbery and win."

Frank grinned. "This is one time that defeat merits a toast." He waved his hand to attract the attention of their waitress and ordered another round of martinis.

Jim drank from his newly arrived glass feeling grateful that the atmosphere had changed for the better. He found added pleasure in being immersed in the exchange of thoughts and ideas, like those that shaped the heated discussions in the university's cafeteria. But the current need to economically fend for himself, made this pursuit empty of any practical value in providing realistic solutions to those concerns that truly mattered now. His reasoning made him want to put an end to this discussion. "Why don't you just write off the events of this past week as just another one of life's demoralizing experiences?" he advised them.

"Here we go again with Jim's obsession—experience," Frank proclaimed with a newfound stridency.

"Well, Frank, isn't life all about our personal involvement with experience?" Jim challenged aggressively, his intake of martinis unbridling any self-constraint over his speech and mannerisms.

"Yes, but what counts," Frank answered, "is how you react to these real life situations." Peggy's silence began to trouble him. He suspected that the subject of their previous discussion might have injured her feelings. In an effort to soothe any such hurt, he turned to her and asked, "Well, what're your thoughts on the subject, darling?"

At first she failed to respond. When she did, however, it was with a slight bow, apparently made unsteady by her intake of martinis. "I've listened to you, friend, and to you, lover." She stopped to give recognition to the role each had played in her life with a short nod in the appropriate direction. "If you'll allow me, I'd like to provide a new insight into Jim's infatuation with life's experience, or his obsession as you've put it, but not so aptly, dear husband."

"Go ahead…I'm listening." Jim stated approvingly.

"For both of you, I'm afraid, that experience is tied to novelty—a unique happening. It seems to me that men have a masculine twist to the word experience. Like young, untested bulls, you want to storm into the ring of life breathing fire with your horns erect." She stopped for a moment to catch her breath, and added, "And every time you do, you expect to make a discovery, or be challenged, by something new. It seems to me that men's response to repeated experience wanes with time."

"Would you have us be any other way?" Frank protested.

She turned to throw a smug look at him before saying, "But, as a woman, I can respond to repetitive experience, whether it's good or bad, with the same intensity of feeling."

"Like lovemaking," Frank offered with a leer.

"Like lovemaking…and I'm banking on it," she said firmly.

"But just a minute, Peggy, I never claimed that every experience had to be different in order to be enjoyed," Jim objected, becoming mindful of a growing lightheadedness.

Peggy disregarded his remark. "Love, in one form or another, generates feelings we treasure, because it's the one human experience that we want to remain unchanged and unbroken." She could have continued justifying her views on women's preference for constancy, but decided against it. Peggy blamed emotional distress, not the drinks, as the cause for her reluctance to do so.

After all, she told herself, the primary ingredients on this wedding day had been a mix of anxiety and tension, flavored by an all-pervasive sense of uncertainty—not the expected jubilation that her youthful longings had invariably promised.

Frank's chin dropped, his eyeglasses slipping from their perch on the bridge of his nose. He stared at her in silent admiration.

"You'll make an ideal wife for a poet, Peggy," was Jim's approving comment.

There was no reaction on Peggy's part in response to his words of praise. She gazed at him with a troubled look instead. "What's going to happen to you, Jim?"

"I'll be heading west with Nick," he replied listlessly.

She was about to ask about his continuing his relationship with Gennie, but some inner sense of caution held her back.

"And with what specific objective do you have in mind?" Frank's words were barbed with a goading sharpness.

"I don't know. But I'll be looking."

"For what?" Frank verbally jabbed at him.

"For something I really want to do."

Seeing that Jim's martini glass was empty, the waitress hurried over to their table and picked it up. He, in turn, ordered another round of drinks. A short time later, she returned with three long-stemmed glasses on a tray and set them on the table, her practiced smile remaining fixed in place as she backed away and left.

In Frank's case, the mix of drink and conversation had helped dampen the emotional hurt inflicted by their recent familial conflicts. What he now found troubling was his friend's decision to journey in search for something vague and uncertain, and in a direction governed in the main by whimsy. Jim, he realized, was too set in his ways to respond to any constructive advice he could offer. All the same, Frank felt compelled to warn him of the consequences of taking a path that led nowhere. This compulsion set in motion an internal quest for some poetic imagery that could admonish but not provoke.

"Friend," he started, the pitch and tone of the single word readily familiar to his listeners and making them aware that Frank's frame of mind had once again assumed its characteristic amiability, "your search will be like tiptoeing on the edge of a giant cup. It may appear graceful and challenging to the viewers, but all it takes is one misstep to hit bottom."

"If that's truly the case, there are two ways one can fall. Yes, on one side it's the bottom alright, but on the other side there may be an endless road with many junctions, and one of them is where I'll want to stop and say that this is where I belong. For me, the risk is worth taking."

"I'm glad that we know exactly where we're heading." Frank's response was a tacit abandonment of his pursuit to dissuade.

They sipped at the remainder of their martinis for a time, quiet and reflective, all acknowledging to themselves that they had imbibed more than was warranted by the occasion. None of them had been mindful of the time they had spent in this unorthodox celebration of marriage, although all three were fully aware that this could be their last get-together for a long time to come, or perhaps forever. The signal to depart came when Frank Colucci held out a door key to Jim Stahr, saying, "Here's a parting gift for our stalwart witness. It's my key to Peggy's apartment."

"Go ahead. Please, take it!" Peggy exhorted, almost begging him to do so. When he did not reach for it, she tried to convince him to take the key. "I still have another one...so take it. The rent's been paid until the end of the month. When you get tired of walking the streets, you can use it to get out of the cold and rest. Go ahead." As an afterthought, she added, "I still have to get all my personal belongings out of there, but that can wait." Smiling broadly, she announced, "We're planning to drive up to Canada on our honeymoon. My car is parked right near the apartment. And as soon as Frank can get his things, we'll be on our way. I'm packed and ready to go." The sound of her words exhibited both eagerness and enthusiasm.

Mumbling thanks, he took the key and slipped it into one of the side pockets of his jacket, thinking that there would never be a real need to use it.

As he was doing so, Frank said, "It's only a key, but it may bring you luck. Look at the prize I've won with it."

Jim's reply was a question. "When's Gennie due back? Did she say?"

"Sometime later today. There was an interview for a job offer that she could not pass up—it was supposed to be an exceptional opportunity. Because of that we felt that it would be wrong for us to insist that she be a witness at our wedding. That would have been asking too much. By the way, didn't she tell you?" Peggy asked with a puzzled look.

The look of surprise on Jim's face provided the answer. When the waitress arrived with the bill, he paid it, overcoming Frank's vigorous attempt to snatch it away.

Chapter 42

They had moved unsteadily out of the restaurant and onto the street. They stood in a tight circle, annoyed by sporadic windy blasts that kept pushing them apart. They were troubled as to what to do or say, the intake of liquor having diminished their abilities to give expression to their feelings regarding the impending end of their long-standing friendship. Yet, the events of this day had only strengthened their bond of camaraderie. They stood facing each other saying nothing. Jim Stahr took the initiative to break the silence.

"I'm sure that we'll end up meeting somewhere and sooner than you think. Good luck." He stepped forward to shake Frank's hand. Peggy Troy reached out to hug him.

Frank stood thinking of what more to say. The only words that came to mind were devoid of sentiment but did have a ring of optimism to them. "We'll meet again, friend. Soon, I hope."

"Until then, take care—of both your wife and yourself." Jim threw a salute, before turning away to head westward toward the Hudson River without knowing why. After going a short distance, he felt the impulse to turn around to take one more glimpse of them, although he long ago resolved never to do so when saying good-byes. It was a personal quirk gleaned in the military, for it was considered bad luck to look back after bidding a final farewell to anyone. This time sentimentality battled myth, and the former came up the victor. When he did turn, he caught sight of Frank leading Peggy by the hand as they slipped and dodged around the passing vehicles. Both were laughing. Frank momentarily took his eyes off the oncoming traffic to look back at Peggy, who trailed after him, perhaps to give some jocose warning, when the bus struck them, the impact sending them hurtling through the air. Upon striking the ground, their bodies rolled along the pavement before coming to rest in lopsided, contorted heaps.

Jim stood frozen in place, his legs refusing to respond to his mind's command to run. His attention focused on the large white envelope containing the marriage license as it went spiraling upward in twisting gyrations, the sharp wind sending it sailing over the tops of the automobiles that had screeched to a halt alongside the bus that had struck them. His gaze was still riveted on it when his legs finally responded. And when they did, his blind dash forward was rudely cut short when his chest tore into the metal support rod of a lowered storefront awning, knocking him to the ground, his head striking the pavement. Droplets of blood slid down one corner of his mouth as he dazedly got to his feet.

A shooting pain tore across his chest. He reached up to rub it. Confused, he was still unsure whether what he had witnessed was nothing more than a cruel hoax of his imagination. He became intensely aware of the dissonance that filled the air, drowning his senses in a quagmire of confusion. The harsh shriek of wheel brakes, the blaring of horns and the blowing of police whistles joined to add mental agony to his physical pain. The most grating sound of all was the voices shouting senseless and fearful commands. This time, however, his mind's attempt to deny reality by deeming it a trick played on him by some inborn maliciousness ended in failure. The collapse of the protective machinery of disbelief released an all-consuming rage. Angry tears blurred his vision. Some hidden constriction began to block his windpipe, forcing his lungs to struggle for air. Still gasping, he dashed forward, impelled by fury. He bolted past the crowd of people rushing to the street corner. Anxiety took hold when he spied the ever-growing line of bystanders blocking his way as he neared the curb.

After thrusting his way through them, he caught sight of the twisted bodies of his friends lying lifeless in front of him. Their arms were still outstretched as if reaching out to take hold of the white envelope that was no longer in sight. Some irrational impulse made him step off the curb and hurry to where they now lay silent and unmoving. He sank down and rested on his haunches within arm's length of them. When he turned to gaze at their faces, he was bewildered by the vision of their contorted and bloody features, which gave them the look of strangers. He began to shake uncontrollably as he stared down on their unrecognizable faces. Some mystifying force rose up directing him to reach out and touch them, but as his fingers drew near, his courage failed him.

The crowd stared at him with fascination and shock, an eerie quiet permeating the center of the irregular ring formed by them. Jim was no longer aware of their presence He sat with his upper body bent slightly forward, arms outstretched, frozen in place, fear paralyzing his wish to stroke and caress, although an opposing force urged him to do so. Mind and senses locked in this hypnotic dialectic, as if time and motion were immobilized and unchanging. The awareness of warm liquid seeping into his pant legs failed to break the firm hold of this trance. Only when an approaching wail of a siren tore through the unnatural stillness around him, did its ripping cries burst the undetectable fetters that had bound him in its cataleptic grip. Again, a violent frenzy took hold. Jim balled his fists, pressed them into the slowly expanding pools of blood forming around him, and clumsily pushed himself erect. Tucking his cheek against his shoulder, he forced his way through the huddle of onlookers.

Once outside of the circle of bystanders, he started racing through the streets possessed by an unwavering obsession to reach the river. As he twisted his way around oncoming pedestrians, the same intense awareness of wrongdoing, which had haunted him once before, now took unchallenged command of his thinking. Back then, he had been witness to others falling in crumpled heaps, the result of their having been cut down by enemy gunfire. At that time, he had responded to the cries of the wounded in the same way that he had to today's pulsing wail of an ambulance. He had run away to make his way to safety, convinced that by crossing a river, his fear would be bested and tranquility restored. The memory of what took place that day never failed to tear through his contrived defenses, which he had evolved over time to absolve him of what he had come to believe was an uncourageous act. Yet, that experience left him with feelings of guilt that still haunted him. Today, however, there would be no need to attend to the wounds of others. His friends lay dead on the street behind him.

He broke into a sprint as he neared the river's edge. His mind was locked in the same silent and repetitious mantra as it had done that agonizing time in the past when the snow-crunching sound of sound of enemy soldiers drawing closer sent him racing away— *Run...coward...run!...Run...coward...run!...Run, coward, run!*

Then, those words had kept cadence with the striking of each army boot against a snow-flecked riverside path. These same words now beat rhythmically, keeping time with the pounding of each shoe as it struck the concrete pavement. When Jim Stahr reached the Hudson's edge, he stood and stared across its wide expanse, overcome by the despair of those who have conceded all is lost. There was no bridge in sight, and the river was too wide to cross.

A short guardrail separated the land from the river. He wiped away the blood that still trickled from the corner of his mouth from the fall he had taken. A feeling of wetness made him glance down at his open hand. Streaks of fresh blood mixed with perspiration discolored his palm and fingers. He erased this image by clenching his fist. But it was instantly replaced by dark stains of encrusted blood that covered the backs of his fingers, blotted up when he got to his feet and started his panic-driven rush to the water's edge. To steady himself, he gripped both hands around the protective railing and stared at the Jersey shoreline, unable to stem the past from forcing its way into the present, bringing with it a need to placate feelings of self-reproach for what he now believed was another unfeeling flight taken without any regard for others— living or dead. Taking a firmer hold of the top rung of the iron barrier, he bent over and vomited into the garbage-strewn water, his distraught thwarting any attempt to mollify an unbearable sense of despair.

Chapter 43

There was no specific point of transition from nightmarish slumber to that of vexing wakefulness, the conscious state making itself known to Jim by a dull thudding in his forehead. His mother could not hide her repugnance when shaking him awake. The clothes that he had worn yesterday now lay in a twisted heap on the floor, filling the room with the rancid odors of alcohol, perspiration, and vomit. She informed him that Nick Grigoris had phoned early that morning, but she had not wanted to wake him. Jim acknowledged that he understood what she said with a muffled groan. Satisfied, his mother left the room.

Instead of getting out of bed, he immersed himself again in the replaying of what had taken place the day before and with the same dizzying repetitiveness that had plagued his sleep. There seemed no way out of this dilemma. His mind was unyielding in its refusal to end its constant repetition of the very events that he was trying to blot from memory.

A short time later, the high-pitched ringing of the phone in the apartment's narrow hallway brought him to full wakefulness. It was sure to be Nick, he surmised, anxious to report, as shocking and new, what already had become afflictive and old. He slid out of bed and walked unsteadily to the phone. When he picked it up, all he could utter was a toneless hello. There was no immediate response to his phlegmatic greeting. When Nick did begin speaking, his voice was colorless, as if he had deliberately rehearsed what he was going to say with the intention of masking any show of emotion.

"I've got some bad news for you, Jim. It's very bad."

"I already know all about it!" he responded irritably. "Don't ask me how."

Jim heard Nick's sigh of relief.

Each waited for the other to continue. The smell of coffee brewing wafted into the room and briefly diverted his attention.

Nick spoke first. "Damn. It's in all the morning newspapers." He then asked tentatively, "Is there anything we ought to do?"

Nick's earnest concern, along with his willingness to be helpful, left Jim with feelings of shame for having spoken to him in such an abrupt manner. "Sorry, Nick, I didn't mean to bark at you," he said by way of apology. "I'm not much good about formalities. So, maybe you could do a better job in dealing with their families."

Nick did not balk at the suggestion. Although it was not a welcome task, there was no doubt in his mind that he could carry it out with his usual efficiency. "Look, I'll do it," he said. "But how about getting together afterward?"

"Yeah, okay. We can meet at Stephan's after you get back." Jim's suggestion lacked any real show of enthusiasm.

"What time?"

Jim glanced up at the nearby wall clock. It was a little past ten. The lateness of the hour left him somewhat startled. He could not remember at what time he had finally arrived home, nor how many hours he had spent drifting through the streets after he fled the scene of the accident.

"I could be there by five. Can you make it by then?"

Without giving it much thought, Jim replied, "Don't worry, I'll be there."

He replaced the phone and ambled back to his bedroom, his mind already rejecting the idea of attending any funeral services. After witnessing friends die in battle, a chaplain's words or ritual prayers—however well intentioned—had never helped ease the pain of their loss. The death of friends like Frank and Peggy was inestimable, and the healing process required time, as well as the need to devise one's own ways of dealing with their anguish.

After having shaved, showered, and put on some fresh clothes, he walked out of the apartment and started for the subway without taking time to drink the coffee his mother had brewed.

On the train, he braced himself against its swaying motion by taking a firm grip on a nearby vertical pole. There were several empty seats nearby, but he was resolved to stand apart from all others. His thoughts shifted to a search for the cause of yesterday's tragedy.

It was almost noontime when he walked out of the subway station. Stuffing his hands into his coat pockets, he crossed Fourteenth Street and entered Union Square Park. The red and orange glow of flames from a fire burning in a metal trash basket stood out in sharp contrast to the sunless surroundings. Children ran past him, armed with assorted pieces of wood and rolled-up newspapers to toss into it.

He sauntered over to stand behind the circle of shouting kids, who stood clapping their gloved hands a safe distance from the flames. Their laughter cut short his introspective enumerating of the possible actions he could have taken to alter events that would have averted the death of his friends. The youngsters pranced around the burning rubbish seemingly free of any cares. A smile crossed his face when he tried and failed to recall the last time he had felt that happy-go-lucky.

While his eyes remained fixed on the children, his thoughts drifted back to unpredictable events that had occurred in the past, when reason proved ineffectual in providing explanations as to what had caused them. At such times, he had to admit, emotions took command and sent his spirits either soaring or plunging into despair.

He wondered how Gennie Connors would react when told of what had taken place during her absence. In all probability, she was now alone in the apartment and with no one to turn to except himself. He walked away from the cavorting children and headed toward a public telephone booth just outside the park.

His call to Gennie Connor's apartment went unanswered. He hung up the phone and stood debating what to do next. More than four hours remained before he was to meet with Nick Grigoris. Hunger, more than the cold, made him enter a nearby restaurant, where he slid into a booth and waited for someone to take his order.

After he finished eating, he stared at his coffee cup, engrossed in his thoughts about the future. The need to leave the city with Nick was no longer a matter for procrastination, he told himself. The collective events of recent weeks had converted what he had once considered as whim into exigent need. It was an action highly desired and crucial. Pushing his coffee cup to one side, its contents having turned cold and tasteless, he stood up and made ready to leave.

He leisurely walked out to the street, hoping for something to happen that would bring an end to the rueful pessimism that now seemed bent on faulting him for having failed to prevent yesterday's tragic turn of events. Logic had given rise to the conviction that had he taken even the most insignificant action, it would have varied the timing of their parting. The principal factor in the catastrophe, he admitted to himself, was the interaction between time and event in which he had played a decisive part. This conclusion left him obsessed with the need to ascertain the various ways he could have acted that would have kept his friends out of harm's way. The exploration of all such possibilities was preceded by a hypothetical *if:*

> *...If I hadn't taken so long to say good-bye...if I had said something more...or less...if I had taken them to another restaurant...if we had not had so many martinis...if I refused to take possession of the apartment key...if...if...if...*

These and other ifs were added to his mind's growing list of imagined scenarios. The futility of what he was doing suddenly struck him. He could not reorder the past, so there was no sense in torturing himself with these ruminations. This realization made him try to fix his mind on something else. The idea popped into his thoughts that maybe a visit to the university's cafeteria, with its familiar sounds of student laughter and conversation, might buoy his spirits.

Crowded around the large table where his group had habitually met were new undergraduates, each taking turns to express feelings or ideas with sophomoric intensity. Their opinions now sounded frivolous and empty of any real purpose. Yet, just a short while ago, the same sort of discourses had constituted one of the most gratifying pursuits of his student days. He stood listening to the diverse views expounded by them and found himself envying their lack of concern about the real pressures that dominated life outside on the streets. There was no way of avoiding the fact that whatever perceptivity he may have acquired from participating in such discussions was yet to be tested. Lately, he had begun to suspect that for some people, the drive to accumulate knowledge as an end in itself might prove an indiscernible opiate, the kind whose derived pleasures had value only for those so addicted. The thought that he may have become such a victim made him hurry out of the building.

He spent the remainder of the afternoon wandering through several bookstores and a public library in order to rest, to keep warm and to pass the time. It was not nostalgia, or habit, that made him return to the same places he had frequented throughout his years at the university. Doing so helped dispel his troubling thoughts. At times, he would make calls to Gennie Connors from public phone booths, but all of them had gone unanswered.

Nick Grigoris was quick to note the dark smudges under Jim Stahr's eyes as soon as he slid onto the bar stool next to him. They muttered their greetings to one another and lapsed into silence, both visibly manifesting fatigue brought on by what each had done this day. Nick ordered some draft beer by pointing to one of the large tap handles behind the bar. Stephan, the bartender, drew down on it, filled two glasses and slid them in their direction. Brooding over the recent ill-fated events dampened Nick's desire to speak. Saying nothing seemed the only panacea for purging his pensive reflections. He sat sipping from his glass until hunger made him break his silence.

"How about some food? I haven't eaten all day," he said.

Jim agreed. His mumbled okay was barely audible.

Grabbing both beer glasses, Nick led the way into a small dining room at the rear of the tavern, its gloomy interior lit by a single, dust-speckled bulb. As they seated themselves in one of the two available booths, the bartender's wife poked her head from behind the open kitchen door and waited to take their order.

"Goulash," Nick requested in a loud voice. Jim ordered the same thing.

Jim looked up to face Nick squarely for the first time since they had entered the tavern. Under the weak light of the room, he noted the drawn and puffy features of his face. This was ample proof that this day's activities had taken a toll on Nick's vitality and spirit.

"Who did you get to see?" Jim asked.

"I managed to see both families." Nick hesitated, uncertain whether to continue relating the day's events.

"Well, how did it go?" Jim persisted, puzzled by Nick's reluctance to say anything more.

"Rough. I didn't stay too long at either place." Nick drew his lips tightly together in a show of agitation. "You know, their parents kept pressing me to tell them what the two of them were doing together when the accident happened."

"What did you tell them?"

"The truth."

"Which was?"

"I didn't know."

An image of the white envelope that contained the wedding license whirling through the air by the gusting wind flashed into Jim's thoughts. It now dawned on him that he might be the only one of their mutual acquaintances, as well as both their families for that matter, who knew that they had become husband and wife. He sat gazing at the empty space ahead of him with a vacant stare, totally engrossed in a mental search as to how best to utilize this information. From the little he knew about their parents, informing them that Frank Colucci and Peggy Troy had wed would only have added resentment to their feelings of grief over their respective loss. If his assumption proved to be a valid one, than prudence cautioned that he conceal the truth. His preoccupation with this matter came to an abrupt halt when Nick reached across and tapped him on the arm.

"Hey, Jim, what's wrong with you?" he asked with a look of concern.

Jim responded by hastily removing his arms from atop the table.

"Sorry. Sorry about that. I was lost in some crazy daydreams for awhile."

"What's troubling you? You've been in a daze ever since you got here."

The bartender's wife brought the goulash, moved the beer glasses aside, and carefully placed the bowls on the table, which gave Jim time to frame a suitable reply.

"Oh, I just got caught up in some memories," he explained. "Maybe I'm still not over the shock of what happened yesterday."

As soon as finished stating his reason for his inattention to his friend's words, he realized that he may have let himself open to possible inquiries by Nick about what took place yesterday. He quickly changed the subject.

"Did you come across Gennie Connors in your travels today?" he probed.

"No. But I did overhear someone say that she was probably out looking for a job. Peggy's folks were anxious to collect her things in the apartment. That's all I know."

"I wonder if her parents can get into it," Jim questioned. He instinctively slipped his hand into one of his pockets and stroked the key given him by Frank Colucci. "Gennie could let them in," he continued, "but I don't believe she's there right now. She never answered any of my phone calls today."

"You'd think she'd be back from job hunting by this time. You ought to try calling her again." Nick words mirrored a growing listlessness, his mind caught up in trying to bring some order to the various happenings that had taken place that day, each event having produced its own particular set of tensions. Exhaustion foiled this effort. The ride back from Westchester had been very tiresome.

Nonetheless, it was while riding on the bus that he had come to the realization that his forthcoming trip was no longer just a matter of seeking a job. What now seemed to him of equal importance was to break away from the routine that had held him captive these past years by the obligatory discipline of study. The last few months had been particularly hectic, the pace of events too unsettling to suit him. He wanted nothing more than to sit in the sun, read something that was not on somebody's reading list, and listen to jazz rhythms stored in his library of memories. But he could not afford that kind of luxury. They were set to leave in a matter of days. He had not told Jim that he had been interviewed this past week by several news organizations and was waiting to hear from them, although he knew that landing a job locally was a long shot at best. Still, he told himself, it would be best to wait for the responses from them before starting his job search outside of New York. Aware of Jim's distraught condition, he set about seeking a plausible excuse to delay their departure.

"Would you like to leave later this month?" Nick probed.

"The sooner the better," Jim replied with an outright eagerness he had never exhibited before.

Nick slid back in his chair with a look of dismay. Without revealing anything about his job interviews, he undertook to dissuade Jim from acting on what he assumed was an irrational impulse.

"What's your hurry? You're not trying to run away from something, are you?"

"Maybe…just maybe." There was no resentment in his reply. Finding the goulash too salty, Jim pushed the bowl away and reached for his glass of beer. The captious tone in Nick's question triggered a nervous search for the true cause of his compulsion to leave the city. Reason, he had to admit, was unable to supply any satisfactory answers. When faced with such a predicament in the past, he always gave in to the idea that some illogical force had intervened.

"Maybe, just maybe," he continued voicing his thoughts, "I'm running away from something I don't know how to deal with in a rational way." He paused momentarily, which gave the impression that he was questioning the discretion of revealing his innermost thoughts to his solitary audience. Pushing his glass of beer to one side, he stated with a show of annoyance, "Lately, it seems that reason keeps getting outwitted by fate."

The words took Nick by surprise and roused him out of his lethargy.

"People are nothing more than its playthings," Jim stated tonelessly. For a moment, at least, his insightfulness seemed fully restored.

Nick made no effort to disguise his look of disbelief. "Since when have you allowed fate to take precedence over logic and reason?"

Jim's responded quickly. "Since yesterday, when they failed me."

"You've changed. Somehow you seem different today." Nick drew a hand across his forehead before adding sympathetically, "Losing Peggy and Frank like we did would leave any one of us searching for answers as to why. Even being a realist, Jim, doesn't diminish the pain." Nick rubbed his chin, his eyes downcast, absorbed in trying to fashion other words of consolation that he felt needed saying. "It's a good thing that none of us were there to witness what happened. Anyway, blame it on anything you want. I'm sure reason had nothing to do with it."

Weariness pressured Nick to try and bring an end to this conversation and start for home. It was apparent to him that talking was Jim's way of venting his anguish. Nevertheless, at this moment, he felt that any break in this discussion would certainly be a welcome interlude. What Jim said next, however, kindled his curiosity.

"There are times when emotions rise up and overwhelm my rational decisions and actions," he declared.

"Well, that makes you like all the rest of us—a compromiser with reality," Nick concluded, his words enunciated with a lackluster hollowness, his mind busily engaged in finding a tactful means to leave.

"I hope that you're wrong," Jim remarked without any show of emotion.

"Anyway, we're right back to where we started—destiny!" Nick concluded, his declaration intended as a prelude to ending the discussion. "Look, Jim, I'll call to let you know when it would be best for us to leave." He got to his feet, shuffled over to the bar and paid the bill. He made his way to the subway station, vexed by having to put up with the dreariness of the long train ride home but relieved that Jim did not insist on moving up their departure date.

The dining room was now silent and empty. Jim stared at the decorative tin sheets that covered the wall, their surfaces a repetitious pattern of raised squares. His attention fixed on the design of a single tree leaf that was stamped into each of them, this monotonous motif no doubt a visual form of tedium at any other time than the present. Now, this sameness, along with the soothing quiet of the room, filled him with a tranquility seemingly long absent from memory. As soon as this sense of serenity began to slip away, he took it as a sign to depart. He got to his feet and made for the bar.

Stephan refused to take his money telling him that his friend had paid for all of it. The bartender waved good-bye and added in heavily accented English, "I'll be seeing you."

Jim walked out of the tavern without making any reply.

Chapter 44

On the street, Jim flipped up his collar and started hurrying toward Second Avenue. When he reached St. Mark's Church, he stopped and peered across the street at the kitchen window of Gennie's apartment, the same one that had served as his habitual post to observe the comings and goings on the street below. It was unlit. From all appearances, she was not at home. He glanced at his wristwatch. It was still early.

Aimless, he walked up to the fence that blocked entry into the church grounds with its row of rigid iron lances. He took hold of a pair of them, pressed his face between them, and focused his attention on the statue of an American Indian that stood guard near the center of the church's graveyard. The light of the streetlamp highlighted its head, its matched braids falling in straight lines down to the perfectly formed chest. He studied the figure awhile, then twisted around, leaned his back against the fence and again gazed up at the kitchen window. Weak flickers of light danced erratically on its dark surface.

He stood watching this bizarre fluttering, puzzled as to its source. Opening his overcoat, he reached into the pocket of his suit jacket and fingered the key to the apartment. Watching these baffling, intermittent flashes gave rise to feelings of uneasiness. The possibility that something terribly wrong could be taking place inside those unlit rooms crossed his mind. He hurried to the other side of the street and finding the entry door of the building slightly ajar, pushed it open and went in. Not wanting to meet anyone in the elevator, he skipped up the stairs.

The door lock turned easily. He stepped inside. In the dim luminosity coming in from the hall fixture, he could see on the floor in front of him books, cartons, pictures, and other household items lying in disarray, and beyond them a quivering light that emanated from what he knew to be the kitchen. He waited for his eyes to become accustomed to the dark. Slowly, he started forward, taking care not to disturb any of the objects that cluttered his way, before carefully moving through the living room and entering the kitchen. Once inside, he spotted a pair of wooden candleholders, each holding two long candles whose flames cast off narrow streams of shimmering smoke. On the table, a bottle of champagne stood unopened in a silver bucket filled with ice cubes. Around it, silverware, napkins, wine glasses and plates were all laid out in a neat and orderly manner.

Perhaps, he surmised, Gennie may have set the table to surprise the newlyweds when they came back to the apartment. He suspected this was the case when he noticed that the candles had not been burning for any great length of time. He considered blowing them out and leaving. The possibility that Gennie may have stepped out to buy something she urgently needed quashed that idea. There were no signs of anyone being at home.

Momentarily lost in thought, he failed to hear Gennie emerge from her bedroom and shuffle barefoot into the living room. She stood rubbing her eyes with a childlike expression of helplessness, then dropped her hands to her sides, and started for the kitchen. As she was about to enter it, she caught sight of Jim standing near the room's neatly arranged table, the quivering light from the candles imparting color and luminosity to his face, which gave off a warm, soft glow against the contrasting darkness that filled the room's interior.

Shock made her step back with a gasp of fear. In doing so, her foot struck a metal object lying on the floor, sending it tumbling across the uncarpeted section of the living room floor. The sudden and unexpected noise shattered the room's silence, startling him. He looked up to find Gennie staring at him, her panic readily apparent.

They stood apart, both recovering from the surprise and confusion that had resulted from this unexpected meeting. Before she uttered a word, however, her expression changed from one of alarm to that of disbelief. Jim's initial astonishment turned to guilty embarrassment. "I'm sorry if I frightened you," he said apologetically.

"Frightened me?" There was an obvious testiness in her reply. "For a moment, yes..." Her voice trailed off as she fought to suppress her anger at his untimely intrusion.

He placed the key on the kitchen table. "Peggy gave it to me."

"When did she do that?" she queried, her look of annoyance still showing.

"Yesterday."

"Were you with them when it happened?" This time she spoke softly, with the kind of gentleness one uses to address a hurt child.

"Yes, I was." He felt no need to be evasive as he had been with Nick Grigoris. He suspected that she knew he would be the one Peggy Troy and Frank Colucci would call upon to stand up for them at their wedding, if she could not. Deception was out of the question. Coming into the apartment uninvited, he now realized, was an act taken in response to a senseless fear triggered by the candlelight's projection on the kitchen window. Once again, he had allowed impulse to take command of his actions. He rebuked himself for again having fallen victim to some impellent force spawned by irrationality. It would have been wiser had he set out for home after meeting with Nick Grigoris instead of coming here.

In her long nightgown, she seemed to float over to him. Placing the fingertips of one hand against his cheek, Gennie tenderly slid them up and down in an effort to soothe any anguish she felt certain he had experienced the day before.

"Jim, please forgive me if I sounded annoyed just now." She bit her lips. "Most of the day was wasted yesterday going to Yonkers for a job interview. I should have gone with them when they asked me to. Things might have turned out differently if I did." Taking her hand away from his face, she stepped back and waited for him to respond to her plea for forgiveness.

"We've a right to be a little touchy today. But I'm not upset with you, or anyone else for that matter…just with myself," he assured her. His remorse was not easy to push aside. But his earlier resolve not to belabor the matter of his role in yesterday's tragedy held, for he added nothing more to what he already said.

Gennie shuffled her way to the neatly set kitchen table and seated herself, the closeness of the candlelight highlighting her features with a shimmering glow. Jim studied her face to see whether the calamity had left any visible marks of grief There were no signs that she had shed any tears. Only her pallor, one that left her face empty of any color, revealed the pain she had suffered at the sickening news of the sudden and unexpected death of friends.

"I've a confession to make." Her voice assumed a lilting pitch.

"If you want to," he answered halfheartedly.

"Well, I tried playing the same old game tonight, Jim. Look—I set the table, waiting for the newlyweds to come back here and celebrate…with me, just me…although I already knew what had happened to them. I wanted no part of reality. So I ran away from it with the help of my old standby—make-believe."

Gennie succeeded in shaping a crooked grin before telling him that what she had done was a childish game, a nonsensical pastime, and confessed that it was a pathetic way of avoiding the truth. "That's one thing that I'll never do again," she proclaimed with genuine conviction.

If she had hoped for a sympathetic reaction from him, it was not forthcoming. Calamity, as it had in the past, had made Jim revert to his wartime habit of suppressing any outward display of affection. Nonetheless, he conceded, his involvement with Gennie Connors these past months had helped to partially unlock this self-imposed hold on his ability to express tender feelings in words.

He found himself proffering a judgment instead of voicing any disparaging criticism. "I guess we all have our own ways for dealing with misfortune. You're inclined to resort to imagination in such situations."

"Yes, it's true. Fantasy is my means for handling any anguish that comes my way," she concluded, no longer smiling.

"Well, in the long run, it may be better than locking up your emotions and throwing the key away." His words, he hoped, would communicate indirectly that he was guilty of doing just that by his failure to display any open expression of grief over the loss of those he considered to be his most steadfast friends.

"I tried calling you a good number of times today," Jim said in an effort to show concern for her feelings.

"I was in no mood to talk to anyone, so I didn't answer the phone."

"Needless to say, I didn't want you to be alone," he told her, hoping to elicit a response that would reveal some appreciation for his efforts to provide moral support in what he knew would be an extremely trying time for her.

A period of silence followed before she made any reply. "You needn't have worried about me. I've been through this kind of loss before. I didn't cry; I just got angry—the same way I did when I lost my parents as a kid."

This time Jim stood mute, not knowing what to say.

"Look around you and you'll see how badly I've mismanaged things." She paused awhile before informing him that Peggy's parents would be coming the next day to pick up her personal belongings, as well as her car that was parked across the street.

"They'll help you get everything organized," he assured her in an effort to boost her spirits. He thought it best to say nothing more.

She watched him walk past her and enter the living room.

Still trying to make up to him for her initial rudeness, she got up from her chair and followed him. He took a few steps across the living room taking care not to disturb any of the objects that cluttered the floor.

"Are you getting ready to go?" she asked.

Her question made him stop and turn to face her. "Yes, it's getting late. And I still have lots to do before I start on my trip with Nick."

Gennie did not plead with him to stay. She offered an excuse for failing to do so instead.

"I haven't been at my best tonight. I'm washed-out from all the things that have happened to me the last few days. The way I feel right now, I'd even find good news hard to handle."

Jim could sense her struggle to control her emotions in the quiet that followed.

"The call from Peggy's mother did me in," she added. Her words dribbled out empty of all feeling.

"I'm also beat," he told her, "so I better get going."

He had never given any thought as to how he was going to part from the only woman who had ever told him she loved him. Logical thinking, he realized, would serve no useful purpose in dealing with circumstances in which emotions took on the dominant role. Reason was again proving to be an inadequate tool in resolving a painful situation, the kind that tears at the very roots of one's spirit. As in the past, this same failing again gave rise to a resolute urgency to circumvent such problematic state of affairs, knowing that he lacked the ability to deal with it effectively.

Taking great care, he moved through the darkened living room toward the opening of the long corridor that led out of the apartment. Unlike yesterday's short-lived indecision about turning back to take a final look at his departing friends, he deliberately stopped and directed his gaze at Gennie who remained standing facing him. Her facial features were now barely visible in the room's dimness, making it impossible for him to observe how she was reacting to what he knew to be an unfeeling way of severing the ties that still bound them. For a moment, he felt stymied as to what to do to amend what she surely would have construed as cold indifference in the manner that he was going about his leave-taking. A feeling of compunction persuaded him to try again.

"I'll probably end up seeing you sooner than you think." The weak glimmer of candlelight was far too distant to let him see her reaction to what he had said. When she did speak, her words were empty of any kind of sentiment, and much to his surprise reflected the composure of someone in full control of their emotions.

"I'd like to believe that, but I've become too much of a cynic—thanks to you—to be taken in by what you said."

"But I'm going to try and see you as soon as I can."

"I find it strange how easily you realists can revert to fiction with such ease whenever you want to falsify reality." There was no anger, hurt or sorrow in her accusation. On the contrary, her opinion was marked with the kind of conviction customarily derived from pragmatic proof. What she said left him uneasy, as if he had been caught in the act of lying. This show of fortitude was not what he thought would result from his leave-taking. What he had expected was the voicing of hurt feelings intended to injure his self-esteem and engender feelings of guilt. She proved to be more in control of herself than he could ever have imagined. Even the tactless manner in which he was parting from her did not seem to faze her, for she still managed to maintain a resourcefulness in the manner in which she contested the sincerity of his alluding to the possibility of their meeting again in the near future.

"Let's be practical," she challenged. "Can you tell me where and when?"

"Perhaps in Minneapolis. But I have no idea of when."

"You'll know where to find me."

"Then there's no need for us to say goodbye," Jim suggested on an upbeat note.

"If that's the way you want it. Then let it be! Let it be!" Resignation was more evident than belief in her impatient rejoinder. Gennie made no effort to go to him. Her failure to do so made him think that some deep-seated insecurity cautioned her not to reach out to him for fear of being rebuffed, although this was far from the truth. Yet, he failed to take the initiative to approach her for the same reason. Apprehension made him retreat into the unlit passageway that led out of the apartment. Remorseful over the unfeeling means in which he had gone about ending their interdependence—one that had helped uplift his spirits these past months—he stopped and retraced his steps partway. From where he now stood, she was barely visible.

"I'll be seeing you," he stated flatly, again failing to make clear his true feelings for her. His hurried search for something more to say was cut short when Gennie responded to his remark by singing a lyric from a popular song: "…in all the old familiar places."

Jim heard her giggle.

"No, it wouldn't be like that at all, I'm afraid." Implicit in her words was the acceptance that this farewell might well be their final one.

It now struck him that his intended departure had failed to reveal the slightest sign of regret on her part. If anything, she had remained unflappable, her self-assurance seemingly intact, or else she had been adroitly using the dark to masquerade her true feelings. The only excuse he could muster for his inability to put forward any caring expressions was the notion that the horror of seeing his friends killed the day before had filled him with a bitterness that now obstructed his ability to convey feelings of any kind. Apparently, he now concluded, yesterday's events had retrieved from the past an emotional shortcoming that he had locked away in his psyche at the war's end, whereby he learned to muffle sentiment whenever tragedy confronted him. Obviously, his endeavor to give her some assurance that they were bound to meet again in the near future did not suffice in mollifying the emotional hurt he probably had inflicted by the insensitive way he was terminating their relationship. It was now essential, he thought, to resort to other means to make it plain to her that his determination to get together with her was not a deceitful ploy on his part. He reasoned that the most effective means of doing so was to be frank and open about his fears concerning the outcome of his planned search, which he hoped would help her to understand that there would be a real need to be with her should his exploratory venture end as she predicted—in failure.

"Like you said, Gennie, there's a good chance I'll not find what I'm looking for," he admitted, the absence of light and the empty space between them giving added vigor to his words.

"There's enough out there to keep you searching forever," she said with indifference.

"I'm not as strong-minded as you think."

This admission struck her as strange and somewhat out of character.

Jim shook off a rising inclination not to elaborate any further concerning this disclosure. "Don't let my outward show of self-confidence fool you, Gennie. I have qualms about what's ahead of me."

"What makes it so frightening?" she questioned, her words emitting an uncharacteristic forcefulness rather than solicitude.

He took a moment to consider the wisdom of revealing a fear that had been haunting him these past weeks with an unyielding intensity.

"I've this nightmare that one day I may be forced to commit the most odious deceit of all." He expected some response from her, but none was forthcoming. Her silence made him have second thoughts about telling her anything more. Nevertheless, he set aside his reluctance, for he wanted nothing more than to elicit an empathetic reply to what he felt was a deep-seated, personal revelation, one he never openly voiced before.

"What I fear most, Gennie, is that in some distant tomorrow, I'll be put into a position of having to hold in the highest regard the very same values that I find repugnant today." He let out a deep sigh. "That would make me just another unidentifiable shadow in that endless march of nobodies."

Another period of silence followed. Her lack of interest in what he said ended his efforts to drive home the critical need for him to resume their relationship if his journey ended up nothing more than a futile venture. He took her indifference as a signal to leave. Saying nothing more, he turned and started toward the door without taking care to avoid striking any of the things that lay heaped around him. This resulted in his accidentally kicking over a pile of books, sending them tumbling to the floor. The string of thuds that followed made Gennie think that he may have tripped and fallen. Reacting instinctively, she moved through the dark in the direction of the long hallway, her feet brushing some objects along the way.

"Jim? Jim, did you fall?" she called out to him as soon as she reached the entryway.

She caught a glimpse of him as he opened the door, a shaft of light from the hallway fixture clearly illuminating him as he made his way out, the corridor again becoming devoid of light after he quietly closed the door behind him. The charade was over. This time, however, her use of pretense may have had a realistic intent, but it failed to wipe away an unsettling sense of loss. The emotions that she had so successfully kept in check now broke free. Her tears began to flow freely. There was no longer any need to disguise her true feelings behind an outward show of calm in response to this painful separation. Jim Stahr had just stepped out of her life. Moreover, she counseled herself, if she was truly going to be a realist, then she had to accept the possibility that she might never see him again. A tiny smile appeared, sending the tears streaming down her cheeks in new directions. What had brought on this contrasting display of emotions was her perception that hard-nosed realists also cry. A teary-eyed look of amusement crossed her face as she made her way through the living room and into the kitchen. The cause of it was the recognition that any use of her imagination to ease the pain of this loss would be so devoid of good sense that it could only be termed as ludicrous.

Chapter 45

Jim Stahr was convinced that early morning would be the most opportune time to tell his family about his plans to leave. At that early hour, both his father and brother would be anxious to depart for work, thus minimizing the number of questions they would get a chance to ask. When they were told, their first response to this news was a burst of effusive glee expressed in congratulatory handshaking and backslapping hugs. But as soon as they sat down for breakfast, the full import of his intended departure began to dampen their initial enthusiasm.

"Do you have to leave today?" his mother inquired, hoping for a negative reply.

"The company wants me to be in Pittsburgh on Monday. I'll need the weekend to find a place to stay," he lied. He stopped speaking in order to gather more fiction to pile atop his initial prevarication. "I'll be doing lots of traveling in the future, but I promise to stay in touch."

They finished eating without any lengthy exchanges, his family accepting his decision to relocate as being irreversible. Before his father and brother left, they shook his hand, snatched their metal lunch boxes and hurried out the door, their footsteps gradually fading as they pounded down the stairs.

He had hurdled a major obstacle by having made a firm and open declaration to depart, although he felt uncomfortable in having used the expedient of a white lie to do so. This was the least complicated means, he judged, for avoiding any vociferous opposition from his family had he revealed the real purpose for his going away. The truth would have been upsetting and senseless to them. The worst had passed. All that remained was to pack and await Nick's phone call.

Once back in his room, Jim pulled a suitcase out of his clothes closet and placed it on top of his unmade bed. He began to take his personal belongings from the various drawers and put them neatly into the suitcase. After he finished packing and had set the suitcase on the floor, his mother came into the room to inform him that she was going to leave. Jim acknowledged the information with a wave of his hand and then went over to sit at his desk. His attention was fixed on a row of textbooks arrayed on a wooden shelf attached to the wall opposite him, a pair of heavy metal bookends holding them firmly in place. He pulled out a volume and began flipping pages, stopping now and then to examine the words and sentences he had underlined in order to highlight their importance. Information that he had once held to be worthy of memorization now appeared to be empty of any real significance, as if some invisible force had drained their power to challenge and stimulate. He snapped the book shut and placed it back on the shelf.

The noon hour passed and Nick still had not called, so he took the initiative and tried phoning him. One of his sisters answered, saying that he was not at home but was due back soon.

Jim returned to his room, made his bed and lay down to rest. He dozed quietly until awakened by the persistent ringing of the phone. Sluggishly, he got out of his bed and made his way to the phone in the hallway. The sound of Nick's voice acted like a stimulant quickly bringing him to full wakefulness, his words spilling out with the enthusiasm of an excited child reporting some novel revelation.

"Hey, Jim, there's nothing but great things to tell you."

"Did they reduce the bus rates?" he shot back with the kind of humor used to bolster one's own spirits.

"No, it's something a hell of a lot better."

"Well, don't keep it a secret. What's it all about?"

Instead of the expected energetic response, Jim heard only the monotonous hum of the telephone. Then, as if words could no longer be contained, Nick burst forth, "I've just landed a job! I'm going to be a copyboy for a wire service."

The news stunned Jim into silence. He stood flustered, unable to think of what to say. When calm returned, instead of extending his good wishes, Jim asked agitatedly, "Where?"

"You wouldn't believe it. Right here in Manhattan."

"Then the trip is off?" Jim asked, already having assumed that this was truly the case.

"Let's admit it, Jim. I'd be a damn fool to turn down a chance like this one. Don't you agree?" Nick pleaded.

"You're right, Nick. Go ahead and take it."

"I already have!" The exuberant delight that first filled Nick's words returned with greater intensity, now that he no longer had to tell his friend that all the planning they had done for their trip was of no consequence to either of them. In the same happy pitch, Nick went on to relate the details concerning his newly found job.

"I've got to start work on Monday. How's that for a lucky break? Can you beat it?"

"No, Nick, it's one break in a million." The dejection that follows an unexpected blow to one's spirits permeated his speech.

"Hey, Jim, I've got a heck of a lot of things to do this weekend, so I'll be in touch with you soon. I have to rush off. See you."

The phone conversation ended as abruptly as it had started. He replaced the phone with the halting movements of someone bewildered by the loss of something highly prized. Shock changed to anger when he realized that Nick had not even bothered to ask what he intended doing now that their trip was called off.

Annoyed and troubled, he went back to his room and lay down. He fought to stifle anxiety and bring order to the tumultuous thoughts that flitted through his mind as he struggled to fashion a new and decisive course of action for himself. The resulting confusion left him with the feeling of being stranded on a secluded road that splintered off in many directions, all of them unmarked and leading nowhere. He settled down onto his bed, folded his hands behind his head, and soon was lost in thought. After a time, he grew weary of his mind's search for a way out of his dilemma. He raised himself from the bed and went over to his desk, tore a sheet of paper out of a notebook, and began to pencil a note to his mother. Unable to think of what to write, he crumpled the paper and flung it into a wastebasket. Jim removed his coat from his closet, put it on and took hold of his suitcase. He walked out of the apartment and shut the door.

As if acting in response to some wild trumpet call of the human spirit, Jim Stahr yielded to its tuneful summons to venture forth into an unstructured future, prodded on by an unwavering quest to find the means whereby he could do and be more than what he characterized as the ordinary. Chance, however, not reason, was the tunesmith that had fashioned the melody, which did not beckon, but rather contrived to thrust him onto a path empty of any markings that could help guide him in this endeavor. He brushed aside rationality's admonishment that such a trek would set him wandering down a road rarely frequented by others and continued on his way to the nearest subway entrance.

Acknowledgments

Elizabeth Thompson Pastore planted the seed from which this novel sprouted. It was Eileen Forrester's editorial skills that nurtured it into fruition and the copy editing task carried out by Carrie Andrews gave a structural luster to the text. I would like to thank New York University archivists Nancy Cricco and Svetlana Sergeevna Kouzmina for retrieving some of the photo material used in the book cover from the university's archives. And finally, Jana Rade masterminded the overall design of the book cover and succeeded in setting the mood of a time and a place in New York City's past.

About the Author

Jules Tragarz is a graduate of New York University and Columbia University and has served with the U.S. Army in the China-Burma-India Theater of operations during World War II. He spent his post-graduate years in a long career of formulating and writing research and development documentation for both government and industry. These tasks entailed the need to travel extensively throughout the United States and foreign countries. He now resides in Pacific Palisades, California.